P9-DCI-333

STRANGERS

ALSO BY URSULA ARCHER

Five

ALSO BY ARNO STROBEL

The Script
The Coffin
The Village
The Flood

STRANGERS

A NOVEL

URSULA ARCHER
AND ARNO STROBEL

TRANSLATED BY
JAMIE SEARLE ROMANELLI
AND STEFAN SCHOLTZ

Minotaur Books
New York

This is a work of fiction. All of the characters, organizations, and events portrayed in this novel are either products of the author's imagination or are used fictitiously.

www.minotaurbooks.com

Designed by Omar Chapa

Library of Congress Cataloging-in-Publication Data

Names: Poznanski, Ursula, 1968– author. | Strobel, Arno, 1962– author. | Romanelli, Jamie Searle, translator. | Scholtz, Stefan, translator.
Title: Strangers : a novel / Ursula Archer and Arno Strobel ; translated by Jamie Searle Romanelli and Stefan Scholtz.
Other titles: Fremd. English
Description: First U.S. edition. | New York : Minotaur Books, 2018. | "First published in Germany by Wunderlich in October 2015"—Verso title page.
Identifiers: LCCN 2017036262| ISBN 9781250113061 (hardcover) | ISBN 9781250113078 (ebook)
Subjects: LCSH: Fianc,ees—Fiction. | Fianc,es—Fiction. | Danger perception—Fiction. | GSAFD: Mystery fiction. | Suspense fiction.
Classification: LCC PT2716.O98 F8613 2014 | DDC 833/.92—dc23
LC record available at https://lccn.loc.gov/2017036262

Our books may be purchased in bulk for promotional, educational, or business use. Please contact your local bookseller or the Macmillan Corporate and Premium Sales Department at 1-800-221-7945, extension 5442, or by email at MacmillanSpecialMarkets@macmillan.com.

First published in Germany by Wunderlich: October 2015
First U.S. Edition: January 2018

10 9 8 7 6 5 4 3 2 1

STRANGERS

1

It's only by chance that I see the entrance light flicker on. Because I happen to glance across at the bathroom window as I blow-dry my hair. Outside, there is light where there shouldn't be any.

Someone must have activated the motion sensor, but I'm not expecting anyone, so there's no way I'm opening the door if the bell rings. In general, I've got nothing against friends dropping by unannounced, but the last thing I'm in the mood for today is Ela turning up on the doorstep with two bottles of red wine and launching into an endless monologue about how she's really going to break up with Richard this time, without a shadow of a doubt.

No. She'll just have to come to terms with her lousy relationship by herself today. But then again, maybe it's just Jehovah's Witnesses.

I switch the hair dryer to a higher speed so I won't even have to lie when I say I didn't hear the doorbell. I ignore the nagging sense of unease gradually unfurling inside me. Sure, sometimes burglars ring the doorbell first to make sure no one's home before they strike. That's what I've heard, anyway. I haven't been in Germany long enough to know how common it actually is. I may speak the language fluently, but when it comes to day-to-day life, there's a lot that's still foreign to me.

Besides, it's silly to think the worst just because of a harmless ring of the doorbell.

For heaven's sake, I'm not usually like this.

A few moments later, the entrance light goes out again.

I turn off the hair dryer, nudge the curtain of the bathroom window aside a little, and peer out. There's no one there. Neither a visitor nor someone trying to break in through the door or windows.

Dad would throttle me with his bare hands if he knew I was living alone in an unprotected house—there are more security cameras at our family compound in Melbourne than at the Pentagon. Another reason I'm glad to be away from there.

For the next few minutes everything is still, and the pressure weighing down on my chest slowly dissipates, giving way to joyful anticipation. There's nothing else standing in the way of a relaxing evening on the couch, and I can't wait. A cup of tea, a warm blanket, and a good book are everything I want from the rest of today—also, maybe someone who'd be willing to massage my back for me. I have no idea where the tension between my shoulder blades has come from.

Vanilla tea. Just the thought of it warms me up. I slip into my bathrobe and open the door to the hallway, then make my way down the stairs. Halfway down, I pause.

There was . . . a noise. A clinking sound. From inside the house. Someone smashing in a window pane? No, it wasn't loud enough for that.

All at once, the uneasiness from before comes crashing back, this time with twice the force. My hand grips the banister. I take a deep breath, try to pull myself together, walk down another step. *You're being silly*, I tell myself, *burglars would make much more noise*. They would snatch as much stuff as they could and try to make off with it as quickly as possible—

Another sound. Not a clinking this time, but a scraping. Like a drawer being opened and closed.

My first impulse is to turn around. Run to my bedroom, call the police. Hide.

Instead, I fight all my instincts and remain there, as I realize I don't even have this one, sensible option. My phone is in the kitchen, its battery almost dead. I had put it on the espresso machine, in plain sight, so I wouldn't forget to charge it.

But the kitchen and living room are precisely where the noises are coming from.

I walk down another two steps. Yes, I can see light through the crack of the living room door.

I take a deep breath to beat back my fear, which seems much too great for the context. The fact that the light's on doesn't mean a damn thing; I'm always forgetting to turn it off. So there's no reason to panic. And besides, the front door is right in front of me. If I need to, I can be outside in five seconds to get help, no matter if I'm in my bathrobe or not.

I hold my breath. Concentrate and listen hard. Now there's nothing but silence. Was I wrong, did I just imagine the noises? My mind considers this to be entirely possible, but my wildly hammering heart says otherwise. And if there's one thing I can't bear, it's uncertainty.

There's a paperweight on the dresser in the hall. Ela gave it to me a few weeks ago. A cube made of blue glass, at least four pounds in weight. I pick it up in one hand, ignoring the junk mail which sails down to the floor, and slowly, slowly, open the living room door.

Nothing. Nobody. At least not in here. The living room is untouched; the terrace door is completely intact; everything is just as I left it.

As far as the kitchen is concerned, though, I'm not sure yet. I can't get a glimpse of it from where I'm standing, and the light's off.

The paperweight almost slips out of my sweaty hand. I grip it tighter and take a step into the living room. Silently. Another step. Until I'm standing in the middle of the room.

Right when I'm starting to laugh at myself for being so foolish, a shadow steps out of the darkness of the kitchen.

The scream which tries to escape from me dies out halfway, as if there were suddenly no breath left in my body. Every part of my body freezes.

Run away is the only thought which makes it to my consciousness, but I'm not capable of putting it into action. My legs refuse to respond.

A man is standing there beneath the light of the ceiling lamp: he is dark haired, broad shouldered. He says something, his mouth moves, but I can't make out a word of it; every sound seems to be coming from a great distance, only the hammering of my heartbeat is worryingly close and loud. Is this shock?

The man says something again, but it's as though I've suddenly forgotten all my German. For a moment, the room spins around me. *Don't pass out now,* I tell myself.

He cocks his head to the side, hesitates. Then he comes toward me. A new thought pounds into my head: *You're so stupid, why didn't you stay upstairs?*

Only when he's close enough for me to smell a hint of his aftershave does the paralyzing shock finally lift. I edge backward, but toward the wall instead of the door. By the time I realize it's too late, he's almost right next to me.

"Get out!" I shout, in the hope of at least startling him. To my surprise, it works. He stops in his tracks.

"Get out, or I'll call the police!" If I shout a little louder, maybe the neighbors will hear me too.

A burglar would run away now, but the stranger doesn't do that, and something inside me has already figured out that the man hasn't broken in here to rob me. No thief wears a suit when he's breaking into a house. But that means there's another reason, that the stranger has a different intention . . . and this thought awakens a completely new kind of fear within me. I take another step back; the floor lamp is right behind me now; I feel it tipping over, almost lose my balance.

"Please," I whisper. "Please don't hurt me."

He is five steps away at most. He doesn't shift his gaze from me, not for a second.

"For heaven's sake," he says. "What's wrong?"

Another step toward me. I duck down a little, as if it could help, as if I could hide inside myself.

"I don't have much money in the house, but I'll give you everything I've got, OK? Take whatever you want. But please . . . don't hurt me."

"Is this supposed to be some kind of joke?" He lifts his hands, baring his palms. They're empty. "Are you feeling sick? Should I call a doctor?"

He's stopped advancing toward me. That's all that matters. I slowly straighten up again. The paperweight. Maybe this would be a good moment to throw it.

"Just go, please. I promise I won't call the police."

He blinks, takes a few deep breaths in and out. "What's going on? Why are you talking to me like this?"

If those were signs of uncertainty, then I have a chance. I'll engage him in conversation. Yes. And grab the first opportunity that presents itself to flee.

"Because . . . I'm scared, OK?"

"Of me?"

"Yes. You've given me a real shock."

He spread out his arms, coming toward me again. "Joanna . . ."

My name. I flinch again. He knows my name; maybe he's a stalker . . . or maybe he just saw the address details on the envelopes that were lying in the hallway.

I take a closer look at him. Blue eyes beneath thick brows. Prominent features, which I would remember if I'd met him before. He doesn't look aggressive, nor dangerous, but the sight of him still fills me with a horror I couldn't explain even to myself.

Now I have the wall behind me. There's no way out; I'm trapped. My pulse is racing; I lift the paperweight. "Go. Right now."

His gaze flits back and forth between my face and the glass cube. Then it slips a little lower, making me realize my robe is gaping open more than I would have liked.

"Joanna, I don't know what you're doing, but please, stop it."

"*You* stop it!" I meant my words to sound authoritative, but in actual fact they sound pathetic. "Stop acting like we know each other and just go, please."

Something about my fear must be enticing to him; he comes yet another step closer. I edge along the wall to the left, toward the door.

"Will you give it a rest already? Of course we know each other." His tone is one of impatience, not anger, but that could easily change. Another seven feet to the door. I can make it; I have to make it.

"You're wrong. Really." With every sentence I say, I'm winning myself time. "Where are we supposed to know each other from?"

He slowly shakes his head. "Either you're playing some kind of twisted game with me, or maybe I should get you to a hospital." He runs his hand through his hair. "We're engaged, Jo. We live together."

I stare at him, speechless. What he said was so far from what I'd expected that I need a few seconds to get my head around it.

We're engaged.

So not a stalker, then. Something much worse. A lunatic. Someone who's living in his own made-up world. Someone who's suffering from delusions.

But why, of all the people in the world, am I the one he's directing them at?

That's irrelevant, I tell myself. You can't reason with someone who's mentally ill, nor convince them with logic. His mood could change at any moment—he seemed peaceful so far, but who knows, a single ill-judged word could be enough to make him aggressive. After all, he used force to break his way into a stranger's house.

I can think of only one way out of this, and I make the decision quickly.

The paperweight traces a shimmering blue flight path through the air as I hurl it at the man. My aim is good, but he twists to the side and I only catch his shoulder, not his head. But it's enough. I run out of the living room, through the hallway, up the steps into the bedroom. I slam the door behind me, turning the key twice.

Then I sink down to the floor, back against the door, staring at my bed. One pillow, one blanket. Nothing more. The bed of a woman who lives alone. But if he really is ill, then his brain will come up with some reason for that. That he's been sleeping on the couch recently, for example.

Everything seems to have gone silent downstairs. I close my eyes for a moment. Safety at last. I hope.

Of course we know each other, the stranger had said, with an almost eerie matter-of-factness. I search my memory, but in vain. Had he come into the studio once? Was he a client?

No, that's impossible. I never forget a face that I've photographed.

A noise makes me jump. A dull thud, like a door being slammed.

I press my ear against the wood of the bedroom door. Nothing. Maybe the paperweight hit the man hard enough to scare him away.

I listen with my eyes closed, holding my breath. My hope lasts for just one minute, then I hear footsteps on the stairs, slow and heavy.

He's coming after me. Now he won't be staying calm anymore.

And I still don't have a phone to call for help.

2

The cockatoo's gone.

I notice as soon as I get out of the car at the house, as the exterior lights go on. It was a present for Joanna's birthday, a welded thing, thirty inches high. A symbolic piece of home. She told me once that Melbourne was full of cockatoos.

As I walk past the now empty spot next to the rhododendrons, I ask myself where it could be. I unlock the door and enter the house. It's dark in the hall, but I can hear a muffled whirring noise coming from upstairs. The hair dryer. Joanna. A warm feeling pushes away my bewilderment about the missing cockatoo.

I walk through the hall. The light from the streetlamps casts a diffused glow through the slim glass pane next to the main door. Just enough for me to be able to make out where I'm going. I open the door to the living room. It's bathed in bright light, as is the kitchen. I can't help but smile. My Joanna. The house is usually lit up like a Christmas tree whenever she's at home by herself. Much to the delight of the power company.

I drop my keys onto the kitchen worktop; they miss it by a hairbreadth and land on the tiled floor, jangling sharply. Tiredness is taking its toll, as is this strange, shitty day I've had. Today it seemed like everyone in the company wanted a piece of me.

I sigh, pick up the keys, and put them in their place.

The opened bottle of Pinot Blanc from yesterday evening is still in the refrigerator. I don't feel like having wine, not yet anyway. Maybe later, together with Joanna, once we've snuggled up on the sofa.

I reach for the carton of orange juice next to it. It's almost empty. I pour the meager amount that's left into a tumbler.

The drawer containing the bags for waste packaging is stuck, and makes a grinding noise when I open and close it. One of the screws holding up the guide rail has probably come loose. I'll take a look at it over the weekend.

After turning off the kitchen lights at the entrance to the living room, I remember that my phone battery is almost empty. So I go back and attach the device to the cable lying on the waist-high cabinet just inside the kitchen. I turn around and jump, startled. Joanna is standing right in the middle of the living room. I didn't hear her come in. But at the sight of her, I get that warm, pleasant feeling again, and from one second to the next my tiredness and irritation are forgotten.

It looks like she hasn't seen me yet. I use the brief moment to take a look at her from the darkness of the kitchen. She's only wearing her bathrobe. It's tied only loosely and is hanging open a bit, revealing the swell of her small, firm breasts. Another sensation, a different one, joins the pleasant feeling, and all of a sudden I feel like a peeping tom who's been caught in the act.

I step out of the darkness and approach her. She hears my footsteps, turns toward me and . . . freezes. The cheerful hello I was about to say sticks in my throat.

I search for a possible explanation for the horror I can read on her face. "Hi, darling," I say carefully. "What's the matter? Are you unwell? Did something happen?"

Joanna doesn't react; she just stands there and looks at me like I'd spoken to her in a foreign language. I've never seen her like this. My God, it looks like she's having a panic attack. Now I feel scared too. Something terrible must have happened.

"Darling," I try again, as gently as I can. I take one careful step toward her; now we're only an arm's length apart. Then she jolts out of her paralyzed stance, her eyes fly open, and she shrinks back from me. One step, then another.

"Darling, please . . ." I whisper involuntarily. As cautiously as I possibly can, I edge forward, trying to reduce the distance between us. The expression on her face suddenly changes; her features contort. "Get out," she screams at me, with such force that I stop in my tracks. "Get out or I'll call the police."

Get out? What the hell's wrong with her? It seems like she's completely lost her senses. A million different things shoot through my mind all at once, and I struggle to put them into something even halfway resembling order.

Is it drugs, alcohol, shock, did someone attack her . . . did someone die? Joanna takes another step backward, and bumps into the floor lamp. It tips over. The glass shade shatters into pieces on the floor.

"Please," she whispers, "Please don't hurt me."

I try to keep my voice even and calm. "For heaven's sake," he says. "What's wrong?"

Another step toward me. I duck down a little, as if it could help, as if I could hid inside myself.

"I don't have much money in the house, but I'll give you everything I've got, OK? Take whatever you want."

For a brief moment I feel irritation flaring up inside me, despite my bewilderment. "Is this some kind of joke?" My voice sounds harsher than I'd intended; I raise my palms to indicate she has nothing to fear. "Are you feeling unwell? Should I call a doctor?"

She shakes her head. "Just go, please. I promise I won't call the police."

I resist the fierce impulse to grab her by the arms and shake her and scream at her, to get her to stop all this nonsense. To be Joanna again. But I need to stay calm, it's important that at least I keep a clear head. I take a few deep breaths, looking right into her eyes all the while. "What is all this? Why are you talking to me like this?"

"Because I'm scared," she says hesitantly. "You know?"

"Of me?"

"Yes. You really scared me."

"Joanna . . ."

Her expression changes in an odd way as I say her name. It's as though she's trying to read my face to find out what I'm thinking.

"Go away. Now." I can feel she's trying to make her voice sound firm. But it doesn't work. She raises her hand slightly, and it's only now I see that she's clutching something. I try to make out what it is. The paperweight from the hallway. This whole thing is getting crazier and crazier. "Joanna . . ." I look deep into her eyes, trying to convey that she has no reason to fear me. "I don't know what you're doing, but please, stop it."

"You stop it," she responds, like a small brattish child. "Stop acting like we know each other and just go, please."

This can't be happening. I'm starting to worry Joanna might have completely lost her mind.

I take another careful step toward her, not knowing how I'm supposed to deal with this bizarre situation. I have to be careful not to lose control. "Will you give it a rest already; of course we know each other."

Joanna shakes her head. "You're mistaken, really. How, in your opinion, are we meant to know each other?"

I've had about enough of this, damn it. "Either you're playing some twisted game with me, or I should get you straight to the hospital. We're engaged, Jo. We live together."

Her features crumble. This isn't a game. She really doesn't recognize me.

Suddenly, her hand shoots up without warning and something flies through the air at me. I turn sideways by reflex, but it's too late. The glass cube strikes my shoulder, and a firework of pain explodes in my entire upper body. I hear myself groaning. I suddenly feel nauseous and, at the same time, like someone has kicked me in the back of the knees. My legs buckle; I crash down to the floor and groan again. Joanna flits past me, just a dark shadow, and, in the next instant, disappears from my field of vision.

Carefully, I feel around my shoulder.

I thought I knew Joanna well by now, but suddenly she seems like a stranger to me, so much so as if it were another woman in her body.

The pain in my shoulder is slowly subsiding. I prop myself up and struggle onto my feet. The living room sways. I take two, three careful steps, until I'm able to lean against the back of an armchair. My eyes wander over to the open living room door. Did Joanna run outside? Maybe she's going to call the police.

She's sick; I have no more doubts about that. Maybe she always has been. Maybe she knows it and just never told me. Maybe . . . yes, maybe I never knew who the real Joanna was until now. No, that's not possible, it *can't* be. I straighten up and take a scrutinizing look around. Nothing's swaying. I'm standing firmly again.

Should I call the police myself? No, nonsense, what could the police do here? There was no burglary. My fiancée has lost her mind, but that's something a doctor would need to tend to. A psychiatrist, even. I could call an emergency doctor. They'd probably commit her to a mental institution right away if they see her like this. And once she's in one of those places . . . what with her being a foreigner and only having a temporary residence permit . . . No, first I have to try to talk to her again. Who knows what happened; maybe she's just completely disorientated. For whatever reason.

I turn on the light in the hallway, and a violent pain surges through my shoulder. I take a deep breath and look around. The front door is shut. If Joanna had run outside, she would have either left it open or hastily slammed it shut, upset as she is. I would have heard that.

So she's probably still in the house. I walk over to the stairs, look up, then pause. Something's not right here, I can feel it. I slowly turn around and let my eyes wander through the hall again. The front door, the dresser next to it, the slip of paper on the floor, the coat rack . . . the coat rack. The realization feels like a punch in the gut, knocking the wind out of me. My things. They're missing. There are two empty hooks where my jackets would usually be hanging. Below them, on the shelf . . . her sneakers, three pairs of casual shoes in different colors, but that's it. They're all hers. What the hell is going on here?

I pull myself together. I have to find out. I rush over to the front door, open it, and take a look outside. Everything's quiet. I close it again and decide to lock up, just to be sure. Then I climb the stairs, taking firm steps. I want Joanna to hear me, I want her to know I'm coming. I want to find out once and for all what's going on here.

I look into the bathroom: nothing, it's empty. With grim determination I approach the bedroom door, firmly grip the handle, and push it down. Locked.

"Joanna." My voice sounds forceful. Not angry, but enough so she'll realize I'm serious. "Joanna, will you stop this nonsense! Open the door so we can talk. I'm not going to hurt you, damn it."

Silence. I wait. Ten seconds, fifteen . . . Nothing. "Joanna, please, will you think about this for a second? If I really wanted to hurt you, do you think this pathetic little lock would stop me from getting into the bedroom? One kick and that's that. But I don't want to break down the door, because it's my door as well, you see? We live here together. And if that doesn't seem right to you, then we'll . . . Joanna. Are you listening?"

I realize I'm speaking very quickly. That's something I always do whenever I have a thought I urgently want to tell somebody about.

"I have an idea, Jo. Are you listening? Ask me something. Something only I could know. Something I'd *have* to know if I really live here with you. OK? Then you'll see. Come on, ask me something, anything."

Again, nothing but silence for a while, but then I hear something behind the door. At the door. A click. The handle is pushed down, the door slowly opens and swings inward. Thank goodness.

Joanna is standing there in front of me, a little off to the side. She's looking at me, frightened, still holding on to the handle. My eyes move past her and into the bedroom. A hand, as cold as ice, reaches for my heart. And, for the first time, the thought crosses my mind that maybe the person who's lost their mind here isn't Joanna, but me.

My blanket, my pillow . . . My wardrobe . . . Everything's gone.

3

I did everything wrong, everything, one mistake after the next. I realize that now. Now, while the intruder is rattling the handle of the bedroom door.

Dead end. No way out. Why didn't I run outside instead of imprisoning myself? Because I felt safer in my own bedroom? What a fallacy. I'm sitting in a trap here; there's no exit, just the window.

"Joanna."

I close my eyes, press the pads of my thumbs against my eyelids. *Go away*, I think, *just go away.*

"Joanna, will you stop this nonsense! Open the door so we can talk. I'm not going to hurt you, damn it."

Of course not. After all, we are engaged.

I feel a sudden urge to laugh, out of pure hysteria, and if I do I know I won't be able to stop. I take a deep breath and bore my fingernails into the palms of my hands until the urge subsides.

What do I know about people with delusions? Nothing, really. That you should agree with them, not provoke them—I think I remember that much.

"Joanna, please, will you think about this for a second? If I really wanted to hurt you, do you think this pathetic little lock would stop me from getting into the bedroom? One kick and that's that."

I immediately back away from the door. He keeps talking, saying something about how it's his door too and that's why he doesn't want to break it down, but I'm well aware that he'll do it sooner or later if I don't open it.

I frantically look around. For a weapon, something heavy. Next time I'll hit the mark. Really take him out. Except there's nothing in here that I can use. I would have to take a curtain rod apart, but there's no way I have time for that.

"I have an idea, Jo. Are you listening? Ask me something. Something only I could know. Something I'd *have* to know if I really live here with you."

I have to get to my cell phone. Or make it out onto the street, but neither of those will be possible unless I open this door. And that would mean taking all the risks that come with doing that.

I feel sick.

"Come on, ask me something, anything." The man on the other side of the door sounds hopeful now.

Maybe he's dazed. The paperweight had hit him, after all, and I'd thrown it as hard as I could. Surely I have a chance against him now.

OK. If I'm going to do this, it has to be quick. Like ripping off a Band-Aid. I turn the key and open the door, and at that moment I realize I'm still standing there in my bathrobe . . . such a stupid, stupid fool.

For a moment the man smiles at me, then his gaze goes past me into the bedroom behind. The smile vanishes all at once, and is replaced by . . . Bewilderment. Disbelief.

Who knows what he's seeing, what his illness is leading him to believe. Maybe he's on drugs.

The opportunity is too good to let slip away because of fear. I edge through the door, squeezing past him, I'm almost at the top of the stairs now, and then . . .

I make it exactly two steps, then he's beside me again, grabbing my upper arm.

"Stay here." His tone sounds more pleading than threatening, but his grip on my arm doesn't slacken. "We'll talk now, OK? Jo? Let's talk, please."

I try to wrench myself free once more. If I could just get to my phone and lock myself in the downstairs toilet . . .

Even though his shoulder is clearly bothering him, I have no chance against him. He pulls me back into the bedroom, closes the door, and leans up against it.

My fear comes flooding back. I could still try to open the window and shout. Hell, I should have done that right away. Instead of unlocking the door.

The stranger doesn't take his eyes off me for even a second. He slowly shakes his head. Breathes in shakily. "You really don't recognize me, do you?"

"No. I really don't."

He laughs for a moment, but it's a laugh that sounds far from cheerful. "Then I guess you also don't know what happened to my things."

What? His things?

My perplexity must have been written all over my face, because the stranger points his finger toward the bed.

"My blanket. My pillow. They were here when I got up this morning. So was my wardrobe. And the shoes and jackets downstairs in the hall." He comes a step toward me, but stops when I flinch.

"If I go into the bathroom, I bet I won't find my toothbrush either, will I? Or my aftershave? My shower gel?"

He must have spun together an entire world in fine detail. A life that doesn't exist.

What if I play along? Simply act like I'm remembering everything bit by bit? Would he believe me, or is it too late now?

I look him directly in the eyes, even though I find it difficult. There is something about him that makes me wish I had a knife. A knife I could stab him with. Again and again.

My God, what am I thinking?

I press my hands against my forehead, and the impulse to use violence to free myself from this situation abates. "You're wrong. I've been living here alone ever since I rented this house. There is no second pillow and no second blanket and there's most definitely no aftershave in the bathroom."

"Damn it, Joanna." He tries to force his mouth into something resembling a smile. "What am I going to do with you?"

The question makes me edge backward again. Nothing, there's nothing he should do with me. He should just go.

"I thought your suggestion before was a good one." My voice was trembling a little. "We'll do it the way you said. I'll ask you questions that you could only answer if you really live here. And if you know me as well as you claim to."

He nods as his eyes flit around over the bed, the walls, the floor. Before eventually locking back onto me again.

"OK." I scour through my memories, searching for something that even the most cunning of stalkers wouldn't be able to find out. Details that don't appear on Facebook or my website.

But the stress is taking its toll, and all I can think of are mundane details, nothing significant. Nothing that would convince me if he knew it.

So I start with something random instead. An old habit. "I'm sure you've found out what I do for work."

"You're a photographer." He says it slowly, but without hesitation. "You're doing an apprenticeship with Manuel Helfrich, because you admire his work so much; that's one of the reasons why you came to Germany. Your pictures are wonderful, I love your portraits. You've photographed me so often . . ."

I try to interject, but he doesn't let me. "You had a favorite photo of me," he says. "You framed it, and until this morning it was hanging right there." He points at the wall, at a spot over the dresser.

"First, that's nonsense, and second, that wasn't my question!" Even as the words are still coming out of my mouth, I realize how reckless I'm being. Just because he hasn't done anything to hurt me so far doesn't mean it will stay that way. Aggravating him is definitely a bad idea.

"Sorry," I mumble. "But I'd like to ask my question now."

He nods and prompts me to continue, with a despondent gesture.

"When I photograph people who are nervous and feel uncomfortable in front of the camera, I always play a song at the start of the session. A very particular song. Which one is it?"

He opens his mouth. Closes it again. "I don't know. I went to see you in your studio a few times, but as soon as the clients arrived, you kicked me out right away. You said that third wheels are just as unwelcome at photo sessions as they are on dates."

I feel my stomach cramping up. He doesn't know the song, as expected—but the rest really does sound like something I would say. Word for word, even.

But that doesn't necessarily mean anything.

New question. Quickly.

"What's my middle name?"

If he knows me, then he'd know it. I would have had him try to guess it, like I do with everyone I get to know, usually over the third and fourth glass of wine. He would have failed miserably, like all the others. But eventually I always give in and tell. Always.

The stranger glances to the side, as if he can't believe what I've just asked him. For a moment I think he's about to burst out laughing. When he starts to speak again, his voice is quiet. "You haven't told me. Not yet. You wanted me to guess it myself, but so far I haven't managed to."

My mouth is dry. What I'd do for a sip of water right now. Once again, the man hasn't answered my question, but once again, what he said lies close to the truth.

You wanted me to guess it myself.

He can't have gotten this information online. Or by following me. He must have spoken to people who know me. Who told him what makes me tick, what I like, what I don't like . . .

He's still blocking the door. His gaze wanders over my face, like he's looking for something he lost.

"One more question," he says. "Something different, something that has more to do with you as a person, with your history, with this house, our life together."

"I asked you two questions, and you couldn't answer either of them."

He closes his eyes, looking tormented. "Please," he says. "Stop talking to me that way. You can't imagine how—" He interrupts himself. "You don't remember what my name is, do you?"

I cross my arms in front of my chest. "I never knew."

A stunned shake of the head. "This is so . . . unbelievable."

"I'm sorry. But I can do the guessing this time if you want." Now the man looks vulnerable, and hope is slowly growing within me that perhaps I can get the situation under my control after all. At least enough so I can flee from this room.

My suggestion makes the stranger's eyes light up. "Yes—that's a great idea! Maybe your consciousness saved some information, then everything else will fall into place." He takes a step toward me. "Just say the first name that comes into your mind," he says in an imploring tone. "Without thinking about it."

I do exactly as he asks, and the result is surprisingly clear in my mind. "Ben."

Wrong. I can see it in his face. In any other situation, his disappointment would have awoken my sympathy. But now it's giving me a further advantage I have to exploit.

"OK, so not Ben. I'll ask you another question. One last one, OK?"

He nods in resignation, in a way that shows he's lost hope.

"There on the wall, above the wardrobe—do you see it? That little round hole?"

No, he can't, there's no way he could from where he's standing. I beckon him closer, even though I don't feel comfortable about it. "There, do you see? What made that hole?"

I take a step back to make space for him. One step, then another, toward the door. By the time he sees there's nothing there, I want to be out of the room already and put as much space between us as possible so he can't grab me again.

"But there was never," I hear him say as I fling the door open and run out onto the landing . . . toward the stairs, quickly, two steps at once, *please don't fall now.*

"Joanna!"

He comes after me, of course, but I'm almost downstairs already, almost at the front door. . . .

Which is locked.

My keychain is hanging on the hook, where it belongs. I grab for it; it slips out of my fingers, falls to the floor with a clinking sound.

"Jo! Please, you can't just run out like this!"

I've got the key in my hand again, and there's still time. I manage to get it in the lock on the first try, turn it once, twice, press down the handle. The cool evening air rushes to meet me.

Then, a jolt. I'm torn backward with a force that pulls me down to the floor. The next moment, the door slams shut again with a loud thud.

I jump up, try to get past him, if he hasn't locked it again I still have a chance, but he grabs my arms so tightly that I scream.

"Do you really want everyone to see you like this?" he yells. "Are you trying to get yourself committed?"

I struggle against him, with all my strength, but I have no chance. So I go slack and just let myself fall.

He wasn't expecting that. I make him lose his balance, he almost falls onto me. At the last moment he turns to the side, without letting go of my wrists.

Only now do I realize I'm crying.

He sees it too. He lays his forehead against mine, his breathing fitful. "You need help, Jo."

He's damn right about that. And as soon as he lets me go . . .

"Look at me," he demands. His voice sounds like he's close to tears himself.

I do what he asks. Our faces are so close now, for a moment I'm afraid he's going to kiss me.

"Let me go."

He shakes his head. "Erik," he blurts out. "My name is Erik." He waits, as though he really thinks his name will mean something to me.

"Erik," I repeat obediently, then feel his grip loosen a little, as though the name was some kind of password.

I wrench my hands away, pull myself up, try to push him away from me, but the very next moment the man's weight pushes me back down to the floor again. His breath is hot in my face.

"Don't do that, Jo. I just want to help you. And I will."

His last word is underlined by a loud ringing. The doorbell. Someone's at the door.

4

I jump, startled. Never has the doorbell seemed as loud to me as it does in this moment. Joanna stops struggling almost immediately, I feel her grow motionless beneath me.

There's a flash of hope in her eyes that someone who'll help her is outside the door. My thoughts tumble through my mind. We're not expecting anyone.

Crazily enough, I feel guilty, and what's more, a twinge of panic. Like I really am a burglar or a madman.

I push the thought from my mind; it's ridiculous, after all. But I don't want anyone to see Joanna in this state. Could she have called the police?

"Please! Please help me!" Joanna's mouth is just a few inches away from my ear. Her screams leave a high-pitched, painful ringing in my head.

"Be quiet, damn it," I hiss at her and resist the impulse of putting my hand over her mouth. In the same moment, I realize I'm going to have to act quickly if I don't want the situation to escalate. I turn onto my side and release Joanna. She jumps up and is at the door, tears it open, and leaps outside, all before I've even managed to fully get to my feet. "Thank goodness," she gasps. "I've been assaulted; this man broke into my house."

My heart is pounding in my throat. The open door is obstructing my view. I take two steps to the side, then find myself face-to-face with Bernhard Morbach. He looks at me, surprised. Joanna is cowering behind him.

Bernhard is a department manager at Gabor Energy Engineering.

He's never been to my house, but the laptop bag hanging from his shoulder suggests the reason for this first-ever visit. Why now, of all times? Today at work was strange enough, not that I could describe exactly why. And if tomorrow Bernhard starts telling everyone about what he's witnessing here . . .

"Erik . . ." Bernhard, clearly confused, turns around to face Joanna, who's pulling her bathrobe together at the collar. He looks her up and down, then looks over at me. "I don't understand. What's going on here?"

Joanna's eyes widen as she hears my name. I can tell she's confused, see her taking a step back, and I realize what's going to happen next. I have no choice. As she turns to run, I've already taken a couple of strides past Bernhard. I fling my arm around Joanna's upper body from behind. "Jo, please," I hiss at her as she tries to free herself from my grip. "You have to come back inside."

"No way! You're conspiring together, the two of you. Let me go." Joanna's rib cage expands as she takes a deep breath, but I press my hand over her mouth before she can scream. I take a quick look around and note Bernhard's incredulous expression, but now isn't the time for long-winded explanations.

"Come on," I pant, and drag Joanna, twisting and turning and kicking at me, back into the house, using all the strength I have. She tries to bite my hand, but I don't let go.

Finally I make it into the hall. Bernhard, to my surprise, actually follows us into the house. I let Joanna go, rush to the door, and slam it shut. Moving quickly, I turn the key and remove it from the lock, while somewhere behind me another door is slammed shut with a dull thud. I slowly turn around and take a deep breath.

"She . . . she went in there," Bernhard stutters, pointing toward the kitchen. "Can you tell me what's going on? I mean . . . that *is* the Joanna you've told us about, isn't it?"

I indicate to him that he needs to wait.

The kitchen is empty. Either Joanna ran into the living room or she's hiding in the pantry. A few steps and I'm at the door. I reach for the handle. It's locked. So Joanna, in all her confusion, went and hid in the only room on the ground floor that doesn't have any windows.

I turn away from the door and walk back to Bernhard, who's nervously pacing up and down the hall.

"She's locked herself in the pantry," I start to explain. "I don't know what's going on, but Jo's all over the place. She doesn't recognize me anymore, not since I got home tonight. I don't want anyone to see her like this, so . . ." I hesitate, thinking that this attempt at an explanation must seem strange to Bernhard. He stands there and looks at me, perplexed.

I shake my head. "I'm sorry that this is how you're getting to meet Jo. She's not normally like this. I don't get it either. You know she's Australian, right, and she's meant to be going back soon, but she doesn't want to because we . . . And I really want her to stay as well. But if anyone sees her in this state, they'll think she's crazy. Then everything will get a lot more complicated, you see? That's why I held . . . That's why I don't want her running around outside and screaming."

Bernhard finally takes his bag off his shoulder and sets it down against the wall next to him. "I see . . ." But his face says the exact opposite. "Has she ever been like this before?"

"No. I've never seen her like this." I look over toward the kitchen. From where I'm standing, I can see a narrow section of the door to the storeroom. What's Joanna doing in there now? What's going on inside her head? Is she sitting on the floor, trembling in fright, thinking about how she can escape the madman who's invaded her house and who claims to be living with her?

I turn away and swiftly wipe my eyes before I look at Bernhard again. "Everything was perfectly all right this morning. She was in a good mood when I set off for work. Something must have happened during the day, something that triggered this . . . confusion. I hope it'll sort itself out again, otherwise I don't know what I'm going to do." I pull myself together; those kinds of thoughts aren't going to help anyone right now. My eyes wander over the laptop bag on the floor. I nod toward it. "Is that the reason you stopped by?"

"What? Oh yeah, it is. I'm flying to London tomorrow morning, but I can't find the presentation that one of your guys transferred over to my laptop from my desktop this afternoon." He pauses and quickly looks over at the kitchen. "But I can see now isn't really a good time, I'll go see if Alex can help."

He's right, it's definitely not a good time, but there's no way I'm having Alex find out about what's happening at my house as well. So I say,

"Oh, nonsense," and point toward the living room. "Come on, let's take a look."

We're both sitting on the sofa as I turn on the computer. Bernhard is eyeing the screen with interest, pretending the system messages that appear as the device starts up mean something to him.

"What are you going to be doing in London anyway?" I ask, to pass the time.

Bernhard hesitates. "Ah, it's because of that new project. You heard about it, right?" He lowers his gaze.

"Oh. That. Yeah, I did hear that it's coming up soon. But only by chance. As I'm sure you know." My anger from that time is flaring up inside me again.

The whole thing is visibly unpleasant for Bernhard. While I try to focus on the laptop again, his gaze wanders toward the kitchen. He's looking for a way to change the subject.

"Not that it's any of my business, but as I've just witnessed this . . . situation, it made me think of an acquaintance of mine. Something very similar happened with her once. It all passed really quickly, but at the time it was happening she no longer recognized anyone. It's just that she got very aggressive too, with herself and other people. Awful, really. Is it the same with Joanna? I mean . . . you said she doesn't recognize you anymore all of a sudden. But did she attack you?"

I find his question bizarre, but then I guess bizarre situations entail bizarre questions. And the things Bernhard's witnessed since he arrived at our front door would probably prompt such a line of inquiry. Also, the whole thing with the new project is clearly uncomfortable for him. At the end of the day, I guess I should be relieved he reacted the way he did instead of just leaving before I had the opportunity to explain.

"She threw something at me, but that was understandable in a way, because she was afraid. I mean, she does seem to think I'm a stranger who broke into her house. There wasn't anything else, but that's enough for me."

Bernhard nods. "Well, then it's different to my acquaintance anyway. Who knows, maybe she'll be all better again in the morning?"

"Yes, I really hope so." I realize I'm staring at the laptop screen and not seeing anything.

Still, it doesn't take me long to find the presentation we're looking for in the recycle bin. Somebody deleted it. Probably Bernhard himself, but if I tell him that, he's going to categorically deny it. Just like all computer users do when they've made a mess of things. Besides, I'll be relieved when he's gone again and I can focus on Joanna.

I restore the file and open it. "Is this the presentation?"

Bernhard clicks here and there a few times, then nods, relieved. "Yes, it is. Thank goodness. Where was it?"

"There's no way you could have found it," I say, sidestepping the question.

I close the laptop and get up. Bernhard hesitates for a moment longer. "Listen, is there any way I can help? I mean, if there's anything I can do for you and Joanna . . ."

"No, thanks. I'm going to go have a quiet chat with her. And I'm sure she'll be feeling better soon. She has a lot of office visits and paperwork looming; maybe she's just stressed."

I hope Bernhard can't hear in my voice just how unconvinced even I am by what I just said. He packs his laptop away into his bag and gets up.

"All right then. If I was you, I'd think twice about coming into the office tomorrow morning."

I hadn't even thought that far ahead yet. What if Joanna's state hasn't gotten any better by tomorrow morning? What if she still believes I'm some crazy stranger who broke into her house?

"We'll see. But I think it will be all right."

I accompany him to the door. He stops in the hall, his eyes fixed on the passage through to the kitchen. "Should *I* maybe try to talk to her? If I assure her she really is living here with you, maybe she'll believe you?"

He means well, but I don't want anyone she doesn't know—genuinely doesn't know, that is—talking to her in this situation. Besides, she did just make it plain that she thinks we're both in cahoots. No, if there's anyone who can manage to recover Joanna's memories of us, then it's me.

"Thanks, that's very kind of you, but I think it's better if I talk to her."

He shrugs and turns toward the door. "All right then. So good luck and . . . well . . . all the best."

"Thanks."

I wait until he's walked a few steps, then I go back into the house. I stand at the entrance to the kitchen for a while and stare at the pantry door. I can't hear anything. Joanna's probably sitting on the floor and listening just as intently. My Joanna.

I approach the door and raise my hand. Hesitate. Then, finally, I knock carefully.

"Jo?" I say, so quietly that she probably can't even hear me. I clear my throat and try again, louder this time. "Jo? Please, I have to talk to you."

5

It's dark, and the light switch is outside. Outside the closed door. That's where the voices are coming from too. The voice of the man who says his name is Erik, and that of the other man, who just stood by and watched as I was pulled forcibly back into the house by his pal.

They're talking, but not very loudly. I wait to hear a laugh, conspiratorial and in unison, but it doesn't come. Their muffled voices sound serious.

It's cramped in here. Packed full. My right hand brushes against a familiar shape, hard and round. A tin can, probably tinned tomatoes. Good. It's a suitable enough weapon, and feels comforting in my hands.

For a while, I try to make out at least some snippets of their conversation, but eventually I give up.

Erik. The man with the bag over his shoulder had used his name so naturally. And he hadn't been surprised to see the stranger in my house, not even for a second—if anything, it was me who had surprised him. Me and the way I was acting.

That means that this . . . Erik guy must have dished up the same insane story to him as he did to me. That he lives here, and that he's in a relationship with me.

So maybe he's not an accomplice after all? I don't know. None of my thoughts seem logical anymore. My head is pounding; I vaguely remember hitting it on the floor earlier during my failed escape attempt.

But at least I can still remember where I store the bottles of mineral water. Rehydrating helps, and my headache gradually dissipates.

A short while later, I hear the front door click into the lock. The man with the bag has gone, I'm guessing, and he won't be lifting a finger to help me.

I huddle into my corner. Any moment now the reprieve will be over and the game will continue. Even though I'm waiting for Erik's next move, the sudden knock on the door still makes my heart skip a beat.

"Jo?" His voice is quiet and insistent. "Jo? Please, I have to talk to you."

That approach again. This time he won't get any answer from me. Stay silent, I tell myself. Play dead.

"Jo? Can you hear me?" More knocking. "Are you OK? Is everything all right?"

And if it's not? What will you do then, asshole?

I don't have to wait long for an answer. I hear a clinking sound; the man is probably rummaging through the kitchen drawer. A brief silence, then the sound, very close now, of metal against metal.

He's found something to break open the door with.

"I'm OK." My voice is hoarse with reluctance, but it's still enough to stop Erik from working on the lock.

"Thank God," he says. "Listen, I'm sorry I was so rough with you before, but . . ." He pauses.

Rage suddenly surges up within me; it's so overwhelming that it completely drowns out my fear. Suddenly I'm almost wishing for the lunatic out there to really break down the door so I can throw myself at him with all my strength. Beat him with my fists until he's no longer moving. Or stab him, if I can get my hands on the big kitchen knife. . . .

The image is so vivid in my mind it takes on a life of its own, and I'm shocked by how much I like it. I didn't know that helplessness and violent compulsions could be so closely interlinked.

So far, though, physical resistance hadn't helped me. On the contrary. It was time to change my strategy.

"Erik?" I make my voice sound as though I'm close to tears.

"Yes?"

"Could you turn on the light for me? Please?"

"What? Yes, of course. I didn't realize you were sitting there in the dark."

The eco-lightbulb under the cheap frosted-glass ceiling lamp flickers on, bathing the packed shelves in a dim light.

The can in my hand really does contain peeled tomatoes.

"Better?"

"Much better. Thank you."

There's a short pause. When the man outside the door starts speaking again, his voice is on the same level as my head. He must be sitting on the floor. Or kneeling.

"Listen to me, Jo. We won't be able to figure this out by ourselves, we need help." He sounds exhausted. That's good. Eventually he'll need to sleep.

"I'd like to take you to a doctor in the morning, so we can find out what happened. Maybe the stress of the past few weeks was too much for you, or . . ."

He left the sentence unfinished.

"To a doctor?" I ask quietly.

"Yes, Jo. Before it gets even worse. If I hadn't stopped you tonight, you would have run out into the street screaming and half-naked, on two separate occasions. I don't want them to institutionalize you, I mean, our situation is hard enough as it is."

His tone is imploring and gentle at the same time, but I'm fully aware of the intention behind his words. He wants me to doubt my own state of mind, not his.

"You can't imagine how much all this is hurting me," he continues. "Yesterday you were telling me you love me, and today you don't even remember who I am."

His voice was becoming quieter and quieter. Either he really believes what he's saying, or he's a really good actor.

"Jo?"

"Yes?"

"I love you, and it's awful to have to do this, but I can't let you out of here tonight. I can't risk you screaming for help out the window, or trying to run away again."

If it weren't so sad, I would have laughed. My cell was of my own choosing. I had imprisoned myself in the very place where I couldn't draw attention to myself. I really am a very cooperative victim.

"But I'm staying here," he adds. "I'm going to lie down here right by the door; I won't leave you by yourself. If you need anything . . ."

I don't answer him. It was obvious, after all, that he would block any escape route available to me.

I take a few clean tea towels from the pile I keep here on the shelves, arrange them under my head and close my eyes. The door is locked from the inside, so Erik can't get in here. I could even risk falling asleep, but I can't get my thoughts to settle. I run through the events of this awful evening in my mind again and again, moment by moment. I can't push them away . . .

And then, after at least two hours must have passed, everything falls into place all at once, forming a picture as clear as glass and logical down to the very last detail.

What Erik wants, above everything, is for me to believe him. For me to think that something is wrong with *me*. That's why he had a friend of his turn up here, acting like Erik's presence in the house was entirely natural. I could probably bet on a few more encounters like these taking place over the next few days.

And then the doctor's visit. The next act, surely, in which I find out from an experienced professional that I have a screw loose. I'd bet anything on it.

At least there's one thing I don't need to waste any more time tearing my hair out over: the motive of my caring fiancé there on the other side of the door. Once someone knows my name, it doesn't take a genius to find out who I am. And, most important, who my father is. Then it's highly possible that someone could come up with the creative idea of wanting to convince me I'm engaged to them. Maybe one day I'd even believe it, and boom—they would have just married into the third-richest family in Australia.

Well. Unfortunately Erik has picked the wrong victim.

I curl up into a ball, try to find a tolerable sleeping position, and close my eyes. At least I don't have to worry about him cutting my throat in my sleep. After all, a billionaire's daughter isn't much use to a con artist once she's dead.

"Jo?" A knock on the door. "It's almost eight, we've got an appointment with Dr. Dussmann in an hour. I just called him, he's fitting us in as an emergency."

Shelves, cans, cleaning products. For the duration of a few heartbeats I'm unable to remember where I am, but then the events of the previous day come flooding back with full force.

"Are you awake, Jo?"

"Yes." My whole body is in pain from lying on the hard floor, I can hardly get up.

"I brought you some clothes. If you unlock the door, I'll pass them in to you."

"I'd like to take a shower." It's not a pretense, but the absolute truth. After the night I've just had, I really need some soap and hot water.

Erik doesn't respond. I unlock the door into his silence.

He is standing directly opposite me, with my black jeans, a green shirt, and clean underwear in his hands. He looks tired, there's no question about that, but his eyes are alert. As soon as I make any quick movement, he'll grab me just as quickly as he did yesterday.

"I won't run away," I say. "I'll go with you to see this doctor . . . What was his name again?"

"Dussmann." Erik doesn't trust the sudden peace, I can see that from his expression.

"Dussmann, exactly. But I want to go to the toilet and take a shower. And I want to do both alone; hopefully you can understand that. I promise I won't make a run for it or call for help."

It's not difficult to read the thoughts that are going through Erik's mind. He is weighing whether he can take the risk. I had the whole night to figure out a plan, and my peaceable behavior could very well be part of that.

So I force a smile. "I think it's a good idea for me to see the doctor. I feel kind of . . . strange somehow. And besides—" I act like I'm not quite sure if I should really trust him with the words I'm about to say. "And besides, during the night I had a kind of memory of you. It was very brief and fuzzy. But if it wasn't just my imagination," I say, furrowing my brow thoughtfully, "then maybe there is something wrong with me. And if that's the case, I want to know about it."

Bingo. All of a sudden Erik no longer looks tired in the least.

"Really, Jo? You remembered me? That's wonderful." He takes a step toward me, and I have to fight my instinct to back away. "Listen, here's what we'll do. You go take a shower, but I'll disable the lock and wait outside. Please don't try to trick me, because then I'd have to come in. For your own sake. You understand that, right?"

I nod, smile, say yes to everything. He gives me twenty minutes, and we both keep to what we promised. Only once we're at the front door and he's turning the key in the lock with his right hand does he reach out with his left to grip my arm.

"That's not necessary." My voice sounds almost tender. "It really isn't, Erik. But I'd like to take my phone with me. If there's really something wrong, I want to be able to call my family."

He looks at me, searchingly. He raises his hand as though he wants to stroke my face, but stops midmovement and grasps my arm again. "As soon as we know what's wrong with you, you'll get your phone and anything else you want. I promise."

In other words, after Dr. Dussmann has played his intended role. This is just what I'd expected. "You're probably right," I say. "OK."

He leads me outside, as if he's afraid I could fall. There's a silver Audi parked in the driveway next to my used VW Golf, one of those limousine-like cars that manager types drive. Shiny and immaculate, without even the hint of a mud stain on the fenders.

I can't help but grin. Anyone who didn't know better would guess that Erik was the more affluent of the two of us.

He opens the passenger door for me and waits until I've put on my seat belt before closing it again. Five seconds later, he sits down next to me and starts the engine.

"We'll sort this out," he says. "You'll see."

6

I steer the car out of the driveway and turn right. For a brief moment, I look over at Joanna, who's giving me a slightly tense smile. Her hands are on her chest, holding the safety belt like she was afraid it might squeeze the air from her lungs.

Just before we turn into the next street, I glance into the rearview mirror and see a man standing in the entrance to our driveway. He's looking in our direction. Is he watching us? Nonsense. I'd better make sure I don't start getting paranoid too.

Houses pass by us on both sides, with cars parked in front. Here and there, different campaign posters for the upcoming elections. Garbage bins, already set out on the curb by overzealous neighbors even though collection day isn't until tomorrow. Life as always in our street. Normal.

Deceptive.

My thoughts wander. I called into work and took a day off. If there aren't any IT projects in the critical phase it's usually not a problem.

Thank goodness Bernhard is in London. I hope he doesn't call anyone at work and let slip about what he saw at our place last night.

If he does, well, there's nothing I can do about it. Joanna said that she remembered me, and at first I was so relieved that I believed her without a moment's hesitation. I willingly clung to her words, because I simply didn't want to accept that Joanna, my Joanna, might suddenly have developed a psychological problem.

Now, though, I'm not so sure anymore. She had a good few hours in the storeroom to think everything through. Maybe she invented having remembered something about me just to placate me.

But at least she's willing to go see Dr. Dussmann with me. I've never been to see him myself, but he was an acquaintance of my parents. The last time I saw him was at my father's funeral, two and a half years ago. The fact that we're loosely acquainted at least gives me hope he'll take Joanna's problem seriously and not just commit her to a clinic.

"How well do you know this . . . doctor?" Joanna threads her way into my thoughts so smoothly that it's almost like I'd spoken them out loud. I shrug. "Only vaguely. He knew my parents."

I look over at her, see her raise an eyebrow. "Knew?"

"Yes, knew. My parents are dead." I only just manage to suppress the impulse to snap at Joanna, to hurl my words at her. *You know that very damn well. Cancer. First my mother, then my father three years later. I told you, right down to the tiniest little detail.*

Surely she can't just have forgotten all that.

The expression on her face tells me otherwise.

The traffic light we're approaching skips to red. I stop, and feel Joanna's eyes on me. Look over at her. Why is it right now, in this bizarre situation, that it strikes me just how incredibly beautiful she is?

"Erik . . . If you really believe what you told me . . ."

She pauses, as though she's not sure she can dare say what she wants to say. But then she comes out with it after all. "Did the thought ever occur to you that *you* might be mistaken?"

I don't understand what she means. "Mistaken?"

She nods tentatively. "Yes. You're claiming something's wrong with me. That I've forgotten you."

"Which you certainly seem to have done."

"That's what you're saying. But maybe it's you who's imagining that you know me and that you live in my home?"

"What? You think . . ." I believe I understand what's happening right now. Her mind is feverishly looking for an explanation that would confirm that nothing's wrong with her. Wouldn't I do the same if it were me? But still . . . "I used my key to get into the house. You have to admit . . ."

"It could be a copy."

"But how do you explain me knowing my way around the house so well? And Bernhard. How come he turned up on *your* doorstep if it's me he wanted to see? I know for an absolute fact that we live together, Jo."

"But that doesn't prove it. Think about it! If that's the case, shouldn't some of your stuff be in the house? Clothes? Furniture? Your bedding? Something?"

Yeah, I haven't found an explanation for that yet either. "I don't know either why—" The angry blaring of a car horn interrupts me. The traffic light. I shift into gear and start driving.

"You say you know that we live together." Joanna's voice is so quiet I can barely understand it. "But I, on the other hand, know that we're neither engaged nor in love. And I know that yesterday evening was the first time I saw you."

"I thought you'd remembered me?" I can hear how much my voice sounds like a petulant child's, and it irritates me.

"Each of us has their own version, Erik," she said, sidestepping the question. "And my version could be just as true as yours. How can you be so sure it's me, that I'm the one something's not right with?"

We're on a busy street now, with lots of traffic. But I still glance over at her quickly. "Because, damn it, I just know." The words come out louder and sharper than intended.

I ask myself if my anger is the result of Joanna's obtuseness, or whether it's because what she's saying might be true. Both of us are sure we're right, but one of us is living in a world of make-believe right now.

Little by little, we approach the center of town. Another traffic light. Joanna is sitting upright in her seat now; her body seems tense to the point of snapping. No wonder.

"I didn't mean to shout at you. I'm sorry."

We're at a standstill now. "None of this is easy for me either, and—" There's a clicking sound, very loud and very close. I twist around. The brief moment my mind needs to process the movement next to me and turn it into something I can comprehend is enough for Joanna to sweep the seat belt aside and shove the door open. My fingertips brush her arm but fail to grab on.

"Jo, don't!" I shout after her. "Damn it, stay here. Jo!"

She ignores my shouting and starts to run. A few feet along the sidewalk, then off to the right, following the intersecting road. Out of my line of sight.

I have to go after her. She can't be running through the city all by herself like this. Not in this state. But the car, the traffic behind me . . .

I don't give a crap. Let them honk.

I try to undo my seat belt but don't manage. Like a man possessed, I pound the lock, curse, scream, take out all of my desperate fury on the goddamn thing while a concert of car horns starts up behind me. Finally, the lock clicks open. I shove open the door . . . and freeze. What the hell am I doing?

If I mindlessly run after Joanna now, I probably won't find her. But my car is blocking a busy intersection. The police will be here in two minutes flat, and they're going to ask questions. I can't have that. Not now.

I pull the door shut again and take a look into my rearview mirror. The guy behind me is throwing a fit and gives me the finger. *Right back at you, asshole.*

I step on the gas. There's that nerve-fraying *ding, ding, ding* sound telling me I have to buckle my seat belt. I need a place I can stop, where there aren't any idiots riding their horns. After driving for about five hundred feet, I find an empty parking space in front of a pharmacy. Finally.

I switch off the engine and get out of the car. Even though it's pointless, I look around for Joanna. No luck, of course. I lean back against the closed car door, rub my hands over my face, and try to force my thoughts back into some sort of coherent order. Being a computer scientist, I should be used to thinking in a structured way, after all. So . . . Joanna's running through the city all alone. What's she going to do? She needs someone, needs to talk to somebody. But who is she going to turn to? The police?

Maybe. But Joanna isn't quite as panic-stricken as she was yesterday evening. Even if she's refusing to accept it, she must at least be considering the possibility that I could be right and that something's wrong with her. And no matter what's going on inside her head right now, she's smart enough to figure out how the police might react.

No, she's going to go to someone she knows first. Someone she trusts. To make sure she hasn't really lost her mind.

Ela. Of course. Ela is her best friend, the only really close girlfriend she has. She's a medical technician in the city hospital, not five minutes from here by car. Maybe fifteen minutes for Joanna on foot. That must be where she's going. If I hurry, we might even arrive at the same time.

I get in the car, wondering why it didn't occur to me earlier to take

Joanna to see Ela. Before dragging her to the psychologist's practice. Then again, I'm under extreme pressure here myself, and that kind of thing tends to stall your rational thought process.

Should I call Ela and warn her?

No, that's pointless. I'll probably have arrived at the hospital parking lot already by the time they've put me through to her on the phone.

Damn it, can't these idiots get a move on? It almost seems like they're blocking my way just for the fun of it.

Another red light. I drum my fingers on the steering wheel. In my head, images from the past are blending with the surreal situation from this morning.

A flea market. *The* flea market. I'd always written off those stories you hear about love at first sight as being overblown tripe from cheesy romance novels. Until that moment, that is.

I don't even know if it was really love I'd felt upon seeing Joanna for the first time. In any case, it was something that had struck me somewhere deep inside, completely turning my emotions upside down. I simply had to be near her; I hadn't been able to help myself. She hadn't seen me; she'd been completely focused on a small, ornate box, so tacky it was beautiful. The seller had wanted two more euros for it than she'd been prepared to pay. I'd listened to her bargaining, to no avail; then I'd put the full amount down on the table in front of the man.

I can still picture her right in front of me, staring at me in disbelief. I think it was in that moment, if not before, that I fell irretrievably in love with her.

After she furiously turned away from me, I had run after her. When I'd cut off her path and stood in front of her, I was scared she'd hit me in the face, that's how angry she had been. But then I held up the box, out toward her. Her eyes had widened in surprise. I said I'd bought it for her. At first she had seemed to want to . . .

Someone's car horn is blaring behind me again. I've had enough of these damn horns now. I step on the gas pedal so hard that the car bounds forward.

Just a few minutes later, I arrive at the hospital. I find a parking space near the entrance. Taking swift steps, I hurry toward the revolving door and glance at my wristwatch. Joanna leaped out of the car just over twenty minutes ago. So maybe she's already here.

I know the way to the lab. Down the hall, past the elevators, then through the door on the left. Up some stairs, through the next door, then one more turn, and I'm there. My pulse quickens as I walk the last few steps. What awaits me now?

I knock, open the door. The young, dark-haired woman in the lobby gives me a friendly look past the side of her monitor. "Good morning."

"Good morning." My voice sounds hoarse. "I'd like to see Ela Weisfels, please."

A hint of sympathy settles over the friendly smile.

"I'm sorry, Ela left already; she was on the night shift."

"OK, thanks," I say, and am about to turn away as something occurs to me.

"Oh, I was meant to meet my girlfriend here, we wanted to surprise Ela. Maybe she was already here?"

Now the smile disappears completely. "Yes, about five minutes ago there was a young lady here who wanted to see Ela as well." She fiddles around with something on her desk, then gives me a strange look.

"Not that it's any of my business, but is everything all right with your girlfriend? She seemed somewhat . . . distraught."

7

I run like I've never run before, not because of panic, but because the sensation of my regained freedom spurs me on with every step I take. The first street on the right, then the next left. A glance over my shoulder—no, he's not following me, but I keep running regardless. I've been given a chance, and there's no way I'm going to let it slip through my fingers.

Only once I'm gasping for air do I stop in a doorway to catch my breath. I ignore the surprised glances of two stroller-pushing mothers walking past. I'm not far from the pedestrian zone, and there's a police station up ahead on the corner. My hand is already on the door handle before it occurs to me that I can't provide any ID. My papers, my visa—everything's in the house, and I don't have the key anymore. That's the first obstacle.

The other is how hurt Erik had looked before, when he spoke about his dead parents. As hard as I had tried to fight it, his disappointed gaze had moved me.

Of course I'm still going to report him, though; I don't have a choice. If I want my life back, then he needs to disappear from it.

But I want to have someone here with me who can confirm my story.

The knowledge of how easy this would be if I just had my phone with me almost makes me storm angrily into the police station anyway. *Soon*, I reassure myself. A few minutes won't make a difference, and the hospital where Ela works is just over a mile away at most.

I set off, taking care to avoid the main streets, but still give a start every time a silver car comes into view.

Would Erik grab me on the street and pull me into his car in broad daylight? Is that plausible?

He would have to be very sure of himself if he did, because of course I would call for help. And resist him with all my strength.

Does he have an ace up his sleeve that would allow him to take the risk?

At the end of the street, the hospital comes into view, towering over all the buildings in the vicinity.

Five minutes later, I find out that my detour was in vain. Ela was on the night shift and went home at seven this morning, the laboratory secretary informs me. The disappointment, paired with the stress of the past twelve hours, pushes tears to my eyes.

"Has something happened? Can I help you?" The secretary's sympathy only makes it worse. I silently shake my head, refuse the glass of water she offers me, and turn around.

Only once I'm already outside again do I realize how stupid I've been. I won't get another opportunity as good as that to call Ela, considering that I don't know her number by heart. The secretary would have had it, and she probably would have given it to me too if I'd gone about things the right way.

But maybe Ela already went to bed hours ago and put her phone on silent.

When it comes to the doorbell, though, she'll definitely hear that.

Normally I'd never wake her up, but this is an emergency.

I have to cross the entire city to get to her apartment. I don't have a single cent in my bag, no credit card, nothing. I can't even afford to get the bus, let alone a taxi. The irony of the situation is striking, given that I could easily buy the entire bus company if I had access to my fortune right now.

So I'll just have to risk riding without a ticket. The bus that goes out to where Ela lives is just pulling in as I get to the bus stop in front of the hospital. Just a coincidence, of course, but it brightens my mood a little. Perhaps things are finally turning in my favor.

It's a twenty-five-minute journey. I lean my forehead against the window of the bus and gaze out. What if Ela didn't go back to her place after work? What if she decided to stay over at Richard's, despite their constant fights?

That's unlikely. He has to be at the office, so they wouldn't have been able to grab any time together.

Nonetheless, I'm incredibly nervous by the time I get off the bus, and even more so once I'm standing in front of Ela's front door.

What will I do if she doesn't answer? What other options do I have? The police, OK. That's my last trump card. But it's one I don't feel ready to play, not without support.

Hesitating here won't help anything. I ring Ela's doorbell for ten, fifteen seconds.

When she answers the intercom, she sounds wide awake. Luckily.

"Yes? Who's there?"

"It's me. Joanna." My voice trembles with relief. "Can I come in, please?"

The door release buzzes; I push the door open, step inside, and close it behind me again. Too impatient to wait for the elevator, I run up the three floors to Ela's apartment.

She's standing in the doorway wearing jogging pants and a sweatshirt. Her dark locks are tied up into a ponytail, and her expression is confused and questioning.

"I'm sorry to burst in on you like this." I give her a quick hug and can smell soap. She must have just showered. "I would have called you, but . . . I couldn't."

"Come in." She pulls me into the apartment. "How about a coffee? You look like you need one."

"No. Thank you." I'm so happy to see her. Her level-headed manner alone is already calming me down.

In the living room, she gently presses me down onto the couch, sits next to me, and takes my hand. "Now tell me what's going on."

I begin, hesitantly at first, but soon the words are just flowing. The strange man in my house who claims his name is Erik and that he's engaged to me; the night I spent imprisoned within my own four walls; my escape.

Ela doesn't interrupt me a single time, but here and there she widens her eyes with disbelief; a deep wrinkle has appeared above her nose.

"That's . . . unbelievable," she murmurs once I've finished. "Give me a couple of minutes to digest it, OK?" She shakes her head, then suddenly pauses. "Oh damn it, I almost forgot." She reaches for her phone and dials a number.

"A colleague," she murmurs apologetically. "I was a bit scatterbrained with the . . . Hello, Sandra?"

I already know that Ela is very laid-back, at least when it's not about Richard, but the way she's responding to my story astonishes me nonetheless. As does the fact that right now, of all moments, something to do with her colleague should pop into her mind.

"Sandra, sorry, I completely forgot to tell you on the handover that the technician is coming to see to the centrifuge this morning. What? Yes, that would be good. OK. Yes. I'll do that. See you then." Ella puts her phone away. "Done." She rubs both hands over her face. "Are you sure you don't want a coffee?"

It's starting to become difficult to hide my impatience. "No, I want to go to the police, and I was hoping you'd come with me."

Ela stares fixedly at the carpet beneath her feet. "I don't think that's a good idea, Jo."

I feel a cold tingling at the back of my neck. "Why not?"

She looks up and makes eye contact again. "Because what you've just told me doesn't make any sense. You and Erik, you are a couple. And a damn good one too."

The cold feeling has suddenly spread through my entire body. *Please don't*, I want to say, *please don't do this to me.*

"I swear to you, last night was the first time I ever saw that man in my whole life," I whisper, seeing in Ela's eyes how uncomfortable this situation is for her. "I live alone, you of all people would know that—you've been over to my place so often! There's no one in my life apart from Matthew, and even he's ancient history now, really."

Ela straightens her ponytail. A gesture of self-consciousness. "You haven't mentioned Matthew for months."

"I know, why would I? I'm content by myself. I love the fact that I'm standing on my own two feet; my job is wonderful; everything is great. Or at least it was until yesterday."

Something twitches in Ela's face. She takes my hand, which feels icy cold against hers. "Listen. I have a suggestion. Instead of going to the police, we'll go to a doctor. I'm sure it's nothing serious. I know a really nice neurologist at the clinic. . . ."

My eyes burn. I pull my hand away so I can wipe the tears before they run down my face. "You think I'm crazy too, don't you?" Even just saying the word was hard. Because that's turned it into a real possibility. *Crazy.* Or perhaps seriously ill; who knows what kind of damage brain tumors could unleash—

I instinctively reach up to touch my head. *Please no, don't let it be that.*

No. Of course not, it's nonsense. I'm fine, I don't have any problems with my vision, no headaches, no dizziness. Just one person too many in my life.

Ela gently strokes my arm. "Try to remember. Do you still know when and where the two of us met?"

Of course I do, I don't have to think about it for even a second. "At *Lorenzo's*, at the bar. You stood next to me while we were waiting for our drinks. I ordered a caipirinha, you got a mojito, and you said you liked the look of the barman."

Ela bites down on her lower lip, nodding at almost every one of my words. "That's all true, except that it was the second time we met. The first time was at the squash club—Erik and I were playing, you came to pick him up, and he introduced me to you." She smiles, and her expression looks both tense and reassuring at the same time. "Do you remember? You guys had only been together two weeks and you were so crazy about each other it was almost too much to watch." She looks down at her hands, interlaced on her lap. "You still are, to be honest. You love him, Jo. Very much." Our eyes meet. "You can't have forgotten him, surely."

By now I can barely breathe. I picture the face of the stranger, the man who I supposedly love. I feel nothing, nothing but the nagging fear which his presence provokes in me.

Ela is still looking at me, her expression full of sympathy. My God, what would she stand to gain by lying to me like this?

I press my fingertips against my closed eyelids until it hurts.

Think. If what she says is true . . .

"Prove it," I whisper, suppressing the panic rising up inside me. What if she can? What if I have to accept that there's something seriously wrong with me?

She thinks for a moment, then nods. She stands up and goes over to a little table with a laptop on it. "I have some photos saved on here, we can both—"

The penetrating buzz of the doorbell interrupts her midsentence, and she whirls around. Now her expression is a mix of relief and guilt.

It takes me a moment to catch on. But then I do. "You called him." My mouth is so dry I can barely form the words. "I'm here telling you how relieved I am to have gotten away from him, and you bring him here to me?"

She looks sad, but I probably can't believe that any more than I could the supposed telephone call to her colleague.

"He's so worried about you," she says softly. "Look, perhaps the three of us can manage to figure this out."

She's already halfway to the door, but turns around one more time. "I want to help you, Jo, you have to believe me."

Please don't do it, I want to say, please don't let him in, please hide me from him.

But she has already pressed the door release button.

8

The door unlatches with a sharp *clack*. Ela opened up for me without any questions. I enter the elevator, even though I hate tight spaces.

Thoughts are tumbling over one another in my head. Hopefully Joanna's still up there. Does she know it was me who just talked to Ela on the phone and rang the doorbell? And what will be in store for me when I come face-to-face with her again?

I told Ela not to let her leave again at any cost. Was she able to convince Joanna that it's better for her not to run away from me? That she urgently needs to get help?

What in the hell has happened to her? I mean, she can remember everything else in her life. Like Ela, whom she met through me. How has Joanna's mind managed to make sense of this friendship without me having been part of it?

Or maybe her head is perfectly fine and she's just playacting? But why would she? That doesn't make any sense.

The elevator stops, and its doors open up onto the third floor.

My heart beats faster with every step I take, and starts racing as the door to Ela's apartment swings inward. Ela looks concerned.

"Is she still here?"

The pounding of my heart has become deafening now.

Ela nods and blinks briefly before stepping aside and letting me enter.

As I step into the small living room, Joanna jumps up and rubs her palms on her thighs. She always does that when she's nervous or very angry.

She's so beautiful. Even in this strange situation.

"Jo, I . . ." I start, but she raises her hands defensively and emphatically shakes her head.

"No, stop. I don't want to hear the same story again, about how we know each other and even live together. It doesn't matter how often you repeat it, it doesn't change anything. I don't know you."

There's that punch to the gut again.

During the night I had a kind of memory of you. It was very brief and fuzzy. Those were her words. And I, foolish as I am, gladly clung to them, like a child being told that Santa Claus exists. She lied to me just so she could escape.

"So then you didn't really remember me last night?" A superfluous, naïve question.

Joanna laughs briefly, with no trace of humor. "Of course not. I can't remember you because I don't know you. Whatever you have planned—it's not going to work. So you can just stop, right now."

She looks past me, and the expression on her face changes. "This man, whoever he is, must have his own selfish reasons for doing all of this. But you, Ela, helping him . . . How much did he promise you in return for playing along with his little psycho game? What's the going rate for betraying your best friend?" Joanna's eyes suddenly grow wide. "Wait . . . Or did this friendship never really exist from the beginning? Was it part of your plan as well? Just so there would be somebody who can confirm this insane story? Is that how it is, Ela?"

"Jo . . . You can't honestly be thinking that . . ." Ela paces a few steps past me and sinks down into one of the blue armchairs. She flips open her laptop and starts tapping away on it. "I don't know what's going on with you, but I can prove that you and Erik are a couple. I have some photos of the two of you right here. Hang on . . ."

Photos, of course. Once again, hope wells up inside me that some sort of trigger will allow Joanna to regain her memories of me.

"You emailed me about a hundred photos just from your vacation last month on Antigua alone," Ela explains, furrowing her brow.

"Photos can be doctored," Joanna remarks snidely.

Ela pauses what she's doing and looks up at Joanna. "But you're a photographer. That means you have an eye for identifying whether a photo's fake or not, doesn't it?" Not for the first time, I find myself admiring

Ela for how calm she is when dealing with difficult situations. Despite the fact that her best friend obviously has a serious psychological problem.

One last click, then she turns the computer around. "Look, Jo. Does this look doctored to you?"

Joanna looks over at the screen. She moves closer, leans over, wrinkles her brow. Stays silent. For three seconds, five, ten . . . ?

I can't take it any longer. I stride over to Joanna's side and look at the photo. It's not one of our vacation photos, but I recognize it right away. Ela took it not too long ago. We had been celebrating her birthday, right here in her living room. Two of her coworkers from the hospital had been here, and another couple who I don't know. Ela had managed to get all of us together on the photo, and Joanna and I are pictured right in the middle. Not that I know a lot about doctoring photos, but I think it would be pretty difficult, if not impossible, with an image like this one. One of Ela's coworkers is blocking a part of Joanna, and I'm sitting on the other side of her. I have my arm around her shoulders. We're both in high spirits, laughing into the camera.

The lighting conditions, the shadows . . . everything fits. I look at Joanna. Wait for a reaction. Eventually she stands up. She must have noticed that I'm looking at her, but she ignores me and looks at Ela.

"It's very well done."

"What?" Ela gives me an uncomprehending look.

"The doctored photo. Must have been made by a pro. I can't see any edges."

"Christ, Jo!" I say, louder than I'd intended. She flinches and retreats from me. "I'm sorry. But this whole situation's enough to drive a man insane, it really is! At some point you'll have to at least consider the possibility that we're telling the truth here. You can't go and dismiss everything as being lies or falsification just because it doesn't fit in with your version of the truth."

I look at the photo again, at the two young women who work with Ela in the hospital. An idea crosses my mind, to suggest to Joanna that we should find these women and get them to confirm the photo's real, that we were all at this birthday party together. But I decide I'd better leave it. She'd just sweep it aside by arguing that those two are in cahoots with me as well.

Damn it.

The vacation we spent together, though; surely Joanna can't have forgotten that. "You really don't remember Antigua? There should be tons of photos on your camera."

Joanna's mouth curls into a sneer. "Yeah. Sure."

"Jo." Ela puts the laptop to one side and gets up out of the armchair. "Come on, think about all the things we've done together. The wonderful conversations we've had. You know so much about me, and I know so much about you. You really think all of that's just one big lie? Is that what you believe?"

I see a hint of uncertainty in Joanna's expression. She looks at the floor. "I don't know." All the aggression has suddenly left her voice; it sounds quiet and thin now. As she looks over at Ela, I can see a moist sheen in her eyes. "I want to believe you, I do. But that means I also have to believe the things this man is saying, and I can't do that. Don't you understand?"

I'm nearly overcome by the powerful urge to take Joanna into my arms, press her against me, stroke her hair, and tell her everything's going to be all right.

"If I've really forgotten the man I'm living with, the man I love, just like that . . . That would mean something's not right in my head."

"Jo, sweetheart . . ." Ela comes up close to Joanna. The two look into each other's eyes. Ela's hands find those of her friend, clasp them, hold them tightly.

"Maybe there really is something wrong. Something that can easily be fixed if we see to it soon. But in that case it's important for you to get medical assistance right away. You do understand that I'm worried about you? Really worried?"

Crazily enough, I feel jealous of Ela in this moment. Right now she's close to Joanna, like I desperately want to be. I tell myself I'm a fool; how can I possibly have these thoughts in a situation like this? The most important thing right now is for Joanna to agree to let us help her. And Ela seems to be very much on the right track . . .

"I . . ." Joanna's struggling.

I want to tell her I love her and that I'll always stand by her, no matter what might come. But my instincts tell me not to interfere right now. It looks like Joanna's actually thinking about agreeing to what Ela suggested.

"Please, Jo." Ela's voice sounds gentle yet insistent. "Go get yourself checked out. After that you can do as you please, I won't interfere anymore, I promise. But please, go see a doctor."

The two of them look at each other for the duration of a few seconds, then Joanna turns to face me and looks into my eyes. Her expression pains me. It's how you look at a stranger who's asking you to do something you don't want to do.

"And what about you? Will you leave me alone as well if it turns out there's nothing wrong inside my head? That in itself would make it worth my while."

I hesitate, just for a second, then nod. "Yes. I will."

I hope she can't tell I'm lying.

9

I had never realized there could be so many different nuances of fear. Frantic, acute mortal fear like I'd felt last night, when I thought the stranger was going to rape or kill me. That was bad enough, but somehow more bearable than what I'm experiencing right now—a creeping, all-consuming fear seeping into every inch of my body.

Because regardless of what lies behind the inconceivable situation that I've found myself in—there's no longer any possibility that it's something harmless. Something that could be quickly resolved with the disappearance of this man. Not anymore.

Ela's reaction has changed everything. She's reduced the number of possible explanations to two, and both seem awful to me. Either I can no longer trust my own mind, or my best friend is lying to me. Her laptop is still open in front of us, the photo filling the screen. Ela chose cleverly. In the picture, the stranger has his arm around a woman who looks like me and who, without a doubt, is sitting next to him on the sofa—but the image of my head could have been skillfully inserted. The woman's bodily dimensions look about right, but she's sitting down, so the specifics are harder to make out. Almost every woman has a little black dress, just like the one she's wearing, hanging in her closet. I have two, and they're almost identical.

Yes. A very clever choice indeed.

"So?" Ela's voice is unusually soft. As if she's taking great pains not to scare me. "Shall we go?"

I turn around to face her. No, *them*. Ela and Erik are standing next to each other, so close that their shoulders are almost touching. United. A team.

"To Dr. Dussmann, right?" My question is directed at Erik, who nods and opens his mouth to respond, but I don't give him the chance.

"No way. And we're not going to see your *nice neurologist* either, Ela. I'll go to see a doctor with you both, but I pick who it is."

They exchange a glance, something between confusion and surprise. So all that preparation was in vain. Well, tough luck!

"Do you know someone you trust?" Ela asks hesitantly.

I grab the laptop and sit down with it on the couch. It's connected to the Internet; the browser page is already open. Perfect.

My search for the combination psychiatrist/neurologist brings back six results for the local area. I settle on a Dr. Verena Schattauer, not just because the photo on her home page looks nice and her practice is open this morning, but above all because, according to her background information, she doesn't work in the same hospital as Ela.

"Which of you is going to lend me their phone?"

Erik, who hasn't said a word for the past few minutes, holds Ela's arm back as she is about to hand her cell phone to me. "I'd prefer it if I could call," he says.

Surprise, surprise. "Are you worried I could call the police?" I ask with a smile.

"No, Jo. I'm afraid you might do something stupid." He sits down next to me, too close for my taste, but I'm tired of constantly backing away. Which turns out to be a mistake, because clearly he takes it as being encouragement. He reaches for my hand, but I pull it back with a jolt. The hurt look comes back into his eyes. "Sorry," he whispers, before finally taking his phone out of his jacket pocket. He dials the number on the doctor's home page and only passes me the phone once the call has been picked up.

"Dr. Schattauer's practice, good morning."

"Hello." My voice is hoarse with nerves. "My name is Joanna Berrigan. I've never been to your practice before, but I need an appointment. As soon as possible. Please." I don't understand why the tears rush into my eyes now of all moments, but there's nothing I can do to stop them.

"We're actually . . ." the receptionist says, but then stops midsentence. "Could you be here in an hour? Then I could fit you in our emergency slot."

My breathing is frantic and uneven. "Yes. In . . . an hour. OK."

"Could you describe your symptoms to me?" The woman's voice is more pragmatic than concerned. She waits patiently as I try to get my sobbing under control. This goes on for about half a minute. "Is anyone with you?" She asks then. "Could you give the telephone to him or her?"

Him or her. The decision is an easy one; I give it to Ela. Not that I still trust her, but at least I know her.

"Yes," I hear her say. "Hmm. My impression? Joanna is very upset, she's suddenly having . . . gaps in her memory. Disoriented? No, not really. What? Yes. OK. Of course I'll go with her."

Ela ends the call and hands Erik back his phone. "We'll take both cars," she says, "and Joanna can choose who she wants to go with. In case it . . . takes a while. I'll need to get some sleep at some point, as much as I hate to say it." She yawns, as if wanting to emphasize her words.

She's planning to leave me alone with him. Just because she's tired!

On the way downstairs, there's not one single opportunity to flee. Not as we leave the elevator, not on the street. They flank me, always close enough to be able to quickly grab me in case I try to run away.

"I'll go in Ela's car."

Her small blue Honda is parked around the corner. I notice that she still hadn't fixed the dent on the right-hand fender. I remember the dent, just as I remember the story of how it happened. I remember everything, for God's sake. I'm fine.

The sentence makes me feel good. I repeat it silently to myself, again and again. *I'm fine.*

As I get into the car, I see Erik gesture in Ela's direction. A twisting motion with his wrist. A signal to lock the car door.

Of course. He doesn't trust me as far as he can throw me. Ela tries to press the button for the central locking as casually as possible, but of course she notices that I notice.

We stay silent during the journey. The Audi is always in sight, either alongside us or in front, a glimmering silver shadow.

Then, shortly before we reach our destination, a new thought shoots into my mind, even worse than its predecessor.

What if this Erik guy isn't the driving force between the events of the last day? What if it's Ela instead? She's known me for over six months; she knows about my family's fortune. We've spoken about money from time to time. I know that she doesn't have much of it, and I also know that Richard has desperately been trying to find start-up capital for his freelance venture for a while now, but without success.

I actually offered to help a while ago, and neither of them had wanted to accept it. But perhaps only because they wanted much more?

Erik could be an actor who Ela has hired and instructed. That would also explain why he keeps tearing up when I push him away from me. Technique. Unfortunately, this is precisely the kind of story that would make me sound completely crazy if I told it to a doctor.

Ela parks the Honda. "Everything OK, Jo?"

I nod and try to get out, but the door is still locked. I hit my hand against it with a force that surprises even me. I pound my knuckles against the metal, again and again; it hurts, but I can't stop.

"What are you doing?" Ela grabs my arms and holds onto them tightly. "Jo! Please!"

The back of my right hand throbs and burns. I feel a strong, almost overwhelming urge to bang my head against the car door as well.

I take a few deep breaths, and it gradually dissipates.

The expression in Ela's eyes is one of utter perplexity.

"Get me to this doctor," I say. "Quickly."

The waiting room is quiet. Just an elderly woman and a young man. And the three of us. Erik sorts out the paperwork with the receptionist; he has my passport and my insurance card. All the documents that I so urgently need.

The elderly woman is called in a short while later. I prepare myself for a long wait. We've arrived early, but I'd rather sit here than in Ela's apartment.

There is a single dark spot on the otherwise immaculate marble-tiled floor. I fixate on it. Count my breaths, in and out. My wrist is hurting more by the minute; it's probably swollen, and the most inconceivable part is that the pain feels good.

Really good.

I curl my right hand into a fist and feel new barbs of pain shoot through it. If I'm not careful, I'll start laughing.

I really hope this doctor knows her stuff.

By my reckoning, Dr. Verena Schattauer is in her late fifties, and right away she forbids Erik or Ela from accompanying me into the examination room. I take an instant liking to her.

Because of this, it's easy for me to give her a summary of what happened since last night. It's not even been a day yet, for God's sake, and my life has been turned completely upside down.

I am as honest as I'm able to be. The only thing I keep quiet about is what happened just now in the car. About the fact that I clearly have an underlying need to injure myself.

"He's utterly convinced that he's right, and now even my best friend is taking his side. And yet there's not a single thing in my house that belongs to him. No books, no clothes, not even a toothbrush. But he's disregarding that, they both are."

The doctor looks at me, her expression solemn. She has made a few notes, but mainly she just listens to me, with an attentiveness that's almost tangible.

"It's . . . as though I'm standing in front of a red wall, and everyone's telling me it's blue. I can try as hard as I want—but for me it stays red. I don't see any other color. I *know* it's red, but I can't prove it to anyone. How could I?"

Dr. Schattauer nods compassionately. "Yes, I understand what you mean. Let's summarize one more time: you can remember everything, you say, short-term memories as well as long-term—everything except this man called Erik."

"Exactly." I suddenly become aware of how it must sound. "I know that if it turns out Erik is telling the truth then I must really be sick, there's no other explanation . . ." My words are too hasty, each one running into the next, stumbling over one another.

"Let's not get ahead of ourselves." The doctor presses the tips of her fingers together and smiles at me. "We'll need to give you a thorough examination, of course, but believe me, there are other explanations for the symptoms you've described."

She pauses and looks at me thoughtfully. "Systematic amnesia, for example. In other words, memory loss that is restricted to specific areas. In some circumstances, specific people." Seeing that I'm about to question her, she raises her hand to stop me. "That doesn't mean that this diagnosis applies to you. It's just another possibility. To start with, we need to rule out all physical causes." She pulls her calendar toward her and flicks through it. "I can fit you in for an EEG appointment here in the practice on Thursday, and I'll also refer you to the clinic for a CT scan." Probably noticing that I flinched in response to her words, she quickly continues. "Even though I don't really believe your problem has a physical cause."

Systematic amnesia. Memory loss, for no apparent reason? I inquire, and Schattauer shakes her head. "There's always a cause. A very stressful event, some trauma that is connected to the thing or person in question."

My mouth is so dry that I need two attempts to form my question. "Meaning that I've suppressed my memory of Erik . . . because he traumatized me? Abused me?"

Dr. Schattauer shakes her head emphatically. "No, it doesn't mean that. It's just one of many possibilities that we should consider. I'd really like to help you, if you'd allow me to."

This thought that my mind has blocked out Erik to protect itself from the memory of something terrible suddenly seems more plausible to me than any other explanation. Then Ela's behavior would make sense. Erik's, too, come to think of it. The way he looks at me, then averts his gaze, the way he's trying to look after me . . . it could be down to a guilty conscience. And then there are those fleeting moments where it seems he's struggling to control himself . . .

"Is the EEG appointment on Thursday OK for you?" asks Dr. Schattauer, interrupting my train of thought.

"Yes. Yes of course." I shake her hand and leave the office. Only Erik is waiting there, he jumps up when he sees me.

"Ela went home. She was absolutely exhausted, so I told her she could go. She'll call this afternoon."

There it is again, that searching, testing gaze. Guilt? It was entirely possible.

"Did your talk with the doctor go well?"

I smile, or at least something close to it. I show my teeth, in any case. "Oh yes. It certainly was."

Dr. Schattauer has followed me out, and positions herself between Erik and me. She looks him up and down before turning to me. "If you like, I can arrange for you to stay in a private clinic for the next few days. You'd have some peace there, and you'd be looked after. Maybe that could help."

Half an hour ago I would have seriously considered the offer. But now I shake my head. "No, I want to go home. And you have all my details, my address and everything?"

"Yes, of course." The doctor's questioning glance tells me that she hasn't understood what I'm getting at yet.

"His too?" I gesture toward Erik, whose surprise at my decision is written all over his face.

"Yes. He even provided his ID."

Ah. Very thorough. So Dr. Schattauer and her receptionist know more about him than I do. His surname, for example. And his address?

I've already taken a step toward the reception area, wanting to take a look at the notes, but Erik steps into my path. He has his wallet in his hand, and pulls out his driver's license. He hands it to me silently.

Erik Fabian Thieben. The photo shows a younger version of the man who is standing in front of me, but it's unmistakably him. In it, his hair almost reaches down to his shoulders; his smile is easy and open and framed by stubble.

There's no address on the driver's license, of course. Maybe I should ask him for his car registration.

I hand him back the document. "Thank you."

"You're really coming home with me?" he asks softly as he opens the clinic door for me. "Voluntarily?"

"Yes." Even I can hear the hostile undertone in my voice.

If there's any truth to the theory of trauma-provoked amnesia, I'll be able to get to the bottom of it quicker in Erik's presence. I doubt that he'll dare lay a finger on me at the moment with the way things are.

If this trauma really exists, then I'll *have* to remember it sooner or later. And if I should find out that Erik was the one who caused it, then God have mercy on him.

10

We leave the building, walking next to each other in silence. There's a lot I want to tell Joanna, and even more that I want to ask her. Like what exactly she told Dr. Schattauer, for instance, and how the doctor reacted. But I don't dare say anything just now. The fact that Joanna is prepared to come home with me seems like a new, frail bond between us, one so delicate that a single ill-judged word might tear it apart. I'm not going to risk that. We've almost reached the car. I click the car remote, open the passenger door and stand next to it. Joanna's gaze wanders from the door to my face, then her eyes fixate on mine. "Still scared I'm going to run away?"

I shrug and, for some strange reason, start to feel guilty for not denying it.

Joanna folds her arms in front of her chest. "I came along to see this doctor because I want to know if there's something wrong with me. I'm coming back home voluntarily. But let's make one thing perfectly clear—you're not locking me up again. Promise me, otherwise I'm not getting in that car."

"I promise," I say, not missing a beat. Not because I'm convinced Joanna won't try to run away again, but because I know I can't watch over her all the time. Neither do I want to. If she still wants to run to the police after seeing the doctor, I won't be able to stop her. All I can do is hope that she won't.

"Are you getting in?" I ask carefully.

"Only once you're on the other side."

I understand. She wants to test if I'll really leave her be. If I trust her.

Is she waiting until I'm in the car to run off? No. She actually gets in the car. Relieved, I sit down behind the steering wheel. She buckles her seat belt and nods her chin forward. "Let's go."

Her voice sounds so impersonal that, in this moment, she really does seem like a stranger to me. It hurts.

I start to drive, eyes on the road, but my thoughts are on us. On Joanna and me. Will there ever be an *us* again? Will it be possible to reverse whatever happened to her yesterday? What if everything we had between us is irretrievably lost?

"Will you tell me what you talked to the doctor about?"

"I told her everything that's happened since yesterday evening. From my point of view."

"And? What did she say?"

"That there are various possibilities."

"Like what?"

She seems to think for a moment. "I can't say just yet. Maybe later. Once I know more about you." *Once she knows more about me?* We haven't been together for a full year yet, but there's barely anyone who knows as much about me as Joanna does.

I feel another, new feeling pushing away the emptiness inside me. It's faint at first, but when I glance over and see the delicate, familiar contours of Joanna's face, which all of a sudden I can no longer caress, no longer kiss, the feeling surges through my entire being like a wave of heat.

Defiance. Rebellion. Anger. At this twist of fate, which is screwing up our lives.

There's no way in hell I'm going to just roll over and accept this, no matter what else may come. I love this woman, and she loves me. Even if, right now, she has no recollection of it.

I'm going to tell her everything. Describe every single day we've spent together. Every hour if need be. I'm going to . . .

"What are you thinking about?" Joanna asks me all of a sudden. She does that often. Usually I have a hard time answering the question. Now, though, it's easy. I quickly glance over at her again, our eyes meet.

"I was thinking that I'd like to tell you about us. Everything, from the very first day. Maybe that will help you remember again."

"Everything, really?" she asks, a strange undertone in her voice.

"Yes, everything I can remember myself."

"All right. I'm eager to hear."

I'd give the world to know what's going on in her head right now. Maybe it's the same for her, too.

I eventually turn into the driveway to our house and park the car. We get out, walk to the front door. It's almost the same as it always was when we came back home together. If only it weren't for this pervasive, nagging sense of fear inside me, a feeling that even my defiance can't suppress.

My eyes wander to the place where the cockatoo used to be. I resist the temptation to go see if any traces of it can still be seen in the soil.

We enter the house. I take care to do everything in the exact same way I always do. Keys onto the shelf, in the same place as always. Shoes next to the dresser, in the place where my black sneakers had been until yesterday morning. Rituals. They might just help.

Joanna goes into the kitchen. That's almost always the first thing she does when she comes home. I'm waiting for the buzzing sound of the coffee machine being switched on, and, sure enough, hear it only a few seconds later.

I walk over to her, sit down at the small breakfast bar where we always eat together in the mornings. I look at her, feeling like I'm watching a film I no longer play a role in. This silence as we're in the kitchen together . . . it's so alien. Joanna usually can't go a single minute without telling or asking me something.

"We met at a flea market." Did I really just say that so loudly? Joanna takes her mug and sits diagonally across from me. Not too close.

"Uh-huh," she mutters, taking a cautious sip of the steaming coffee.

She sounds so uninterested I have to force myself to keep talking. "Yes. I bought a little box right from under your nose. You were pretty angry with me."

"That, at least, I can imagine quite well."

"I gave it to you afterward as a gift. You didn't want to take it at first. Until I told you I'd bought it for you."

Another sip from the cup, which Joanna is now clutching with both hands as if she was trying to warm them on it. "When was that?"

"Nine months ago."

"And how long have we allegedly been living together?"

Allegedly . . . "For six months. You had a one-room apartment, and my place was too small for the two of us. We went looking for somewhere new and finally found this house." Even as I'm uttering the last sentence, something occurs to me. "The lease! Joanna. We both signed the lease. It's in the green file, in the cabinet in the living room with all the other documents."

Without even waiting for her to react, I slide off my stool and practically run into the living room. My heartbeat quickens. If Joanna sees both of our signatures on the tenancy agreement . . .

Except—what if that's disappeared as well?

I open the top right cabinet door, and find the green file right away. Joanna wrote IMPORTANT on the white tab at the back of the file in permanent marker. My hand is shaking as I reach for it and pull it out of the cabinet. The lease must be somewhere in the middle, in between the other documents. With nervous movements, I leaf through the papers, already fearing that the document's gone, but then I finally have it in front of me. I take it out of the plastic sleeve, hastily flip it over and heave a deep sigh of relief. Our signatures are there on the lower third of the last page, next to the date.

Joanna looks at me warily when I hold the agreement out toward her.

"There, look at it," I prompt her, unable to suppress the triumph in my voice. I put the paper down in front of her and point at the spot. "Here, you see?"

Joanna only eyes the document for a moment then looks back up at me. "The signatures were added with two different pens."

This can't be happening. "Christ, Jo, we both had our own pens. That's not exactly unusual."

"Do I really have to point out that you could have added it at any time after the fact?"

This is driving me crazy. My hand slams down on the breakfast bar with a bang. "Yes, damn it. At the end of the day you can question everything, even when you see it with your own eyes. Come on, think about it. If everything really was phony, the photos, the contract, evening visitors, even your friendship with Ela . . . just think about how much of a hassle it would have been to set it all up? And what could possibly justify all of this? Jo? Why would I be doing it?"

Again, I get one of those strange looks from her. One full of suspicion, mixed with anger. But now it seems there's a new element in the mix. Something I can only read with difficulty. Like she knows more than I do. It almost seems disdainful.

She must have inherited it from her father. From the stories she's told me, he's a . . . A thought flashes through my head. Why am I only thinking of it now? "Your father!"

"What? What about my father?" She looks irritated.

"You told him about me, Jo. You put it off for a long time, but . . . Call him. Please. He'll confirm it."

This next look irritates me even more. She's hiding something from me, I can feel it. But right now it's more important for her to speak to her father. She'd believe him.

"All right." She gets up. "I'll call him."

I'm so relieved I could kiss her. "Thank you."

I'm tempted to jump up as Joanna, very matter-of-factly, walks over to the shelf behind her where her phone is, but I decide not to. She picks it up and tosses it back down again seconds later.

"Battery's empty. Can I use yours?"

"Yeah, sure." I fish my smartphone out of my pocket and hold it toward Joanna.

To my surprise, she sits back down on the stool as she's dialing. I was expecting her to leave the room for the call to her father. Like she usually would.

I nervously wait for someone to answer. This should be the breakthrough moment. If Joanna's father confirms that we live together, there's no way she can have any more doubts. Then, of course, there will still be the problem that she can't remember me, but once this awful mistrust she holds against me is gone, things will look totally different. I feel like we can get through this.

"Hi, Dad, it's me, Jo." Her voice sounds harder than usual. Is it because she's speaking English rather than the German she speaks with me, or because it's her dad she's on the phone with?

"Good, thanks, and you?" She laughs briefly.

"Same old, same old . . . Oh, thanks. Tell him I said hi. . . . No, he hasn't been in touch. But that's fine." There's a longer pause, during which she's only listening. "I don't know yet." She looks over toward me. "I'll discuss it with Erik."

My heart is pounding. I watch her face carefully. Another strange look, then Joanna gets up and leaves the kitchen. I watch her go, perplexed. Why is she leaving now?

She pulls the door to the hall shut behind her. If she leaves the house now . . . I push the thought aside, try to calm myself down, tell myself her father must have said something about me that she wants to talk over with him in private. Maybe he's trying to convince her to come back to Australia. After all, that Matthew guy is waiting for her over there.

Man, how long is this going to take? I consider following her, but discard the thought. I want her to feel that I trust her.

Finally, the door opens. The way Joanna looks at me brings my world tumbling down even before she opens her mouth.

"My father didn't know who I was talking about when I mentioned your name. He doesn't know any Erik."

11

It's just after nine in the evening in Melbourne, and Dad only picks up after the seventh or eighth ring. That probably means they have guests, because then my father only answers the phone very reluctantly.

"Hi, Dad, it's me, Jo." I try to hide my nerves.

"Jo, sweetheart." Yes, I can hear voices in the background. Laughter. "How are you?"

"Good, thanks, and you?"

He clears his throat. "Everything's fine. The McAllisters are here right now, and Max Cahill with his new wife—do you remember Max?"

Yes. A bald-headed lawyer with buckteeth and a laugh that could make milk curdle. "Mom's away for a couple of days," Dad continues. "The usual charity stuff. She'll be sorry to have missed your call, you know how much she likes to hear about your adventures in her homeland. Paul had a fight with Lisa but then they sorted things out again; other than that . . ."

"Same old, same old," I finished his sentence for him.

"Yes. And Matthew sends his best."

"Oh, thanks. Tell him I said hi." Matthew. The fiancé who I definitely can remember, maybe even a little too well. The man whose life consists of a steady stream of fulfilled wishes, the man for whom I—everyone agrees—am the perfect match. One empire marrying another, just like it was two hundred years ago. The fact that I had felt the need to put a few continents between us hadn't particularly fazed Matthew—

after all, he would get me for the rest of my life once I was back, he had told me as we said good-bye.

The match is very close to Dad's heart too, unfortunately. "Have you heard from him?" he asked.

"No, he hasn't been in touch. But that's fine." Erik doesn't take his eyes off me even for a second. He's following our conversation, no question about it. He works as a computer technician, so his English must be better than average.

"You could give him a call yourself sometime, you know." Dad's tone sounds accusatory. "Or come here for a surprise visit! Or even better, just come back. Seriously, Jo, this Europe nonsense has gone on for long enough. Don't get me wrong, I think it's fine that you want to experience things—in every sense—but don't lose sight of your real life in the process. Right then." His voice has taken on the tone he usually uses for business negotiations. The George Arthur Berrigan tone, which it's advisable not to argue with. "So I'll just send you a plane. When?"

This is my chance to leave all this nonsense behind me. If I hand the reins over to Dad, I'll be out of this situation in a few hours. Except then I would never understand it. And I would be *his* Jo again, irreversibly. Daughter, heiress, business capital that can be married off.

"I don't know yet." I rest my gaze on the stranger sitting opposite me at the kitchen counter. Then I summon up all of my courage. "I'll discuss it with Erik."

Silence, one or two seconds that seem to last forever. Then my father's voice again, dangerously quiet now. "With whom?"

I manage to stop the smile from appearing on my face as I slip down off the barstool and leave the kitchen. I shut the door behind me, stand there in the hallway. The paperweight is back in its usual place.

"Erik. I told you about him, remember?" My father is the last person who would deceive me, or anyone else for that matter. He would regard such a thing as being miles beneath him. So I wait for his answer like it's a judgment from God.

"No you didn't, not once, I would have remembered. So who in God's name is Erik?"

If only I knew, I feel the urge to yell into the phone. *I have no idea, but he's sitting in my kitchen and he cosigned my rental contract, and my best friend here says that we're in love.*

It's too late to backtrack now. "A man I met a while back."

"Goddamn it, Jo." Dad doesn't shout, but lowers his voice to a tone so deep it resembles the sound of distant thunder. "You remember what we agreed, don't you? You can have your fun, but only to the extent that it doesn't endanger your relationship with Matthew."

Oh yes, I remember the conversation. That unbelievably embarrassing conversation.

"So I really didn't mention Erik to you?"

Now Dad does raise his voice after all. "No, and I never want to hear about him again! End it and come back home! And without any gold-digging Germans running after you!"

He hangs up before I can.

For a moment, I stand there indecisively holding the stranger's cell phone in my hand; then I open the contacts list. Yes, there's my number, as well as Ela's. And the number of the photography studio. Other than that, just names I don't know, apart from the Chinese restaurant in the pedestrian zone, and my favorite pizzeria.

I go back to the kitchen. Only once I've opened the door and see Erik's expectant expression do I realize it would have been much better to check the text messages instead of the contacts list.

Too late now. I stay at a safe distance and look him directly in the eyes. "My father didn't know who I was talking about when I mentioned your name. He doesn't know any Erik."

He doesn't look surprised; he must have known, of course he did. For a moment he just closes his eyes, as if he's exhausted. When he opens them again, there's not a single trace of guilt. Just anger.

"You promised me. I know how afraid you were of having the conversation, but I thought you'd gotten it over with." He turns his head to the side, slams the palm of his hand down on the bar. The spoons in the coffee cups clink.

"You said you had, anyway. You said it was hard but that in the end your father accepted it. Unwillingly, but he did." He laughs. "You also said that we still had a lot of hard work ahead of us. Well, Jo, maybe I should have asked you what you meant by that."

I open my mouth to retort, but he doesn't give me a chance. "So you already lied to me when your memory was still intact, and about such an important thing at that. But who knows—maybe you're just pretending not to know me? If that's the case, there's no need to go to all this effort. If you're so eager to get rid of me, you can just tell me." Erik gets down from the barstool and stretches his hand toward me. He wants his phone back. I give it to him. And all of a sudden I'm picturing the knife again, long and shiny and sharp. It's not just in my thoughts, it's actually close to hand. I would only need to take five steps into the kitchen and I could pull it out from the wooden block, eleven inches of Japanese steel, and plunge it into the stranger's body.

I instinctively edge back to the door, which makes Erik shake his head in resignation. "No, I'm not going to hurt you. Maybe you'll finally realize that." He puts the phone into his jacket pocket and raises his hands, looking dejected. "If you want to run away, then run. If you want to call the police, do it. I'm going to the office to get some things, I've got a change of clothes there." He gestures down at his body. "I don't have anything to wear here anymore, you know? Not even any underwear. So I'm going to go shopping, that could take a few hours. If you're still there when I get back, I'll be very happy. If not . . ." He takes a step toward me, warily, and brushes his hand across my cheek. "If not, then have a good life, Joanna."

He goes without locking the door after him. He left my cell phone here too; I plug it into the charging cable and turn it on.

Seven missed calls. Once the battery has started to fill up again, I listen to my messages. Five of them are from Manuel, each one angrier than the last. Why didn't I show up to the photo studio when I had clients booked in? Don't I realize that it's his business and his reputation that I'm damaging if potential clients leave disappointed? The last two messages are from Darja, who's also working as an assistant for Manuel, and she sounds much more concerned than he did. Is everything OK, she asks, adding that I was usually so reliable.

I decide to call her back instead of Manuel. I tell her I woke up with a migraine so bad that I couldn't get up and use the phone.

"And are you better now?" she asks.

"Yes. Please tell Manuel I'm very sorry. And that I'll be there on time tomorrow."

I spend the next two hours turning the house upside down, searching for some clue that I don't live here by myself. There's not a single text message from Erik on my phone, nor any emails on my computer.

There are no photos of him on either of the devices, nor on any of my SD cards, and of course there's also no trace of Antigua. But there are at least fifty pictures of Matthew. Playing polo, at the wheel of his damn yacht, in the enormous waterscape he calls a pool. Always grinning and tanned. I'm itching to delete the photos, but I stop myself. It's possible that my memory is uncertain territory, so I shouldn't destroy anything that I might later forget.

After I've searched through all the rooms, I'm bathed in sweat. I found precisely three things that I don't know the origins of: a green USB cable under the bed that I definitely never used and certainly never bought. In one of the chest of drawers there's a comb, not like the ones women use—black, narrow, and wholly inadequate for long hair like mine. And the final object, crumpled up in a corner of the basement, a gray T-shirt with oil stains on it, most definitely neither my size nor my style.

Nothing specific. In theory, they could all be things left behind by the previous tenant. Except that the house was unfurnished when I took it, so the theory can't be applied to either the cable or the comb.

I glance over at the kitchen clock. Even though Erik has a lot to do, it won't be much longer before he comes back. He'll hurry, no doubt about that. By then I want to have showered and changed.

My glance falls on the knife block again, and I pull out the knife, the one I keep thinking of. The blade shimmers dully, alluringly . . .

And suddenly an idea comes into my mind, one that makes sense to me but which at the same time is so terrible I almost can't bear to acknowledge it.

Systematic amnesia, as Dr. Schattauer described it, is unleashed by trauma. One that is probably connected to the person who the consciousness is now blocking out.

This knife, the knife I can't get out of my head—is it possible that Erik threatened me with it? Or even hurt me? Or held it to my throat while we had sex because fear turns him on? Is that conceivable?

I try to search for a memory, to force something back, but there's nothing, so I put the knife back into the block and run up the stairs into the bedroom. I undress to my underwear and search my body for injuries. Cuts, scars.

Nothing. Just some bruises, one on my upper arm, two on my left thigh. And a graze on my right knee.

I have no idea where they came from. Probably from the struggles yesterday during my unsuccessful attempts to flee.

A quick glance out of the window. There's still no sign of the silver Audi. I'll just have to hurry in the shower.

Normally I can count on the cascading water to clear my thoughts, but *normally* seems to be a thing of the past. I'm barely under the shower for two minutes before my head starts pounding, as if I were getting the flu. Just what I needed. It was only a lie to explain the client appointments I missed, but now my body seems to think it has to turn the lie into a truth.

I take a deep breath, but the only result is that I feel sick.

Very quickly.

Very intensely.

And then the world goes dark.

12

The headquarters of Gabor Energy Engineering are located a few miles outside the city limits. It takes roughly half an hour before the modern eight-story building appears in front of me. I try to remember the details of my drive here, but in vain. My thoughts were revolving around Joanna the entire time.

My parking permit opens the barrier to the underground parking garage. I park the car, walk the thirty feet to the elevator, swipe my company ID on the reader, go up to the fourth floor. Routine, all of it. If it weren't for the chaos in my head.

As I exit the elevator, Nadine walks toward me. Nadine, of all people. She stops, raises an eyebrow. "Hi, Erik. Everything OK?"

"Yeah, all good," I say as complacently as possible. "There was something urgent I had to take care of."

"Problems?"

"No." *None that I'm going to tell my ex-girlfriend about, at least.*

I can see that she doesn't believe me, but I hope she'll leave it at that.

"You're to report to the boss once you're here."

Hans-Peter Geiger is the vice president in charge of IT, office administration, and accounting. All in all, he's a fairly agreeable guy. After the shitty day I had yesterday though, I do wonder what he might want from—

"The Godfather," Nadine interrupts my train of thought.

The Godfather. That's what we call G.E.E.'s proprietor and top executive. "Gabor?" I ask incredulously, and feel something tightening in my stomach. Conversations with Gabor tend to veer in directions I don't find entirely comfortable. He's a difficult man with strange viewpoints. "Do you know what he wants?"

She shrugs her shoulders. "No. Frau Schultheiss called you at around ten or so. And when she couldn't reach you she called me. I said you weren't at work yet and would probably be here a bit later."

I try not to let on how much it annoys me that everyone turns to Nadine whenever they can't reach me. The question is whether they only do so because she's the department secretary, or because we were an item for so long.

"Five minutes after that," Nadine continues, "she called back and said you should report to Gabor immediately after you arrive."

Report to Gabor immediately . . . the tightening in my stomach intensifies. Could it have something to do with me having called in sick today? No, I don't think so. Gabor has more than a hundred employees; he doesn't concern himself with such trivial issues. It has to be something else. Well, I guess I'm going to find out very shortly.

In my office, I take a small suitcase out of my closet. My emergency luggage. It's always there, all packed and ready to go, with all the essentials for last-minute business trips of two or three days' duration. Toiletries, fresh underwear, socks. There's also a spare shirt hanging in the closet.

I freshen up a bit in the bathroom next door and put on the shirt. Twenty minutes after arriving at the office, I head to the eighth floor to see Gabor.

As I enter the lobby, Eva Schultheiss looks me over in a way that seems to say she takes personal affront at my turning up here. Does she perhaps know the reason why Gabor has summoned me, I wonder?

"There you are at last," she says indignantly. "You'll have to wait, he's in with someone right now."

"No problem," I respond, attempting a smile. I know that falling out of favor with Gabor's secretary isn't a smart move.

She reaches for the telephone, announces my arrival, and points toward the two leather armchairs by the opposite wall. "Take a seat."

I nod and sink into one of the armchairs. Watch Frau Schultheiss tap around on the keyboard, a grave expression on her face.

* * *

Damn it, what the hell's happening in my life all of a sudden? For two months now I haven't been able to rid myself of the suspicion that Gabor's trying to keep me down. And I only got wind of the fact that apparently I'm not even going to be involved in the closing of an important contract, by pure coincidence.

About three months ago, Gabor had been having problems with his private laptop. It had crashed. Instead of informing someone from first-level support, he'd summoned me, the head of the IT department.

It had been a malfunction in the energy saving mode, a minor issue, which had turned off the monitor.

I'd only caught sight of the open email for a few seconds before Gabor quickly closed it. But it was long enough for me to suspect something was going on that I wasn't meant to know about.

The sender of the email, HvR, had been cryptic, and the subject line had read *Phoenix completion.*

There hadn't been much content:

> Munich central station, October 18th. 1:10 PM. More details to follow.
> Contractual basis: At least 100. Confirmation expected by September 15th.

October 18th. My birthday.

At first I had jokingly asked Gabor if "Phoenix" was the code name for my birthday present. But from his reaction I could clearly see how uncomfortable it was for him that I'd seen this strange email. There could only be one reason for that: Gabor wanted to keep me out of this deal, and there could be no doubt that it *was* a deal—in fact, with a contractual basis of a hundred stations it was the biggest one G.E.E. had landed yet.

Usually I'm always there when contracts like this are concluded, because every large project presents new demands on the IT department as well. But, this time, I hadn't been informed.

The phone rings, the door opens almost simultaneously, and a man leaves Gabor's office. He's old, over eighty for sure. His white, still fairly full hair is meticulously parted, his dark suit perfectly tailored. Bespoke. A cane made out of dark wood is hanging from his crooked right arm.

The man's eyes sweep over me briefly with the same amount of attention you would accord to a flowerpot standing in front of a wall somewhere.

He nods at Gabor's secretary, giving a hint of a bow; then he's already past me and leaving the waiting area.

I look over at Frau Schultheiss, who's just putting down the phone handset. "You can go in now."

Seconds later, I enter the enormous office.

There's an immense floor-to-ceiling window, offering a wonderful view of the woods nearby. Six black leather chairs grouped around a dark wood table form the centerpiece of the room.

Gabor is sitting behind his large, modern desk, smiling at me openly as I approach him. His open laptop is in front of him. "Erik, nice to see you." He gets up and walks around the desk toward me. That's unusual. My sense of unease is getting stronger.

"Please, have a seat." He gestures toward the furniture in the middle of the room. I opt for the chair closest to me.

Gabor crosses his legs and looks at me. In a friendly, but contemplative way. It seems like he's considering how he should start the conversation.

Just as the silence is beginning to get uncomfortable, he sits up straight and sets his forearms on the desk. "Erik, you know that part of my philosophy is that my coworkers are more than just employees. Their well-being is very close to my heart. It's not entirely selfless of me, of course, as I know people who are content are more efficient and, most of all, more productive than people with problems."

There's that contemplative look again. Four seconds, five . . . I don't know how I'm supposed to react, so I simply nod. Is this the part where he drops the bombshell?

"I'm going to come out with it, Erik. Our colleague Morbach called this morning from the airport in London. He was very concerned about an incident at your house yesterday evening."

So that's it. Bernhard. How dare he discuss my private affairs with Gabor? This has nothing to do with the company. I have to pull myself together to stifle my anger.

"Oh, that." I act in a pointedly casual way, even though I'd like nothing more than to jump to my feet. "My significant other, Jo, she was a bit confused yesterday evening. Nothing serious. She's feeling better already."

Gabor remains silent. Then he says, "I'm happy to hear that; that puts my mind at ease a bit. It sounded completely different on the phone this morning, though. Morbach said your girlfriend was trying to run away from you, wearing only her bathrobe. He said she didn't recognize you at all."

Bernhard, you fucking asshole. "Like I said, Jo was a bit disoriented yesterday. But it's already worn off. She's back home now, recovering."

"All right. But still." Gabor leans forward even farther, like he's wanting to tell me a secret. "You're one of the leaders here in my company. It's important to me that you're well in your private life, too. If there's any way I can help, please do let me know. No matter what type of problem it is."

"Yes, I will, thank you very much. But I think we'll manage."

That look again. "What would you say to a few days' vacation? Take some time, take care of everything at home and recuperate. Isn't it your birthday soon? So having some time off work would be well-timed, right. . . . What do you think?"

"Oh yes, my birthday." I can't bite back the comment. "Well, there'll be a couple reasons to celebrate, right? Though maybe not for me . . ."

That needed to be said. Because somehow, I have the creeping suspicion he wants me completely out of the picture so I don't see the contract being concluded at all, and now he's seizing the first available opportunity. He probably wants to use the time to prepare my severance and appoint my replacement.

"Herr Thieben." Gabor is now adopting a fatherly tone. "I can tell you're under a lot of stress. I mean, you don't usually react like this. You know what? I'll just give you a week off. With full pay."

"Thank you, that's very generous. But I don't think it's necessary. I enjoy my work, it's good for me. I'm going to end up getting frustrated if I just sit around the house all day."

"All right then, Erik." Gabor gets up and straightens his tie. I get up too. "I haven't met your significant other, but do give her my regards. And if you need any help—my door is always open."

"Thank you," I say, gripping his hand. Then I start making my way back downstairs. A vacation. If Gabor thinks it'll be that easy to sideline me, he's dead wrong.

In my office, I log on to my computer and check my emails. A few appointment requests, messages from external project staff, offers from various companies. The usual. My coworkers in the office next door are all busy; there aren't any problems. Fortunately, Nadine refrains from asking me in front of all the others about what Gabor wanted.

I answer the most important emails, but find it hard to concentrate. My thoughts keep straying back and forth between Gabor and Joanna. I really want to call her and ask how she's doing, but I leave it. I don't want her to think I'm keeping tabs on her.

I still need to go get some clothes. I take the suitcase containing my toiletries and the things I've been wearing with me. Roughly an hour later, I have two new pairs of jeans, three polo shirts, and two work shirts. I also buy a couple of three-pair underwear packs and five pairs of dark socks from another store. With all of that, I should be well-equipped for the next few days.

The journey home takes far too long for my liking. The closer I get, with every few feet I drive, the more nervous I get. How's Joanna doing? Is she even still there? And if so, will she be by herself? Or will there be a couple of policemen waiting for me as well, wanting to find out what the deal is with this bizarre story Joanna's just told them?

It's half past five when I park next to the Golf and walk to the front door, my knees shaky.

In the hall, I stop and listen. I can't hear anything apart from my own pulse.

"Jo?" I don't know why I'm calling her name out so faintly, so I try it again, louder this time.

"Jo? Are you there?"

Nothing.

She's actually gone. Despite everything that's happened, I didn't really expect she'd actually run away. On foot. Her car is still outside, after all.

The sensation of immense loss starts spreading through me. It feels like it's draining all my energy. I have difficulty standing upright from one moment to the next; I just want to lie on the ground and stop moving altogether.

But wait—I haven't looked upstairs yet. Maybe Joanna just went to lie down? With everything she's going through right now, she must be exhausted.

Without missing a beat, I run to the stairs, take two steps at once. I stop at the top, pause for a moment, then continue as quietly as possible. I don't want to startle her.

The bedroom door has been left ajar. I carefully give it a push. And in the very same moment I see the empty bed, I also hear a crashing sound. It sounds like it came from the bathroom. Only now do I notice the pattering noise in the background. The shower.

Five swift steps, six. The bathroom door isn't locked.

A cloud of warm steam billows toward me. The large mirror is all misted up, the plexiglass shower only in parts. Joanna's contorted figure is lying on the shower floor.

"Jo!" I scream. I jerk open the shower stall door. Water sprays in my face, soaking me through and through in mere seconds. "Oh my God, Jo."

My movements erratic, I turn off the water and bend down. My hands slip off Joanna's wet body; I bang my elbow on the edge of the shower. Finally I manage to pull her up a bit. I look over her body. No visible injuries. Her eyes are closed. I carefully lift her out of the shower, and at the same time realize I'm starting to feel nauseous. My head hurts. What's happening to me?

My eyes wander through the bathroom. Sink, closet, hot-water boiler . . . the boiler? I try to stand up, and slip on the wet floor. Finally I manage to push myself up, make it over to the window, and yank it open. Don't throw up. Not now.

I quickly lean out of the window, take a deep breath, another; then I turn around. I've got to get Joanna out of here. I grab her by the hands and drag her across the tiled floor out of the bathroom. Across the hall, into the bedroom. The first thing I do there is open the window; then I heave Joanna onto the bed. Panting, I set my ear onto her chest. She's breathing. Her breaths are shallow, but she's breathing. Thank goodness.

I want to collapse down next to her on the bed, but I need to go back into the bathroom first. I hold my breath as I close the gas valve on the boiler.

I stagger back into the bedroom, needing to brace myself against the wall in the hall as I go. Then I fall onto the bed next to Joanna. What should I do now? I have to call an ambulance. Arduously I push myself up to go look for the telephone.

At that moment, another thought hits me. The boiler in the bathroom. It was serviced just three weeks ago. And now it might have almost killed Joanna.

How is that possible?

13

Light.

A wall. A window. Out of focus. It's hard to keep my eyes open.

Too hard.

Someone touches my shoulder. Shakes me.

"Jo! Don't fall asleep again! Stay awake, OK? Look at me!"

A dark silhouette over me. A face. A stranger's face.

Or no . . . Not a stranger. Worse than that.

A hand caresses me, my head, my cheek. "The ambulance is almost here. They're coming as fast as they can. Are you feeling sick? Can you breathe?"

I try to focus on my body. The answer to both questions is yes. The silhouette above me becomes blurry; the room spins. I can breathe, but it still feels like the air I can get into my lungs is far too little. . . .

"Jo!" Another shake. Then a few soft slaps on my cheek. "Please! Look at me, OK?"

Suddenly the image becomes clearer. Erik, leaning over me. "That's it. Just look into my eyes. I'm with you, everything's going to be OK."

He wheezes. In his right hand he is holding a bundle of . . . fabric, which he now stuffs into the drawer of my nightstand.

"Did you do this, Jo?" He pulls me into his arms, pressing me against him. The shirt he is wearing is soaked through, just as I am, and slowly the memory of what happened comes back. The shower. The dizziness. Vomiting.

Erik is still holding me. The thought that I should put up a struggle pops into my mind, then goes again. Too little strength. Too little air.

I feel his rib cage rising and falling laboriously, feel his hand entangling itself in my wet hair. His breath on my neck.

Then he lets me go. He supports himself wearily against the bed as he straightens up, and walks over to my wardrobe with shaky steps.

"They'll be here any minute now. I should put some clothes on you." Panties, a T-shirt. I'd like to be able to dress myself, but any movement I make worsens the dizziness and breathlessness, so I let him dress me, as if I were a doll.

Then the sirens, moving closer, coming to a halt in front of the house. Erik stumbles over to the window. "The door is unlocked," he calls out; then he sits down on the edge of the bed and reaches for my hand.

Suddenly the room is full of people, all of them wearing respirator masks. Voices come from everywhere around me. A flurry of activity. Someone pulls Erik away from me, shines a light in my eyes, feels for my pulse.

"Carbon monoxide." I keep hearing the words again and again. An oxygen mask is placed over my mouth and nose, and suddenly breathing becomes a lot easier.

I turn my head, see Erik sitting on the floor, also with a mask on his face. His eyes seek mine, he nods to me.

They lift me onto a stretcher, place a blanket over my body, and I close my eyes.

"Is this your house?" I hear someone say. "The boiler is really old, when was it last checked, OK, and by the way we need to take you to the hospital as well."

The stretcher is tilted at an angle on the way down the stairs, then there's a gust of air as we arrive outside. I open my eyes, see the dark evening sky above me. The stars.

I think I can finally sleep again now.

A huge, tubular object. Hyperbaric oxygen therapy, the doctor explains to me. "After all, you don't want any long-term damage, do you?"

I weakly shake my head. No. What I want is to turn back time, to the point when my life was still familiar and I didn't have to be afraid all the time.

Inside the chamber, tubes protrude out of the walls, running into blue masks. One of them is pulled over my face. "Just breathe," says the doctor. Then he leaves me alone.

I try to remember what happened. I was searching the house, then I took a shower—and collapsed. Erik must have found me and pulled me out of there, hence his wet shirt.

Did you do that? he had asked me. Whatever he meant by that.

After an hour, they bring me out of the tube again. I'm feeling a lot better, but they still don't want to let me go home. "First, because the fire department is still there, and second, because we need to keep you under observation."

At least my insurance gets me a private room in the hospital. The oxygen mask is still my constant companion, and it's a good excuse for staying silent. I stare at the wall and try to block out the cheerful doctor sticking electrocardiogram contacts onto my upper body. "Gas boilers are so dangerous," she chatters away to me. "You're lucky that your husband reacted so quickly. Just a while longer, and . . ."

She leaves the sentence unfinished, but it's clear what she means.

My husband.

Without a doubt Erik had pulled me out of the shower, he had rescued me—but what would have happened if I had showered half an hour earlier? Would he have been there? Had he just been waiting for an opportunity to be my knight in shining armor?

Or would I be dead?

I lie there, and watch the zigzagging lines that my heartbeat is projecting onto the observation monitor.

Did you do that, Jo?

The pain in my wrist is no longer as acute as it was this morning, but it has spread. It now goes from my knuckles to the tips of my fingers. I can remember clearly the feeling of euphoria that filled me when I hit my hand against the door of Ela's car. It had been so painful and yet, at the same time . . . good.

Something isn't right with me; maybe I should start to face up to it. If I'd recently felt the need to inflict harm on myself, then it was also plausible I had tampered with the boiler in order to do something much worse.

Except that I have no idea how to go about doing something like that. And I don't remember having even been near the device. But by now I guess I shouldn't be that surprised by gaps in my memory.

Or maybe I should. It could be that all of this has been staged to bring me to exactly the conclusions I'm drawing now.

But how could someone stage my newly acquired urge to self-harm?

Maybe it had simply been an accident. A maintenance error. Something that could happen anywhere. The bad thing, though, is that this possibility seems the least likely to me.

I close my eyes. Block out the world. Concentrate only on the oxygen streaming into my body.

The next morning, even before the pitiful hospital breakfast is brought to me, there's a knock at the door and Ela comes into the room. She looks pale, shaking her head again and again, and sits down on the edge of my bed.

"What on earth is going on with you guys?" she says as she takes my hand." Do you realize how close it was, Jo? With carbon monoxide poisoning, two minutes can mean the difference between life and death. Sometimes even less."

I'm still wearing my oxygen mask. I don't have to say anything, but I reciprocate the squeeze she gives my hand.

"I'm so glad Erik got there in time," she murmurs. "He did exactly the right thing."

She correctly interprets my questioning glance. "Yes, I talked to him, he's here in the hospital too. He didn't have a mask, after all, so it got him as well." Was that a trace of accusation in her voice? "Not as badly as you, though. They're already discharging him today." She smiles; I guess she means for it to be encouraging. "Is there anything I can do for you?"

Yes, as a matter of fact there is. I lift my oxygen mask for a moment. "Call the photo studio. Please. Tell them that . . ."

"That you'll be away for a while. Of course."

She strokes my arm, biting her lower lip. It's clear she wants to get something off her chest, but doesn't know how to say it.

Eventually she comes out with it. "Have you thought about whether you might want to stay here for a while to get treatment, once you've made it through this part, I mean?" She tries to hold my gaze. "Not in this department, of course. In the psychiatric ward. Just to be on the safe side, you know?"

I abruptly pull my hand away from hers and turn my head to the side. Not because I find the idea so unreasonable; on the contrary. I had the same thought during the night. But Ela's suggestion makes it real, and makes me realize that it's the last thing I want. To be locked away, be put on medication, confronted with a diagnosis.

Cleared out of the way.

"I'm sorry," I hear Ela say. "I don't want to push you into anything. I really don't. But do you remember what happened in the car yesterday? That's just not like you." She sighs, and I close my eyes.

Go away, I think.

Ela stands up, as if she heard my silent plea. "I'm just afraid that you could be a threat to yourself. Or maybe you already are. To yourself and Erik."

She strokes my head. I let her, lying still like I've fallen asleep.

"I mean, you're my friend. You're important to me. Both of you are important to me. I don't want anything to happen to either of you."

Erik comes by a quarter of an hour after the doctor's made his rounds. He pulls up a chair and doesn't say anything for a long time, nor does he touch me. He has his elbows propped on his knees and his hands folded in front of his mouth. A waiting position.

But if he's hoping that I'll be unable to bear the silence and start a conversation, then he has a long and frustrating wait ahead of him. My oxygen mask is my protective shield.

His voice is soft when he eventually speaks. "I was so worried about you, Jo. And I'm so glad you're getting better."

I force myself to look him in the eyes. Was there ever a time in my life when I had felt so torn? I should be thanking this man, should be down on my knees with gratitude, for the fact that he had risked his own life to save me. And I'd do it too, without hesitation, if it wasn't for this other possibility. The possibility that I wouldn't even have needed to be saved if he weren't here in the first place. The possibility that he intentionally put me in danger, all just to extort gratitude from me.

I decide to lift up my oxygen mask after all. "They're saying it was the boiler?"

Erik hesitates for a moment, then nods. "It's not just what they're saying. That's what it was. And—Jo . . ." He buries his face in his hands, rubbing it, then looks up again.

"I found the scarves."

I have no idea what he's talking about. "The scarves?"

"Yes. The boiler's exhaust vent was blocked with three bunched-up scarves, the large ones that you like so much. That's why . . ."

That's why.

It wasn't a technical defect. Or a maintenance error. Someone took my scarves out of the wardrobe and used them to build a little deathtrap.

"I took them out before the firemen arrived. They were really puzzled, because the exhaust should have been vented normally. They said that accidents like this can happen without the boiler being blocked, but in those cases the carbon monoxide only gets pushed back down into the vent when it's humid outside and the air pressure is low."

Erik doesn't say any more, but I'm well aware of what he's thinking. It wasn't humid yesterday. And I was alone at home for hours. I would have had time to do it.

He probably talked with Ela already. Hence her suggestion earlier.

"It wasn't me," I say, and even I can hear how flat my voice is. Exhausted. Unconvincing.

I clear my throat and try again, making an effort to sound stronger. "Believe me, Erik. I didn't do it. I wouldn't even know how to; I've got no idea about gas boilers and vents and . . ." I run out of air, and press the oxygen mask back down over my face, for three, four breaths. "I'm not trying to kill myself," I say then. "Neither myself nor you."

He doesn't smile. Staring at the floor, he says, "I hid the scarves; maybe that was stupid of me. But I didn't want you to get into trouble with the police, or for them to lock you up in a psychiatric unit." Now he looks up, and for the first time since I've known him, I feel the urge to take his hand. To hold it and squeeze it.

I don't, but when he reaches for mine, as if he can sense my thoughts, I let him.

"I still believe that we can get over our problems," he says. "But you have to want it, Jo. You're making it so unbelievably difficult for me right now. I'm doing everything I can, but you have to help me. Please."

I don't know why I nod. Probably because I'd like to believe what he's saying. Because I need something to hold on to, too. Or someone.

And maybe that's exactly what he was after the entire time. If that's so, he's achieved his goal.

14

"You were lucky." The ward doctor looks up from the clipboard holding my patient chart, and puts it down at the foot of the bed I'm sitting on, all dressed and ready to go. Lucky? That seems like an absolute mockery, given the chaos of the past few days.

"All in all, your blood levels are OK. Your paperwork is being prepared as we speak, and after that you're free to go. I'll write you a sick note for the next two days. You should use the time to recover."

He gives me a firm handshake. Then I'm by myself again.

I can go. Leave this room with its whitewashed walls that threw back my thoughts like an echo when I was staring at them, for hours on end, searching in vain for answers. .

But I'm still reluctant about the prospect of leaving the hospital. About leaving Joanna, who's lying in a room only a few doors down from mine.

If I leave now, I won't be able to protect her. From . . . from what, really?

From herself? From me?

What if it's not Joanna who has mental problems, but me? How can I be so sure her head is the one that's out of whack? She's fighting the idea that something's wrong with her just as desperately as I would be. As I am. But maybe it really was me who plugged the boiler's vent, and I just don't remember it? I do know where you'd have to stuff the scarves to block it, at least.

"OK, Herr Thieben, here's your sick note and the letter for your doctor."

A rotund nurse is holding an envelope out toward me. I get up and take it from her. "Thanks," I say, and I truly do feel thankful. Because she showed up at exactly the right moment and pulled me out of these frightening thoughts.

"And that's all. You can go now. Get well soon." She gives me an encouraging smile, and a moment later she's gone. Next patient, next smile.

I leave the room, turn to the left, and walk to the room five doors down. I decide not to knock.

Joanna seems to be asleep as I carefully shut the door behind me and go over to her bed. I stand there and look at her. The oxygen mask over her pale face, the tubes, the monitor next to her bed. Three jagged lines, one underneath the other. Green, blue, white. Some numbers as well. Blood pressure, oxygenation, ECG, heart rate. She looks so incredibly helpless, so fragile. I scream silently on the inside. I desperately want to take her in my arms, hold her against me. Whisper into her ear that everything's going to be OK. That I love her more than words can say, that we'll get through everything together. Everything.

If only I could at least hold her hand.

But I leave it. She needs her rest.

Get well quick, I think. *I'll be back later.* I leave the room on tiptoe. Hallway, elevator, foyer, and reception. I register them all as though they were props in this nightmare I'm stumbling through, this horror film in which I'm inadvertently playing the leading role.

I get into a taxi and tell the driver my address. Stare out the window as we drive off in silence, leaving the hospital behind us. The concrete faces of the suburban houses gawp at me with cold indifference.

I've been put on sick leave for two days, but I don't want to sit around the house, especially not now, when things are quite clearly going off course for me at work.

On the other hand, it would give me the chance to look after Joanna without having to invent any stories. Stories that would give Gabor, or Bernhard, even more reasons to speculate.

"You want me to drive up there?" The driver points at our driveway.

"Yes, please."

I pay, get out, and pause in front of the spot where the cockatoo had been standing until two days ago. Already it seems so long ago that our world still made sense. I realize now how we always took it for granted, never wasting a single thought on how it could all be different one day.

I close the door behind me and slump back against it. The house seems empty to me, almost like it belongs to a stranger. It was only on rare occasions that Joanna wasn't in the house when I got back. And even then I knew it wouldn't be long before I'd hear the door click into the lock and a cheerful "Hi, darling, I'm back."

Will I ever hear that again?

Frau Schwickerath from HR explains to me over the phone that it will be fine if I bring the sick note with me when I come back to the office; it's only two days, after all. Then she wishes me a speedy recovery.

I make myself some coffee and sit at the kitchen table, the steaming cup in front of me. Again and again I go over the events of the past two days, desperately searching for just a hint of an explanation. But all that comes to my mind is irrational nonsense.

After a while, my mind wanders to G.E.E. and Gabor. Not a very pleasant subject either, right now, but still I follow the train of thought. Because it's something different, at least. What had made Gabor exclude me from this huge contract? All the projects I've headed over the past few years have gone well. Of course there were delays here and there, which we simply couldn't have reckoned with during the run-up. But that's normal, and it happens with all the larger contracts. It was certainly no reason to give me the cold shoulder all of sudden if something big was coming in.

Maybe Bernhard has something to do with that? After all, he called Gabor from the airport and told him about what happened at our house.

If I was you, I'd think twice about coming into the office tomorrow morning, he'd said to me, pretending to be concerned. Asshole.

By now my coffee's just lukewarm swill. It seems I've lost my sense of time as well.

I walk into the living room, without really knowing what I intend to do in there. So I go back out into the kitchen, then the hallway. The boiler pops into my mind and I climb the stairs, my heart thumping.

It looks like a bomb exploded in the bathroom. There are towels lying on the floor, some of Joanna's cosmetic products scattered among them. The bottles and small tins on the shelf next to the sink have fallen over. What exactly were the firefighters up to in here?

The lower section of boiler has been bared; the cover is lying on the tiled floor in front of it. The tangle of copper tubing, fittings, and wires looks like a body that's been cracked open, ready for autopsy.

Had someone been here who tampered with it, or was there another explanation for the scarves in the exhaust vent? And who were they trying to get at? Joanna? Me, maybe? Or didn't it matter?

Which once again brings up the crucial question of why. I walk down the stairs and stop in the hall. Stare at the door. It's possible that a stranger was in our house. In our most intimate place. It feels like an act of desecration. Maybe he was in our bedroom as well, touching the covers we'd pulled over our naked skin after we . . . No, he didn't. If he did, he could only have touched Joanna's covers, as mine are no longer there. It's enough to drive someone insane.

I go into the kitchen again. This turmoil inside me; I feel like I'm losing my mind. I look at the clock and try to figure out how much time has passed since I got out of the taxi. Although, for that, I'd need to know what time it was when I got out. And I have no idea.

"Fuck it."

Did I just say that out loud? Yes, I think I did. Does that count as talking to myself? A sign that my mind's giving up?

I can't bear to be in this house anymore. It feels wrong to be here while Joanna's lying there in the hospital, poisoned. Left all alone with the terrible fear she must be feeling.

She's going to need fresh clothes. Underwear, towels.

Half an hour later I'm behind the wheel and on my way to see her.

That afternoon and for the next two days, I'm with Joanna most of the time. I only leave the hospital in the evenings to sleep and at some point during the day to go get food.

I tell her a lot about us. At first, my sentences always start with the words, "Do you remember . . . ?"

She silently shakes her head every time. After a while I decide to stop using that painful introductory question.

Sometimes I just sit by her bed in silence and watch her sleep. Or pretending to sleep. I can tell the difference from the way she's blinking, but I let her rest.

As for Joanna, she only speaks very little, apart from on one occasion when she tells me about Australia. About her childhood and her friends. She barely mentions her father. I don't interrupt her; I simply listen.

On the afternoon of the second day, when I get back from a walk through the small park next to the hospital, Joanna is sitting in the chair where I've spent the majority of the past two days. She's dressed.

"I'm allowed to go," she says. She doesn't say *I'm allowed to go home.*

I take one big step toward her and pull her into my arms. I can't help myself. I expect her to push me away, but that doesn't happen. She doesn't hug me, but neither does she resist being close to me. I close my eyes. It's amazing how little you need for a simple moment of joy when there's no longer anything you can take for granted.

We don't talk much during the drive. Joanna sits there looking out of the window on her side, and I'm scared that a single unmindful word could destroy the small moment of joy I just experienced.

Finally we're home. I carry the bag with her things and instinctively put my hand on her back as we're walking. She doesn't push me away this time either, but I can feel her body tensing up, and quickly drop my arm again.

Joanna tells me she's very tired and wants to go lie down for a while.

Half an hour later, she's back down in the kitchen with me. She can't sleep, she says, even though she's so tired.

I suggest I cook something nice for the two of us. "Are you good at cooking?" she asks.

"I'm best when you're helping," I say, but she shakes her head and sits down. "No, please, it'd be nice if you cooked something for us. I'll watch you."

I agree. The notion of cooking something for her feels good, like something that could help break down the distance between us.

Our freezer is in the pantry. I've just pulled out a large ice-cold bag of shrimp when the doorbell rings.

When I come out of the storeroom, Joanna has got up from her chair. I recognize fear in her expression. "Who could that be?"

"I don't know. Maybe someone else from work who's deleted a file from their laptop," I say dryly.

Joanna follows me as I leave the kitchen, but stops in the passage to the hall and holds on to the doorframe as if afraid she could topple over.

I open the door and stare in surprise at the person opposite me for some time before finally finding my ability to speak.

Standing on our doorstep, with a smile on his face, is Dr. Bartsch, the company psychologist at Gabor Energy Engineering. I say hello haltingly and feel anger rising up inside me. Is this another attempt to give me the boot?

"Good evening, Herr Thieben," he says, grinning ever more broadly. "I just wanted to drop by briefly to check if everything was all right with you. May I come in?"

15

The man is of average height and wiry, and I immediately notice that Erik can't stand him. He takes two deep breaths before inviting the visitor into the house with an abrupt jerk of his hand. "Dr. Bartsch. What brings you here?"

Another doctor? I instinctively edge backward into the kitchen.

The man strokes his trim beard. "Herr Gabor sent me, he wanted me to check in with you. Naturally he heard how close you came to a tragedy . . ."

As he says these words, he looks over at me. Studies me with blatant interest. "You must be Joanna, is that right?"

I'm so tired. I don't want to make small talk with this doctor, and if he's capable of even just the tiniest bit of empathy, he should notice that. But before I can answer, Erik is by my side. "Jo, this is Dr. Bartsch, our company psychologist. I didn't ask him to come here, if that's what you're thinking; I know you want to rest today."

Perhaps it's just the tiredness, but I find myself unable to grasp what's going on. Is this visit about me? What do I have to do with Erik's business? Over the past few days he's told me a fair amount about himself, including his work. It has to do with renewable energy—an emerging market, my father would say.

"No." Bartsch looks serious now. "Erik didn't ask me to come here, that's true. But our manager thought it would be a good idea if I check in on you. Perhaps there's something I can help with, and if that's the case, I'd be very happy to."

It's clear that Erik is struggling to contain himself. "Come on, we both know why you're really here," he says quietly. "You're looking for some reason which would allow Gabor to can me."

I give Erik a sideways glance. He hadn't mentioned he was having problems at work.

The psychologist shakes his head with a smile. "But why on earth would Gabor want to do that? You're doing an outstanding job, Herr Thieben, and believe me, he knows that too." He nods toward the living room. "I'd like it if we could sit down. I won't keep you long, I promise."

Even though everything in me is fighting against it, I nod. Yet another stranger in my living room.

Bartsch sits down on the couch and crosses his legs. He looks over at us expectantly.

I pull myself together. "Would you like something to drink, perhaps?"

His expression softens. "Oh, that would be wonderful, thank you. I'd love a glass of water."

I go into the kitchen, where the pack of shrimp is lying next to the stove, slowly thawing. I can completely understand that Erik wants the man out of the house as soon as possible; I feel the same way. He has that penetrating psychologist's gaze, which gives me the feeling that he's able to look right through me. And, ultimately, that he knows more about me than even I do.

Not a difficult accomplishment right now, admittedly.

Feeling a chuckle creeping up my throat, I quickly take a glass out of the cupboard and fill it with water.

"Thank you," he says, as I place it on the coffee table in front of him. He takes a sip, not averting his eyes from me for even a second, then leans back. "Joanna. I'm very happy that you came through the accident unharmed. How are you feeling?"

It's not just the stare, it's also . . . his voice. It's not unpleasant, but nonetheless there's something about it which makes me want to leave the room and hide.

"Leave her be," Erik answers for me. He takes my hand and interlaces his fingers with mine. "If you want to cross-examine me, then go ahead, but leave Joanna out of it."

Bartsch shakes his head once more. "I really don't know what gave you this idea, Herr Thieben." Without waiting for an answer, he turns to me again. "How long have you been living here?"

For . . . I have to concentrate. "For six months. Roughly."

Bartsch gives the pictures on the wall an appraising glance. "Did you choose the furnishings together?"

No, that was just me. I feel the urge to pull my hand away from Erik's grasp—what am I supposed to say to that?

Bartsch's gaze wanders back to me; he's wondering, of course, why it's taking me so long to answer such a simple question. "Yes," I whisper.

"Very tasteful." He reaches for the glass, rotates it between his hands. "It's a shame that we're meeting under such regrettable circumstances. Why haven't you come to any of our office parties with Erik? They're much less boring than you'd expect, almost all the employees bring their significant others."

I never went because I've only known him for the past five days. The response lies on the tip of my tongue, but there's no way I'm going to say it out loud. Erik's grip on my hand has tightened significantly.

"I was always busy," I say, hating myself for the fact that my voice sounds so weak. "I often work until late in the evening," I add, a little louder now.

"I see. Yes, that's understandable." Bartsch takes a large gulp of water.

My heart is hammering a little too hard in my chest, and I don't know whether it's down to the psychologist's voice or to the fact that he just gave me a clue that my original suspicion was correct. If I really was engaged to Erik, I would have gone with him. I'm a curious person; I would have wanted to see who he works with.

Bartsch speaks up again. "As I said, I don't want to disturb you for long. And of course you know why I'm really here. Bernhard Morbach was at your house recently and told us afterward that you had tried to run away from Erik, Joanna."

The man with the laptop bag. Erik's grip on my hand becomes so tight that it's almost hurting me.

"That was . . . a misunderstanding," I stammer.

The psychologist gives me a penetrating stare. "He said it seemed as though you were terrified."

Erik lets go of my hand and jumps up. "Oh, that's what Bernhard said, is it? That's very interesting. If he was so worried about her, then why did he just go and leave Joanna alone with me?"

Bartsch stares at Erik, his expression unchanged. "No one is accusing you of anything, Herr Thieben. But the scene which Herr Morbach described to us was, at the very least, unusual and stressful for both of you, I'm sure. And now, in light of recent events . . ."

Erik has gone pale. He is standing close to Bartsch, no more than two feet away, and his hands are balled into fists. "What do you mean, in light of recent events? Come on, let's hear it."

The psychologist doesn't look at Erik, but instead at me. "An unusual accumulation of problems. I'm sure you would agree with me." Speaking in an ostensibly calm tone, he leans over toward me. "Joanna, would you answer a few questions for me? Only if you want to, of course, but perhaps we might find out why you were so afraid?"

I try to make eye contact with Erik, but he's not even looking at me. He's standing in front of Bartsch, looking as though there's nothing he'd like to do more than go for the man's throat. "You're meddling in my private life."

"That's a sign of esteem, Herr Thieben." There's still not even a glimmer of impatience in Bartsch's voice. "We are offering you help, and I promise you that every single word spoken here will be treated in confidence."

Erik laughs contemptuously. "You don't even believe that yourself!"

Is it because of the stress of the past few days, or is he always this undiplomatic at work? I discreetly try to wipe my sweaty palms on my pants. I'm not sure why this situation is making me so nervous—whether it's Bartsch or Erik's blatant rage, I only know that I want it to stop. And the quickest way for that to happen is probably if I agree to speak with Bartsch; I might even be able to say a few things that put Erik in a better light than he's putting himself in right now. Whoever he is, whatever our connection to each other is—he was so caring with me when I was in the hospital. So willing to help. There's no harm in trying to return the favor.

"Ask me your questions, Dr. Bartsch."

Erik wheels around to face me. "You can't be serious!" He sinks down next to me on the couch. "But you're doing better, Jo. You don't need him, we already have help . . ."

I smile at him. *My God, I'm so tired.* "It's just a few questions, it's not like I'm agreeing to a therapy session."

"Exactly," Bartsch affirms. He has pulled a small notebook and a pen out from his jacket. "Bernhard Morbach said that you didn't recognize Erik the other day. Is that correct?"

This is beginning differently than how I had imagined. A little too direct for my taste. Nonetheless, I nod. "Yes."

Bartsch makes a note. "But now you recognize him again?"

No, I don't. I've been unable to find anything that Erik has told me over the past few days within my own memory. There has been no sudden flashback of shared experiences. But never mind, that's not what matters right now.

"Yes," I lie. "Everything's OK again."

He looks at me for a little too long before noting down my answer. As if he doesn't completely believe me.

"Could you tell me what happened before that evening? Before you were so distraught about Erik's presence?"

I shrug my shoulders in a vague gesture. Everything that came before that seems as though it's months ago. "I was working, I think. I cleaned up a bit and then took a shower. I was planning to make tea and read something."

On the couch. Right where Bartsch is sitting now.

"That was everything?"

"I think so, yes."

He makes another note. "What about before the accident with the boiler? Can you still remember what you were doing before that?"

Before I can answer, Erik places his hand on my arm. "What are you getting at? Are you accusing her—"

"I'm not accusing her of anything," Bartsch interrupts. "It's a completely harmless question. I don't know why you're so against this conversation, Herr Thieben. Why you're so determined to refuse the help being offered. You said yourself that your girlfriend was confused. Both to Herr Morbach and Herr Gabor."

I don't know why, but his last two sentences hit a nerve with me. Until now I had thought that the psychologist was here because this Bernhard Morbach guy saw me running out of the house in my bathrobe, but now it turns out that Erik has been discussing our situation with his coworkers. So I'm *confused*, am I?

Who knows who else he's talked to about me. If we really are a couple, then that's an unforgivable breach of trust, and for some strange reason it really feels like one too.

I press my hand against my eyes. If I start to cry now, can I blame it on how tired I am?

I feel an arm around my shoulders. "Please go, Dr. Bartsch," I hear Erik say. "You can see for yourself that she's not back to full health yet."

I straighten up. Turn around to face Erik. "Who else have you talked to about me?"

A frown forms above the bridge of his nose. "What do you mean?"

"I'd like to know: who else did you tell that I'm supposedly *confused*?" My tone doesn't sound accusatory, but exhausted instead. And now tears are welling up in my eyes after all, as if the impression I'm giving didn't already look pitiful enough. I turn away, away from Erik's embrace, and wipe the back of my hand over my face.

"Jo . . . I didn't say anything that Bernhard hadn't already spread around. Believe me, if he hadn't turned up here, no one would know anything about this."

The sound of a throat being cleared from the other side of the coffee table. "There's really no reason to be annoyed at Erik. He wasn't gossiping about you, he was just concerned—"

Erik jumps up, and this time it really does look as though he's about to launch himself at Bartsch. "You stay out of our business, you hear me? I don't need your mediation or your professional support. Unlike Joanna, I know exactly why you're here, and I'm not going to play your game."

Bartsch waits for Erik to finish, with a calm demeanor that must be the result of years of training. Then he turns to me. "Joanna. The most important thing here is you and your safety. Do you want my help?"

If I say yes now, it's an open declaration of war on Erik. But I would do it regardless, if I thought I had something to gain from it. And if my stomach hadn't started to cramp up. Is that still the lack of oxygen? But my tests were fine. So now what's wrong?

"Joanna? Take your time."

I can feel both of them waiting. Bartsch full of patience, Erik full of impatience. I take a deep breath in and out, fixing my gaze on the kitchen door.

All of a sudden I can't bring myself to tear my gaze away from it. As if there was something there that I need to resolve. Urgently.

All of a sudden I realize how I must look.

Confused.

I summon all my strength. "No. Thank you, Dr. Bartsch, but I don't think you're the right person for me to talk to. If I need help, then I'll find someone myself."

I hear Erik breathe out a sigh of relief next to me. Bartsch looks a little concerned, but doesn't make any move to get up.

"Can I ask you something in return?" The words are out before I even realize that they've formed in my mind.

Bartsch inclines his head lightly. "Please do," he says politely.

This time I know what I want to say, but I'm not sure why. And I'm sure the two men in my living room will feel equally clueless, no doubt about it.

"Is your first name Ben?"

Bartsch blinks briefly, but that's all. He covers up his surprise very effectively. "No. My name is Christoph."

"Ah. OK."

I wish I'd gotten myself a glass of water too. My mouth is dry, and the hammering behind my temples is announcing the arrival of a headache.

"Tell me, Joanna . . ." begins Bartsch, but this time Erik doesn't let him finish.

"No. That's enough now. Please go. Tell Gabor whatever you want, but leave us in peace."

"Herr Thieben—"

"I said, get out!" Erik pulls Bartsch up from the couch by the arm, then roughly pushes him out of the living room. "I've fucking had it with you. That's at least three times I politely asked you to leave, and you've ignored me every time. If you don't leave now, I'll throw you out myself. Get out, you inconsiderate piece of shit!"

His voice is loud, too loud. I manage to suppress the urge to cover my ears, but I can't stop my hands from trembling.

"Good-bye, Joanna," I hear Bartsch say from the hallway. Then the door is opened and a few moments later slammed loudly shut.

We are alone once more.

16

The sound of the door slamming shut echoes in my head, intermingling with the hammering of my pulse. I'm finding it hard to formulate a clear thought.

Hot rage consumes me like wildfire. And the realization that Bartsch, that grinning asshole, managed to make me lose my cool, is like an accelerant for the blaze.

"Why did you do that?" Joanna's voice reaches my ears, sounding like it's coming from far away even though she's only standing a few feet from me.

"What?" I say loudly, wheeling around to face her. My voice sounds severe, I know, but I'm not sorry. I look at her, see fear, despair, helplessness in her eyes. I ought to feel bad about it, really. But I don't.

I love this woman more than I've ever loved anyone before but . . . damn it. I can't even find the words to explain to myself what's going on in my head right now. Explosions. It feels like a succession of mental explosions. Making it impossible for me calm down, I'm so unbelievably furious. And the sight of Joanna right now is making it even worse.

"Why did you tell people in your company I was confused? If we really are a couple like you keep claiming we are, that's a huge breach of trust."

"What do you mean, tell people?" I roar, and see Joanna flinch. "I didn't have to tell anyone anything, Jo. Because my boss asked me about what was going on at home, right to my face. After Bernhard went gossiping around about what he saw when he was here."

"But that's no reason to—"

"Sure it is," I say, cutting her off again, and I'm not sorry about that either. On the contrary, I'm getting a feeling akin to satisfaction with every word I say. It feels relieving. Kind of like a pressure valve was being opened somewhere.

"It is a reason, in fact, it's the reason for everything, Jo. Do you remember? No? I wouldn't be surprised if you don't. Let me help you. My coworker Bernhard was on our doorstep here when you ran outside, screaming, half-naked in just your bathrobe. You hid behind him and begged him to protect you. From me, Jo. The stranger who'd broken into your house. Do you really think it would have been necessary for *me* to tell people at work anything, with you making a scene like that? Do you? Me saying you were confused wasn't a breach of trust, damn it, it was damage control. Your insane behavior is the reason for everything that's happened over the past few days."

It's getting worse and worse. There's a voice somewhere in my head, whispering to me that I have to stop this. That I'll work myself into a raving frenzy if I don't try to fight back this surge of anger.

"My . . . insane behavior?" Her whispered words are in such marked contrast with my screaming, it makes me feel even angrier, like I might snap any second.

She's doing it on purpose. She still feels like I'm not treating her fairly, even after everything I went through with her over these past days. It's hopeless, all of this.

Calling on all of my inner strength, I soften my voice. It sounds breathless, barely composed, even to me. "Jo, don't you realize that's exactly what Bartsch wanted? Gabor sent that bastard to stir things up even more. To have a reason for firing me. Can't you see that he used you and intentionally put you at odds with me? Come on, you have to see that! I feel like I'm going to go crazy if you don't understand this."

"My insane behavior, Erik?" she repeats stoically, making something inside of me shatter. *It's over!* I hear the voice inside of me, shouting those words, see them in front of me like they were written on a poster. *It's over.* And I surrender myself to the impact.

"Yes, exactly. Your totally insane behavior!" I scream at her. "What in the hell else would you call this stunt you've been pulling here for days?"

"That's . . . Do you realize how unfair that is, Erik?"

Is she really doing this? Making herself out to be the victim in this whole fucked-up situation? My head is threatening to explode. I want to scream. Scream in desperate anger, until my lungs burst out of my chest.

Next to me on the floor, the umbrella stand . . . I stride over and kick it with such force that it clatters loudly over the floor tiles until coming to a rest a few feet away by the front door. Joanna lets out a soft scream, and I wheel around, grab her by the arms and grasp them tightly. Her eyes grow wide. "Ow, you're . . . you're hurting me."

I let her words bounce off me and clutch her even more tightly. I want to yell in her face. But I do the exact opposite. My voice goes completely calm. "I came home without a clue, Joanna. After a shitty day in that shitty company. I wasn't feeling well, and the only thing I was looking forward to, the only thing I really needed, was a hug from you. To be close to you. Some comforting words. Instead you made a scene that I could only describe as being totally insane. You claimed not to know me. Threw a paperweight at me and wanted to throw me out of *our* house. You ran away from me and locked yourself in the bedroom. Then you made a complete idiot out of me in front of Bernhard, and in front of the entire company as a consequence. You're destroying everything about the life we shared, all with your crazy behavior. Maybe you even tried to kill yourself. And me along with you, because once again I wanted to save you. Five days, Jo. I've been going through hell for five days. I feel like I don't even know myself anymore. Like I'm living someone else's life. And still, I stuck by you the whole time, defended you against everyone and everything, no matter how much your behavior hurt me."

I have to yell again all of a sudden. I don't want to. I *have* to.

"And now you're standing there and whining about a breach of trust?" I shout so loudly that my voice cracks. I've unwittingly started shaking Joanna hard, much too hard. At the very same moment I realize that, it's all over. The anger, the screaming, the shaking. My arms slump by my sides. No more strength. No energy. Nothing.

Joanna's crying. She crosses her arms in front of her chest, rubbing her arms where I'd grabbed her. I can see redness. Without looking at me, she keeps backing away until she bumps into the wall. She slides down it, as if in slow motion, and slumps down onto the floor with her legs tucked in. She stares past me.

I did this.

The love of my life is sitting there on the floor in front of me. A pitiful sight. Totally overwhelmed by my yelling. Handled far too roughly. Hurt in every sense.

My rage still hasn't dissipated completely, but I'm starting to realize that I went too far. I squat down in front of her, put a hand on her arm. "Jo, please . . . I didn't mean to . . ."

She shakes off my hand with a sharp jerk.

"I didn't mean to get carried away like that," I try again. "I'm sorry, Jo, please . . ."

"No!" She shifts over, pushes herself up, then takes a few steps to create distance between us. "Go away."

I get up angrily.

"You want me to go? Fine, if that's what you want."

I turn around, open the door. A cool wind hits me. The door clicks shut behind me. Not loudly, though, I realize. I didn't slam it shut. Only let go of it. I've got no strength left.

The driveway, the street.

I just walk. Mechanically, with no purpose, no destination, just for the sake of walking.

The tips of my shoes appear alternately beneath me like big brown bugs. I observe their race. Every second, the one in the lead changes.

Two streets on I sit down onto a waist-high garden wall. I reflect for a moment. What have I done? I screamed at the woman I love. Said terrible things to her, physically hurt her, even. Completely lost control.

While she's probably just sick and none of what's happened is her fault.

How did I end up losing my temper so badly? With her, of all people? Has something like this ever happened to me before? No, I don't think so.

Instead of supporting Joanna in this difficult situation, I completely lost it. Without any sense of compassion or responsibility.

I'm ashamed of myself.

I need to go apologize to her. But first I have to give myself time to recharge my batteries. To think. About her, about me. About the things happening around us. Gabor, Bartsch, Bernhard.

I feel like I'm stumbling across a field full of smoldering fires. And I don't know which one to put out first. Or if I can put any of them out at all.

I'm cold. I stand back up, keep walking, and rub my arms. I should have worn a jacket.

After a few feet I turn into a small side street. We've been living here for a few months now, but I've never been in this street, even though it's only about three hundred feet away from our house.

Thus far we hadn't really paid much attention to the neighborhood we'd moved into. We were just busy with ourselves, so fixated on each other that the two of us were enough. We didn't need anyone else; why would we? They would just have disturbed our intimacy.

It's only now I notice that I'm crying, and I don't care. I don't even attempt to wipe away the tears. To hide them. Let everyone see; they don't know me anyway. I've never been here. And even if someone does recognize me, who cares? Maybe we won't be living here much longer anyway. Maybe . . .

I stop walking. Is she still there in the same place in the hall, staring at the wall, I wonder?

Or maybe she isn't even in the house anymore? Did the way I acted confirm her belief that I'm not the person I say I am?

I couldn't blame her for that. No, in fact I could even understand it. Would someone who loves her as much as I claim to act like this? Screaming, grabbing hold of her, raging, and taking off when she's at her most helpless?

I have to go back. Right now. Maybe she's still there. Maybe, in spite of everything, she'll believe I really am the person I say I am.

My steps speed up; I start to jog. I turn into our street, running now, as fast as I can. Every second counts all of a sudden. A few more feet, then I slow down. Stand still.

Go away.

Joanna wanted me to go. She shoved me away when I tried to apologize to her.

I listen to my thoughts, feel how stirred up I still am.

What if she shoves me away again? Then how would I react?

After what just happened, I can't know for sure. Am I capable of seriously hurting her if what she says and does makes me as angry as before? Or angrier, even?

No, I can't go back to her.

Not yet.

17

The door falls into the lock again, but gently this time. As though it were a counterpoint to the scene that just took place. Erik is gone, and I sink slowly, very slowly, down the wall and back down to the floor.

I should be happy now. After all, he yelled at me, shook me, called me crazy. Since the first time I encountered him, all I have wanted is to be rid of him. Now he's gone, and something within me is balking at the idea.

This is clear proof of the fact that I'm not myself right now. I wipe the tears from my face, then gently inspect my upper arms. They hurt. By tomorrow the bruises will appear, and the police would have to take me seriously if I filed a charge.

But it's not my arms which are hurting the most. It's . . . I'm not even sure. Where are the feelings coming from?

The way he looked at me. His exhaustion, his vulnerability, everything that had just broken through, was far more convincing than his tenth or twentieth *but I love you*. Some things can't be faked. Whether he's lying to me or not, whether we really are engaged or not—he definitely has feelings for me, and very strong ones at that.

My own feelings on the other hand . . . I'm unable to make sense of them. His outbreak of rage was unforgivable and it has doubtlessly torn a new rift between us, but for one confusing moment, where he put his arm around me to protect me from Bartsch, I had to fight the urge to move closer to him. To simply let myself fall into his embrace.

It would have been so simple. It would have felt so good.

But the part of me that stopped me from doing so had clearly been right. Just a few minutes later, Erik had shown what he's capable of. Rage. Lack of self-control. Violence.

I can't let the fact that, seconds later, he was even more shocked than I was count as an apology. No more than I can accept his pitiful attempt at a genuine apology.

Instead, I should see it as being evidence. It's entirely possible that this isn't the first time he had handled me roughly. Dr. Schattauer's attempt at an explanation is becoming more and more plausible—that I know Erik, but have suppressed all my memories of him because of trauma. Systematic amnesia.

How bad must it have been; what he had done to me? And—did Dr. Bartsch already suspect? "The most important thing here is you and your safety," he had said, before expressly offering me his help.

Was it possible that Erik's problems at work are also rooted in the fact that he's unable to control his rage?

If that were the case, then it's not surprising he couldn't wait to get rid of the company psychologist. Or that he interrupted the man again and again.

Yes, it all paints a logical picture—with a few flaws, nonetheless. I stand up slowly and go over to the window. The silver Audi is still parked in front of the house, meaning that Erik left on foot. So he will be coming back, at some point this evening.

His car is here, but that's all. Erik's things—his shoes, his books, his photos, all the small things of daily life—I haven't suppressed the memory of them, they are simply not there. So how can I believe that we live together? How could he, indeed, how could *anyone* believe that?

On the other hand, there are some things I'm feeling which I don't understand. The disappointment that he told people at work about my supposedly confused state, for instance. If a stranger had done that, I don't think I would have cared. And before, when he had shouted at me and shaken me—I'd been shocked, yes. But if I really listen to my heart, I wasn't afraid he could hurt me. Unlike the first time he had appeared here in the house, when I'd felt nothing but fear. Cold, overwhelming fear.

That was five days ago, and these days were among the worst I had ever experienced. How can it be that I could have built up trust, in so little time, with the very person who had set off all of these events? Were the two days he had spent sitting by my bed in the hospital enough for that?

I don't know.

I really don't know.

I also have no idea what I should do when he comes back. Throw him out again? Talk to him? Lock myself in the bedroom and put the problem off until tomorrow, or get out of here and find a hotel room?

I glance out of the window again. There's still no sign of Erik. That gives me time to think, to put together a plan.

The half-full glass of water left by Dr. Bartsch is still in the living room, along with the scent of his aftershave.

I know the brand, but can't think of the name. Too sweet for my taste. And with a note of tobacco which I find nauseating.

Picking up the glass, I go into the kitchen and wash it; all normal actions, and they do me good. I concentrate on the task, and start to feel calmer.

Dr. Schattauer. Maybe I can call her tomorrow—no, it'll be Saturday. Never mind, I'll get through the weekend, and then put my energy into resolving this crazy situation. Waiting for things to come to me—that's not how I do things, and there's no way I'm changing now.

The pack of shrimp is still lying next to the stove, and by now a small pool of water has formed beneath it on the work surface. They must be at least half-thawed by now.

Earlier, when Erik had offered to cook for me, I had felt relaxed for the first time in five days. Had I been looking forward to the meal and a conversation with him? His company?

Maybe. I'm not sure. In any case, the sight of the packet gives me a melancholic feeling. It's probably just a result of my tiredness. Exhaustion, really, because I am exhausted, even if I don't want to admit it, not even to myself.

Maybe I'll lie down on the couch for a few minutes. With a magazine; I don't have the concentration span for a book right now.

But what if I fall asleep? And Erik comes back?

The thought unsettles me, but doesn't scare me. The man had pulled me out of the shower when I was unconscious and risked his own life in the process. He had . . .

All of a sudden, my mind is made up. When he comes back, we'll talk. I'll tell him what I'm thinking, all of it.

I turn off the kitchen light. Feeling the cool air, I rub my upper arms and wince. Yes. We'll talk about that too.

The pain comes so quickly, so unexpectedly, that I only realize what's happening once I hit the floor.

My head pounds, tears shoot into my eyes, but I don't need to look around to see who it was that attacked me.

I know it was me, that I bashed my own head against the doorframe. With full force, because by the time I realized what I was doing, it was too late to stop myself.

I prop myself up on my elbows, lift my upper body a little, and immediately slump back down to the floor. The living room becomes blurry in front of my eyes; everything is spinning. I reach up to touch my right temple, and feel a lump starting to swell.

More tears. Not of pain, but despair. *What am I doing? Why am I doing it? Why can't I control it?*

I try to push myself up once more. I have to get into the living room, I'm safer there. I don't know why, but I know it's true.

But my arms are trembling, the room spins around me again, I lose my balance.

The fact that I fall is unintentional. The fact that I turn my head so that it's my right temple that hits the floor, on the other hand, is steered by a small, manically gleeful part of myself.

The pain explodes in a white flash of light. It adds to and multiplies itself with the pain that was already there. The scream which reaches my ears, sounding like it's muffled in cotton padding, must be my own.

Lie there calmly. Don't move.

That's the only thought I allow myself once the pain gives me room to think. Stay calm. Stay lying down.

I focus on that. I have to stop it from happening again. Next time I could give myself brain damage, if I haven't already. Or a fractured skull.

Once again, there's a small part of me that likes the idea.

I cradle my head in both hands, because of the throbbing pain, but also to protect it.

Wait. I can't stop crying. Erik is right. He said it, plain and simple. Called it *my insane behavior.*

Admittedly he doesn't even know how crazy I really am. A danger to myself, no question. Maybe even to others. Or to him.

Suddenly, the idea that I might have tampered with the boiler myself doesn't seem so implausible. They were my scarves, the ones which had been stuffed into the exhaust vent. Even if I don't know anything about the technology or how to tamper with it—maybe it's a different matter when it comes to my subconscious.

I bite my teeth together. It won't happen again, it won't. Slowly, exerting all of my powers of concentration, I crawl out of the kitchen on all fours. And yet I can barely manage to drag my gaze away from the doorframe, which simultaneously entices me and frightens me to death. I actually do almost stumble, practically as soon as I turn my eyes away from it, but this time I at least manage to turn my head to the side, and it's only my shoulder which bangs against the edge. It hurts, but it's a partial victory nonetheless; I've managed to resist the urge to harm myself more. Limited the damage.

Once I'm in the living room it gets better. Nonetheless, I don't dare to stand up yet. I don't trust myself, not even a little.

I straighten up just once, to pull one of the cushions off the couch. I keep the edges and corners of the coffee table completely in my sights, even though they frighten me less than the doorframe.

It feels liberating to lay my head on the cushion. Even if I should feel the urge to hit my head against the floor again—now I won't be able to hurt myself that badly.

When I straighten the cushion a little, I see a red stain on the yellow fabric. Blood. Not much, but it's there. Just seeing it gives me a worrying sense of pleasure.

I tightly grasp the cushion and force my eyelids shut. I count my breaths, and hope that Erik will come back quickly, hope that he'll be here again soon.

Out of the two of us, he poses the lesser threat by far.

18

I can't even recall how I got to the small park. All my thoughts have been tangled up with Joanna and the past few days.

Clearly my subconscious hasn't just taken over the control of my legs but the navigation too.

Now I'm sitting on this wooden bench with my eyes closed. I've shut out the world. Not that I'm feeling any better for it.

Nadine! All of a sudden her name pops up in my head. Why, of all people, am I thinking about her? Because these thoughts, about everything that's happened, everything that's been said, are crushing me? Because I feel the pressing need to talk to someone who knows me really well? Is it crazy that I would think of my ex-girlfriend?

No, I think it's more because Nadine, despite all her faults, has always been a good listener. And she usually finds the right words to pick me back up when I need it.

At work she'd asked me if I was having problems. She'd seen it in my face. No wonder, really. We were together for almost five years; you learn to read your partner's moods in that time.

"Are you OK?"

I jump, and find myself looking into the eyes of a white-haired woman. The years are engraved in her face as furrows; deep ones on her forehead and at the corners of her mouth, but not quite as pronounced around the eyes. Her expression is one of concern.

"Yes, thank you, I . . ." I don't want talk to her. Even if she does mean well. "I'm very tired, that's all. I'm fine."

She hesitates. Eventually she nods and leaves.

My thoughts return to Nadine. I ended our relationship back then because I couldn't deal with her jealousy anymore. Her keeping tabs on me all the time; having to justify myself for every conversation, for every time I'd go for a drink without her.

We were almost always together. At work during the day and at home during the evenings and at night. I had felt like I couldn't breathe anymore.

Nadine wouldn't accept I was leaving. Again and again, she would profess just how much she loved me and that she'd change. But it was too late.

Once she'd realized, she'd put some distance between herself and me. At first anyway.

Two months later, there she was all of a sudden, right in front of me when I went to my car in the company parking lot. Could I spare just half an hour for her, she'd asked. Just one drink at the bar around the corner. I didn't want to go, but when she assured me she wouldn't try to talk me into getting back together, I went with her.

She said she knew that she'd made a lot of mistakes and that we wouldn't be able to get back together. But she wanted to be friends. After all, you couldn't simply sweep away five whole years just like that, she said.

I hadn't been able to promise her a real friendship, but I said we could interact in a friendly way at least. Maybe a drink or a chat here and there.

Sure, I mean why not? Five years. That's a really long time, after all.

The view in front of me becomes blurry; the different shades of green flow into one another. A tear rolls out of the corner of my eye, slowly trickles over my cheek and down to my chin.

My phone's in my pocket; Nadine's number is saved on it. Two rings and she picks up.

"Erik! Thank goodness. How are you? I'm glad you called. I heard about that awful business. The boiler. What happened, tell me?"

Damn it. I wasn't expecting that. What an idiot I am. Of course she's going to ask me about that. Everyone at work will probably have heard about it already. Now what am I going to tell her?

"I . . . don't know, exactly. The fire department's not sure either.

They said that it was probably the weather conditions pushing carbon monoxide back into our bathroom. An accident."

My voice sounds uncertain and hoarse.

"How's your girlfriend? Is she at home?"

"Yeah, she's feeling better again. She was . . . *We* were lucky."

All of a sudden there's a pause, I can almost physically feel that Nadine's waiting. Waiting for me to tell her the reason for my call. I don't usually just call her out of the blue, I haven't done that for over a year.

In the end she can't hold back the question. "Why are you calling?"

"Because I wanted to talk to someone."

"Well, it's very nice that you thought of me. Where are you? At home?"

"No, I'm in a park."

"Do you want me to come over to you?"

"No. Let's talk on the phone."

How do I start? *Where* do I start?

"You probably heard at work that we're having some problems at home."

"Apart from the thing with the boiler, you mean?"

"Yes. I'm sure Bernhard must have told everyone."

"No, he didn't. Not me, at least. What exactly do you mean?"

Is she telling the truth?

"It's about Jo. I . . . Christ, it's idiotic of me to be talking to you about problems that Jo and I are having."

"No, it isn't. As I said already, I'm happy you called. And that means something, don't you think? I always knew there was still something there from the time we spent together. More than just being superficially friendly to each other."

This conversation is taking an unpleasant turn.

"That's not what this is about, Nadine. Jo has . . . gaps in her memory. She can't remember certain things. Things concerning us. Her and me."

That was the understatement of the century right there, but something inside me is fighting the impulse to tell Nadine the whole truth. It feels like by telling her, I'd be exposing Joanna. Betraying her, even, to Nadine of all people, the bitterly jealous person from whom I had always wanted to protect her. I even went to all the work parties by myself to prevent the two of them from meeting each other. I know Nadine well enough to know that her meeting Joanna would inevitably lead to trouble.

"That would never happen to me. I haven't forgotten a single second of the time we spent together."

"Nadine . . ." Fuck. Calling her was a mistake.

"Never mind. So? Did she already go to see a psychiatrist? Something's obviously not right in her head."

My first reflex is to snap at Nadine for the insensitive remark. Unfortunately, though, she's probably right.

"The doctor reassured us and explained there could be several reasons. But it's a difficult situation, because the things Jo's forgotten are really essential. She . . . well, I'm feeling really desperate right now. We just had a fight, and I left."

"You left? Did you leave her?"

"Leave her? No. I . . . I left the house because I felt like I needed to be alone."

"Oh . . . That doesn't sound good at all. I did see it coming though, remember? I'll admit, I feared from the very start it wouldn't work with the two of you. Because you still have feelings for me, Erik. But you'd never admit that to yourself, because then you'd have to accept the whole thing with Jo was a mistake."

"No, for God's sake. I just needed to talk to someone."

There's a short pause.

"Erik?"

"Yes?"

"My door's always open for you, I just want you to know that."

"This again, really? I love Jo. That hasn't changed."

Her voice has an edge now. "You *think* you love her. But you don't really. You're only using it as an excuse because you hope it'll help you get over the two of us, but it's not going to work. And she doesn't love you either, Erik. Not like I do. *I'd* never forget anything to do with you. Not for a single second."

"OK. Let's stop this. I'm going to go back now."

"Wait," she says hurriedly. "Don't hang up. There must be a reason you called me. You were thinking about when we were together, right? How good we had it and how much we loved each other."

"Come on, Nadine, that's just . . ."

"No, listen to what I'm trying to tell you. I've been holding it back for more than a year now. Every day I see you at work, and it stings me every time. And the only thing that lets me endure it is the certainty that one day you're going to realize how much there still is between us. And now you're calling me because your Joanna forgot some things that concern the two of you. Is there anything worse you could do to your other half than forget the things you've shared?"

This call was most definitely not a good idea.

"Think about it, Erik. You really think she's the right person for you? I don't."

"I do," I say and hang up.

I hope, I think to myself.

It takes me a good fifteen minutes to get back to the house. Outside the front door I take a deep breath, then I step inside. I walk through the hall and into the kitchen. Even before reaching the passage to the living room I see Joanna lying on the floor. I freeze momentarily, then dash to her side. Her head is lying on a pillow, her eyes are closed.

"Jo! What's the matter?"

I kneel down beside her, see her eyes flutter open, see her blinking at me.

"My God, I thought something had happened." I put my hand on her head, wanting to stroke her hair, but Joanna groans and pushes my hand aside. "No, please . . ."

She raises herself up a bit, turns her face fully toward me. It's only now that I see the swelling. It stretches down from her right temple to above her eye, giving her entire face a misshapen appearance.

"You're hurt! What happened?"

"I tripped," she explains, and sits up, her face twisted with pain. "The doorframe. I crashed into it with my temple."

"Did you ice it yet? Do you want me to get ice from the kitchen?"

"No, leave it. I don't want to touch it again." Joanna lowers her gaze. "I think I did it on purpose."

I don't understand. "What? How do you mean, on purpose?"

Her eyes fix on me again. She looks awful. "Maybe I wanted to hurt myself."

Now I get it. *Oh no. Not this as well.*

"But . . . If you did . . ." I shake my head. "How is this possible?"

"I don't know."

A thought flashes through my head. I stare at her. "Jo, you didn't do this because we were fighting, did you? To punish yourself, or me? Something like that?"

"I don't know." Her voice is so quiet I don't really hear what she says, but I can guess at it.

Inside me, the urge to take her into my arms fights against the voice telling me to call an ambulance and have her brought to a psychiatric clinic right away.

"All of this is very . . . difficult," I say, and I can hear how weak my voice sounds. What I should really tell her now is that things will surely go back to the way they were and that I'll stand by her. That we can get through anything together.

But I'm no longer certain. Utter chaos, not just in my head, but in my heart as well. Things are no longer like they were six days ago. Yes, I love her. I *want* to love her. Despite everything. But I've got no idea if I'll have the strength to do so much longer. And if it's my presence that's making her do all this—

"How would you feel about me checking into a hotel? Maybe for a couple days? So you get a chance to straighten yourself out? Maybe you'll remember me again if you don't see me every single day?"

I'm completely aware how idiotic that sounds, but I don't have any other ideas right now. The look in Joanna's eyes changes, but the swelling makes it difficult to read her expression.

"Don't do that, please. Not now."

"I get the impression I'm only making things worse for you right now."

"No. When you showed up here five days ago I was scared. But right now I feel safer when you're here with me."

"I didn't show up five days ago. I've been living here for more than six months. With you."

"Yes, OK. Still, for me you've only been here for five days. Come on, it's not my fault. Erik . . ."

"What do you want from me, Jo? For days you've been telling me to go away. And when I finally realize, after these five shitty days, that it would probably be the best thing for me to do, all of a sudden you'd prefer it if I stayed. I can't deal with this constant back and forth anymore."

She reaches for my hand. I'm suddenly aware it's the first time she's done that since the start of all this. Is it because she really wants me near her? Or does she have an ulterior motive?

"Stay. Please. Let's talk to each other. OK?"

"How long for? Until you tell me to go away again? I promise you one thing—the next time I will. For good."

19

He stays. And if I'm being honest with myself—I wouldn't have known what to do if he had gone. Apart from, maybe: call an ambulance. Have myself committed after all, but I'm still afraid of that option. I don't want people feeding me pills to keep me under control; I want to know what's wrong with me.

The pain in my head is raging. Erik says that if I start to feel sick, we should go to the hospital, because it could mean a concussion. Just the thought of ending up there again is almost enough to turn my stomach.

Erik convinces me to take two aspirin and let him put the cold pack against my forehead. If I'd been even slightly in the mood for joking around, I would have suggested he use the pack of shrimp instead so it's good for something at least. But I can barely get a word to cross my lips. Again and again, I catch myself taking his hand and holding it tightly. Because, at this moment, there is nothing I'm more afraid of than being by myself.

Perhaps Erik senses that it's this fear, above all, which is bringing me closer to him; in any case, he doesn't look pleased by my sudden trust. He takes care of me, changing the cold packs at regular intervals, squeezing my hand dutifully, but his thoughts are clearly somewhere else.

After just half an hour, I'm feeling better, at least enough to get up and go to the bedroom.

He helps me to get undressed, pulls the covers over me, then drags a chair over to the bed and sits down next to me. As if he were a father and I his child.

"I wanted to tell you again that I'm sorry about how I behaved earlier," he says. "It was wrong to shout at you like that, and even more so to be rough with you. It was just . . . too much, all of a sudden. I know that's no excuse, but . . ." He doesn't finish the sentence. He just stares at the floor.

I would nod, if it didn't hurt so much. "OK," I say instead.

"Then good night." He moves to stand up, but I've reached out for his hand again. "No. Please."

Now the expression on his face is one of disbelief. "You want me to sleep here?"

Yes. No. What I don't want is to sleep alone; I don't want my subconscious to completely take control and provoke me into jumping out of the window or doing something just as crazy.

"I want you to stay with me," I whisper.

He looks at me for a long while. Gently touches the lump on my right temple. "You know how much I'd like to do that. But all this back and forth has to stop, Jo, it just hurts too much. I'm telling you, honestly, I'm at my wits' end here."

"OK." I try to smile at him. "There's a blanket, over there in the trunk and . . ."

"I know where our things are," he interrupts me. "But thanks."

Five minutes later, he's lying next to me. Enough of a distance away not to be able to touch me, not even by accident. But on one occasion during the night, when I wake up for a moment, I feel his arm around my waist, hear his calm breathing behind me, and hope for a few seconds that I might be able to retrieve some memory of him after all. But there's nothing. Nothing at all.

The next day I feel better, in every sense. The pain has subsided, along with the fear of losing control over my actions again.

As soon as he notices I'm awake, Erik gets up. "I'll make us some breakfast." He goes into the bathroom, and a few moments later I hear the shower being turned on. My stomach cramps up, but I remind myself that the scarves are gone now, the boiler is fine.

Ten minutes later, as I hear Erik go down the stairs, I get out of bed.

The sight of my face in the bathroom mirror is a shock. The swelling has gone down considerably, sure, but the right side of my face is bruised purple, from my forehead to the top of the cheekbone. The slightest of touches makes me wince. The fine jets of water shooting out of the shower head feel like pinpricks.

Should I put makeup on to cover up the bruises? I decide against it. Not unless I have to go out, be among people who might ask questions I can't answer. *I fell down the stairs.* The classic response of abused wives.

But I will brush my hair so it covers part of my face, so Erik doesn't constantly have to be reminded of my *insane behavior* every time he looks at me.

The scent of coffee drifts up toward me from downstairs, and I realize that I'm really hungry. A good feeling. A normal feeling.

"Sit down," says Erik, pointing the spatula toward the already set table. "I'm making ham and eggs. Would you like some orange juice?"

My favorite mug, the foamed milk almost spilling over the edge. Ham, a little plate of cheese—everything the way I like it. Is it possible that he does know me after all?

He has barely set the plates on the table when the doorbell rings. My heartbeat quickens at once. Damn, is every noise going to throw me off like this?

"Maybe it's the mailman," says Erik with a sigh. "But whoever it is, I'll get rid of them. Dig in, otherwise it'll get cold."

I nod, lifting the first forkful to my mouth, but let it sink again as soon as Erik leaves the kitchen.

What if it's that psychologist again?

"Good morning!" A woman's voice. "Yes I know, this is a bit of a surprise, but I thought I'd check on you both. I've brought rolls. And croissants!"

A few seconds pass before Erik says something. "Listen, I thought I'd made myself clear."

"You did. You guys aren't doing too well, that was quite clear. And that's why . . ."

The sound of heels clicking on the floorboards. "Hey, that smells delicious."

She is already standing in the kitchen doorway. Dark curls, short skirt, high heels and an almost aggressive cheerfulness. She gives me a beaming smile, teeters over to me, and stretches out her hand. "You must be Joanna, right? I say we go straight to first-name terms. After all, you guys in Australia are quite informal, aren't you? It's lovely to finally meet you!"

I let her shake my hand, completely overwhelmed in the face of so much energy. I notice how her gaze hovers over the right side of my face and then, as if I'd caught her in the act, glides away again.

Erik appears behind her, with the rolls she brought in his hand. "Jo, this is Nadine."

He says her name like it should mean something to me, until my expression makes it clear to him that it doesn't. "She's a colleague. And—"

"We used to be an item," Nadine interrupts. "But I'm sure you know that." She turns to look at Erik over her shoulder. "Would you be a darling and make me a coffee too? That would be great, thank you."

Just one glance at Erik's face is enough to tell me that he wants to end this visit as soon as possible, but without the same means he used with Bartsch yesterday.

"Milk?" He asks. "Sugar?"

Her smile widens. "Come on, you know exactly how I like it."

It sounds like she means something completely different. If my problems weren't overshadowing everything else, including my vanity, then I'd be wondering about the contrast between Nadine and myself, in terms of our appearances. She's obviously made an effort; her makeup is perfect, her blouse and skirt fit her so well it looked like she'd been poured into them.

Quite a lot of effort just to bring some breakfast to a good friend on a Saturday morning.

And it certainly couldn't be said that I'd made an effort. A washed-out T-shirt and an old pair of track pants, along with the bruises on my face—I look as though Erik had picked me up off the street.

But I don't care, as I realize with some amusement. The only thing that matters right now is that I'm able to look at the doorframe without feeling the need to ram my head against it.

Erik puts a full cup of coffee down in front of Nadine, a little too forcefully; a few drops slosh over the edge.

We all act as though we didn't notice. "It's great that you two have made up," Nadine says, beaming at me. "Erik hates arguments." She sips at her coffee, which is the same color as her hair. "I was really worried, he sounded so distraught last night."

"Nadine!" A single word, but it contained both a warning and a great deal of repulsion.

"What?" She turns around to him, crossing her legs. "But it's true. You didn't call me just to say hello."

He called her? Talked about me with someone who is a complete stranger to me, poured his heart out to her? Described my *insane behavior* to her, even? I clench my teeth and avoid Erik's gaze, but at the same time tell myself how silly it is to be so sensitive. It shouldn't bother me in the slightest what his tarted-up ex thinks of me. He needed someone to talk to yesterday. And it's not like I don't understand that; after all, I could do with someone to talk to myself.

When I look up again, Erik is shaking his head silently. Apologetically. "I'd prefer it if you just go now," he says, looking at Nadine. "Thank you for the rolls. But we'd really prefer to be alone."

She nods, smiles. Puts on an expression of understanding. "Can I finish my coffee first?"

"If you must."

Now, as she looks at Erik, she looks genuinely hurt. "Your tone was completely different yesterday. But I understand why my being here is uncomfortable for you." Now she's openly staring at the right side of my face.

I almost grin. "You're wrong."

She understood exactly what I mean, but she feigns innocence. "Wrong about what?"

"That my injuries have something to do with Erik. That *is* what you're thinking, isn't it?"

She hesitates only briefly. "It all adds up though, doesn't it? He calls me, completely beside himself, and when I try to check up on you the next day . . ." She makes a vague hand movement in my direction. "Erik was never violent when he was with me," she adds more quietly.

It's clear now that she's crossed a line. Erik comes over, positions himself behind me, and puts his hands on my shoulders. "You're totally right, Nadine," he says, in a dangerously low tone. "I wasn't. And I never will be violent, especially not with Jo, for whom I feel much more strongly than I ever did with you."

She recoils as if he'd slapped her in the face and takes a few seconds before she answers. "Oh really? Then—no offense—but your taste has gone downhill of late. I didn't know you went for the boring, pale, and frumpy look nowadays."

Even while she still speaking, she realizes she's making a mistake, I can see it in her eyes.

"OK, I shouldn't have said that," she adds, giving me an apologetic smile. "I know that you've only just got out of the hospital. But it's still unusual—normally Erik goes for a completely different type."

I can feel his grip tightening on my shoulders. "Do you want to hear it again? You do, don't you? I love Jo, and I think she's beautiful. I told you so yesterday, and I can tell you again, as many times as you want to hear it."

Now Nadine visibly gears up for an attack. "And I told you that the two of you don't match. You told me she forgets things about you. What kind of relationship is that?" She looks me up and down quickly, this time without any trace of sympathy. "And you're clearly hitting her. Even if she denies it, but apparently that's quite common in codependent relationships. And just look at the way you're holding on to her now. Pushing her down, to be more precise."

Erik laughs, but Nadine doesn't stop. "It was never like that with us. Don't you remember? We had our differences, but more than anything we had fun and a wonderful trusting relationship and—"

"This is unbelievable," Erik says, interrupting her. "Did you really come here to tell me that, first of all, I'm mistreating Jo, and, second of all, that you're the better choice for me? Have you lost your mind? How did you think this was going to go? That I'd have a quick think about things, break up with Jo, and go back to you? Really?"

There's no way she can say yes in response, and she doesn't try. "I came here to remind you of the fact that a relationship doesn't have to be like the mess you're in right now. Regardless of who it's with. If you didn't want my help, then why did you call me?"

"To be honest, I'm wondering that myself," Erik replies. "I'm very aware of the fact that it was a mistake. To be fair, I already knew that yesterday, even while we were still on the phone. Now, Nadine, would you please leave?"

She takes a sip of her coffee, acting as if she didn't hear him; she's probably thinking up a new strategy.

I watch her in silence, feeling a little bewildered. Suddenly she turns her attentions on me again, her eyes narrowing. "Erik says you have gaps in your memory, specifically in regard to him. You know, I think that says a lot. It may well be that he loves you, but do you feel the same way?"

Her question actually makes me feel embarrassment. The answer that lies on my tongue—*I barely know him*—is not one I can give. To say no, in this situation, would be completely heartless and disloyal to Erik. And . . . I'm actually beginning to like him. Maybe that's inadvisable, risky, or even crazy, especially considering his fit of rage yesterday, but it's true. He's still standing behind me, the warmth from his hands on my shoulders spreading through my whole body. Just like Nadine, he's waiting for an answer.

"I don't think I need to give you an account of how I feel," I say, lacing my tone with the appropriate level of sharpness. "I don't know you. My feelings for Erik are none of your business."

She laughs. "Well, if that's the case . . . Then have a nice life together. But I know Erik, and I've known him longer than you. He's not in a good place, and if you're the reason for that, then you won't be part of his life for much longer."

Erik takes his hands from my shoulders and moves a step toward Nadine. "You don't know me quite as well as you think. Otherwise you'd know just how pitiful I find this whole act. You wanted us to stay friends, didn't you?" He leans toward her, propping his hands on the surface of the table. "Well, there's no chance of that now. And I'll happily spell it out for you again: I love Joanna, and you're the last person who could do anything to change that."

Now there's so much raw hurt in her expression that I even feel sorry for her. "OK," she mumbles. "I only meant well, I wanted to . . ." She stands up, reaching for her handbag. "Whatever. I guess I was wrong."

In the doorway she turns around one more time, looks at Erik, then leaves without another word.

20

I feel that Nadine showing up here has unleashed something. Maybe for Joanna as well, but definitely for me in any case. Within me.

That special warmth I used to feel when Joanna was close to me, when we looked at each other, when we talked . . . I couldn't feel any of it yesterday. I was searching for it, hoping it was still there. The fear that it might have vanished forever—that was probably what was making me despair the most.

But now the warmth is back. I can feel it quite clearly.

"I'm sorry," I say, and they're not just empty words, I really am. "Calling Nadine was a stupid mistake. I was just . . ."

"It's OK." Her voice, her gaze. How could I think, even for just a second, of giving this woman up? Whatever happened to her, it's not her fault. At this difficult time, she needs me more than ever.

Was I really going to abandon her?

"She's still in love with you." There's no accusation, no anger in her voice. It's an observation.

No. I don't want to talk about Nadine now. She's a nuisance, especially at this moment, when all these feelings have come back.

"That's not important. *She's* not important and hasn't been for some time. She never meant to me what you do, Jo. No woman ever has. And none ever could. I only wish you wouldn't just believe me, but that you'd know it again for yourself. Just like you did only a few days ago."

"Yes, I wish that, too." She takes a couple of steps toward me. She hasn't done that even once these past few days. Every movement had always been away from me. Our eyes are fixed on each other, joined as if by some invisible bridge, over which this wonderful warmth seems to be flowing from her body into mine.

"I believe you, Erik. I still can't remember any of the things you told me about us. But I believe you. There's this sense of familiarity. Maybe that's the beginning of a memory."

"That would be nice."

Another step. Only a couple of feet are separating us now.

"I'm frightened. You understand that, don't you?"

I think about the situation she's in. She doesn't know whether she's being completely deceived or whether she's simply losing her mind. Or has already lost it, perhaps.

"Yes, I understand very well, Jo."

"I believe you, but I'm still terribly frightened of getting involved with you. If I do that and it turns out you're . . ."

I can feel her looking for the words to describe what she means without hurting me.

"That I'm lying to you?"

"That you're pulling the wool over my eyes, for whatever reason. I wouldn't be able to deal with that. It's hard enough as it is. The uncertainty, the doubts. The fear that I'm going insane."

Just one step between us now, and I'm the one who takes it. As my hands search for hers, they brush her thigh. She doesn't shy away. Our fingers meet, become entwined. My heart is beating so quickly Joanna can probably see the artery in my neck pulsating. How often have we stood like this before, looking at each other, touching each other? And yet it's completely different this time.

There's that sense of excitement that comes at the first touch, that sense of anxiety about whether this tentative attempt to get closer will be reciprocated. But also, the certainty of knowing how it will feel when the hands you're holding are stroking your skin, all over your body. It's a paradox, a crazy mixture, a state of being I've never experienced before.

My heart is set to burst out of my chest when her face, suddenly, is only mere inches away from mine. Not only can I feel her breath, I suck it in, almost as soon as it's left her slightly parted lips. It soothes me, numbing the glaring emotional pain I had felt just moments before.

Something pulls me in even closer to her, a vortex I can't resist, don't want to resist. Across the now almost nonexistent distance between us, her eyes look ever so big. Like misty blue oceans, and I let myself fall into them.

Our lips touch, tentatively at first, almost shyly. We breathe into each other's mouths, slowing time down to a mere fraction of its normal pace. It no longer meanders along in seconds, but by the same rhythm to which we breathe, taking each other in. Her hand pulls away from mine; two heartbeats later I feel it at the nape of my neck. The tip of her tongue playfully traces over the contours of my mouth, but immediately withdraws like a timid animal when I try to respond. It's back the next second, as if she were trying to tease me.

Everything within me is pushing me toward Joanna, wanting to get as close to her as possible, with an intensity I've never known before. And yet I willingly surrender myself to the gentle play of her lips and tongue. A tentative exploration, the way it would usually be on the first kiss.

The events of the past days, the pain, the despair, the anger, they all become meaningless for that one moment. I don't know if we've been standing here like this for minutes or seconds when she finally lets the tips of our tongues touch. Time becomes insignificant. Everything around us completely loses all meaning as our timid game turns into an intimate kiss and we succumb to each other.

My hands move around her waist, stray to her back, and pull her closer toward me. I feel her body next to mine, hear her breath getting quicker. We kiss with increasing passion; our hands glide over each other's bodies. Caressing, feeling, exploring. My lower abdomen is pushing against hers; there's nothing I can do to stop the grinding of my hips, and I don't want to either. I feel her adjusting to my rhythm, letting me lead her like we were dancing. Not only do I hear her moaning, I can feel it on my lips. It fires me on; our kiss becomes ever more intense, ever more expectant.

Then, all of a sudden, it's over.

Joanna's lips jerk away from mine. Her hands drop to my chest and push me away from her.

"Jo," I rasp, reluctant to loosen my arms, which are still around her waist.

She shakes her head and exhales heavily.

"That was wonderful. But . . ."

I don't finish her sentence this time, but wait until she's found the words she's looking for. I'm still so worked up I can't even guess at what might be going on inside her head.

Maybe the kiss stirred up a memory? Maybe she thinks it was a mistake? I don't know.

"I'm so confused. And afraid."

"Of me? Still?"

"No, Erik, not you, I'm afraid of myself."

"I don't understand."

She looks at the floor and briefly touches her temple, the blueish bruise. "I don't either. I get moments where I'm as much a stranger to myself as you are."

"Still no memories? Not one?"

She shakes her head. "But now I can imagine having fallen in love with you."

At least she isn't rejecting me anymore. Maybe she can feel there's something connecting us, that . . . All of a sudden she's close to me again, and I feel her lips on mine. Not shy and playful this time, but the way we always kissed. Tender and passionate.

She's smiling when she draws her head back again.

"It was still very nice, though."

Sometimes, I reflect, you don't need much at all to turn a feeling of anguish into relief. I don't feel like I'm free from all my worries, but what I do feel all of a sudden is a sense of optimism. The hope that we'll get to the bottom of this and that things will take a turn for the better.

"Yes," I say, returning her smile. "It was wonderful."

"I want to go outside, get some fresh air. Can we go for a walk?"

An image appears in my mind's eye. Joanna and I, strolling through the small park all wrapped up in our jackets, in a tight embrace, heads tilted toward each other . . .

"I'd love to."

Our walk ends up taking quite a long time. We don't talk much, nor do we walk in a tight embrace, but our hands keep touching. Again and again they brush against each other, as if by accident, and a gentle shudder goes through my body every time.

Joanna suddenly stops and looks at me when we've almost reached the house again. "Would you give me your number?"

I'm confused for a second. "Yes of course, I . . . I thought you had it but . . . yes."

"Not, not until now. But I should have it, right?"

A short while later we're sitting in the living room, on the couch. The look Joanna is giving me no longer contains the suspicion of the past few days, when it seemed that she was trying to read me, decipher my thoughts.

"Tell me about us again, please?"

"Yes, I'd love to," I say, and take her hand.

"What would you like to know?"

"Everything," she answers. "I'd like to know everything."

21

It's already dark by the time we finish talking. Only now do I realize that I haven't eaten anything since breakfast; my stomach is making itself heard, gently but insistently. "How about we cook something together?" I turn to Erik and trace the contours of his face with my finger. Foreign yet at the same time strangely familiar. And gradually becoming more and more so. "You wanted to, remember, yesterday."

He smiles. "I still want to."

The way he looks at me when I touch him. There's so much emotion in it, and it's increasingly spilling over to me. Is that a good thing? Is it careless?

The fact is, I no longer want to be asking myself these questions. Now that I no longer see Erik as an acute threat. I've become aware of how attractive he is, this man who I'm getting to know bit by bit. The man who is there for me night and day. Who hasn't let my memory loss scare him away.

And who kisses like . . .

"Why are you laughing?" He takes my face between his hands, carefully, without touching the bruised parts.

"I'm not telling you."

His mouth on mine again, his tongue, gentle at first, then enticing, then insistent. I playfully bite his lower lip. "I'm hungry."

"I can see that." He smiles, takes my hand, and pulls me into the kitchen. "Let's see. We'd better leave the shrimp, but what would you say to turkey skewers? With that special tomato salad you make? We've got everything we need."

Just the thought of it makes my hunger grow twofold. "Sounds wonderful."

He takes all the ingredients out of the cupboard. "I'll do the meat, you do the vegetables. That's how we usually do it, do you remember?" I can see that he regrets the last three words even as he's still saying them. I shake my head. "No. Unfortunately not. But that sounds like a good plan."

His eyes are trained on the worktop; the fridge is still open behind him. "Usually," he repeats. "Unless it was steak, you're better at that."

I can see how desperately he wants to be able to share these memories with me, but as hard as I try, the images just won't come into my mind.

"Probably because I always made them on the barbecue with my father, since I was a young child," I say. That memory *is* there, crystal clear. Daddy and his beloved, gigantic sirloin steaks.

"OK then." Erik gets the skewers from the drawer and begins to cut the turkey fillet into even pieces.

I wash the tomatoes under hot water. Nothing tastes worse than ice-cold tomato salad.

Erik hums as he works, a melody which I don't recognize at first. With a bit of imagination, though, it kind of sounds like "Strangers in the Night." Singing along under my breath, I pull the knife out of the wooden block. I don't need to exert much pressure, it glides through the tomatoes as though they were butter. Perfect, fine, wafer-thin slices. Red and juicy.

It's easy and fun. In just a short time I've already cut five tomatoes into slices and pushed them into the salad bowl, without the white fleshy part with the seeds breaking away.

The bottles of olive oil and white balsamic vinegar are standing there at the ready, but . . . the onions are missing. I hope I still have some in the fridge, at least one; one would be enough. All I need to do is get it, but I can't pull my eyes away from the tomatoes in the bowl. From that red color.

I feel so light, inside. I feel like humming and singing and almost like dancing. All the pressure from the past few days is gone; it's faded away. No more worries. No more thoughts.

And then, suddenly, there's a silvery arc, so beautiful, like a curved bolt of lightning shooting up into the sky, one I've created with a single, smooth movement.

There's a pause, for the duration of half a breath. And then . . . falling, plummeting, jabbing. Like I was a falcon swooping down, with a clear target, one I don't want to miss at any cost.

The spot on his back, not far from the spine, beneath the shoulder blade. At last.

Time slows, almost standing still. I see the knife going downward, looking at it both with joy, the like of which I've rarely felt before, and with a fear which almost makes me lose my mind.

Part of me wants to stop the movement, but the rest of me is stronger. It wants to see the knife plunging into Erik's back, not just once, but again and again.

At that moment Erik turns his head; his eyes widen, he moves his body to the side and the knife catches his right upper arm, raised in self-defense.

Red. Glistening, flowing red.

For a few seconds I stare in fascination at the stain which starts to spread on the sleeve of Erik's shirt; only then do I begin to understand what just happened.

What I did.

No, please no, please . . .

It is me who screams, not him. I let the knife fall on the worktop, this knife which has been haunting my thoughts for days, the knife which I just used to stab Erik. Just like that.

"My God . . . I'm so—I'm so sorry!" I take a step toward him, but he flinches away. With an expression that I've never seen in his eyes before. Full of disbelief, horror, and disappointment which pains me all the way to my soul.

Then, in just a few seconds, all of that is gone. It turns into the opposite. I try to go over to him again.

"Stay where you are." His voice, so full of emotion just moments ago, is now like ice. And it's no wonder, I understand it, understand him, but . . .

The first thing I can get my hands on, that seems to make sense, is a roll of paper towels. I move forward to press it onto his upper arm to make a dressing, but this time he yells at me. "I said, stay where you are! Come any closer to me, and I won't be held responsible for my actions!"

The blood has already seeped through his sleeve and is now dripping to the floor. Erik presses a hand over the wound, and it seems as though the pain is now kicking in.

"I'm so sorry," I repeat, and hate myself for the fact that I also start to cry. For the fact that I seem incapable of uttering anything but this laughable, completely worthless apology. As if my words could make up for what I just did. As if anything could ever make up for it.

And I don't understand. I don't understand *myself.* There was no reason to do that, everything was going well between us . . .

"You're completely insane." Erik shakes his head in emphasis to every word he says. "Insane and dangerous. No, don't come any closer." The iciness in his tone has been joined by something else. Disgust?

I could understand that, of course. If I say what's on the tip of my tongue right now, which is that I have no idea why I did this, because I was actually in the process of falling in love with him, it would only make things worse.

Insane and dangerous.

He's right. It's now glaringly obvious, if it wasn't before, that I have to get myself admitted to a clinic. As quickly as possible.

But first Erik needs help. "I'll get the first-aid kit. We have to make sure that we stop the bleeding and—"

"*We* don't need to do anything at all, not anymore." He fixes his gaze on me. "You were going to stab me right through the back with that knife, weren't you? If I hadn't turned around, I'd be dead now. You would have . . . stabbed me in cold blood."

Everything he says is true, despairingly true. And, at the very least, he has the right to know it. I nod.

"Why, Jo?" Now, for the first time, I see something resembling grief in his eyes. Grief for how things once were, maybe, even if I can't remember. Grief for what we could still have had.

"I don't know." My sobs swallow my words. "I really don't know," I repeat. "It just happened. I barely knew what was happening myself, and I know how that sounds. Even to me. But that's how it was. Like I was outside of my own body, watching myself doing it. I never wanted to harm you and yet I almost killed you. You're right. I am crazy."

He doesn't disagree, but he doesn't say anything to reaffirm it either. My attention goes back to his arm; the bleeding has slowed now, but not stopped.

I gesture hesitantly toward the kitchen roll, then walk past Erik, out into the hall and up the stairs. My legs are shaking so hard that I can barely manage the steps.

In the bathroom, the first thing I see is the boiler, the cover of which hasn't been replaced yet. Yes, so I guess that was me too. It must have been, if there was any logic at all behind the past few days.

If he hadn't turned around, then—

Then I would be sitting over his dead body right now, covered in even more blood, the knife sticky in my hand. Without the slightest idea how it came to that.

The image squeezes the air from my lungs. I squat down on the floor until the black spots in front of my eyes gradually clear.

Close. So close.

With clammy fingers, I get the first-aid kit from the cupboard, find the disinfectant spray and sterile swabs. I bring everything downstairs.

Erik is now sitting on one of the barstools. He's taken his shirt off and is pressing it against his arm. His face is pale. I place the first-aid kit down on the bar and move to tend to the wound, but he shakes his head. "Don't even think of touching me."

"But you can't do it by yourself—"

"Yes I can." He jerks his chin, silently telling me to back away, then begins to clean the wound.

A deep, gaping cut; blood is still seeping out of it. It needs stitches.

Struggling a little, Erik puts a dressing over the wound and tries to wrap an elastic bandage around it, but it's practically impossible with only one hand.

"Let me help you. Please."

He doesn't answer; instead he intensifies his efforts.

As I step closer to him and take the roll of bandage from his hand, he finally relents. He holds the dressing as I secure it.

"Please let me drive you to the hospital."

He laughs. "Not a chance."

"But you have to get stitches."

Erik moves his hand over the bandage, checking it. For now, it's holding. "Yes, I know. But the last thing I'm going to do is get in a car that you're driving."

He glances over at the torn, blood-soaked shirt on the floor. "I'll change clothes, and then I'll go. Alone."

When he stands up, he teeters a little, but then regains his balance.

I step into his path. "Let me come with you."

"No."

"In the passenger seat. Please. I can't let you drive like this." I'm fully aware of how ironic my concern must seem in light of the situation. But I want to do something; I'd undo everything that happened if I could, but as that's not possible then I at least want to . . . be of help.

"I'm going by myself. I don't want to have you next to me and constantly be afraid that you'll grab the steering well and drive us into a wall. Or pull another knife out of your sleeve. Or off yourself in front of my eyes, jump out of the car while we're doing a hundred or something like that." He looks at me. "It's over, Joanna. I hope you get help, for your own sake. But there's no way I can be with someone who I can't turn my back on without having to worry they might stab me."

He slowly makes his way over to the stairs. "I'll come by in the morning and pick up my things. The little that's left of them, anyway."

I follow him, and try to take his hand, but he pulls it away. "I mean it," he says sharply. "Don't touch me. Stay away."

And so I let him go. I retreat back into the far corner of the hall, wondering why this good-bye feels so painful. No chance of an answer, though. And I should probably hand the task of figuring out the inner workings of my mind over to the experts as soon as possible.

Five minutes later, Erik comes back downstairs. The new shirt he's put on is already beginning to turn red above the stab wound.

I say nothing else.

He says nothing else.

He leaves the house without turning around even once.

22

I sit down carefully in the car. Waves of white-hot pain are surging through my entire upper body from the wound on my arm.

What's just as painful, perhaps even more, is the bitter disappointment, the crushing realization that Joanna's lost her mind once and for all. That she's beyond recovery. And that there's nothing she, or I, can do.

She wanted to kill me.

The mixture of physical and mental agony is starting to dull my senses. I blink several times, shake my head, and wrench my eyes open. Don't faint, not now. No, I can't let myself escape into that merciful darkness right now. I have to go get the wound treated.

I start the car and take a final look over at the front door. It's closed. Who knows what Joanna's doing in there right now. Maybe she's attempting to take her own life again for a change. Insanely enough, when that thought crosses my mind I feel the urge to get out of the car and check, but soon shake my head in disbelief. I can't really be that stupid, can I?

The house seems like it's swaying as I reverse the car down the driveway. This surreal kind of image is something I usually only see in bad dreams. But this isn't a dream. There's no hellish pain in dreams.

Scratching sounds. A voice from some recess of my mind tells me I just clipped the hedge that separates our property from the street. I don't care.

I don't care about anything.

Turn the wheel, shift gear, drive.

What am I going to tell the people at the hospital? The truth? The piercing sound of a car horn tears me from my thoughts. I just cut somebody off. I think.

Focus, Erik. Damn it.

I have to go left. What was I just thinking about? Oh yeah, the hospital. So what am I going to tell them? The truth? What is the truth?

Joanna tried to kill me. She really did. With full intent. She wasn't just trying to hurt me. She actually wanted to end my life.

Damn it, I can't see anything anymore. Everything's turning blurry. I step on the brake, turn the steering wheel to the right. There's a rumbling sound, then the car comes to a stop. More car horns blare, several times in a row.

I wipe the tears out of my eyes, groan because I jerked my arm up to do so. This fucking pain's just about driving me out of my mind.

By now, most of my sleeve is stained red. *Hospital. Stitches.* I have to keep going.

I even remember to check the rearview mirror before driving down off the sidewalk and back onto the street. Good. Pay attention. Don't cause any accidents now.

Joanna. I hate you. I love you. I . . .

Where am I? What's the way to the hospital again? I think I have to go left here, leave our neighborhood. Yes, that's it; that should be the right way.

This dizziness isn't good. Not at all. I need to keep myself alert, need to think. If the mind's busy, it'll stay awake.

Why? What could possibly be so horrible that Joanna wants to kill me for it? What did she go through? And with whom? With me?

The last few houses in our neighborhood roll past the side window. At least I notice; that's a good sign.

A country road. No streetlamps. No illuminated shop windows. Just the brief stretch of road that the headlights are snatching back from the darkness ahead of me. A short gray runway which I'm driving along without ever reaching its end. And a corridor on either side, each one several feet in width.

It's relaxing for my eyes.

And yet there's something disturbing the picture. A car is approaching from behind. Its headlights are on full beam, so bright that even the reflection in the rearview mirror is irritating. I try hastily to adjust the mirror, and shout out in pain. Used the wrong arm.

In a fraction of a second, I feel nauseous. My car swerves; I overturned the steering wheel. I take my foot off the gas, try to get the swerve under control. Which is really goddamn difficult with just one arm. I have to concentrate so I don't vomit.

Finally I get the car straightened up again, and I accelerate. The jabbing pain in my arm has made way for a dull, hot, throbbing pain. I don't know which of the two is worse.

Those lights behind me . . . they're getting closer, and very rapidly at that. The driver must be speeding. What an idiot.

Joanna. Again and again, Joanna's there in my head. She cuts into my thoughts like the edge of a knife. A knife. How fitting.

But what am I supposed to . . . Goddamn it, is the guy behind me insane? What's he trying to do? The headlights of his car are growing in my rearview mirror at breakneck speed. *Just drive past me already, asshole. The lane's clear!*

Then he crashes into the back of my car. The jolt hurls me forward, then back against the seat again; my head slams into the headrest and I lose sight of the street. Only for a moment, though; then I manage to focus again. The Audi, thank goodness, stays in its lane. There's only one headlight in my rearview mirror instead of two. The car drops back a bit but stays behind me.

Should I stop? Will the guy do that too? Apologize, maybe? No. He's probably drunk as a skunk. If I stop now, he'll probably crash into me again.

I have to keep driving until I reach a residential area. Somewhere where there are streetlamps. Then maybe I'll be able to make out the car brand and the color. And the license plate.

It's not far now. A mile, maybe, one and a half at most.

Out of the corner of my eye I notice something's changed, and I look into the mirror again. The one-eyed car behind me is getting ready to pass me. Good. I'll be able to see everything I need. I look into the side mirror. Now he's next to me, but at an angle; maybe in a second I'll be able to see the driver. Suddenly the headlight jerks to the side and there's another loud crash. As I feel the Audi busting apart at the rear, there's an excruciating explosion of pain in my arm. The steering wheel is torn from my hands and turns wildly; I get pushed up against the door; then total chaos. Left is right, up is down, all the dimensions shift in a deafening cacophony of booming, crashing, pounding.

I'm just thinking that my senses might not withstand such a massive onslaught; then a gigantic black talon reaches out to grab me.

I emerge out of the nothingness into a shapeless interplay of dark colors with even darker ones. I try to move. Pain, everywhere. In my arm most of all. The first memories begin to flicker back to me. An accident. Chaos. There was this headlight behind me. The crash. Everything spinning . . .

My vision becomes clearer, my eyes adapt to the surroundings. I make out a shapeless, brighter surface. The airbag. It opened, and is now sagging over the steering wheel and dash. The windscreen isn't there anymore; an icy wind blows away the last slivers of the fog in my head. I turn my head to the side. Everything's twisted, dented. Like a Dalí painting.

I carefully move my right arm. I manage, but it hurts like hell.

It takes me a while to check all my limbs and determine that I'm probably not seriously injured. The driver's door won't open; I have to shift over to the passenger side. Doing that involves a fair bit of effort and more pain, and then I roll out of the car and slide down onto wet, sandy ground. *I was lucky.*

No sooner than I formulate the thought, I hear myself giggling, in a way I myself could only describe as insane. But is that a surprise? Given all the nonsense my mind's coming up with?

My fiancée tried to murder me; I only survive by chance. On the way to the hospital, some piss-drunk asshole catapults me off the road and I get into a serious accident. And the first thought that comes into my goddamn mind is that I was *lucky*?

I try to get to my feet, but then pause. There's something over there. A parked car, and someone's getting out of it. There are about thirty feet between me and the vehicle; its motor is still running, the headlights are on. Two headlights, I'm relieved to see.

My eyes scan the surrounding area for the other car, the one that forced me off the road. Nothing. It's gone.

The person is approaching me; the light behind gives him or her a dark, two-dimensional appearance, like they were cut out of paper.

The figure stops just in front of me. I still can't make out a face.

"What happened?" A man's voice, young-sounding, and panic-stricken. "Are you hurt?"

"Yes," I answer. "But I don't think it's too serious."

"Well, it all looks pretty horrendous. I'm going to call an ambulance, OK? And the police. You wait here. And don't move." He raises a hand as if he had to reassure me somehow. "I . . . I'm just going to go back to my car, my phone's in there. Just a moment . . ." He hastily turns away, runs back to his car.

My arm throbs, a reminder. My arm. Ambulance. And the police. What am I going to tell them about the wound? I know the answer even as I'm formulating the question in my mind. It's so easy.

I just had an accident.

I feel my arm. The fabric of my shirt sleeve is wet. I grasp it around the shoulder, dig in my fingernails, and yank it strongly, tearing the seam. The second time I pull, I tear the fabric apart as well, baring my upper arm. But now there's the dressing to deal with. I loosen the end and start to unravel it. The white-hot stabbing pain in my arm is back. It takes all of my energy, but then it's done. I glance hurriedly over to the vehicle on the side of the road. The young man is standing next to it, still on the phone.

I realize that I'm in the process of covering up Joanna's attempted murder. Which answers the question from just now once and for all. But what am I going to do with the stupid bandage? If I leave it around here somewhere, someone's going to find it. Into the pocket of my pants, then, and I'll see where I can get rid of it later on. I have to stretch a bit, but then the piece of cloth vanishes into my pocket.

Why I'm covering for Joanna after she tried to kill me is something even I don't understand. Maybe it's a reflex. An urge to protect her, still.

"The police and the ambulance will be here shortly."

I hadn't even noticed that the young man had come back.

"Thanks," I say in a strained voice, hoping he's right. I need a shot of painkillers. A tablet. Something.

About ten minutes later, the police and the emergency ambulance arrive together. While I'm still being hoisted onto the gurney, one of the two uniformed officers asks me how the accident happened. I tell him about the headlights behind me, about the first collision, which I managed to get under control, and about the second one, that swept me off the road.

No, I wasn't able to make out either the car make or the color. No, couldn't make out the license plate either.

"Maybe it was some drunk," I tell the officer.

"Yeah, maybe. Have you been having any problems with anyone lately? An altercation, maybe?"

"What? I don't understand." And I genuinely don't.

The man cocks his head. "Could it be that someone deliberately tried to force you off the road?"

I feel the pain in my arm. Think of Joanna. *Joanna?*

I just manage to stifle the *yes* before falling back into darkness.

23

I almost can't bring myself to go back into the kitchen, but I know it's unavoidable. Erik has been gone for a good ten minutes now, and since then I've been cowering in the hallway with my hands pressed against my eyes. Sobbing. Thinking. And none of it has helped even in the slightest.

I would have killed him. With the knife that haunted my thoughts from the very first evening Erik came into my life. And today it was as though it took on a will of its own, seeking its target without any help from me whatsoever.

No. Don't be a coward, not now. Don't make up laughable esoteric theories. It was me and me alone who did it; I had fixated on the spot on Erik's back that looked the most promising, where the knife would cut the deepest.

And I'll take responsibility for it. I stand up, immediately see black spots flickering in front of my eyes, am even pleased about it for a few seconds. If I faint now, I wouldn't have to think anymore, maybe never again . . .

But I stay conscious. I'm not the type to faint easily. Holding my breath, I take a step into the kitchen.

It's a battlefield. Blood is splattered across the worktop and walls, and there's a smear of it across the front of the fridge too, from where Erik was leaning against it. But most of it is on the floor.

The knife is lying where I dropped it, on the cutting board right next to the tomatoes.

I see it all, and don't understand any of it. All I know is that I can no longer trust myself, because the next time I might shove some child into the street or drive the car into a group of pedestrians or something like that. It's understandable that Erik didn't want me to take him to the hospital. It's better that way.

I get a cloth and bucket from the cupboard containing the cleaning products, fill the bucket with hot water, and start washing away the blood. After that, I scrub the floor with a brush as well, cleaning it more thoroughly than anyone ever has before.

It's not because I'm hoping to hide what happened; on the contrary, I'm assuming that Erik will report me as soon as his wound has been seen to. I'm even happy about that in a way. If they lock me up, I'll no longer be solely responsible for myself. I'll be kept away from everyone, able to breathe, and I'll no longer have to be afraid I could hurt someone. Not even myself.

I clean the kitchen walls until my arms hurt and there's no longer a trace of blood to be seen in the entire room. After that, I find myself wanting to carry on; the task is stopping me from having to think, saving me from the images, the guilt, the unspeakable fear of this . . . thing in me, that has moved me to . . .

The knife. I still haven't cleaned the knife. It's in the sink and has left a red smear on the silver basin. The stain on the blade shows how deeply it cut into . . .

I only just make it to the toilet in time. I throw up until my stomach is empty and the exhaustion numbs my senses. Now I can wash the knife; I'm able to bear the feeling of having it in my hand. Fear that I could suddenly turn it on myself and plunge it into my stomach or neck takes hold of me for a moment, but passes quickly.

I polish it until it shines, then put it back in the block.

Erik must have arrived at the hospital a while ago now. Maybe they've already given him stitches and are keeping him there overnight, on an antibiotic drip.

My phone is still on the coffee table, next to the sofa where we spent the afternoon. Laughing. Kissing.

I dial the number I saved in it earlier. Erik probably won't pick up, but I could at least leave him a message. Tell him I'll bring his things to the hospital if he needs. Tell him I'm sorry. So unbelievably sorry.

The number you dialed is not available.

That's unusual. If I knew Erik better . . . or remembered him, then I'd know if he usually turns his voice mail on or not, or whether this is just an exception. Maybe he was on the phone? Or had no reception at the hospital?

I try again five minutes later, then again after ten. The same result.

What if the bleeding got stronger? If Erik lost consciousness at the steering wheel? If he . . .

I run up the stairs, into the study, and open my laptop. Which hospital was Erik most likely to have gone to?

I try the closest one, even though there's no emergency department there.

"Good evening, my name is Joanna Berrigan, I'm looking for Ben . . ."

My God, what am I saying? Ben? Why does this name keep popping into my head?

"Sorry. I'm looking for Erik—" I am so anxious I can't remember his surname. The one I only recently learned. It starts with a T, I'm sure of that, but then what? Thaler? Thanner?

"Who is it you want to speak to?" The woman at the other end of the line already sounds irritated, and although I don't really care, it's still enough to break down my composure.

"I'm looking for Erik . . . Thieben. Erik Thieben! He has a wound to his arm and was going to drive to the hospital. Is he with you? I can't reach him on his phone and—please tell me if he's with you."

The woman clears her throat. "I can't give you any information over the phone."

"Why not?" Now I'm almost shouting. "Please! He's my fiancé." It feels like a lie. But if it is, then it's *his* lie.

"If you want any information, you'll have to come by in person with your ID."

I hang up. Look for the next number, and try to sound calmer this time. But the result is the same.

Number three on the list is the hospital where Ela works. Ela. She wouldn't brush me off, I'm sure of it. But first I'd have to tell her, admit what I've done. And I'm so ashamed. After all, she was the one who suggested I have myself committed. If I'd done that, none of this would have happened.

I pull myself together. Ela will find out anyway, so it's better if it comes from me. Without any sugarcoating or hesitation.

She answers after the third ring. Even though I try to sound unemotional, she interrupts me after the first few words.

"What on earth is wrong, Jo? You sound awful! Did something else happen?"

My fingers grip the phone so tightly that its edges cut painfully into the palm of my hand. "Yes. Erik is injured. He drove to the hospital, and I can't reach him."

"Which hospital?"

"I don't know."

I hear Ela exhale loudly. "You don't know? OK. Tell me exactly what happened."

It feels as though I'm leaping, out of a window or off a cliff. From the moment I can no longer feel the ground beneath my feet, it's as though things just take on momentum of their own, going faster and faster.

I confess everything to Ela, from the moment when we went into the kitchen, to when Erik drove off.

After I finish, there's nothing but silence on the other end of the line for a few seconds. "You attacked him with the knife," Ela whispers, so quietly I can hardly hear her.

"Yes. Even though we were getting along so well. Even though I was really starting to like him . . . What's happening, Ela? What's wrong with me?"

She doesn't answer for a while, and when she speaks again her voice is cool. "Let's deal with your issues later. First I'm going to try to find out where Erik is, and I'll get in touch again afterward. Please try not to cause any more chaos in the meantime, OK?"

I can hear as much contempt in her words as I feel for myself. I mumble good-bye, then curl up on the sofa and close my eyes.

And see nothing more. Hear nothing more. Feel nothing more. I manage to go into a merciful semiconscious state, and it's only the ring of the telephone that pulls me out of it again. Ela.

"I found him. He had a car accident on the way to the hospital. He says the car's totaled."

"Oh my God." And I let him drive alone, in the state he was in. Instead of calling an ambulance. "Is he badly injured?"

Coldness resonates from Ela's voice again when she answers. "The stab wound you gave him is the worst injury he has, but of course he has some extra scrapes and bruises now. Nothing too bad, luckily. But he has to stay overnight." She hesitates before continuing. "And he doesn't want to see you. He forbade me from telling you where he is."

I understand, very well in fact, but it still hurts. Even though that's illogical.

The memories of this afternoon are suddenly all around me again. His lips, his hands. The way he looks at me.

"But he does want me to look after you," Ela continues. She doesn't sound too enthusiastic about it.

"You don't have to, I—"

"I'm doing it for him," she interrupts me. "Do you realize he's covering for you? That he's claiming the wound on his arm is from the accident?"

"No," I whisper. "How could I know that?"

Ela sighs. "I'm coming to get you now. Erik is worried about you; he doesn't want you to spend the night alone in the house. He's an idiot, obviously, but he's one of my best friends. Be warned, though, I might just hit you for almost killing him."

"Do it," I say. "As much as you want."

She laughs, at least. "OK, Jo. Pack what you need for the night. And when we get back to my place, we'll talk, OK? You need psychiatric treatment, you see that now, don't you?"

"Yes. See you soon."

I spend the evening on one of Ela's armchairs, with my legs pulled up to my chest and my arms wrapped around them. As if holding on to myself that way was enough to stop me from doing something else uncontrolled. Ela gives me a list of experts that she's printed out, along with a few case reports about people with systematic amnesia whose stories align with mine in some ways, but are completely different in others. None of them became violent.

I listen with one ear, but my thoughts are with Erik. He didn't report me. I wonder if I'll still get the opportunity to thank him for it.

24

They let me leave just before midday. Neither the X-ray nor ultrasound yielded any findings.

"You were lucky," says the doctor, indicating the fresh bandage on my upper arm. "Something with a very sharp edge did that. If it had been your chest or your neck it went into when you crashed . . ."

I'm fully aware of what would have happened if Joanna had caught me in the chest or neck with that sharp knife. But he doesn't know anything about that. Thank goodness.

Yeah, I was lucky, when you stop and think that it could have been worse. Things could always be worse.

Two men appear just as I'm about to leave the room. They identify themselves as police detectives and ask their questions. I say that I can't tell them any more than I told their colleagues right after the crash. We agree that it was probably some drunk who forced me off the street.

They're going to go look for witnesses, they tell me. Put a notice in the local section of our daily paper. Then they note down my personal details and bid me good-bye.

Outside the hospital, I get into a taxi and have the driver bring me home.

Home.

After paying and getting out of the car, I pause in our driveway and contemplate the white housefront. For the whole time we were here, I saw this house as being exactly what it was supposed to be: a temporary solution until Joanna and I either bought or built our own place together.

Nonetheless, it was our home, and I was always happy to come back here, be it in the evenings after work or after business trips. Because I lived in this house together with her. Because she'd almost always been there waiting for me.

Now I'm standing here in front of it, and it feels unfamiliar. Not just this house, but also the fact that I'm standing here at all. Thoughts about what happened here only a few hours ago are blanketing everything that defined my existence over the past months. Everything about my life with Joanna now seems to be so far away.

I hesitate briefly before putting the key into the lock. Is Joanna still here? Could she be lying in wait for me, to finish off what she failed to do yesterday?

Nonsense. I asked Ela to take care of her. Did she take Joanna back to her place? Or could both of them still be here, even?

The clicking sound when the latch of the lock snaps back, something I've probably never taken note of before . . . now seems overly loud to me. I enter the hall, listen while holding my breath. Nothing.

A few minutes later I'm certain: Joanna's not here. I enter the living room, open the bottom right door on the cabinet. That's where we keep our liquor. I can't remember when this door was last opened during daylight hours.

I opt for vodka, half-filling one of the heavy whiskey glasses from the shelf above the bottles. The alcohol leaves a fiery trail as it makes its way down into my stomach. It tastes disgusting this early in the day, but it still helps.

My eyes sweep over the entrance to the kitchen and linger there. Without thinking much, I approach it, the glass still in my hand.

Bewildered, I stop for a second when I see the sparkling clean countertop. I walk closer, carefully inspect the spot where Joanna attacked me.

I don't know if I still expected there to be blood everywhere. I don't know if I expected anything at all, but still, the meticulous cleanliness leaves me stunned. Joanna tries to kill me, then she just up and cleans the place as if she had all the time in the world . . .

Stop! I tell myself. Joanna's in an exceptional situation; her actions can't be explained by logic. And it might just be that Ela cleaned up the place. Or helped Joanna. I push aside the thought, flickering in my mind, that maybe Joanna cleaned up the crime scene to erase any traces of it.

I go back into the living room, collapse onto the sofa, and take another sip from the glass. When I lean forward to put it back on the table, needles of pain jab me in the back. The aftereffects of the accident. If it was an accident. Was it really that some drunk had lost control over his car? And first crashed into the back of my car, then into the side of it with his second go? How likely is that?

Or did someone ram me on purpose to push me off the road? And not long after Joanna . . . Hang on. Is there a link between what happened in the kitchen and the car crash? Was that her plan B in case she didn't manage to kill me?

But that would also mean her attack on me wasn't in the heat of the moment, triggered by her confused state and without any conscious intent on her part, but a well-devised plan instead. One including a backup plan.

I fight these thoughts back, search for a counterargument, but my mind refuses to let me lose sight of the logic. I feel like screaming. Just sitting there and screaming until the despair, anger, and disappointment are gone.

I want my life back. I need an anchor.

Work. Gabor. I'm going to have to report back at some point anyway.

I'm just about to lean to the side to grab my telephone when I pause. Is this the right thing to do right now? Things have changed for me at G.E.E. as well. This project, the one I'm not supposed to be part of, the one Gabor's excluding me from. With the help of some of my so-called workmates as well, apparently. Is that really going to help me right now?

Plus, it's Sunday today. Which means I'd have to call Gabor at home. Not that it's a problem; just like every other department head I have his cell number. For emergencies.

I pull myself together. *Fuck it, why not? Right now.* If all this shit isn't an emergency, I don't know what is. And if anyone has some explaining to do around here, it's definitely Gabor. I'll tell him what I think of all this secrecy bull-crap about the big contract; I'm going to give it to him straight. Now or never.

Gabor picks up after a single ring. I make an effort to greet him in a halfway normal manner.

"Herr Thieben!" he calls down the phone line. "How nice to hear from you."

I don't buy his cheerful manner. He's overdoing it.

"How are you doing? Have you recovered at all from that awful business? My goodness, what a terrible affair. The boiler . . . Just like that. How's your partner doing? I heard from Herr Bartsch that you were a bit . . . displeased that I sent him to your home."

I'm so fixated on the project that I need a moment to remember what he's talking about. Then it comes flooding back. The company psychologist, at our house. Funny, I'd completely blocked that out.

"Well, his behavior wasn't that great either," I curtly explain. I don't feel like talking to him about Bartsch right now. "I'm calling about something else."

"But you haven't answered my question yet. How are you doing?"

I take a deep breath. "Not so good. I was in a car accident yesterday. Someone forced me off the road."

"Good Lord. Everything's happening to you all at once, isn't it? I'm sorry to hear that. Were you hurt? Were you in the car on your own?"

"Yes, I was on my own," I explain, feeling irritated. "Must have been some drunk. The police are looking for him. I'm doing OK."

"Things really don't seem to be going well for you at the moment."

"Certainly seems that way. That's also the reason I'm calling."

"Oh, do you need more time off? That's no problem, take as many days as—"

"It's about the big contract," I cut in. "I'd like to know why I'm being overlooked."

Gabor only hesitates a couple of seconds. "Come on, what do you mean overlooked? It's perfectly normal not to involve you in every new deal—"

"No, it isn't normal. As head of IT I've been involved in every new project from the very beginning."

"Not every project. Only those where IT support was necessary." It sounds halfhearted.

"And it's not necessary for this one? The way I see it, this is the biggest fish G.E.E.'s reeled in yet. Someone from my department will have to be involved in some way."

He hesitates. "I reckon you should recover before you do anything else, that's the most important thing. And once you're fully back with us in two or three weeks' time, we'll see what's what. I'll put you on paid leave until then. What do you say to that?"

You'd like that, wouldn't you?

"I feel well enough to work. Sitting around at home just makes me jumpy."

Gabor seems to be thinking, and I let him. The ball's in his court. It takes quite some time, but then I hear him breathe heavily.

"Very well then, Herr Thieben. If you really want to work instead of recovering, that's fine with me. Honestly, I only meant well."

He pauses. I don't know if he's waiting for me to say something, and I don't really care. I say nothing.

"You wanted in, so you're in. For starters, you can go pick up our two business partners from Munich central station tomorrow. I was actually planning to do it myself, because the two of them are probably the chief negotiators. But you can do that just as well. As my representative."

Tomorrow's my birthday. The date from the email. OK then.

"So where are the two of them coming in from, if they're arriving by train?"

Gabor clears his throat. "They're in Stuttgart for some other business first, and they've set their minds on making their way here on the express train instead of in a comfortable limousine." He lets out a quick laugh. "Don't forget, these people invest in environmental protection."

"What's the project about?"

"Something big."

"I realize that, but when do I find out the details?"

"Tomorrow morning, before you drive to Munich. Make sure you're here at nine. The two of them will be arriving in Munich just after one. You can't afford to be late, at any cost."

I can't claim to be feeling good again all of a sudden, but . . . at least I'm part of the project. And it was much easier than I'd expected. Maybe Gabor's even telling the truth and he really didn't mean any harm when he left me out at first. At least the professional part of my life seems to be slowly getting back on track.

"I'll be there. And . . . thank you for reconsidering."

"Come on, Herr Thieben, stop it. Reconsider . . . I never had any intention of shutting you out. I didn't realize it was so important to you to be involved in every project. Especially at the moment, since things in your private life aren't exactly . . ."

"Now's the perfect time," I respond.

"All right, see you tomorrow morning then. And do be on time."

He ends the call.

I absentmindedly put the phone down next to me on the couch, reach for the glass, and drink the rest of my vodka in one gulp. All of a sudden, my thoughts are revolving around Joanna again. Against my will and against all reason, but I can't help it.

Is it because of the conversation with Gabor? Because of the glass of vodka? No idea, but I want to know how she's doing. Right away.

Unlike Gabor, Ela takes a fairly long time until she finally picks up.

"It's me," I say. "I'm at home. How's Jo?"

Ela doesn't respond right away, and my hand clenches the telephone. "Ela? Is everything OK with her?"

"Well, I wouldn't exactly say that, after everything that's happened. But she's decided to have herself admitted to a clinic. I think she's very afraid of what she could do to herself."

25

The night on Ela's couch is the worst I can ever remember having. Worse than the one in the pantry, worse than the one I spent hooked up to the oxygen tank in the hospital. It feels as though I only sleep for a few seconds each time before waking up again. Every time I start to drift off, I see Erik before me, with his arm raised and an expression of disbelief on his face; and every time, the knife slices that silvery arc into the air. Except sometimes I don't plunge it into his arm, but into his chest, his stomach instead. Sometimes even into his face. And every single time I jolt upright, my heart racing, feeling like I'm losing my mind.

At least I know I don't scream when I wake up, otherwise it would have roused Ela in the adjoining room by now. My horror is a silent one.

By the time I finally give up on sleep, the blue light display on the Blu-ray player is showing 3:16 a.m. I sit up, pull the blanket tightly around my shoulders, and try to make a plan for the day.

Except that it's Sunday. I won't be able to get hold of Dr. Schattauer, nor, probably, any other leading doctor. Ela's assertion that the psychiatric unit in her hospital is particularly good doesn't convince me. If I'm going to check myself into a clinic, then I want it to be the one with the best experts in amnesia that this country has to offer.

And before that, I want to see Erik one more time. Apologize to him and make sure he's doing as well as can be expected.

There's just one problem: I don't know where he is.

I must have fallen asleep again, because when I next open my eyes it's already light outside, and I'm no longer sitting, but lying slumped on the couch, the pillow pressed against me like a talisman. I can smell coffee.

Shortly after, Ela comes in and puts a tray down on the table. A basket of bread, marmalade, butter, and a little bit of cheese.

The memory of yesterday's breakfast comes back to me against my will. Of Nadine's surprise visit and the way Erik stood behind me. Without any hesitation.

And of the kiss afterward. And the wonderful afternoon that followed.

And then . . .

Every step I take to Ela's breakfast table is unbelievably arduous. The thought of eating is almost unbearable, but the coffee helps. Black, hot, strong.

"Are you taking me home?"

She looks at me, aghast. "I thought we were driving you to the clinic. Yesterday you even said yourself that it was the only right thing to do!"

Her abruptness makes me feel defensive and contradictory. "Yes. I did. And I still think so, it's just that I'd like to pack my things in peace today, make a few calls. I'll go to the psychiatric clinic tomorrow, and by then hopefully I'll know which one as well."

Ela stirs her coffee, a little too forcefully. "I don't think that's a good idea. At the moment you're feeling relatively OK, right? But that could change very quickly if you're confronted with the place where it happened so soon after . . ."

It sounds like an excuse. She avoids eye contact, confirming my suspicion.

"It's because of Erik, isn't it? He doesn't want me to come home; he doesn't want to see me."

Ela denies it at first, but when I persist, she eventually shrugs. "And can you blame him? Do you know what he's gone through this past week? He's in a really bad way, Jo, and he needs to get his feet back on solid ground again." She gives me a warning look. "Without you crossing his path, knife or no knife."

Hopping yellow smiley faces grin up at me from my coffee cup. If it didn't belong to Ela, I'd smash the thing. What are a few more broken shards in my life right now, after all? "He called you?"

"No. But I've known him longer than you have." She takes a sip of coffee and reaches for the sugar. "Is it so hard to believe that he might want to have some peace if he's discharged today? Not another confrontation with the woman who went from loving him to no longer recognizing him, then let him come close again, only to almost stab him to death."

I lower my gaze to the stupid smilies.

"If you need some things from the house, I can get them for you. And you can make your calls from here; I'll give you all the privacy you need."

I agree to everything, acquiesce completely to what she says, finish my coffee, and then curl up on the couch again. I pretend to be asleep. Ela's phone rings three or four more times during the morning, and each time she goes out of the room to talk. Is she talking to Erik? I'm longing to ask her, but don't dare to. I sit on the sofa until just before two o'clock, then I can no longer bear it.

I shower, change, throw everything into the small travel bag. I call a taxi from the bathroom.

"I'm sorry, Ela. I'll tell Erik you did your best. But I have to see him and apologize before I go into the clinic."

She shakes her head, but doesn't try to stop me. She'll probably call Erik as soon as I leave.

The closer the cheerful taxi driver brings me to my destination, the more nervous I become. Do I really want to see Erik? What's the point of apologizing for something that's inexcusable? No matter what I do, it's not going to undo what happened.

It's the fear of being rejected, of the repulsion in his eyes; I realize that shortly before we turn onto my street. I'm afraid of seeing my feelings toward myself reflected in his face.

I give the taxi driver an overly generous tip, partly to compensate for my bad mood and partly from my desire to make at least somebody's day a little better.

Only my car is in front of the house. Of course. Erik had an accident with the Audi. *Totaled.*

My hand trembles as I take the key out of my bag; I can barely get it in the lock.

Maybe Erik isn't even there. Maybe they'll only discharge him tomorrow. But as I walk into the hall, I see his shoes on the floor and his jacket hanging on the hook.

The door to the living room is ajar. Before I lose the courage and simply turn around and leave, I push it open.

Erik is sitting on the sofa, staring straight ahead, toward the terrace door. He doesn't turn his head to look at me as I walk in; it's as though he didn't even hear me coming. There's an empty whiskey glass on the coffee table in front of him.

"Hello." Two syllables, and they sound so pathetic. Like I'm about to burst into tears.

He doesn't answer. Nor does he move; he just keeps staring outside, where it's just started to drizzle lightly.

Fine then. I'll say what I have to say and then disappear upstairs, into the bedroom. Get out of his way and out of his sight.

"I know you don't want to see me, and I understand that, but I really wanted to tell you once more how sorry I am about what happened."

No, not about what *happened.*

"About what I did," I correct myself. "I've tried to understand what was going on inside me, but I simply don't know. I realize that I need help. I'm going to check into a psychiatric clinic tomorrow and only leave again when the doctors say I can."

My voice gets stronger with every sentence I speak, but now my throat starts to close up again.

"I'm sorry," I repeat helplessly. "About all of this."

At the very moment I'm about to turn around and leave, Erik turns to face me. "All of it?"

It's neither a harmless inquiry, nor a peace offering. From the cold expression in his eyes, it's clear that he's getting at something specific.

"Yes." I swallow in an attempt to ward off the tightening in my throat. "Of course."

"If that's so, then please be so kind as to tell me who that was last night, in the car behind me."

I don't understand what he means. "What car?"

"The car that forced me off the road." He straightens up and faces me. The outline of a bandage is visible beneath the right sleeve of his shirt. "It wasn't just an accident, Joanna. It was another attempt to kill me. The car rammed me from behind first, then from the left, until it pushed me completely off the road."

He narrows his eyes. "It's too much of a coincidence, isn't it? First you tried to stab me, and when you don't manage, someone else causes me to have a car accident. Just half an hour later."

I want to say something in response, but I don't know what; I had thought the accident happened because of the state Erik was in at the time.

"You got pushed off the road? Ela didn't te—"

"Don't bother," he interrupts me with a smile. "Any idiot could figure out that there's a connection. I might have been naïve for a long time, but that's over now."

There's a good reason I have a guilty conscience, but this is unfair. "I had nothing to do with that, I swear! I don't know anything about anyone wanting to push you off the road."

Erik laughs. "And even if you don't—how much would that say? What *do* you actually know for sure, anyway?"

The fact that he's right makes it worse. What he's saying feels so unfair, but it's true. I can't remember him, I've lost control over my own actions—who knows what else there might be.

Suddenly I wish that it were already tomorrow, that all I had to do was lie down in a freshly made hospital bed, close my eyes, and let the doctors do their job.

I feel so tired. "If you really believe what you're saying—why don't you report me? Why didn't you do it yesterday?"

Now he lowers his gaze and, for a moment, looks so vulnerable that I long to go over to him and hold him. We were so close, for a short time.

But the rift I've opened up between us with my knife can no longer be healed. If I were to give in to my impulse to embrace Erik, he would push me away. He would have every right to.

And he does it as well, using words. "I didn't report you because I have this insane need to protect you. And, believe me, even I'm finding it more and more laughable with every day that goes by."

He looks me in the eyes, and there's an iciness in his expression that I've never seen in him before. "Maybe I still will. The more I think about what happened, the clearer it is to me that *I'm* the one I need to protect."

26

I see Joanna's eyes moistening as she struggles to maintain her composure. She's motionless, wordless. Reduced to silence, and by me.

Why did I say that? I'm not going to report her to the police. I think I just wanted to hurt her, to see in her face that what I'm saying causes her pain. Because I'm right, every damn word. I . . . wanted to get back at her for what she's done to me.

But despite everything, it was wrong, I know that. And yet, seeing the pain in her eyes felt good. A second ago, anyway. Not anymore. Now it feels more like I'm a total scumbag.

An inner voice badgers me, tells me I should jump up and take Joanna in my arms. Tell her . . . well, something comforting I guess. After all, it's still Joanna who's standing opposite me, and she's never been as low as she is right now.

A different voice whispers that I should first make sure she's not hiding a knife behind her back, to plunge into me as soon as I'm close enough. I have to stop looking at her the same way I used to back then. She's a different person now from who she was a week ago. I have to get my head around that.

"I understand," she says, her voice sounding like a stranger's, then quietly repeating herself a moment later. "Yes, I understand. Really."

I don't respond; I can't think of anything to say. Maybe I'm scared of coming out with more scumbag talk.

For a while, time seems to be suspended in the silence between us, until Joanna finally stirs again. "I'm going upstairs to lie down."

She turns and leaves the room, silent as a ghost. I sit there for a few moments, staring at the spot where she vanished around the corner, then sink into the sofa and tilt my head back. Stare at the ceiling, where there's nothing to see. The throbbing in my arm doesn't hurt nearly as much as the knowledge that Joanna and I are over.

Saying good-bye. It feels like a foreign body in my soul, and yet . . . it's real. For days I've been leading a life that seems like somebody else's, even to me. Now, this life feels like my death. I don't know how it can go on without Joanna.

At some point I feel a tear tickle my ear. How long has it been since I last cried? One day? Two? In any case, it was for the same reason as now.

Before that? Nothing for years.

My eyes are falling shut. No wonder, really, after the past few days. I can feel myself slowly drifting off to sleep, gradually slipping into the darkness. Then a thought suddenly hits me and makes me sit up with a jolt.

What if Joanna's overcome by murderous intent again while I'm asleep? I'd be defenseless. At her total mercy. I look around; the living room door can be locked but not the entrance to the kitchen. The door between the hall and the kitchen, however, can be.

On my way to lock it, I remember that Joanna won't be able to get anything to eat or drink if I lock the door. I brush the misgiving aside. My life's at stake here. She can drink water; after all, she only has herself to blame.

That's another scumbag thought.

After barricading myself in my living-room-kitchen fortress, I lie down on the sofa and pull up over me the blanket that was folded on the upholstered backrest. A relic from a normal life.

Sleep creeps back immediately, like a thief that had been briefly hiding behind the wall of my consciousness.

Once it's reached me, it no longer creeps. It pounces on me with all its force.

It's nighttime, and it takes a while for my head to clear so I can remember where I am. I'm lying on the sofa in the living room. I only vaguely recognize the objects surrounding me; it's like looking through a dark veil that turns the contours into a velvety blur. Table, cabinet, chair . . . The faintest glimmer of light falls through the wide glass panes from the terrace.

All right, I know *where* I am, so now I have to figure out *what time* I'm at. Judging by the darkness, I've slept for a good few hours in any case. I hear myself groaning as I push myself up and search for the display on the telephone. It says 6:13 a.m.

When did I fall asleep? It must have been around four in the afternoon. Fourteen hours. Madness. But then again, maybe not, considering everything I've . . .

Joanna.

Has she been downstairs in the meantime? Was it a knock on the door that woke me, even?

I switch on the floor lamp and walk to the living room door. Before turning the key, I hold my breath and put my ear against the wood. Try to detect sounds on the other side. As I open it, my heartbeat quickens. My hand still on the door handle, I look out into the empty hall in front of me, and breathe a sigh of relief. What did I expect, really? Joanna to leap out at me as soon as I open the door? That's crazy. Or is it?

I briefly think about going upstairs to see if she's asleep, but discard the thought again. The last thing I need right now is another confrontation with her. I have to be at work at nine; Gabor's counting on me. I want that part of my life to be normal again, at least.

By half past seven I'm in a cab, wearing a suit and a new shirt. Good thing I'd hung everything up in the wardrobe. I didn't see or hear Joanna at all. *Good*, I tell myself. I have to learn to resist the urge to take care of her.

I don't encounter many people when I enter the company building. Most of my coworkers usually only arrive between eight and eight thirty. Flextime.

I stop in the doorway to my office and look around. My desk with the two monitors and a stack of documents on top of it, the cabinet . . . A bit of normality, almost as though my life wasn't completely out of control.

All right then, professionalism is the order of the day.

I sit at my desk and boot up the computer. Let's see if I can find anything about this new project on the company network. What usually happens for stuff like this is that a dedicated directory gets set up, which all the involved departments have access to and where everything connected with the project gets filed.

I can't find anything. Either there really isn't any information available, or I don't have access to the directory. Which is quite unlikely, since I'm the head of IT and should have administrator rights for . . .

"Knock knock."

I jump, startled, and find myself looking into the duplicitous, smiling face of trouble personified. Nadine.

"Good morning," she warbles at me, as though we were a lovestruck new couple.

"It was, until now." I pointedly train my eyes on the monitor. "What do you want? We don't have anything left to talk about."

"I just wanted to tell you I'm sorry about the whole thing at your house. I—"

"Well, you certainly disqualified yourself once and for all with that performance," I snap at her. It takes me a great deal of effort not to raise my voice.

She takes two careful steps toward me, kneading her fingers as she does. "I *said* I was sorry. Can't we just forget about it? I'll call Joanna and apologize to her as well if you want."

I prop my hands up on the desktop and half stand up. Nadine shrinks back. "Don't you dare call our house or show your face there ever again."

"OK, fine . . ." She pauses briefly. "Could we at least be civil around each other here at work? We *do* work together, after all."

She's right about that, even if everything inside me balks at the prospect. She is Geiger's assistant, so we often have to interact. Not to mention that . . .

I grudgingly nod and sit back down. "All right, as long as it's about work. And while we're on the subject of work, what do you know about this big new project?"

Nadine raises her eyebrows. "What big project?"

"Phoenix or something. Gabor says it's a big deal. I'm about to drive to Munich to pick up the chief negotiators. Surely you know something about it?"

"No, no idea. I don't know anything about a big new project. Phoenix, really?"

I study Nadine's face and decide to believe her. This whole thing keeps getting more and more confusing. Part of Nadine's job is to prepare contract negotiations and take care of everything that's needed. From meeting room reservations to catering to hotel booking for potential business partners. If even she hasn't been informed about the whole thing . . .

"That's very strange," I say, more to myself than anything.

Nadine shrugs. "It can't be that important, otherwise I'd know about it."

I see it differently. If a hundred units isn't a large project, what is? But maybe it's all still so vague that Gabor doesn't want to go shouting from the rooftops about it? Is that why he left me out? That would make sense. And it's reassuring to have finally found a plausible explanation. It was, however, stupid of me to mention it to Nadine.

"Well, it doesn't matter anyway," I say, trying to downplay the whole thing. To ensure she doesn't probe into it anymore, I add, "In any case, I agree that we can maintain normal contact while we're working. Outside of work, though . . ."

I leave the rest unsaid.

"All right . . . so I guess I'll be going back now." She still hesitates, as if she was waiting for something else I was going to say. I stare intently at the monitor. She finally turns away and leaves my office.

At five minutes to nine, I'm sitting in Gabor's lobby, watching Frau Schultheiss sliding some papers from one side of her desk to the other. At nine o'clock on the dot, I'm summoned in to see Gabor.

He's standing in front of the window, and turns to face me. Unlike last time, he's not smiling; instead he seems stressed. I try to ignore the tugging sensation in my stomach.

"Good morning, Erik. Take a seat." Gabor nods over to the seating area. I select the same place I had during our last meeting.

"I've arranged a car for you from a rental company. An E-Class Mercedes. These men aren't going to sit in one of our tiny company cars. You can drive it until you find something to replace your Audi. Hand in the rental invoice and the gas receipts afterward, we'll take care of all that."

He sits down opposite to me and crosses his legs.

Gabor's putting a luxury ride at my disposal until I have a car of my own again? And covering the gas as well? Is he feeling bad about something and trying to make up for it? Suddenly a thought pops into my mind, and I wonder why I'm only thinking of it now. "May I ask why you're not sending your driver to Munich?"

Gabor looks at me blankly. "My driver? Hardly. I would have gone to pick them up myself if you, as a representative of the management, weren't taking care it. Anything less would be an insult to these gentlemen."

"Strange people," I comment.

"Indeed. And that, as I already said, is why it's extremely important for you to be at the train station on time. These people will take it to be a slight if you're late by even a minute. You'll need about an hour to get to Munich, and then another thirty minutes to the station at least. You'd best set off at half past ten so you have time to spare."

Gabor gets up and starts pacing up and down the room. He seems very nervous, an indication of just how important this whole thing is for him.

"Frau Schultheiss will prepare the documents containing all the project info for you while you're out. The negotiations will begin in earnest tomorrow before noon, so you have the rest of the day to read up on the project. The first meeting will be tomorrow after lunch."

Gabor stops his pacing and sits back down behind his desk. "That should be it, I think."

My cue to exit the stage.

At the door I turn around again to face him. "Thank you, Herr Gabor."

"For what?"

"For making me part of the project team after all. I was getting worried."

"Go already. I'm counting on you."

"Should I get a cab to the rental company? And how will I recognize them?"

"Frau Balke will drive you. She'll also give you a sign with the negotiators' names and the information about the platform and their exact arrival time."

Nadine, of all people. Figures, though. She handles work trips, travel expenses, and rental cars.

We don't talk much on the way, and the few words we do exchange are strictly business. Thank goodness.

I get into the black limousine at half past ten.

Nadine has given me the sign with the names and a slip of paper with the arrival time and railway platform.

Eleven minutes past one, platform sixteen. I can hardly pronounce the two names on the letter-size sign, they sound Arabic—which explains a few things. After all, they are the kind of people who can put up the money for one hundred of our solar power units, when a single one alone costs several million. And it's also no wonder Gabor doesn't want to go around shouting about a big deal like that prematurely.

When I imagine how difficult it must be for him to negotiate with these people, on an equal footing at that, I can't help but smirk. Even the cleaning staff at G.E.E. are exclusively German. Gabor's ill-concealed racism has always sickened me, sometimes even to the point where I'd been unable to hold myself back from commenting, even at the risk that it might cost me my job. It's interesting that he's prepared to set aside his convictions, though, when the money is right.

About twelve miles outside of Munich, the traffic comes to a standstill. An accident involving a truck, as I hear on the radio. The expressway has been completely closed. Today, of all days.

I look at the clock. Quarter past eleven. My phone is lying on the center console. I can call Gabor if worse comes to worst. But I'm only going to do that in the most extreme of emergencies. There's still time.

At around noon, I start to get nervous. I haven't made even one foot's worth of headway. Yet again I reach for the phone and make sure there's still reception to make a call if necessary. Just as I'm about to put it down again, it starts ringing.

I see Joanna's name on the display, and I don't know what to do. I finally pick up after the fourth ring.

"Yes?"

Three or four seconds elapse, accompanied by a quiet static noise in the background.

"You were gone, just like that." Her voice is quiet and defensive. I fight the emotions welling up inside me.

"Yes," I simply reply.

"How . . . well . . . are you all right? Your arm?"

"As can be expected under the circumstances." I want to end the conversation as quickly as possible; the holdup is already making me nervous enough and I'm neither able to nor want to deal with Joanna right now.

"Will you tell me where you are?"

My sigh conveys more annoyance than intended. "In the car, I'm driving to the train station in Munich for work, to pick up some VIPs. Well, if this fucking traffic jam breaks up in time, that is."

"OK." She sounds unemotional, her voice no longer scared. Strange, she never used to react to my bad moods in an acquiescent way. "I won't keep you then. Drive safe."

Drive, as if. People are walking around all over the expressway, in between the stationary vehicles. I get out, too, and take my phone with me.

Twenty past twelve. Damn. I have to call Gabor and tell him I won't make it on time. He's going to be furious and will probably kick me off the project again. That was that, then. All right, just a few more minutes.

I break into a sweat, even though the temperature outside is anything but warm. If the Arabs really take a lack of punctuality as an insult, maybe the entire project will fail because of me. Gabor pointed out several times just how important it was for me to be there on time.

I get back in the car, fidget around on the seat. Damn it, I *have* to call him now. I select his name from the contacts, I have my finger on the call button already . . . and I pull it back again.

Twelve twenty-six, and we're moving again. Hallelujah. I can still make it if nothing else comes up now. Nothing else *can* come up, surely; I've been through enough bullshit these past days.

But on the outskirts of Munich, the traffic is at another standstill. Twenty-one minutes left. I stop and start from traffic light to traffic light, cursing, hitting the steering wheel. Why the hell aren't these idiots driving? Are there only brain-dead people on the road today, or what? Finally things start going at a quicker pace. Right up until the next red light.

A minute past one. This is going to be pretty damn tight. But come on, surely they're not going to make a fuss if I'm late by just three or four minutes? If the train's even on time, that is. Yes, exactly, who's ever heard of the German railway being on schedule?

Ten past one. I turn into the street leading to the station. The last turn, I can already see the large building in front of me. Just two hundred, maybe three hundred yards and I'm in the parking area and actually find a space near the entrance. I snatch the name sign, leap out of the car—it's twelve past one—and sprint into the building. I'm almost on time.

I feel a tinge of elation spreading through me . . .

Then the world is torn apart.

27

Yet another terrible night's sleep. I wake up with a start at what seems to be thirty-minute intervals, and every time I do it takes forever before the pounding of my heart subsides again.

Is Erik asleep? Is he even still here?

Maybe he called Nadine to come and pick him up. After all, he no longer has the silver Audi at his disposal. And he has an ally in his ex-girlfriend, one who's available at any hour of the day or night, one who would willingly assure him that he was doing the right thing in cutting me out of his life as quickly as possible.

I could go downstairs and see if he's still here.

It feels good to stand up and move around a bit. First I creep into the study, which occasionally serves as a guest room, to see if Erik has pulled out the sofa bed. But the room is empty.

Then he must be in the living room. Or gone.

The uneasy feeling in my gut as I make my way down the stairs brings back the memories of that evening a week ago; no, it wasn't even a whole week yet, when I saw Erik for the first time. According to my memory, in any case.

I feel my way over to the living room door. It's locked. So is the door to the kitchen. So he's still here, and smart enough to lock himself in, out of reach of the knife-swinging maniac.

So maybe at least he can get some sleep. I catch myself stroking the wood of the living room door with my hand. Wishing I was on the other side of it. In Erik's arms, or in the arms of anyone who cares about me and can convince me that everything's going to be OK.

Maybe tomorrow. After all, Erik is still here, so there's a chance we could have breakfast together, talk. That is, if I can bring myself to look him in the eyes; I've never felt so ashamed before.

Last Monday I would have given anything to get the strange man out of my house. Now, the thought that he really could go was painful.

If someone really had manipulated me into this situation, then they've pulled off quite a feat.

I start to formulate sentences in my mind for tomorrow, things I can say to Eric so we can engage in a sensible conversation. But I must have fallen asleep in the process, because the next time I look around, it's already light. I glance at the alarm clock; it's almost eight.

I walk down the stairs once again, hoping that Erik is already awake and that he's unlocked the doors . . .

Yes. They're wide open, and Erik is not just awake, but gone.

I don't know why I hadn't considered that possibility. I had assumed he would take it easy today. Recuperate. But from the look of things, his priority was getting away from here.

Maybe he went to the police, to report me.

I realize that, without even registering my actions, I've turned on the espresso machine, filled it with fresh water, and grabbed a mug from the cupboard. My body is going through the motions while my thoughts are somewhere else. Was that how it was with the knife?

No. With that, part of me had been paralyzed and condemned to just watch while another part of me was highly active. It wasn't the same feeling. Not this . . . zoned-out feeling.

I need to find a clinic. That's the priority for today. I take my coffee and go up into the office, turn on the computer, and type *Amnesia specialist Germany* into Google.

The result with the most hits is a Prof. Dr. Hendrik Luttges from Hamburg, who, I read, has been involved in memory research for years.

Hamburg. If I were there, Ela wouldn't be able to visit me, nor would Darja, my colleague from the photography studio, nor . . . Erik. All the other acquaintances I've made in Germany don't really matter; I don't know them well enough to be able to share even half of my problems with them anyway.

But—I could have Professor Luttges come to Munich. For a price, of course. I could finance his next research project in exchange for him finding out what's wrong with me.

No. Stop. It's though I can hear my father thinking. He always solves his problems with money. After all, we have more of it than we have of anything else. One of the reasons why I had come to Germany in the first place was because I was so sick of this mind-set.

But it would be foolish not to use all the tools at my disposal. Wouldn't it?

I search the Internet for more experts—there was someone in Bielefeld, but that's not exactly just around the corner either.

Should I just entrust myself to any old neurologist? Or to a psychiatrist? Should I take Ela up on her suggestion after all, and get treated in the clinic at her hospital?

I rest my forehead on my hands and close my eyes. I'm still too accustomed to other people solving my problems for me, and that's coming back to haunt me right now.

But I can organize it myself; I just need some time. If Erik really is gone, then there's no immediate hurry.

My research and the reading of a few complicated academic articles lasts over an hour; the coffee that I barely even touched is now ice-cold.

So, back downstairs to make another one. I keep glancing at my phone while waiting for the machine.

I wish I could speak to someone, right now. Is there some kind of hotline for amnesia patients?

I sink onto the living room couch with my phone and coffee, but that turns out to be a mistake. The surroundings are enough to bring the scene from yesterday back into my mind. Erik, confronting me with every last bit of his justified distrust. Accusing me of having hired a killer. *Which I would be able to afford, after all.* The sentence had been lying in the air between us, unspoken.

Had money been an issue for us before? This nonsensically large fortune which I've never earned, which is far too much for one single person? Had I picked up the checks in restaurants or had he? Had we shared? Assuming, of course, that this *before* really did exist.

I turn on the TV in search of distraction; I'm so fed up with the dead-end thoughts running through my mind. The first channel is showing cartoons; the second has one of those unavoidable political interviews which are just as omnipresent in Germany as they are in Australia whenever there's an upcoming election. I zap through the channels until I find an animal documentary—about the rearing of orphaned otter babies.

Just watching something and no longer having to think feels good. A program about penguins comes on after the otters. My thoughts begin to drift away again.

It's almost half past twelve. Did Erik maybe go back to the hospital in order to have the dressing changed? My phone is in front of me on the coffee table, and, without stopping to think, I've typed Erik's name into the contacts search box. If he doesn't want to speak to me, he doesn't have to pick up.

A ringing tone. Once, twice, then a crackling sound after the third ring.

"Yes?"

"You were gone, just like that." I try not to let it sound like an accusation, but instead it comes out as though I'm afraid of being alone in the house. My God.

"Yes."

"How . . . well—are you all right? Your arm?"

"As can be expected under the circumstances."

OK, so calling him was a bad idea. I'm desperately searching for words, and Erik clearly has no desire to talk to me. Maybe he's already on his way back and will be here soon.

"Will you tell me where you are?"

He sighs, as though my question is the last thing he needs right now. "In the car, I'm driving to the station in Munich for work, to pick up some VIPs. Well, if this goddamn traffic jam breaks up in time, that is."

And then on top of it all I have to deal with you. The words he's clearly thinking remain unsaid.

"OK." At the very least my guilty conscience is gone. "I won't keep you then. Drive safe."

The conversation hasn't made anything better, in fact very much the opposite, but that's my own fault. What did I expect, really?

I lean back on the sofa, ready to spend the day with the documentary channel. To not have to think. Or make any decisions.

A new program has just started, and I find myself unexpectedly moved by it. A documentary about dingoes in New South Wales.

Home.

The pictures of the Australian mountain landscape and Sturt National Park awaken within me, for the first time in months, a sense of burning homesickness. *Is my father right? Do I belong there after all?*

I hardly know the places rushing past me on the screen, but they still feel so familiar.

Here, on the other hand, if I'm completely honest, I still feel like an outsider. Especially given my current situation.

Suddenly, I know who I really want to talk to.

It's half past ten at night in Melbourne now. It's late, but I still want to try my luck. If there's anyone in the world who'll be there for me, then it's her.

The phone rings three times, four times, then someone picks up.

"Hello?"

"Mama." I'm filled with such a sense of relief, I almost start to cry. No. I can't do that. I don't want her to worry.

"Hey, sweetheart! How wonderful to hear your voice." Her transition from English to German no longer sounds quite as effortless; she briefly pauses at times and has a soft, light accent. Maybe it's because of the late hour, or the fact that she only rarely speaks her native language these days.

"How are you?" I try to sound cheerful. "Is everything OK there with you guys?"

"Oh yes. We miss you of course, so much—but other than that we're good. Daddy's blood pressure counts are finally OK, and I'm going to give a presentation about my projects at the nutritional congress in Sydney soon. Isn't that . . . fabulous?"

"That's wonderful, Mama."

"But now tell me: how are you doing? What's the news?"

Well, the day before yesterday I almost stabbed someone to death. Imagining how my mother would react to such a revelation almost makes me break out in hysterical laughter.

"Really good. Although, health-wise I'm a little run down at the moment, but . . ."

"Ah yes, the German autumn." She sighs in a way that sounds nostalgic. "You just need a few more layers, darling; buy yourself a few chic jackets."

"I will." If I don't get to it soon, we'll drift off into small talk. "Mama, can I ask you something?"

"Of course."

"Have I ever had problems with my memory before? Like, gaps in it?"

There are thousands of miles between us, but I know exactly how her face would look right now, in the three or four seconds she stays silent. Her forehead wrinkled in thought, her lips pursed just a little. She is trying both to find an answer to my question and to figure out why I'm asking in the first place.

"No, Joanna. On the contrary, you always had the best memory of all of us. Do you still remember that time when Dad forgot the code for the new pool house? You were the only one who could remember it, even though you'd only used it once or twice, and it had six figures. Or that time in the hotel in Sydney . . ."

I let her talk, let her tell one anecdote after the other. Soon the conversation is no longer about my memory, but simply about shared memories. Beautiful, familiar snapshots from a world in which I thought I was invulnerable.

My mother is enjoying the conversation, I know that. With Dad, she doesn't get that many chances to talk; he likes the sound of his own voice too much.

But after a while I interrupt anyway. "Have I mentioned an Erik to you at any point over the past few months?"

"No." She didn't pause for even a second before responding. "Why? Who is he?"

"Doesn't matter. Not anymore."

"Aha." Seldom has anyone placed so much weight on just two syllables. A short pause follows.

"It would be lovely if you'd come back home soon, Jo," she says then, hesitantly. She knows that I don't want to be put under pressure. "I mean, Germany can still be your second home, you could spend a few months there every year, perhaps I might even come with you someday."

I don't respond, so she hastily goes on to say what I'd feared she would. “We’re not complete without you, Dad especially; he really suffers from not seeing you.”

I’m unable to hold back a snort. If there’s anything he’s suffering from, then it’s not having me under his direct control. After all, here I can make my own decisions, ones that could go against his interests.

“I don’t want to push you into anything.” Now she sounds sheepish and it makes me feel bad. “But you know how happy we would be if you were back with us. . . .”

I’m only listening with one ear now; my gaze is drawn back to the TV screen. There’s a news ticker announcing a special report in five minutes.

“. . . just spoken with Jasper and Ashley, they send their best—”

“I’m sorry, Mama,” I say as I read the words running along at the bottom of the screen, read them again and again. Unable to believe them. Unwilling to believe them. “I have to go. I’m sorry.”

I hang up without another word, and the phone slips from my hand. Instead of picking it up, I go over to the television and kneel down in front of it.

The news ticker is still running. And then the first pictures come.

28

There's a deafening explosion; something throws me to the ground, compacting my lungs, making it difficult to breathe. Air . . . I need air. I feel sharp pain. In my back, in my arm, everywhere. Pieces of debris are raining down on me, a strange hail of destruction. I curl up my body, protect my head. Suddenly it stops. A brief moment of muffled silence, then chaos. Screaming, shouting, grinding and crashing noises. Dark clouds are all around me, shards of glass, shredded objects. And dust, everywhere. It settles in my nose and my throat; the need to cough becomes unbearable and I give in to it. I'm lying there, coughing, wheezing, gasping for breath, trying to understand what has happened. An explosion, maybe gas . . . maybe a bomb?

I have to get away from here. Get out of this building. Maybe there are more explosions to come? I carefully raise my head. The world is nothing but dust now, gray and grim. And in the middle of it all, scenes straight out of a nightmare. Shadowy figures appear as though out of nowhere, hunched over, climbing clumsily over the rubble. Some of them stumble, others run past, some fall over again, crying . . . And all this screaming. Coming from everywhere. Some of it from very close by.

Someone trips over my foot, falls to the floor next to me. A man. Covered in dust. He groans, forces himself back to his feet, limps onward.

I tuck in my legs, move my arms. A thought comes to me, of major importance: *I have to get out of here.* Slowly I straighten up, until eventually I'm standing in an expanse of shattered glass, chunks of concrete and mortar, wood . . . A man is next to me. Gray dust on his coat and his hair, his face covered in tiny dark marks. He's looking at the rubble with his eyes widened in fear. Motionless. In shock.

And on top of it all, these awful screams. A woman shouts out, very close by. "Oh God! Oh my God!"

More and more people are crawling out of the devastation. I see blood on their hands, their arms and legs. Another woman staggers toward me, her face nothing but an expanse of gray. Her dress is torn; a long, dark wound gapes open on her forearm. Black blood. Everything here is black and gray. The explosion has blasted all the color out of the world.

The woman's knees buckle. I take a step toward her, try to catch her, but get caught on something and topple down to the floor with her. I nearly black out from the pain. The wound on my upper arm . . .

The woman lands on top of me. Absurdly, I ask her, "Is everything OK?" as I twist out from under her.

"Gerhard. My . . . my husband." Her voice sounds hoarse. "I was dropping him off at the train."

I manage to get back on my feet. My gaze keeps falling on her blood-smeared arm. She's looking past me, over to where the exit is. A bright speck in this gray dusty hell. "I want to get out of here, please." I help her get up. Once we've managed it, she walks away without another word, and vanishes seconds later.

I should follow her. Get out of here too.

The station hall is filled with distraught shouting, with groaning and, again and again, with ghastly cries of pain—even very close to me.

About thirty feet away from me, a man is twisting on the ground. He's holding his thigh; I can't see the rest of his leg in the chaos. A stooping figure teeters past him, but doesn't help him. Nobody's helping him.

There's a towering pile of large fragments from the display board next to him. Behind it, a fire is blazing amid the rubble from a wall that's collapsed. The platforms are all located there, somewhere. That's where the explosion seems to have happened. I approach the screaming man, climb over a massive wooden beam, slip, and take a hard knock, of course to my injured arm.

What the hell am I doing here anyway? There was an explosion directly up ahead; the people are all running away from there. Maybe there's a gas leak and there is going to be a second blast any second? I should get out of the building as quickly as possible too.

But . . . the man. He's screaming his lungs out. His leg seems to be jammed somewhere; I have to at least try to help him. A few feet farther on I have to climb over stones and splintered wooden beams. My body convulses into a coughing fit, incapacitating me for several minutes.

It's only when I reach the man that I discover his lower leg.

It's on the floor about seven feet away from him, the foot sticking out of a brown shoe.

I've never seen a severed limb before, but I can't get squeamish now, no matter what. The man doesn't even seem to be aware I'm there. His hands are clutching the tattered stump of his leg, the rubble underneath the hideous wound is glistening darkly. His life is leaking out of him; he's going to bleed to death.

His leg needs to be tied off; I've seen them doing that in the movies about a million times. I pull my belt out of the loops on my pants and kneel down beside the man, who's only whimpering now. He seems to realize I want to help him. I raise the hand holding the belt, and don't know where to apply it. This is no damn movie.

I manage to get some words out. "I'll help you. You have to let go of your leg so I can tie it off." There's no sign he's understood me. His hands are still clenched around his thigh. Now what am I supposed to do? How should I . . .

A hand comes down on my shoulder and squeezes. "Are you a doctor?"

"No," I answer, even before I see who's standing behind me. I turn around and, to my relief, see the orange and silver jacket of a paramedic.

"Then please step aside, I'll take over here." The man is still young, I can see the horror in his face and hear it in his voice. He's making an effort to look experienced. "Are you injured yourself?"

Am I? "No, nothing serious, I—"

"Then please leave the building. My colleagues will be arriving outside soon, they'll take care of you. Please go, now."

"What happened here?" I ask, not really expecting him to know.

"No idea. An explosion, that's all I know. Go, please."

I try to get up, but don't manage right away. The young paramedic clutches my arm tightly, right where the wound is. I utter a cry, and he withdraws his hand.

"So you *are* injured?"

"No . . . Yes, but not from this."

As I'm getting back up, the paramedic is already down on his knees beside the man. He takes a quick look at the bloody stump, then starts getting things out of his bag.

I look over at the train tracks. The dust has settled a bit; visibility is improving. A shattered food stand, several unmoving bodies on the floor next to it, some of them in grotesquely contorted postures.

Farther back still is where the train platforms start. Or what's left of them, anyway. I can only see them in parts, but what I can see is horrific. A dented express train engine car, blackened with soot, is lying at an angle over one of the platforms, flames lashing out of the conductor's cab.

An enormous steel girder has fallen onto the engine, crushing it like a tin can. The casing has been torn open in a few places, and insulating materials and cables hang out like organs and veins. Pieces of luggage and objects I can't place are scattered all around the scene. Human bodies as well. Some of them, a few, are moving, while most of them are lying there motionless. Like corpses. I want to turn away and leave the building like the paramedic told me to do, but I can't bring myself to move. Only when somebody appears at my side, hastily shouting at me that I should get outside, quickly, do I tear my eyes away from the horrible scene. The man who addressed me, wearing a transport police uniform, has run past me in the meantime.

As I look around one final time, I see the young paramedic hastily throwing his things into his emergency case. The man on the floor next to him isn't moving anymore. His eyes are closed.

I don't have to ask. I know he's dead.

As I realize that, the scene of destruction around me starts to sway. The figure of the paramedic is also losing its sharp contours; all sounds become muffled. Then, only darkness.

"Hello, can you hear me?"

Yes, I want to say, but I have a feeling I'm only thinking it. I open my eyes. The image that presents itself is a blur. It becomes clearer after I blink a few times, but also more confusing. The face right in front of mine seems too big. The perspective is strange. The eyes looking at me worriedly belong to the paramedic; his head is hovering over me.

As I try to straighten my upper body, my surroundings immediately start swaying again. I quickly close my eyes, wait a moment, then open them again. Better.

"You fainted," the man explains, a little unnecessarily. "Everything OK now?"

He helps me get to my feet. I look for the injured man. The dead man. He's lying ten feet away. The paramedic follows my gaze. "There was nothing I could do," he explains and draws himself up. "He'd lost too much blood. I . . . I have to keep moving here."

"Yes," is all I say. He shoulders his bag and heads in the direction of the train platforms.

More and more paramedics, firefighters, and police come running into the station hall. The world is no longer in slow motion like it was right after the explosion, having given way to the organized, busy activity of the emergency crews and rescue teams.

Around me, many other people are also heading toward the exit. Grimy, blood-smeared, horrified faces. A teenager runs past, crying; a firefighter with feverish red spots on his face hurries to my side and tells me to go faster.

I have to wait for a brief moment at the entrance, as several uniformed helpers are carrying a large case inside. Then, I've made it. I suck in a deep breath of air, and although my lungs burn, I'm sure I've never tasted anything more precious. Someone puts a blanket over my shoulders and pulls me along, talking to me all the while. I don't understand what he's saying; my mind isn't able to process his words. Then I'm gently pushed down, to sit on a small wall. A hand extends out toward me. Holding out a plastic cup.

I take it and lift my head up; a woman is standing in front of me.

"How are you feeling? Any pain? Are you injured?"

She's pretty. And with her clean, white clothes, she's in complete contrast to the interior of the train station, almost to the point of absurdity. An angel in hell.

"Yes. I'm fine. Do you know what happened in there?"

"No one knows for sure right now. Can I leave you on your own for a moment? There's still too few of us."

"Yes, thank you. I'll manage."

She nods at me and turns away.

I try to comprehend what happened. I keep thinking of that man. I see him before me, screaming from all the pain, hands clenched around the stump of his leg. I never would have thought a human being could scream like that.

Suddenly, Gabor appears in my head. And the reason why I'm here, the two Arab men. What happened to them? I was a few minutes late . . .

I was a few minutes late.

Had I been on time, I would have been standing right where the explosion took place. If I'd been on time, as Gabor kept telling me I had to be, again and again.

I start to feel nauseous. The reason for this sudden nausea is something I feel, rather than something I can put into words just now.

I've just escaped certain death by a hairbreadth, because I wasn't in the place where, had it been up to Gabor, I was meant to be when the explosion happened.

I stand up, feel the blanket sliding off my shoulders. I don't care. Something's dulling my thoughts. Something that's making them slower.

I obey a voice inside me telling me I should leave this place at once. And that I should leave the car Gabor got for me. It seems alien, this voice, but it's crystal clear and commanding. I leave the parking lot behind me; there's now a steady stream of new emergency vehicles and people arriving.

No one takes notice of me. Someone who can walk unaided doesn't need attention right now.

The voice in my head is telling me about a defective boiler and an attempt to run me off the road.

And then it repeats the content of an email I saw on Gabor's laptop by accident.

Munich central station, October 18th. 1:10 p.m. More details to follow.

Not a word about any chief negotiators arriving. Just a date and a time. Exactly the time at which the explosion happened.

29

It's Munich. The train station.

I'm kneeling in front of the television as though it were an altar, staring at the images, unable to comprehend what's happening.

The camera captures stumbling, dust-covered people, running emergency service workers, and a half-collapsed building. All of it in a flickering blue light. The journalist, standing in front of the station, is shouting to make himself heard over the blaring sirens in the background.

"We still don't know the details, just that there were at least two explosions which rocked the central train station in Munich and partially destroyed it. There are a number of people injured, and from what we can make out there have also been casualties."

The man steps out of the path of two ambulance workers running past with a stretcher. It's evident that it takes all of his strength and professionalism to keep his eyes fixed on the camera.

Casualties. I'm struggling to breathe. Erik was on his way to Munich station, he was in such a hurry . . .

My phone is still on the floor. I reach down to pick it up, fumbling because my hands are shaking so much. Only on the second attempt do I manage to bring up the recent calls. I dial Erik's number.

Please.

Please.

Please pick up.

It takes a while before I'm connected. Except that it doesn't put me through to him.

The number you have dialed is not available.

It can't be, it can't. But maybe the network is just overloaded because everyone is trying to reach their family and friends. To let them know they're all fine. And at the same time, everyone else is trying to contact their loved ones who they think are at the station. Just like I am.

Try again. Wait. Don't let your thoughts get carried away, don't let the images push their way into your mind. . . .

The number you have dialed is not available . . .

If it's not the network, then it must be the phone itself. Lying in pieces under the rubble, along with its owner.

No. I can't let myself think that. Because it's not like that. It can't be.

Another attempt. The same result.

As I dial Erik's number again and again and again, the live report continues, the red news ticker announcing: *Special report: Explosion at Munich central station +++ Number of victims not yet known +++ Terrorist attack not ruled out.*

After the tenth or fifteenth attempt, I give up. I crawl even closer to the television, try to spot Erik among the people running and limping on the screen. Many are propping each other up, almost all of them are crying, but they're all too far away to make out any faces. Somewhere in the background, heartbreaking screams. "Mama! I want my mama!"

Then the reporter again, his pale face staring into the camera.

"We've just received more information. It seems that the detonation took part right on the platform, directly next to the express 701009 train which had just arrived from Hamburg. According to eyewitness reports, the explosion must have been very powerful, destroying not just the train but also a large part of the station building."

In the background, a man passes by who is built like Erik, but his face is unrecognizable because it's white and gray with dust, with just a sharp, blood-red line across his forehead.

No. Now that the man's closer to the camera, I can see that it's not Erik.

"We have an eyewitness who was in the station when the explosion took place," the reporter is saying. An older man comes into the picture, visibly struggling to breathe.

"Could you describe for us what you experienced?"

The man coughs. "It's indescribable," he croaks. "I was just inside the main entrance and suddenly there was a bang, an unbelievably loud bang—and then fire, and smoke. I turned around, but before I did I saw part of the ceiling collapsing inward. On top of . . . people." He turns aside, wiping his hand over his face. "If it had been three minutes later, I would have been standing right there. My God. Those poor people."

"Thank you," the reporter says, and the camera sweeps to the side, to a medic who is just getting into an ambulance. Then back to the building. A mixture of smoke and dust is still billowing out from it.

I know they aren't allowed to film inside. Or at least, not to broadcast what they're filming. Luckily.

They switch back to the studio, where the presenter gives an emergency hotline number for those worried about loved ones. As I note it down, my hand shakes so much that I can barely read it.

But first I try to reach Erik's phone again directly, wishing nothing more than to hear his voice, so that I don't have to keep imagining his dead body underneath the rubble.

Nothing. Just the network message again. *The number you have dialed is not available.*

The hotline, then. The first time I call it's busy, and on the second try I'm placed on hold.

Waiting, in this situation. Doomed to uncertainty and helplessness. I know I won't be able to stand this for much longer, and at the same time I'm surprised, wondering where this strong reaction is coming from.

The man I'm worrying about is . . . No, not a stranger anymore, but neither do I know him well enough to feel this much fear at the prospect that something could have happened to him.

Would I be this upset if it were Darja? Or Ela? I've known both of them longer than Erik, have a kind of friendship with both of them. But all the same—my panic wouldn't be as great as it is right now. I would be terribly worried, sure, and I would try to find out if they were OK, but not with desperate urgency like this.

Ela. Thinking of her raises my spirits a little. If I can get hold of her, that's better than any hotline. She can make inquiries with her friends in the hospitals—I know she would. She cares about Erik a great deal, she would do anything to find out if he's OK.

But she doesn't pick up either. I should have guessed; all of the hospitals far and wide must have put their emergency procedures into action, and with all likelihood there's chaos at the lab as well.

But at least Ela's voice mail activates after the fourth ring.

"Erik," I stammer into the telephone. "He was at the Munich station, and I can't get hold of him. Did he get in touch with you?" Even that's a shimmer of hope. With the way things stand, his first call would probably be to Ela, not me. "Please try to find out. And then call me as quickly as you can, OK? Please."

Half an hour passes by, an hour. The special report on TV keeps showing the same images over and over, with summaries for anyone just tuning in, as well as experts being interviewed in the studio. Explosion experts. Terrorism experts. They all remain guarded, saying it's best for everyone to wait until the responsible group steps forward.

Because by now, everyone is in agreement that it's a terrorist attack.

Ela doesn't call.

My phone shows that I've tried to call Erik forty-seven times. Each time with the same result.

He would pick up if he could, I know that. Despite my knife attack. Despite everything. He wouldn't do that to me.

By now, there is talk of there being at least thirty-two fatalities. The emphasis being on *at least*, meaning that this was the number of bodies which had been discovered so far.

I follow the reports in a daze. Some protection mechanism in my head has taken the edge off the panic, stopping me from breaking down completely. I still have no answer to the question of where this intense connection to Erik has suddenly come from, I just know it's there. Without a single doubt.

When my phone rings later that afternoon, I almost burst into tears. Ela's name is on the display.

For the duration of a heartbeat, I contemplate not picking up. What if she found out that Erik is dead? What if the uncertainty gives way to a truth I'm not able to cope with?

I pick up anyway, feeling the tears welling up in my eyes before Ela has even said a word.

She doesn't know anything, I find out after the first few seconds of talking with her. She's only just listened to her messages.

"Why was Erik at the station?" Her voice is shrill over the phone. "Did he get in touch? Do you know anything?"

"No." The word is no more than a breath, my voice is as powerless as I am. "I've been trying to reach him for hours, but—"

"Oh shit. Shit." I can hear that Ela is close to tears. "I'll start calling around right away. I'll find him. I'll be in touch." She hangs up before I have a chance to respond.

I cower back down on the floor in front of the TV, my arms wrapped around my knees, my head resting on top. I only look at the screen every now and then; I've already seen all the images being shown, they repeat them at half-hour intervals, and only rarely is there ever any new information. Blue flashing lights in the approaching dusk. Interviews with eyewitnesses who saw everything from the parking lot, from one of the houses opposite, from a car.

Then they show a cell phone video; someone just happened to catch the moment of the explosion by chance, from outside.

An orange glimmer, then windows bursting, flying rubble, walls crashing down.

They repeat it in slow motion, and I imagine Erik in the station, holding his hands over his face for protection, being hurled across the station by the explosion until he crashes against a wall or into a train. Then, part of the ceiling falling in and burying him underneath.

The images aren't real, but like daggers they pierce the protective layer I've built up around my insides. The pain has me doubled over; I hear myself sobbing, want to pull myself together but I can't.

There's no point pretending any longer. If Erik was OK, if he hadn't been at the station, then I would have heard something from him by now. The explosion happened over six hours ago. The six most torturous hours I can ever remember having. But he hasn't given me any sign of life. Because he can't. Because he . . .

Still, I forbid myself from thinking the word. Like thinking it would make everything true. Like it hadn't already been decided long since.

Around eight o'clock I call Ela again, but just get her mailbox. I leave a message made up of desperate stammering.

I have no idea how I'll be able to get through the night. Call my mother again? No, that's a bad idea. I'll end up needing to comfort her, reassure her, convince her that nothing will happen to me.

And then she calls anyway; she heard about the attack in the morning news. Wasn't it close to where I am, she asks.

Yes, it was. But I'm OK. I'm fine, yes, don't worry.

At nine o'clock there is still no word about anyone claiming responsibility for the attack; there have been no messages, no videos. That's unusual, the experts are in agreement. Especially given such a violent act of terrorism. The number of victims is being constantly updated, right now the count is at seventy.

Politicians announce that action will be taken, without knowing against whom; a national state of mourning is announced.

At around nine thirty, I finally struggle to my feet. I have to drink something, but I can't even get two gulps of water down; my stomach protests, bringing everything back up. I only manage on the second attempt.

I prop myself up against the sink with both hands. With some luck, I should be able to stomach a little vodka, too. One glass should be enough to give me four or five hours of merciful unconsciousness.

I am just opening the fridge when a key turns in the lock of the front door.

My body moves before my brain has a chance to think. Out of the kitchen, into the hall.

He is standing there. Motionless, as the door falls shut behind him. His suit is torn, there's a cut across his left cheekbone, the dust and dirt on his face has been wiped away haphazardly.

I can't get a single word out. My legs only hesitantly obey me; slowly carry me toward him, much too slowly, but then I'm standing in front of him, I put my arms around his neck, press him against me, much too tightly. I want to feel, want to know, that it's really him, that he's alive. I want to hear his heartbeat, but instead all I can hear is the sound of me bursting into tears, sobbing, and there's nothing I can do to stop it. Instead of hugging Erik I grip onto him, burying my face in his chest, which smells of smoke and metal. It takes me a while to realize that he's not hugging me back.

I try to pull myself together. Take a few deep breaths until the sobbing subsides. Then I pull back from Erik a little, not much, just enough so I can see his face.

His expression is hard, and at the same time so hurt that my heart almost breaks.

When he speaks, it's only to say two words.

"Go away."

30

Very slowly, Joanna lets go of me. She finally takes a step backward, moving in slow motion, creating a distance between us which feels both relieving and painful. Then she just stands there, looking at me. Her forehead and nose are streaked with gray, dust her skin picked up from my jacket.

"I'm so glad you're alive," she says, her first words since I entered the house. I watch her carefully, search her face for signs of deceit. But in vain.

"Oh really?" My voice sounds cold and sharp, even to me. "Are you sure about that?"

"Erik . . ." She pauses, then begins speaking again, her voice firmer this time. "You think I don't know what happened in Munich? It's all over the news. I was expecting the worst, picturing all sorts of horror scenarios. And then all of a sudden you're here, and you're alive. Yes, for God's sake, of course I'm *sure*!"

For a brief moment, my entire being is pushing me toward her, with the burning desire to pull her close to me and forget everything around me. Then, the terrible images flood back. A knife, plunging down toward me. The train station. People screaming. Dead bodies, no longer recognizable as human beings.

"I'd like to believe you, Jo, I really would. But I can't. Not anymore."

She lowers her gaze, looks down at the floor tiles, and fixates on a spot for a few seconds. Then she shakes her head and walks away.

I wait until she's reached the top of the stairs, then I sink down to the floor. I don't want to go into the living room, nor the kitchen, I don't want to be here and don't want to be elsewhere either. I don't want . . . anything at all. Is that possible? To not want anything? Is it possible to think of nothing at all? To just . . . be?

What's the use of this nonsense? Am I losing my mind once and for all? But . . . is someone who's genuinely losing their mind aware of the process, do they think about whether it's happening?

I feel the last of my energy seeping out of my body, lean back against the dresser, slump down like a soulless rag-doll imitation of myself.

My eyes drift through the hall. I know the things I'm seeing, and yet they all seem strangely foreign to me. The small watercolor painting on the wall next to the entrance to the kitchen, the tall blue glass vase on the floor containing fronds of pampas grass, the curved sheet-metal umbrella stand on the other side . . . Things I'm familiar with, but which I suddenly don't want to be part of me anymore.

What actually remains of everything that, until a few days ago, made up my life, that *was* my life? What does that woman who just went upstairs still have in common with my Joanna? What's this house still got to do with me? And even my employer . . .

I close my eyes, opening them wide again when the image of the screaming man, and of his leg several feet beside him in the dirt, immediately comes rushing back. I shake my head to make sure the scene dissipates. It'll come back again though, I know. It hasn't let go of me since I left the train station.

And yet, despite the clarity of that memory, I can no longer remember how I got back home. I know I just started walking, it didn't matter in which direction, as long as it was away from the terrible chaos. I left the car because . . . yes, why did I leave the car? Because I wouldn't have been able to get it around all the ambulances and fire trucks? Yes, probably. And because there was a voice inside me telling me it was better to leave it.

People were coming toward me. A lot of people. They'd all been going to the train station, while all I'd wanted to do was to get away from there. Far away. Again and again I'd had to stop and hold on to something when things around me started to sway. Or when some loud noise would shake me to my core and make me jump in fright. And I kept on seeing these images in front of me. These awful scenes from the station. I'd tried to find a cab, but no luck. That was when the idea of using my phone had first come to my mind.

It's crazy. You get so used to the device that you don't go anywhere without it. And when you get a chance to really make use of it, you forget it exists.

It had still been in my inside pocket, but the screen was completely smashed. I'd put it back in my pocket. That's all I can remember, that and suddenly finding myself in some courtyard. The old, rotten wooden bench in the corner, almost impossible to make out in the darkness. I'd collapsed onto it and closed my eyes. The explosion, the screaming . . . I'd reexperienced all of it, again and again.

When the old man had asked me if he could help me at all, it was already late evening. He'd called a cab for me.

I close my eyes, know there's something sitting in a dark corner of my mind, just waiting to be formulated into conscious thoughts.

Gabor.

Was it really possible that he sent me to Munich so I'd die in the explosion? Right now, here on this wooden floor, the thought seems completely absurd. Looking back, the entire day seems completely unreal. The explosion and the debris, fire, people screaming and blood everywhere . . . and yet, all I have to do is look at my hands and clothes to know I really was there.

But Gabor? The only reason he sent me to Munich was because I kept insisting he include me in the project. He even put a limousine at my disposal, paid for by the company no less. Although now I'm wondering why the car was leased under my name if G.E.E. are bearing the expenses. That's unusual. And then there are all those other strange things that have happened over the past few days.

It can't be a coincidence, not anymore. There isn't that much coincidence to go around. I don't understand the meaning of it all, but whatever the reasons may be—Joanna's involved. And if both Joanna and Gabor have something to do with these incidents, then they're in cahoots.

My stomach rebels at the thought, and it turns out I have enough energy left to struggle to my feet and reach the guest bathroom.

Once the retching finally stops, I wash my face with cold water and collapse onto the couch in the living room. I can't think anymore; I don't want to think anymore. I want to run away from all of this, although I probably wouldn't even if it was possible. I'm so dreadfully tired; I close my eyes, getting ready to open them again once the horrible images come flooding back. But apart from the merciful darkness, all I make out is a tiny glimmer of light coming through my closed eyelids.

I push aside the thought that all the doors are open and that Joanna might come into the living room, knife in hand.

All of a sudden, a memory of my mother comes into my mind. It's as though she's standing there in front of me and looking at me with her soft smile. I can't recall having ever seen her angry, not even when she had all reason to get angry. She never lost that smile.

The image touches me with such an intensity that even the strange coldness inside me shrinks away from it. It's nice, seeing my mother this close to me. Recently I've been finding it more and more difficult to picture her face. Her image has become more blurry, more abstract over the years. Like she was drifting away from me, just a little bit further every time.

This time it's different. Her fan-like laugh lines, the green of her eyes, even the tiny scar on her forehead from her childhood, it's all clearly in front of me. I feel the urge to take her in my arms, no, to let her take me in her arms. To let her comfort me, the way she always comforted me as a child whenever I needed it.

More images appear, and I willingly seek refuge in them. Scenes from my childhood, beautiful things I experienced together with my parents. Weekend trips away, going skiing in the wintertime; they even took me camping because I was so hell-bent on going. Although the two of them weren't in the least bit enthused about spending the night inside an uncomfortable tent.

Of course, it wasn't all sunshine and rainbows. We did have our problems here and there, but we were never angry at each other for long, not even in difficult situations.

I open my eyes and stare at the ceiling.

My parents aren't around anymore. Joanna's my family. *Was* my family. And now? A stranger. Work, Gabor, Bernhard . . . my social circle. All strangers.

I push myself up, realizing as I do that there's almost no part of my body that isn't hurting. I prop my elbows on my thighs, drop my head, and bury my fingers in my hair. What on earth am I going to do?

"I have to talk to you."

I jump, and notice Joanna in front of me; she's standing in the middle of the room. I hadn't noticed her come in.

"What do you want?"

"I just said: to talk to you."

Something about her has changed. Her voice sounds different than before. More assertive. All traces of constraint or remorse have disappeared.

"I don't know what I'd possibly have to talk to you about," I say, with emphasized abruptness.

She comes closer. "Really? One catastrophe after the other happens to us, and you don't know what we'd talk about?"

"No. I said don't know what I'd possibly talk about to *you*."

Joanna sinks into the armchair next to me, but without breaking eye contact. "I've been sitting upstairs racking my brain about all this. Your brain usually seems to work quite well, so use it, would you? Then you'll see it's not someone who wants to kill you, but someone who wants to kill us both."

I let out a quick laugh. "The only thing that's sure here is that *you* wanted to kill me."

Joanna leans forward and props her hands on the table. Her gaze is very intense now; there's not even a glimmer of uncertainty, fear, or despair.

"That's what I mean when I say you should use your head. If I really wanted to kill you, Erik, you'd be dead by now."

31

Dead. The word hangs in the air between us. Erik's eyes narrow, like the word was causing him pain, and I think I know why. He was surrounded by death today; in fact he's probably very close to a breakdown. His view of the world can never be the same again as it was this morning. To be precise, nothing can ever be the same again for him.

"If I really wanted to kill you, I would have had so many opportunities, Erik." I feel the urge to stroke his hand, but I know that's not a good idea. "You slept next to me for a whole night, we were . . ."

"The fact that you didn't succeed doesn't mean that you wouldn't have tried," he interrupts me. "And you almost did succeed, as we both very well know."

I sit down next to him on the couch, but at the other end. "So you think I'm so hell-bent on killing you that I'm prepared to off myself in the process? Because if your theory is right, then the thing with the boiler must have been me too. Right?"

He closes his eyes for a moment. "I didn't say that what you're doing is logical, so don't try to win the argument with logic. After all, you're hurting yourself as well, did you forget?" The fingers of his right hand are clutching one of the couch cushions. I don't think he even notices.

"For me, the worst thing," he says, so softly that I can barely hear him, "is the thought that you're probably involved with what happened today. My boss sent me to the exact spot where the bomb went off, at the time of the explosion. But I was late, unfortunately. For him. For both of you. And before that . . . the car accident, your knife attack, the scarves in the boiler." He swallows, shakes his head. "I don't understand how he managed to talk you into this madness. Certainly not with money, because I imagine you have a lot more of it than he does."

I had resolved not to interrupt him, but now I can't stop myself. "I don't even know your boss. My God, I don't even really know you. You can rest assured though, I could never . . ."

I could never be involved in such terrible crime, I wanted to say.

But the truth is, I can only hope that I'm right. My hand instinctively moves up to my right temple—it doesn't hurt so much now when I press it, just enough to remind me how little I can trust in what I think I know about myself.

Nonetheless. Some things are inconceivable, no matter what the circumstances.

I look Erik straight in the eyes. "I had nothing to do with the attack in Munich. I swear, on anything you want."

He returns my gaze. Silently. Searchingly. Until his eyes moisten, then he looks away.

"If you had any idea . . . of what it was like. Of the things I saw. A man bled to death right in front of me, and a little farther away, by the tracks—"

He stops, takes a shaky breath. "I couldn't see clearly, the air was full of dust, but between all the rubble, I . . . they didn't even look like dead bodies, just like . . . chunks. Chunks of flesh. That had been living, breathing people not a minute before, picking up their friends from the train, or their parents, or . . ."

Tears are running down his face now, trailing clear lines on the thin layer of dust which still covers his skin.

He doesn't seem to feel the tears; his eyes are fixed on the wall, but I'm sure he's not seeing it, that he's back in the station again, back in the middle of this hell of screams and death and destruction. Back in the place where he will continue to spend a lot of time.

The trembling starts in his hand, which is still clutching the cushion. From there, it spreads, taking hold of his entire body. He tries to say something but doesn't manage; he tries to stand up, but I don't let him; instead I wrap my arms around him, prepared for the fact that he'll resist. He does, but only halfheartedly. He tries to pull away from my embrace, shakes his head, but I hold him tightly.

After a few seconds he gives up and rests his forehead against my shoulder. I hold him, feel the trembling grow stronger, then slowly subside, ebbing away until it's barely noticeable.

I stroke his hair, his wet face; I want to say something but I can't find any words.

He does, after a while, even though it's just one, whispered.

"No."

This time, when he pushes me away, I let him.

"Don't come near me again, Jo. I can't bear the thought that someone who helped these murderers is touching me. Even if it's you. Especially if it's you."

"But I didn't, I—"

"I believe that you're convinced you didn't. But we both know the state your mind is in, and who knows—maybe you suppressed your part in the whole thing just like you've suppressed the part I play in your life."

Everything inside me balks at this theory. It's wrong, it has to be. The images on TV left me devastated; I wouldn't have felt like that if I had been involved in the attack in any way. Or if I'd known about it.

Except . . . What did I really know for sure?

"If you think I'm one of the maniacs that caused this, then report me."

In spite of my inner turmoil, my voice sounds completely calm. "I'm serious. Do it, maybe that will give us some clarity. Tell them about me attacking you with the knife, about the car that pushed you off the road, and about the fact that your boss wanted you to be at the station at that exact moment, tell them whatever you think is relevant. I'll admit to everything I can remember."

He leans over, his head in his hands. When he looks up again, he appears more lost than ever before. "I can't." There's no strength left in his voice. "Do you know what they would do to you, Jo? Not just the police, the media too—do you know how quickly they'd come up with the idea that you used your money to support terrorist organizations and God knows what else?" He clears his throat, coughs, shakes his head again. "You would immediately be the face of the attack. The billionaire terrorist from Australia." When he looks at me again, his expression is softer than before. "If I knew for sure that you were involved, then I wouldn't hesitate for a second. But like this . . . I can't. You're—"

My phone rings, cutting him off midsentence. It's not one of the ringtones I've assigned to the people I know. I glance at the display. Anonymous.

"Don't you want to answer it?"

I shake my head. "There's no way it can be as important as our conversation."

"Ah." The hint of a smile flickers over Erik's face. "If you'd like some privacy I can go out of the room."

At the moment I realize what he's implying, the ringing stops. "You think that it's my accomplices, right? That they want us to get together and drink to our fireworks show?"

"I didn't say that. I just think it's interesting that you—"

Again, the phone rings. Again, it's an anonymous caller. This time I don't hesitate for a second, I pick up and turn on the loudspeaker.

"Yes?" I sound harried, nervous.

All I can hear from the other end at first is loud breathing. Then a tcnsc voicc. "Joanna? Is that Joanna?" A man.

Erik's eyes have widened; he silently mouths a word that I can't make out.

"Yes. Who am I talking to?"

"Are you alone?"

I should say no, that I have lots of friends around me, but my instinct tells me that the man would hang up.

"Yes. Now will you tell me who this is?"

"This is . . . Bernhard. I'm a colleague of Erik's; we met briefly about a week ago."

The visitor with the computer bag. "Yes, I remember. Where did you get my number?"

"It doesn't matter. Just tell me . . . Have you heard from Erik? Do you know if he's OK?"

I look up, see Erik shake his head decisively, and realize there's an enormous opportunity offering itself up here for him.

"No." I try to inject as much despair as I can into my voice. It's surprising how easy it is. "I can't get hold of him, even though I've been trying for hours, again and again."

"So it's true." Bernhard too sounds as though he's struggling to hold back tears. "I didn't want this to happen, please believe me! I didn't know what would happen, not exactly. They lied to me."

"Who? Who lied to you?" There's no way I can let Bernhard end the conversation now.

Silence.

Is he still there? If I scared him off now with my stupid, overly direct question, then I also blew the first real shot at shining a little light into the darkness surrounding us.

But he is still there. A little more composed than before. "That doesn't matter anymore. It's too late for Erik, but not for you, Joanna. You have to disappear, as quickly as you can. Please believe me. This isn't a joke, you have to get yourself to safety."

Cold fear grips my insides, quicker than my mind is able to wrap itself around what he's saying. "But—who wants to hurt me? And why?"

Silence again, I hastily glance over at Eric, who is visibly trying to stay calm. To not give himself away.

"Tell me what's going on!" I can't stop my voice from breaking. "Please."

Bernhard doesn't answer again, but I can hear that the place he's calling from has changed. Street noises, a car horn, and, in the distance, an emergency vehicle going past with its sirens on.

"It's too complicated, I don't have much time. The part you're playing in everything that happened is too big for them to simply leave you in peace." A dull thud, like a car door being slammed shut. "All the information you want is available, and if you stay alive long enough you'll get it too, but for now you just have to believe me. Get yourself to safety, otherwise you'll soon be dead, just like Erik."

32

I can see that Joanna's struggling to keep her composure as she puts the phone aside, her hands trembling. At the same time, I'm trying to take in what I just heard Bernhard say.

"What . . . does he mean by that?"

How the hell am I supposed to know, I think. "You're asking me?"

"He said I play a big part in it. I know how that must sound to you right now, but I have no idea what he was talking about. You have to believe me." Joanna wipes her face with a jittery hand. "I really don't know."

I listen to my gut and realize that my common sense is working again, in spite of this ever more ludicrous situation. Or maybe because of it. Either Bernhard *and* Joanna are in cahoots with Gabor and this phone call was some madcap attempt to convince me of their innocence, or Joanna's really in great danger. I stare at her intently. "Where did Bernhard get your number?"

She shrugs her shoulder and shakes her head in exasperation. "I don't have a clue."

After spending a few moments thinking about what has just happened, I finally nod. "All right. I believe you."

She seems surprised. "You believe me? Why now of all times, just after that phone call? I thought now you'd have even less reason to—"

"If you'd arranged the whole thing, you would have had an explanation for how Bernhard knows your number."

She raises her eyebrows, making wrinkles appear on her forehead. "*That's* why you believe me all of a sudden?"

Yes, I think, *and probably also because I want to believe you. Despite everything.*

"Bernhard said you were in danger," I say, ignoring her question. "So he knows what's behind all this insanity."

"But he also said he didn't exactly know what would happen, and that someone lied to him."

"Yes, and he thinks I'm dead. He knows something, maybe he knew that I was going to be killed, and did nothing to stop it. But either way, I'm about to find out."

I jump to my feet angrily and reach for Joanna's phone. The sudden movement causes waves of pain to surge through my body. I ignore them. Finally there's a small chance of finding out what it is that's turned our life upside down. And I'm not about to let it slip away. Bernhard, that two-faced bastard, he's in for it now. "I'm going to give Bernhard a call. And he's going to tell me what he knows, no matter how long it takes. I'm sure he'll make time when he hears that I'll report him to the police otherwise."

"Don't!" Joanna gasps quickly, making me pause. "He thinks you're dead, remember?"

I give her a grim nod. "Perfect. So he's going to be all the more surprised when he hears my voice."

"No, Erik, don't you understand? Whatever all of this means, if they think you're dead, then they're not going to be looking for you."

"But they will be looking for you. Bernhard just said so loud and clear. That you're in great danger. So what sort of difference does it make if they're just looking for you or for the both of us?"

"I . . . oh, I don't know. I just have this feeling that it's best if he thinks you're dead. We don't know if we can really believe him."

Joanna's right. It could be advantageous if they think I'm dead.

"All right. But Bernhard said you had to get out of here right now. If he was telling the truth, that could mean they might be here any sec—" The phone in my hand begins to vibrate.

Joanna doesn't have the caller saved in her contacts, of course, but I know the number showing on the screen regardless.

"It's Nadine," I say, staring at the sequence of digits. "What does she want? And at this time of night too?"

"Don't answer it," Joanna implores me.

I nod and place the smartphone onto the table, slowly and cautiously, as if Nadine would be able to notice overly hurried movements on her phone even without the connection having been established. I can guess at what's going on inside Joanna's head. "You think Nadine might be in on it too?"

Joanna purses her lips. "I find it strange, at the very least, that she should call now, of all moments. And how does she have my number anyway?"

I shrug resignedly. "If Nadine wanted your number it'd be easy for her to get it. She's probably had it for months."

The phone stops ringing. First Bernhard and now Nadine—it's like they'd arranged it. But whatever, I'm going to take Bernhard's warning seriously. "We have to get out of here."

Joanna nods without hesitation. Her eyes wander through the living room like she was saying her good-bye to this place, a place in which I've spent wonderful times with her, even though in Joanna's mind it was probably just her home and nothing more. Thinking about that is still unsettling for me. More so, probably, than everything else happening around us right now.

I have to know what's behind all of this. Why Gabor sent me to Munich and what he and Bernhard have to do with this explosion. Nadine too, maybe.

In some far corner of my mind, a voice whispers that I still can't be sure Joanna's not in cahoots with Gabor. It's quiet, this voice, but insistent. I don't listen to it.

"You should call Gabor."

"What? Why would I do that?"

"He probably assumes you know about me driving to Munich, and that I was meant to pick someone up from the train station. By now, pretty much everyone will have heard about what happened there. So you would know I was at the station when it blew up. And I'm not home yet, nor am I picking up the phone. Wouldn't it be normal for you, my fiancée, to be calling around frantically if you can't reach me? Especially to my office? But no one's there at this time. So you'd think of something else."

"Yes, I most likely would. In fact I really *was* in that situation when I turned on the TV. I almost went crazy with worry."

When I think of the moment I came back home, of her reaction, her relief—I really want to believe her.

"This Gabor, what kind of person is he?" she asks as she picks up the phone from the table.

"The more helpless you act, the easier you'll have it with him."

"Oh yes, I know the type all right."

I know Gabor's number by heart. I tap it into Joanna's phone. "One more thing—when you talk to him, at least *imagine* we're engaged and that you love me."

She gives me a look I can't decipher. "I'll put it on speaker again, OK?"

"Yes, but hold your phone to your ear all the same when you're talking; that way he won't notice anything on his end."

The phone only rings twice, then he picks up.

"Hello, this is Joanna Berrigan." Joanna's talking very quickly. She really does sound worried, almost hysterical. "You probably don't know me. I'm Erik's fiancée. Erik Thieben. He was meant to go pick someone up for you from Munich central station today. Where that explosion happened. I've been trying to reach him for ages, but he's not picking up his phone. I'm . . . I'm really worried. Have you heard anything from him?"

Several seconds of silence; then Gabor calmly says, "Good evening, Frau Berrigan. That's right, he was meant to pick up two business partners from the station. He hasn't checked in yet. We've already called the police, but they haven't been able to tell us anything yet. But . . ."

There's a pause, then Gabor keeps talking, in a breathy tone. "That doesn't mean something's happened to him."

You goddamn phony, I think, feeling a strong urge to knock the teeth clean out of his mouth.

"He told me he was meant to be at the station just after one. That's exactly the time the explosion happened." Joanna's doing very well indeed. Her despair sounds convincing.

"Yes, that's right, but it doesn't necessarily mean anything. The police said not all of the wounded had been accounted for yet. That also goes for those with minor injuries, who were sent to the hospital for observation. It could take until tomorrow, they said. And it's also possible that he suffered a shock, if he really was close by when the explosion took place. I know it must be difficult for you right now, but all we can do is wait."

"Wait? But how can I just sit around and do nothing, I—"

"Are you at home, Frau Berrigan?"

I violently shake my head and wave my hand to indicate no.

"No, I . . . I couldn't stand being at home anymore, I went to see a friend."

Very good. That buys us some time.

"That was a good idea. Whereabouts? Is it nearby?"

Joanna gives me a questioning look, but before I can react, she says, "You have my number on your screen, please call me if you hear anything. I'll contact you again tomorrow morning." With that, she hangs up, takes a deep breath, and puts the phone aside.

"That was very well done," I say. "It sounded real."

The look she gives me is defiant. "All I needed to do was remember this afternoon. It *was* real."

33

Pull down the blinds, draw the curtains, turn off the main lights. From outside it needs to look like nobody's home. Ideally, I would go around and knock on all the doors in the neighborhood, to check whether anyone has seen Erik, but that would probably be overdoing it a little.

There are other things I can do, though: like call the hotline for next of kin, and beg the woman at the other end to tell me whether my fiancé has turned up anywhere. Yes, I'm sure that he was there at the time of the attack. No, I haven't heard anything from him yet, nothing at all. Yes, of course I'll leave my name, address, and telephone number.

"Please call me as soon as you know anything, it doesn't matter how late it is," I say in a choked whisper before hanging up.

Erik looks at me thoughtfully. "I had no idea how convincing a liar you can be. It's astonishing. And scary, to be honest."

I open my mouth to respond, but then decide to stay silent after all. My day wasn't as horrific as his, but it was still terrible. Right now my nerves are so raw that I could come out with any conceivable form of emotional outburst: hysterical laughter, or fits of tears. Or an attack of rage.

I don't dare to even try to explain it. It's better to stay quiet.

My next call is to one of the biggest hospitals in Munich, where I get through to someone on the switchboard after the third attempt and give another acoustic breakdown performance. This woman, too, notes down my details.

The more frequently our names turn up on the lists of the missing and those searching for them, the better. If Gabor were to report Erik missing, then he might find out that Erik's fiancée already called. Multiple times. Everywhere. Right now, an open display of worry is the best disguise.

The next hospital. And then the next. At some point Erik stands up, gets a bottle of wine from the kitchen, and opens it. He hands me a half-filled glass, but I wave my hand to reject it. I need a clear head; it's already after midnight. The fact that I'm ignoring my exhaustion doesn't mean it's not there.

So Erik drinks alone, lost in his thoughts as I call hospital number four and am kept waiting in the phone queue for ages. When someone finally picks up, I have to make a considerable effort to sound desperate instead of irritated.

By the time I finish the call, Erik has closed his eyes and leaned his head back. The glass in his hand is empty, as is the second, intended for me.

"You know what I find interesting?" he says, without looking up.

"What?"

"It's possible to interpret your sudden flurry of activity in two different ways. That you're trying to fake my death in order to protect me. Or—"

"Or?" My voice sounds irritated. *Pull yourself together,* I order myself silently.

"Or you're getting everything ready for my actual death. If you wanted to kill me, you'd never get such a great opportunity as this again. No one officially knows whether I'm still alive or not, so if I don't turn up again, the police won't make any effort in their investigations." He opens his eyes again and leans forward, to grab the bottle of wine and pour what little remains of it into his glass.

"They won't find my body at the station, that's the only flaw. But then again I could have been right next to the bomb and pulverized. Right?"

For a few seconds I just stare at him, lost for words. If it wasn't for the episode with the knife, I would have every reason to be outraged. But . . . his train of thought wasn't illogical. It's clear I'll never be able to convince Erik that he's wrong.

I get up from the couch, go into the kitchen, and pick up the tapas cookbook from the shelf. Toward the back of it, there's an envelope clipped between the pages. I pull it out and take it into the living room, where I throw it on the coffee table.

"There. There's twenty thousand euros in it; that should keep you going for a while without having to worry about bills. If you really think I want to kill you, then take it and go to the airport, get on the first plane out of Germany, and hide somewhere."

Erik barely glances at the envelope, his eyes have narrowed. "You think I'll take your money?"

"It's not about money, it's about you being able to feel safe. Money isn't the solution here, interestingly enough it never is, but it helps."

I can see the gears turning in his head, contemplating whether my suggestion can in any way be linked to the theory that I'm in league with Gabor.

"There's no way I'm going," he says eventually. "Bernhard said you're in danger; you really think I could just take off?"

I pick up the envelope and put it back into the book. "It depends on whether you trust me. Despite what happened with the knife, which I'm still unable to explain. Really. And for that reason, I can't promise you that it won't happen again, but I swear to you that I don't want to hurt you. Not in my conscious mind."

Erik rubs both his hands over his face. He's pale, says nothing, and just nods.

I can't let myself forget what he's been through. Not just today, but in the past few days as well, when he looked after me almost around the clock. It's only fair I take charge of things now.

And apart from that it feels good—it fits with the version of Joanna I've always considered myself to be.

"You sleep upstairs, in the bedroom, you can lock the door there. I'll take my things and make up a bed on the couch."

He halfheartedly tries to protest, but I wave my hand dismissively. "It's the only sensible solution. That way nothing can happen."

He's not convinced, but his tiredness wins. "Don't open the door to anybody, Jo, OK? And if you hear any noise outside, come upstairs right away."

I promise him. I grab my things and get set up on the couch, trying to beat back the uneasy feeling that's creeping up inside me.

What if Gabor didn't believe that I'm spending the night at a friend's place? What if he sends someone by here to check?

Sleep eludes me. Every sound in the house makes me nervous. I listen for steps outside, for cars passing by—are they slowing down or is it just my imagination?—and even to my own pulse.

It's past two o'clock in the morning when I finally give up and turn on the television. I keep the volume so low that even I can barely hear it.

There are still special reports about the attack on Munich station, and now the government is speaking up. Security services are on high alert, is the general gist of it, so the population don't need to be afraid of any follow-up attacks. The only different opinion is that of the chairman of a right-wing populist party, who claims to have seen this coming for a long time and says that Germany is already at war. In between, there are live reports from the station and the same material from this afternoon. It will probably go on like this for the whole night. By now I've looked at the images so often that they're almost familiar. So familiar, that despite the horror in them, I manage to doze off.

It feels like I haven't slept any more than three or four hours, but when I open my eyes it's almost ten o'clock. The television is still on, showing new images of the destruction; this time the large station hall can be seen from the inside. I stare at the images for a few minutes, only now realizing what Erik must have gone through. And all of a sudden I realize what we have to do next.

We can't just bury our heads in the sand. Erik is convinced that Gabor at least knew about the attack, even if he wasn't involved in it. Bernhard's call was practically an admission of conspiracy.

We can't keep all that from the police.

Or *I* can't, to be precise. Because Erik has to stay dead. Until we're somewhere safe.

A few minutes later I knock on his door. I feel my heartbeat quicken as it stays silent on the other side. Could something terrible have happened up here while I was asleep downstairs?

I knock again. Harder. Louder.

"I'm awake." His croaky voice says otherwise.

"I'm sorry I woke you, but we have to discuss what we're going to do next. I'll make us some coffee, OK?"

A quarter of an hour later we're sitting in the kitchen, each of us with a steaming mug in front of us. I've turned off the television; who knows what the sight of the images might provoke in Erik. I need his complete attention and concentration now.

"We have to inform the police." He opens his mouth to interrupt me, but then stops as I shake my head. "We can't get to the bottom of this by ourselves, and if we just sit around and wait, it could cost us our lives. I don't think Gabor will wait too long before attempting to get rid of us again. Or to get rid of me, to be more precise."

Erik stirs his coffee; for a few seconds the clink of the spoon against the inside of the cup is the only sound I hear. Apart from a car engine outside. A diesel engine, idling. Not driving past.

In my mind I picture men in black sunglasses taking photos of the house; maybe one of them will get out and try to peer in through the blinds . . . Everything inside me wants to get up and quickly look outside, but that would be the stupidest, the worst thing I could do . . .

I've barely finished the thought by the time the driver of the car steps on the gas. The sound of the engine becomes quieter, before disappearing completely.

Erik still hasn't said a word.

"I'll speak to the police, given the circumstances." The certainty of my voice surprises even me. "But it would be very helpful if you could give me all the details again. Every moment of doubt you had about Gabor and his people."

I've made notes for my phone call to the station so I don't forget anything. I'm guessing that the conversation will be recorded, so I have to sound convincing, particularly in terms of being worried about Erik.

"My fiancé was at Munich station yesterday at lunchtime," I sob, when I finally get someone on the phone. "He hasn't been in touch since, I can't reach him, and no one knows what happened to him. . . ."

The officer tries to calm me down, and I let him. After a few moments, I continue with a softer, more composed voice. "It was so strange yesterday. You know—I think Erik suspected that something wasn't right. There were a few attempts on his life in the past few days. And looking at it in hindsight, it seems to me like his company could be involved in the attack. I also got this very strange call from one of his coworkers yesterday. He warned me, you know."

"Really?" The officer is now listening attentively, but with caution as well. He probably gets ten people an hour calling him with some conspiracy theory. "Would you come to the station and go on record about your suspicions?"

I was afraid of that. "No. I'm sorry, I don't want to leave the house right now. I don't know if I'll reach you alive."

"Fine. Then we'll send someone over to you. This afternoon around two; please make sure you're available, on the phone as well."

I give him the address and hang up.

The three hours until the scheduled arrival of the police feel like three days. Just before twelve, Ela calls, distraught, wanting to know if Erik has turned up yet, saying that she can't find him on any of the lists—neither the survivors list nor the casualty list.

It hurts to have to lie to her, but if I want to keep Erik's cover intact, there's no other way. "No. No sign of him." I whisper into the phone. "I don't know what to do."

"I'll come by."

"No." That was a little too quick. "Please don't. I didn't get a moment's sleep the whole night and I just took a sleeping tablet. Maybe tomorrow, hopefully by then . . ." I didn't finish the sentence, but Ela understands.

"Oh God, yes. Hopefully." I can hear her hesitating, like she wants to say something else but doesn't really know what. "You sound almost like you used to before. Like you care about Erik. So do you? Are you remembering?"

He is sitting opposite me, and looks up when he realizes I'm staring at him. Tries to smile.

"No," I say. "Not even a little. But I'm still so terribly worried about him. And no, I don't understand it either."

We promise that we'll contact each other right away if we find out anything about Erik, then Ela hangs up.

When the doorbell rings shortly after two, it almost takes superhuman effort for me to open the door. The two men I can see through the spy hole could just as easily be Gabor's people. Dark pants, dark jacket. Only when one of them holds up their ID do I open the door.

We sit down in the living room. I wanted Erik to wait upstairs until the policemen are gone, but he insists on hearing as much of the conversation as possible. So he's sitting in the pantry, and I hope there's nothing in there that makes him sneeze.

I've prepared myself for this. Among other things by covering the remainder of the bruise on my forehead with concealer. I don't want the police to ask the wrong questions.

But they barely ask anything anyway; instead they let me speak, and I tell them everything. About the boiler which almost cost us our lives, about the car accident that pushed Erik off the road. "There are police reports and hospital files on both of these incidents, which I'm sure you'll be able to take a look at. The day before yesterday, Erik said that he suspected Gabor Energy Engineering were behind all of it. But he didn't think anything of it when they asked him to pick up some business partners from Munich station on Monday. His boss specifically told him that he had to be there at ten minutes past one, and not be late."

I look at first one, then at the other policeman, seeing their faces blur before my eyes. Tears, at exactly the right moment. "And it seems he was there on time."

The policeman sitting opposite me and to my left has been making notes the whole time. Now he lays his pen aside. "If all of this is the case, Frau . . ." He glances at his notepad. "Frau Berrigan, why didn't you report the suspicion previously? Why didn't Herr Thieben?"

"We didn't have any proof." I wipe the back of my hand across my face, taking care not to touch the part with the concealer. "Do you think Erik would have been able to keep his job after that? And besides, we didn't know whether we were right, it all seemed so implausible. And there wasn't even any reason for Gabor wanting to get rid of Erik."

The two policemen exchange a quick glance.

"You said on the phone that one of Erik's coworkers called you yesterday and warned you?"

"Yes." I pick up my phone from the coffee table and open the caller list. Hopefully the officials will also see my forty-seven unsuccessful attempts to reach Erik; that can't hurt.

"This call here at half past twelve, that was Bernhard Morbach, a close colleague of Erik's. He's never called me before, so I have no idea where he got my number from. He seemed to want to apologize more than anything. He said that he hadn't known exactly what was going to happen, that he should have warned Erik, and that he was sorry. And then he said that I should disappear, hide as quickly as possible. Otherwise I would soon be dead too."

Another quick exchange of glances between the two. The one on the right makes a note. "Thank you, Frau Berrigan, this information could prove to be very helpful. It would probably be a good idea if we take you to a safe place until we've checked the details of your statement. We don't want anything to happen to you. Would you agree to that?"

I hesitate, then shake my head. "For now, I'd rather stay here. In case Erik turns up again."

The man shrugs regretfully. "We'd like to station someone here to protect you, but right now we need everybody we've got. So it's best if you don't open the door to anyone and call the police if anything strange happens. Maybe you have some friends who could stay with you for a few days?" I don't answer and just shrug instead.

"OK then. If you change your mind . . ." He presses a card into my hand; I take it with a grateful smile.

No place the police could offer me would be as safe as the one I'm going to get us to.

Just another day, then everything will be over.

34

I exit the pantry. At last. I felt like a criminal, hiding in there.

The fact that Joanna knowingly lied to the police officers is arousing a feeling of discomfort inside me. After all, these men are some of the people we're hoping will help us. But she's right, it had to be done.

Roughly another minute passes before she calls from the hall. "You can come out now, their car is leaving." She stops in the passage through to the kitchen when she sees me sitting at the table.

"You did that really well," I say.

She sits down opposite to me. "What else—"

The doorbell. Again. I shoot her a querying look, and she does the same to me.

"The police," Joanna guesses and gets up.

I follow suit. "Yes, maybe they forgot something. Sneak over to the door and take a look. But don't open it if it's somebody else."

She nods at me. I see the fear in her eyes. Can she see it in mine too? She sneaks into the hall and I position myself by the door to the storeroom, ready to vanish into it again.

Nothing happens for quite a while, then Joanna says something. So the policeman really did come back. I pull the storeroom door shut behind me until only a small strip of light falls through.

Joanna's voice again; I can't understand what she's saying. I hear it again, more muffled . . . no, that's not Joanna. It's coming from outside. Another woman. She keeps talking, quickly and excitedly. I think I hear my name, and suddenly I can understand everything that's being said.

Joanna has let the woman come into the house.

Then I recognize the voice. Nadine. I clench my teeth so hard it hurts my jaw. This simply can't be happening. Nadine, of all people. What if Gabor sent her? Ever since her performance here the other day, I wouldn't put anything past her. I hear the front door being pushed shut.

"Thanks for letting me in," I hear Nadine say. "Despite the stupid way I acted a few days ago."

"If you really wanted to talk to me, you could've just called." The way Joanna's talking to Nadine leaves no doubt about the fact that she's not particularly thrilled by her showing up here.

"I did, but you wouldn't pick up. That's why . . . I just need to know about Erik. Also, I—" She pauses. Formulates a new sentence. "I've been here for a while. The two men arrived almost at the exact same time as I did. I hid and waited until they'd left again. So that's how I knew you were home. Who were they?" Nadine's voice still sounds agitated.

"Why do you want to know?"

"Because I . . . was it someone from my work?"

There's a brief pause. Joanna's thoughts are probably racing right now, just as much as mine are. What's Nadine up to? And—if she knows where Joanna is, does Gabor know as well?

"No, it wasn't anyone from work. Come on."

The sound of footsteps moving away, then immediately coming closer from the other side. They're in the living room.

"Have a seat."

"Thanks. So who were those men, then?"

Another pause. Then Joanna's voice. "That's none of your business. I've got other things to worry about right now; I don't have time to play games. So, will you please stop asking me questions and tell me why you're here?"

Careful, Joanna. Don't be so abrupt. You're sick with worry about me, remember? Nadine isn't stupid.

There's silence for a while, followed by the sound of someone forcefully blowing their nose. Then Nadine's voice again. It's tearful now, interspersed with sobs.

"I think it's terrible that we still don't know about Erik. And I rented the car he took to Munich, too."

More sobbing. Joanna cuts in after a few moments.

"Does anyone know what happened to the people Erik was meant to pick up?"

"I don't know anything. Lately everything's changed at work." Nadine slowly seems to be getting ahold of herself again. "Erik told me about a new project that I didn't know about. That's never happened before. I've . . . I've always been in charge of project administration, and now all of a sudden there's a project I don't know a thing about? I talked about it to Herr Geiger, that's my boss. Erik's boss as well. His reaction was very strange. He said he didn't know anything about a project, but he was lying; I noticed right away."

"How so?"

"He started making phone calls the minute I left his office. I can see it on my phone display. I stood next to the door and eavesdropped. Although I couldn't understand much, Geiger was speaking very quietly. But my name was mentioned, and so was the word *Phoenix,* two times, even."

Phoenix. There it is again, the name of that ominous project. I have to force myself to stay quiet, to not throw open the door and run into the living room.

"Phoenix," Joanna says as Nadine pauses. "I've not heard anything about it. What is it?"

Very good, Joanna.

"I don't know. Erik mentioned it to me when he asked me about the project. And, I got a call this morning from Bernhard Morbach. You know him, right? He was all nervous, like he was in a real rush. He wanted me to come meet him, outside the office at that, and I was supposed to bring him a USB flash drive that was taped underneath his desk. I didn't want to at first because the whole thing seemed weird, but then he said it was a matter of life and death, so I agreed to do it."

She pauses.

"And then?" Joanna's tone is more gentle than before.

"We met at the edge of the parking area. Bernhard looked awful. Pale, unkempt, just not like himself. And the way he was looking at me. He had this crazed expression, somehow. He said that Erik . . ." Sobbing, again. "He said he thought Erik was dead. And that they were after him."

"They?" Joanna asks, when Nadine doesn't continue.

"I don't know who." Nadine is almost wailing now. "Probably those Islamists."

"Islamists?" Joanna repeats loudly.

"Yes, the ones who blew up the train station. There's that video, you know, where they declare it was them. Didn't you see? It was on the radio and in the papers this morning. Probably on TV too."

A video claiming responsibility. This is getting more convoluted by the second. What does Gabor have to do with Islamists? Gabor, of all people, a man who practically refuses to get into a cab if there's a foreign person driving it. How the hell does all of this fit together?

I have to see this video.

"No, I . . . I haven't turned the TV on today," Joanna explains.

"Bernhard's involved in the whole thing from the looks of it. He said he didn't know how far they'd go. And that I was in danger as well, since I asked about the project and they believe Erik must have told me something."

"But what's he meant to have told you?"

"I don't know." Nadine's voice sounds composed all of a sudden. "I thought maybe he'd talked to you about it."

"No, he didn't. I'm afraid I really can't help you, Nadine."

"Are you sure?" I'm familiar with this habit of Nadine's, of persistent questioning. She's not going to let it go easily now. "The attack, it was Islamists who did it. Our lives mean nothing to them. So please, you *have* to tell me what you know. Everything."

Joanna sighs. "There's nothing to tell. All I can tell you is that Bernhard called me yesterday evening as well. And he told me something similar." There's a pause. "Recently, things haven't been easy for Erik and me. I was all over the place for a while, as I'm sure you know. We hadn't discussed his job in weeks; there were other things we had to talk about. More important things. Our relationship was on the line, we didn't really have time to chat about work projects or things like that."

Joanna's really good at this. Maybe Nadine is telling the truth and she really is scared, but it could just as well be the case that she's in cahoots with them. That Gabor sent her to find out if Joanna knows anything. I'm more inclined to assume the latter, and Joanna obviously sees it the same way as me.

"Would you leave then, please? I think we've talked over everything, and I'd like to be by myself now."

"But . . ." I can picture Nadine's expression, searching for a reason to stay. "I mean, we're in the same boat here. We're both worried about Erik."

"You're wrong about that," Joanna responds coolly. "We're not at all in the same boat."

"I was hoping maybe I could—"

"No. Leave now. Please."

I'm out of the pantry as soon as the front door clicks shut, and in the living room with a few swift steps. I turn on the TV, zap through the channels. Series, soaps, but also special broadcasts about the attack. The video is mentioned but never shown.

"You think she's telling the truth?" Joanna asks from behind me. I turn to face her.

"I don't know. I'm trying to find that video. Islamists and Gabor. I can't get my mind around anything anymore. He doesn't just hate them, he despises them, with all of his heart. If he's really in league with them, he must have made a tidy sum out of it."

Joanna nods. "Anyone can be bought. It's just a matter of price. If there's one thing I learned from my dad, that's it." She indicates toward the door with her chin. "Hang on, I'll get my laptop, we'll definitely be able to find the video online."

We sit next to each other on the sofa when she gets back. I watch Joanna navigating through Web pages. "I don't trust Nadine. I wouldn't be surprised if Gabor sent her."

Joanna's found the video on a news platform in the meantime. She glances over at me and clicks on the play button.

Symbols in Arabic appear onscreen, red against a black background. Flames around the edges. The image becomes indistinct; then a figure can be made out, all in black and hooded but for a narrow eye slit. A black flag is wafting away in the background. The man starts talking, and I can't believe my ears—his German is flawless, with no trace of an accent.

He's talking about a great deed for defending his Arab brothers and freeing sacred sites. And about an act of revenge.

"You supported the American butchers when they came for us. By doing so, you played a part in killing our families. You bombed our cities, brought fear and misery upon us. You thought you were safe, so far away from all the misery and death. But not anymore. Now you too will know fear. You too will witness the death of your wives and children. Fear will be at your side no matter where you may be. Because now your cities will burn too; your train stations and airports will explode. And you will not be able to do a thing about it, for my brothers will overrun your land. We will bring you the one true faith. Believe, or you will die."

More phrases follow, but I only catch snippets of them. My thoughts are spinning at a greater and greater speed, and I try to comprehend how it can be possible for Gabor to support everything I've just heard.

Ever since the thought that he might be involved in the whole thing first came to my mind, my anger at him has grown and grown. If I think about what he did to me, did to *us* over the past days, that he tried to kill us several times . . .

But if he's really in league with these guys, there can only be one explanation. Money and power, lots of it. I don't know if I've ever felt anywhere near as much contempt for a person in my life as I'm feeling for Gabor right now.

The video has finished. Joanna slumps back against the couch, stunned. "This can't be happening."

"It is. And Gabor's a part of it. But what I'm finding increasingly difficult to understand is why he wants to kill us? How exactly are we involved in all this sick, fucked-up bullshit? It just doesn't make any sense."

We're both silent for a while, each of us immersed in their own thoughts. Then, Joanna leans forward, flips her laptop shut, and turns to face me.

"There's something I understand even less. Why can't I remember you?"

35

It's already past two in the morning in Melbourne, but I can't worry about that now. I let the telephone ring, on and on, relentlessly. Until, finally, there's a crackle and I hear my father's sleepy voice.

"Jo? Is that you?"

I could cry with relief, but at the same time it makes me feel embarrassed. Soon I'll be slipping back into the old behavioral patterns which have shaped my whole life until now. When things get tough—just call Daddy. I was so intent on moving past that. But right now, the thing I want most is to survive.

"I'm coming home, Dad. Please can you have me picked up as quickly as possible."

"What?" I can hear that he's wide awake now. "Jo, my darling, finally. That's wonderful, of course we'll have you picked up. I'll send Gavin first thing tomorrow. . . ."

"Not tomorrow. Right now." Even I realize that I sound like him. The same commanding tone. A little too late, I add a "please," but it's one that doesn't sound very patient.

"What happened?" My father isn't stupid; it was obvious that he'd ask this question. I hesitate briefly, then decide to tell him a half truth. I know him. As soon as he has even the tiniest inkling that his precious daughter might be harmed in any way, he won't hesitate for a single second.

"I guess you heard about the attack at the train station in Munich? All hell's broken loose here, everyone's afraid that it was just the beginning."

That's not enough to explain why I'm suddenly in such a hurry—but there's no way I'm explaining the real circumstances on the phone. "And this morning I noticed some suspicious movement around my house. Maybe it's just a coincidence, but . . . either way. I want to get out of this country as quickly as I can. Right now, ideally."

For a few seconds Dad remains silent, but then I hear something creak, followed by the sound of his footsteps and a door being closed.

"Yes, of course. Munich. We all heard about it. OK, listen. Gavin will set off within the next two hours, maximum, and he'll take a security team. Get ready; I'll let you know when you'll be picked up."

"OK." That's the quickest it can be, I know that—but still I'm afraid that by the time the plane arrives, it could be too late. The flight will last at least twenty-two hours; it will need to make a stop, probably in Dubai. Suddenly it seems an unbearably long time. Like it was impossible that we could make it through another day unharmed.

We.

"Dad? I'm bringing someone with me, you should know that."

He takes a deep breath. "This guy you spoke of recently?"

"Yes. Erik."

A brief pause. "I'm not OK with that."

If I show even the slightest sign of weakness now, I've lost. I know my father—he only takes people seriously if they stand up to him, if they don't let him influence them. So I put all the decisiveness I can muster into my voice.

"He's coming with me. If you can't accept that, you don't need to send the plane."

Dad clears his throat. "What about you and Matthew?"

"There is no me and Matthew, not anymore." I had found the right tone now, the one that doesn't allow any discussion. "Matthew is in the past, and I'm sure he won't be heartbroken over it." As if that were my father's concern on the matter.

He remains silent for a few seconds. I prepare myself for a counterattack, but he surprises me.

"You really care about this Erik?"

"Yes." I pay attention to my body's gut reaction to my response, and realize I've told the truth. I close my eyes before I continue, without knowing whether what I'm about to say is really true. "We're engaged."

I hear Dad exhale sharply. There are a good ten thousand miles between us, but I can still picture his reaction as clear as day in front of me. His eyebrows suddenly furrowing, his lower lip tensing over his teeth.

"You make a decision like that without discussing it with me first?"

I can't let myself be intimidated by his tone, now dangerously soft. "Yes. Because it's a personal decision."

"Personal. Well, well."

"Very much so." I'm fully aware of the fact that this conversation will be continued as soon as we're in Australia, that it's going to be unpleasant, and that Dad will use every weapon at his disposal to talk me out of my decision of marrying a nobody.

But by then it won't matter; we'll be safe, far away from Gabor and his henchmen.

"Fine." I can tell how much Dad is struggling to stay in control of himself. "I'm very intrigued to meet this Erik. OK then, you'll find out tomorrow at what time the plane will land, and Gavin will pick you up from the house in a limousine. Is that all clear?"

"Yes. Thank you, Daddy."

I hang up and go back into the living room, where Erik is sitting on the couch and rotating his coffee cup between his hands. I don't know how much of the telephone call he overheard.

I sit down next to him. I wait for him to look at me, but he doesn't, and only turns his head toward me once I start to speak.

"Tomorrow," I say. "My father is sending a plane, with a bit of luck it will be here within the next twenty-four hours. Then we'll have made it. You'll be able to safely make contact with the police once we're in Australia; I'm sure Gabor's arms don't reach that far." I smile at Erik, but his expression remains unchanged. "And even if they do," I continue, "I'm quite sure that his contacts are nothing compared to my family's."

"Great." He shakes his head. "I never wanted to go to Australia, you don't remember that anymore now of course, but we had this conversation a few times. You agreed with me then; you said on more than one occasion that your family would destroy our relationship within a few weeks. And now we don't even have a proper relationship anymore. What do you think our chances are of building it up again over there?"

I try to say something, but he stops me with another shake of his head. "I know that it's for the best in our situation. I'm not stupid. But I'll lose you there, once and for all."

I want to respond, to say something, but I can't find the right words. My feelings for him aren't even half a week old yet; his for me, on the other hand, date back almost a year. If everything that he says is true. Some moments I still have my doubts, but this isn't one of them.

As though my silence was proof of the fact that his fears are justified, Erik turns away again. "You mentioned Matthew earlier."

"Yes. I told Dad that it's over between us."

"But you do remember him?"

So that's it. Erik is upset by the fact that, for some incomprehensible reason, he's the only person my memory has suppressed. The fact that everyone else got to keep their place in my head.

I would give so much to know the reason why. The trigger. *A very stressful event, some trauma that is connected to the thing or person in question.*

See, I can even remember Dr. Schattauer's explanation word for word. Except that I can no longer imagine Erik being violent. On the other hand, unfortunately I now know that a violent Joanna does exist, one which was previously unknown to me.

"Yes, I remember Matthew," I say softly. "But not fondly."

The mood remains tense for the rest of the day. Erik is silently brooding, watching the terrorist video over and over on the laptop. Whenever I refer to the fact that this time tomorrow we'll probably be sitting on the plane and have left all this madness behind us, he only responds with a tired smile.

Maybe it's because my words sound halfhearted; most of my attention is focused on the noises coming from the street outside. Every time a car slows down near the house, my heartbeat quickens. At some point I hear male voices outside, and it's only when I start to feel dizzy that I realize I'm holding my breath. By then the men are long gone and can no longer be heard.

The closer evening comes, the more Erik becomes withdrawn. I gradually realize why: his life is falling apart. Not only am I no longer an anchor in his world, but he's also about to lose his job and his home, as well as be haunted by the scenes from yesterday.

It's dark in the living room, and despite the approaching dusk I haven't turned on any of the lights. I sit down on the couch and put my arm around Erik. I feel his muscles tense. He shakes his head, pushes me away from him. "Don't."

I try not to let show that his rejection, against all logic, hurts me. "It will be better in Melbourne than you think," I whisper. "We don't have to live on my family's land, there are other possibilities. And besides—"

The ringing of my phone interrupts me. A number that seems vaguely familiar, it's not Nadine's, it's—

"Gabor." Erik has reached for the phone; the light of the screen illuminates his face and makes him seem even paler.

I hold out my hand. Erik briefly hesitates, then places the phone into it. Nods to me.

"Frau Berrigan!" Gabor sounds as though he's incredibly relieved to hear my voice. "How are you?"

"I'm . . . not so good," I stammer, turning on the loudspeaker of the phone.

"I'm very sorry to hear that. Then I guess there hasn't been any sign of life from Erik?"

"No." It probably says a lot about my state of mind that I now tend to start crying any time I'm not consciously holding back the tears. "What about you?" I sob. "Have you heard anything?"

"Unfortunately not. But we still can't give up hope." He clears his throat. "Listen, Frau Berrigan, did the police come to see you too?"

I exchange a quick glance with Erik. Should I lie? Or tell the truth? If Gabor is having the house watched, then he'll know that I'm here and have had two visitors today.

Erik shakes his head gently.

"No," I whisper. "I'm not at the house, after all. But I did speak to an officer over the phone, because I wanted to know if there was any news."

"I understand." Gabor sounds thoughtful. "Where are you then, Frau Berrigan? Is someone looking after you?"

"I'm with friends," I say, a little too quickly perhaps. But using the plural is good. "They're taking great care of me; I have everything I need."

"That's very reassuring to hear." Gabor's voice has sunk an octave.

"But you should be prepared for the police getting in touch again. I had a visit from some officers this afternoon, because someone came up with the absurd theory that my company might be involved in the attack." He laughed briefly. "I'd love to know where they got that idea from; I think I could make it abundantly clear to them that it's complete nonsense. It's shocking how far some people will go to hurt others."

I don't say anything, I fear my voice might betray me. . . . Does he know? Or suspect it, at least? Is he indirectly asking me if I was the one who tipped off the police?

"In any case, you should know they'll be wanting to speak to you too. After all, Erik did . . . I mean, he *does* work for me."

He corrected himself hastily, but his slip of the tongue doesn't escape me, and it's by far the best thing about this conversation. For Gabor, Erik is a thing of the past, he believes he's dead.

"Yes," I say. "Thank you."

"If you need anything, please contact me at any time. Will you promise me that? I'd really like to help you; after all, I'm the reason why Erik was in Munich . . ." He sighs. "Believe me, I'm struggling a great deal with that."

I see Erik's jaw muscles clench. "I can imagine," I reply. "Thank you again, I really appreciate your offer."

Erik springs to his feet soon as I've ended the call. "That asshole! The way he's always trying to find out where you are!" He turns around to me. "We have to be careful, Jo. He definitely thinks it's possible that you set the police onto him, and then he'd also have to assume that you know more than is good for him. Maybe he doesn't believe that you're staying with friends. He might send someone by to check."

I find myself holding my breath again. I listen for sounds from outside, but everything is quiet. "What should I do?"

36

How often have I asked myself that very question these past few days? What should I do? What *can* I do? Although, until now, it had mostly been about Joanna not remembering me. Now it was about our survival.

Our. In the past, I'd never been truly conscious of how far-reaching the consequences of this one single word could be. It's only now, where the *our* I'd taken for granted had suddenly broken up into a *she* and an *I*, that I recognize its true meaning. How fundamental it is, that feeling of being loved.

"Maybe we should hide somewhere in the house for the night. Who knows what Gabor might be planning."

Joanna brushes a strand of hair back from her forehead. "You really think he'd send someone over here?"

"I don't know, Jo. I couldn't even hazard a guess anymore at what he's going to do or what he's capable of. The fact is, we have to hold out until tomorrow evening. Until then, we should try to avoid taking risks wherever possible."

"But if he'd go that far, wouldn't he have—" The doorbell rings, stopping Joanna midsentence. We look at each other, as if each of us thought the other must know who it is. Joanna is about to turn away, but I put my hand on her arm.

"Wait," I say, quietly. "Don't go to the door, I'm going upstairs to see who it is."

I sneak through the hall and up the stairs, carefully but swiftly, taking two steps at a time. As I go reach the window in the bathroom, the bell rings again. I tentatively open the curtain a tiny bit, just enough so I can peer down through the gap.

Two men wearing jeans and short jackets are standing outside the front door. I don't know either of them, I'm certain of that.

"Who is it?" Joanna whispers from behind me.

"No idea. Maybe it's those policemen again? Could you take a look and see if you recognize them?"

She comes over to the window, takes a look outside, and shakes her head. "No. I've never seen them before."

"They could be Gabor's men. Nadine must have blabbed, and now they want to check if you're still at home."

"And what are they going to do if I don't open up?"

I look down again, just in time to glimpse the two men disappearing around the corner. "They're leaving."

"Thank goodness." Joanna slumps down on top of the closed toilet lid. I turn to face her. "But that doesn't mean they're really gone. Maybe they'll be back again later, and maybe this time they won't settle for just ringing the doorbell. We should definitely hide."

Joanna looks around the bathroom as though searching for a suitable hideout. "Where, though? If someone does break in, won't they search the entire house for us . . . for *me*? Not to mention . . ." She looks at me candidly. I can guess what she's about to say. "Aren't you scared I might try to harm you again?"

Should I be? I want to ask her in return, but I realize her answer would remain the same: she'd never knowingly try to hurt me, but she can't vouch for any of her actions at the minute.

"I just said we should try to avoid risks wherever possible," I tell her instead. "So this is something that can't be helped."

Joanna doesn't reply. But what could she really answer to that, anyway? She wanted to kill me the other night, and neither she nor I know if, or when, she'll try again.

I can tell that I'm in for a sleepless night.

"OK then, let's head back downstairs and think about where we'll spend the next hours."

The pantry, in contrast to the basement, is warm and dry, and it's proved successful as a hiding place so far. Of course, someone searching for Joanna would take a look in there as well, but if things were moved around a little, it could still work.

I open the door to the narrow, long room and switch on the light. As I look at the tall freezer standing at the back, an idea comes to mind.

"Do you want us to hide in there?" Joanna asks from behind me. "That's the first place they'd look."

"Yes, but if we turn the freezer around so the front is facing the entrance and put one of the shelving units beside it, we can section off a small part of the room. It's probably not going to be very comfortable, but I think if anyone looks in from the door, they wouldn't notice that the room goes on a bit farther behind the freezer and the shelves."

Joanna takes a look around the rear part of the room. "That could work."

"All right. Let's move the stuff."

It takes us about ten minutes to move and position the freezer and the shelving unit to create a space behind it, roughly five feet in length to the back wall. The room is about six and a half feet in width, now all blocked by the shelf and freezer apart from a narrow gap of less than an inch. We stack supplies and boxes onto the shelves to leave as few gaps as possible, then leave things a little askew. Squeezing through the gap on the side is just about manageable. I ask Joanna to give it a try. Then, together, we pull the shelving unit straight again. Once we're done, I turn off the light and go to stand by the entrance to the room.

Perfect. You'd think the freezer and the shelf were backed up right against the rear wall in the storeroom. It was unnoticeable that, beyond it, the room goes on a bit farther.

"It's better than I'd expected. And if we put a few blankets on the floor, it might even be halfway comfortable."

"I hope all of this won't turn out just to be a pointless exercise," Joanna says from behind the shelving.

Shortly after midnight, we're huddled up inside our hideout on top of some wool blankets. At first I was planning to bring some sort of weapon, but then I discarded the idea. I have to share this narrow space with Joanna after all, and there are times when it's better not to tempt fate.

I've left the door to the storeroom wide open, so as not to create any sort of impression that there might be a hiding place here. We're plunged into total darkness. The blinds on the kitchen and living room windows are fully closed, so not even a glimmer of light can get through, making the storeroom all the more dark.

Although we're both totally exhausted, neither of us even contemplates going to sleep in the first hour. We don't talk much. Every now and then, one of us strikes up a conversation, only for it to fizzle out after just a few sentences. The reason why we're cowering here on the floor, in the farthermost corner of our storeroom, doesn't get mentioned for quite some time.

After a while, Joanna feels about for my hand and moves closer to me. Ever since she attacked me, her touch has been evoking such contradictory feelings within me that I shrink away from her almost instinctively.

"I can't take much more of this, Erik."

I don't ask exactly what she means by that, deciding instead that her words apply to the entire fear-inducing situation.

"I know. I feel the same way."

"Just tonight and then less than a day. We can manage that, can't we? And then we'll be safe within a few hours. The people coming to pick us up are professionals. My father's entrusted them with my life several times. Even back when I was still a child."

"That's good to know," I say, and feel her shifting around next to me, changing position. There's a rustling sound. I wish I could see if she's reaching for something, a bottle for instance, or a can of something. The shelf in front of us is full of that kind of stuff.

With all my concentration, I listen for sounds that might let me ascertain what Joanna's doing, but everything's gone quiet again.

After a few minutes, her breathing steadies. She's fallen asleep. I lean against the wall, my back hurting. A short while later, Joanna shifts down a little and rests her head on my thigh. I close my eyes. It makes no difference; the darkness stays the same.

They arrive just before three.

I hear them as they enter the kitchen, conversing at a whisper. How did they manage to break the door open that quietly?

The pressure from Joanna's head on my legs lifts. She's heard them too. I carefully feel around for her, find her arm, and gently squeeze it to let her know I'm awake.

I hear a rustling that's hard to place, then more whispering.

A nervous glimmer of light appears in the room, quickly dances to and fro, then lingers on the shelving unit, where it dissipates into thin strips of light that cut through the gaps between the boxes, the crates, and the packaging, drawing patterns in the darkness.

My heart is pounding so violently that I'm scared it can be heard all the way to the kitchen. Joanna's hand feels around for me with erratic movements, digs into the flesh of my forearm so tightly that I barely manage to stifle a gasp. I can't help but hold my breath. Two seconds, three . . . then the cone of light swivels away from the shelves. I let the air exit my lungs very cautiously, and am just about to breathe a sigh of relief when suddenly the light gets brighter. The flashlight isn't pointing directly at the shelf anymore, but the beam is still darting around the storeroom.

Steps, barely audible, approach the spot where we're cowering. I break out in a sweat. If they've found us, it's all over. They've come to kill Joanna, there's no doubt about that. They'll be surprised when they see me squatting on the floor back here as well, but it'll be their chance to finish the job they didn't succeed at a few times before.

Then again, the fact that they don't expect me to be here could be an advantage. I'm not going to make it easy for them. They're going to have to pull the shelving unit aside, and while they're trying that I'll jump up and throw myself against it with all my strength. It will keel over and, with some luck, bury them underneath. Maybe I'll be able to use the moment of surprise and tackle them. Maybe . . . I hear more steps, brisker now, less cautious. The second guy. He approaches quickly, stops just in front of us.

Was I really just thinking about tackling those two? I'm frozen in fear.

"There's nothing down here." A hissing voice. "What are you still doing down here? Come on, let's go upstairs."

"Calm down. I'm just having a look at all the good stuff they're hoarding down here."

"Come on already."

It gets darker; the flashlight appears to be aimed at the exit. The steps fade, get quieter, then vanish completely. The last shimmer of light goes with them.

Darkness. Silence. Joanna's grip loosens, a relief. I hear her inhaling deeply, then she completely releases my arm.

They didn't find us. They're still in the house, but they were just standing right in front of us and didn't see us. There's nothing I've felt before that can compare to the relief I feel now. But there's something else. Something I absolutely have to tell Joanna once those two have cleared off. If they don't end up finding us after all.

I'm just having a look at all the good stuff they're hoarding down here, one of them just said. He didn't say what *she's* hoarding, he said what *they're* hoarding. So they know Joanna had not been living here by herself. It's not even clear to me why I find it so important to point this out to her, so important that I would notice it right now, in our current situation. Especially since she herself probably knows by now that we *have* to have known each other for some time. But there are still so many damn inconsistencies. The fact that all of my stuff has vanished from the house, for instance.

Neither of us dare to say a word while the men are still in the house. Then I finally hear the dull thudding sound of the heavy front door being pulled shut. They're gone.

"That was close," I gasp.

Joanna's hand finds my forearm again, but her touch is more tender this time. "Do you think they're gone for good?"

"Yes. They didn't find you, so why would they stick around? But maybe they're sitting outside in their car, waiting for you to get back."

She leans against me, tentatively; she probably expects me to push her away again any second now. "Are we staying here for the rest of the night?"

"Yes. I don't think they'll be back tonight but who knows . . ."

"Sure. Who knows." She takes a deep breath. "Erik? I still don't remember our time together. But I'm feeling more and more comfortable when you're close."

"Try to get some sleep now," I say, and close my eyes.

37

I think it was Erik moving that woke me, but it could also have been the pain in my neck.

I wasn't sleeping deeply, and it doesn't take three seconds before the situation we're in rushes back to my mind. Strangers were in our house last night. And they nearly found us.

I struggle to straighten up; it's not just my neck that's hurting, the rest of my body, too, is paying me back for the night on the hard floor, wool blankets or not.

I have no idea how late it is. Since we've been keeping all the curtains and shutters closed, we've lost all sense of time. But according to the display on my phone, it's six thirty in the morning, so there's less than twelve hours to go until the phone call that will save us.

With the pale light from the screen I see that Erik is awake too. Did he even sleep at all? Would he dare to, in my presence?

Just before I turn off the light again, I see him rubbing his eyes. I listen in the darkness. The sounds of the dawning day make their way in to us. Cars driving past, the wind. Deceptive normality.

"What time is it?" Erik's voice sounds throaty, he must've slept after all.

"Almost half past six. We should . . ."

The sound of my phone vibrating interrupts me. I'm still holding it in my hand, and for one irrational moment I hope my father has somehow managed to defy the laws of nature, that he's somehow made the plane arrive in Germany in half the time.

But it's not his name which shows up on the display, it's Ela's.

I press the button to reject the call; I need to be properly awake before I can act well enough to convince her I still haven't heard from Erik. And I want to be sure that there's no one still in the house.

If there is, they will figure out now, as we push the shelving unit to the side, that they're not alone.

But everything remains silent. No footsteps, no voices.

"Wait in the kitchen," whispers Erik, as he takes a look in the living room. "I'll check upstairs."

He is back downstairs within five minutes, and finds me huddled up on the couch. "There's no one here, I've checked everywhere." He smiles at me, but his face is deeply lined with fatigue again. "Should I make us some breakfast?"

Before I can answer, my phone vibrates again. Ela again, this time I pick up.

"Morning," I say, "I'm sorry, I didn't hear the telephone earlier—"

"Jo!" Just one syllable, but even that is barely comprehensible. Ela isn't just crying, she's sobbing loudly into the phone, barely able to catch her breath. My first thought—that she has confirmation that Erik is one of the victims—is, of course, complete nonsense. After all, he's standing right in front of me, with a questioning frown on his face, pointing at my phone.

It takes me a while to understand what he wants. The loudspeaker.

Now Ela's despair fills the entire living room. "What happened?" I say tentatively, and then, even though it makes me feel bad: "Is it about Erik? Do you have any news?"

She gradually gets ahold of herself. "No. No, still nothing, but—" She struggles to breathe. "Nadine is dead. I just found out. Her mother called me."

I can see Erik grasping for something to hold on to, his left hand finding the back of one of the barstools, putting his right hand over his mouth, as if he wants to make sure he doesn't make a sound.

"Oh my God." There's no need for me to act devastated. I wasn't particularly fond of Nadine, but then I hardly knew her . . . which brings me to the question of how the news could reach Ela. A moment later I answer my own question: Ela and Erik have been friends for years, and he was with Nadine for a long time—so of course they knew each other.

"How did it happen?" *Boiler, car accident?*

"She killed herself." Ela begins to cry harder again. "She jumped out of her bedroom window. On the ninth floor. The doctors said she died immediately."

I can't drag my gaze away from Erik, who is clearly using all of his strength to keep his composure. Is he thinking of how he threw Nadine out of the house? Was that their good-bye, their last encounter? Hopefully not.

"That's . . . unbelievable," I stammer. "She was just here. Yesterday. She wanted to know if there was any news about Erik."

At the other end of the line, Ela takes a shaky breath. "Her mother thinks that's why she did it. Because she thought Erik was dead. Apparently she had been getting her hopes up again recently."

I find myself wanting to turn the loudspeaker off, because it's obvious how hard each of Nadine's words is hitting Erik.

"I spoke to her on the phone myself yesterday," she continues, "and she was . . . sick with worry, just like I was, but not despairing. Do you think she found out something about Erik during the night? Is it possible that she knows more than we do?"

Oh yes, that's entirely possible, but in a different way to how Ela means it. I would even bet on it. "Was there a suicide note?"

"No. The police didn't find one."

Of course not. How could they have? Had our two nocturnal intruders made a stop at Nadine's place after coming here? Or perhaps they had been there first.

I try to remember our conversation from yesterday—Nadine was afraid of the Islamists and was saying something about Project Phoenix . . . but I was far too busy trying to get rid of her to listen in any detail.

"If you spoke to Nadine on the phone recently," says Ela, interrupting my thoughts, "then it's possible her mother might call you too. She's calling everyone Nadine had contact with in the past few days, she wants to understand, why . . ." Ela's voice fails her again.

"Yes, of course."

The ninth floor. That would be enough time to realize what's happening. And to know that it's all over.

My stomach cramps up. "I'm going to hang up now, OK? Thank you for letting me know."

After I've put away the phone, the silence in the room is tangible. Erik is leaning against the wall, his arms slung around his body, staring into nothingness. For the very first time, it's as though he's not even aware of my presence.

I want to comfort him, but I don't know if he would want me to. Or if it's the worst thing I could do right now.

Because you don't know him, the familiar thought pops up. *Unlike Nadine, who didn't forget him, but who instead was in love with him until her very last hour, and who is now dead.*

Is Erik having similar thoughts?

Better not to ask him, I decide, and get up to turn on the espresso machine—we have to keep our wits about us and concentrate on what lies ahead of us today. We can't make any mistakes on the home stretch.

"No."

I turn around to face Erik, his voice sounds surprisingly calm.

"We are not going to do anything else here that isn't absolutely necessary. We can't even risk the smell of coffee drifting outside." Erik brushes his hair from his forehead, his hand trembling. "Nadine didn't kill herself. I'm sure of it. I wish, I . . ." He closes his eyes.

The words on the tip of my tongue sound too cliché to be spoken out loud. *You couldn't have known. You didn't do anything wrong. There's nothing you could have done.*

Erik abruptly pushes away from the wall. "Stay here, I'll be back in a moment." He runs up the steps, and I hear him opening the bedroom door.

When he comes back, his face is even paler than before. He sits down next to me on the couch and grasps my shoulders. "They're here. I looked down at the road through the curtains—a little way up on the other side there's a car with blacked-out windows, one that I've never seen in our street before."

"But that doesn't necessarily mean—"

"Yes. It does." Erik's grip tightens. "It makes complete sense: they didn't find you in the house, but you'll have to come back at some point. So they wait. I'd be surprised if Gabor doesn't contact you again soon and try to lure you back here. And if your father's people pick us up from here, those men outside will know. I'm sure they won't let us get away that easily."

That's the least of my worries. As soon as Gavin and his team get here, we've won. But until then . . .

"We're not going to wait," Erik says decisively. "We'll go out the back, through the terrace and the garden and then along that little path. No one can see it from the street, and they won't be expecting it." Only now does he let go of my shoulders. "I'll go crazy if I have to stay here and sit around."

I nod halfheartedly. I can let Dad know on the way, of course, we can change the meeting point—but I feel safer here than out on the open street.

I relent nonetheless, because I can see how much effort it's taking Erik not to peek out through the shutters and check whether the car is still there.

"OK." I put my hand on his arm. "Then let's go now."

We don't need to take much with us. Passports, my phone, money. All of it will fit in my handbag.

The fact that Erik's fears were justified becomes clear, if it wasn't before, while I'm tying my shoelaces. Erik is already waiting for me at the open terrace door; that's why he doesn't hear the scratching and scraping at the entrance.

Someone is there, and they're trying to get in.

I grab my bag and dash into the living room past Erik. And out into the open air.

He catches on without me even having to say a word. He pulls the door shut behind us and hurries me ahead to the fence, helps me over, then clambers up and over himself.

Then we run. Without looking back. Along the path, then the first right, then immediately left and inward, past a playground, into the adjacent park.

There, I stop for a moment, propping my hands on my knees, gasping for air.

Erik pulls me over to the side, into the shade of a small group of trees, and peers over in the direction we came from. We stayed on footpaths the whole time, avoiding the roads—so no one could have followed us in a car.

And it seems that no one followed us on foot either. We wait for three or four minutes, but there's no sign of anyone.

"They didn't see us running away," says Erik. "And they didn't expect you to be in the house anyway. Maybe the car on the street is starting to become too obvious, and they're posting someone in the house, to welcome you when you get home."

Yes, that sounds plausible. I ask myself whether they would go through all this trouble if they knew how little I understood of what was going on. How little I know.

The morning sun peeks out between the clouds and illuminates the colors of the autumn leaves. It must be just before eight o'clock. Too early for the airport still, but then we can't stay here either.

I look at Erik from the side. "What do we do now?"

He blinks up at the sky, looks around him again in every direction, and then reaches for my hand. "I know a place we can go."

38

We leave the park and turn right. I estimate that going by foot will take about twenty minutes. Joanna walks next to me in silence. She's feeling just as anxious as I am, I'm sure. She rubs her arms. It's quite cool outside, even with the sun appearing for a few brief moments every now and then. It's already so low in the sky that some of its strength has ebbed away. But we'll be in the warm soon.

Again and again I find myself looking around frantically. I think I see movement where there is none. The shadow of a small tree makes me jump in fright when the sun peeks out from behind the clouds for a few seconds.

You're paranoid, a voice whispers to me.

You're not paranoid, this is deadly serious, another one retorts.

Joanna's looking around now too.

"Was something there?" she asks.

"No," I reply tersely.

"How much farther is it? And where are we going, anyway?"

"Just come with me. We'll be there in fifteen minutes."

Fortunately, she seems satisfied with that answer. If I tell her now where we're going, she's going to ask me questions I'm really not in the mood for. We already discussed that particular topic some time ago, but of course she won't remember that.

I push the thought aside, focus on my surroundings again. I keep a lookout for men hiding behind a corner or a wall, waiting to kill us. *Kill* us. My God, how can all of this be happening? A bombing at the central train station in Munich, and I was almost right in the middle of it. Men breaking into our house at night, trying to finish us off. It's just impossible. That kind of story belongs in an action movie, not in my life.

And Nadine, too. She's dead. That seems even more unreal than everything else. Ela said that apparently she jumped out of a window. Because she couldn't deal with the news of my demise.

No. Not Nadine. I think, no, I *know*, that she loves . . . loved me in her own particular sort of way. But I know for sure there's nothing that could make Nadine take her own life. Not even my death.

No, if she really fell from a window, somebody had a hand in it. The thought of how ruthless people can be sends a cold shiver down my back.

And in the middle of it all, my boss. The man who I'd always seen as the epitome of normality, of everyday life. I'd thought my life with Joanna to be the same. But none of that's true anymore. Some sick twist of fate has torn me from my real life and dropped me in this poor, evil imitation of it. And from the way things look, there's no way back.

We turn the next street corner, and we're there. Only a few feet separate us from the large building. I stop and look up at the weathered facade.

"A church?" Joanna says next to me, as puzzled as I'd expected.

"Yes. It's always open. It's warmer inside, and I definitely don't think they'll look for us in there."

She looks at me from the side. "Are you religious? I mean . . . do you believe in God?"

I take a deep breath. "No." I nod toward the entrance. "Let's go inside."

As soon as I've closed the heavy door behind us, I stop for a moment and take in that distinctive atmosphere that abounds in nearly all Christian churches. Daylight falling through the colorful ornamentation of the stained-glass windows and bathing the interior in a unique kind of half light, the faint smell of frankincense, exalted silence in contrast to the exterior world with all its sounds . . . A seemingly tangible sense of spirituality. It slows the flow of time. It creates the space for a journey into our innermost being. Even without a god.

I came here often after my parents died. Not because I'd wanted to be close to some tacky, white-bearded god, but because of that particular atmosphere. Here I'd felt like I was close to them.

"Shall we sit?"

I jump, startled, then look at Joanna. "Yes, let's go to the nave up front," I whisper, without knowing why. "If anyone takes a look inside the church, they won't see us up there right away." We opt for the aisle on the left and sit down on one of the pews toward the back of the nave. Joanna takes a look around, contemplates the stone figure of a saint perched on a pedestal by one of the enormous columns.

"You're right, they're definitely not going to be looking for us in here."

I don't say anything, but instead wait for the question that will surely follow.

"Why don't you believe in God?"

Oh, I know her so well.

"I do believe in something," I say, looking at the nearly life-size likeness of Jesus on the cross behind the altar. "But not this type of god." I decide to nip the whole conversation in the bud. "I like being in this church because I like the atmosphere. And because I can find a special peace in here. I don't need a god to do that. I know that you're not overly religious, but that you do believe in God. And that's fine."

"But if you don't believe in him, aren't churches just huge halls that smell funny?"

I'm really not in the mood for this discussion, even though it was obvious to me that it would come up.

"We talked about this several times already, Joanna. The notion of a god in human form is simply lost on me, even if I do come into this church at times."

She turns toward me, gives me a serious look.

"Is it because your parents died so young?"

Exactly the same question she asked me before when we were talking about this. And my answer was the same then as it is now. "No. I felt like that before as well. I just don't believe in his existence."

We sit there in silence for a while, dwelling upon our individual thoughts. Joanna seems to be satisfied with my answer. Then she digs around in her purse, pulls out her phone, and unlocks it. "I have to call my father and tell him we're not at home anymore, that they should pick us up from here."

I nod.

"Hi, Dad," Joanna says. "Just wanted to let you know we're not at home anymore. We thought it would be better not to stay there . . . No, I'm fine . . . In a church . . . Yes . . . To the airport? A bit more than an hour . . . Yes I do . . . A cab? But why aren't we . . . Because we didn't feel safe there anymore . . . I don't think anyone will find us here . . . Yes, that's right . . . So straight to the GAT? . . . OK . . . Yes. Bye, Dad."

Joanna lowers her hand, still holding the phone. "My father wants us to take a cab to the airport. He thinks the lounge of the General Aviation Terminal will be safer than this place. That's the terminal for private aircraft. He'll make sure they'll take us in there."

"Hmm . . ." I think we're actually quite safe in this church. On the other hand, the thought of a lounge with something to eat and drink is quite pleasant, too. And it'll make the time pass more quickly if we take a cab to the airport.

"OK, fine by me. When should we leave?"

"Right now. Actually, I'd be glad if we can get out of here a bit earlier."

"Can you call us a cab?"

She makes the call. Then she puts the phone back into her handbag and gets to her feet. "OK, let's go. It'll be here in two minutes."

We wait inside the church. I've pulled the door slightly ajar and look outside every couple of seconds.

The cab must only have been a few streets away when Joanna called; it doesn't even take two minutes before it pulls up.

The driver cocks his head when we tell him the destination. "I'd have to charge a special rate to go there."

I don't understand. "What's that supposed to mean? You have a meter."

"Yes, but I have to drive back the entire way without a fare because I'm not allowed to pick up passengers at the airport. It's outside my area. I have to charge thirty euros extra to go to the airport."

"Fine. Just drive," Joanna says, agitated.

The taxi meter reads 184.60 euros when we arrive at the glass-roofed GAT hall an hour and five minutes later.

Joanna thrusts two hundred and twenty euros into the driver's hand and gets out of the car. She waits until I'm alongside her, then nods toward the building. "It's best if you let me talk to them, OK?"

We walk toward the entrance side by side, and I suddenly feel as though I'm just a hanger-on. As we go into this fancy terminal, it's like we've left the pitiful remainder of the world we shared behind us for good and entered another world, one that's completely normal to Joanna but completely foreign to me. The world of rich people.

The hall is bathed in a warm light, the atmosphere very inviting. Joanna heads over to the information desk. She talks to a friendly young woman who, after finishing the conversation, reaches for her handset and speaks to someone on it.

I reckon I'll probably have to show my ID at some point as well. Hopefully my name won't be on any lists relating to what happened at the train station. Who knows what ideas the investigators might get in their heads if someone who was allegedly at the station during the explosion has vanished, with no trace of a body.

"You coming?" Joanna tears me from my thoughts and points at a brightly lit passageway labeled *Passport Inspection/Federal Border Guard*.

"Dad's sorted everything out. We're expected up in the VIP lounge."

It seems I'm not on any sort of list, as the rotund border guard checks my passport silently and impassively, then hands it back to me and nods. I can go through.

Joanna walks purposefully toward a set of stairs with a white railing, I traipse after her. Two minutes and twenty-six steps later, we enter another world altogether.

The modern yet tasteful atmosphere of the VIP lounge envelops us. Joanna shows her ID to a young staff member, who gives us a knowing nod and leads us past dark, comfortable-looking leather environs to a table laid out in white. Apparently Daddy's organized a late breakfast for us while he was at it. Though, when I see all the food being wheeled to the table on top of two trolleys, I wonder how many people he was assuming would be here.

I make a remark to this effect, and immediately feel Joanna's discomfort. She's visibly struggling with having slipped back into the role of the well-heeled daughter.

"You're going to like being in Australia," she says while I'm eating my scrambled eggs.

"Yeah, maybe," I reply. "But how do you think your father . . . or indeed, how are *you* going to like showing up back home with a complete stranger in tow? A stranger to your family, and to you as well?"

Joanna stares at her knife for a while, then puts it aside and gives me a candid look. "Erik, I really don't know. But what's important for now is that we're safe. Don't you think?"

"Yes," I say quietly, feeling completely despondent all of a sudden. Maybe it's sheer exhaustion after all the things that have happened over the past days. I feel like crying, and all I want to do is curl up into a corner and pull a blanket over my head, and neither see nor hear anything.

"If you've finished your breakfast, our relaxation room is at your disposal next door," says the young man, who must have noticed the look on my face.

We sit at the table for about another half hour. Joanna uses the time to tell me about Australia. Most of it I know already, but I don't interrupt her. I'm happy to play the role of the listener and not have to think about anything for a while.

The relaxation room turns out to be a comfortable space with enormous leather armchairs that turn into bed-like loungers upon reclining. We've barely even made ourselves comfortable before the young man brings us pillows and blankets and assures us he'll be there if we require anything else. Less than ten minutes later, I'm asleep.

When Joanna wakes me, it takes me a while to get my bearings in this strange environment. Judging by her tousled appearance, she's only just woken up herself.

"It's late afternoon, six o'clock, almost."

"What?" I sit up with a jerk. "That means we've slept for seven hours."

"Yeah. Guess we needed it. And I probably would have kept sleeping if they hadn't woken me up. My father's plane is just landing."

There it is again, the feeling of being a stranger. Very soon I'm going to be sitting inside the private jet of a man I don't know in the slightest. A billionaire. Who is also Joanna's father. How's he going to respond to me, I wonder?

"There they are," Joanna says. She's in front of the glass window that offers a view of the airfield. I walk over to her and behold the sleek, white aircraft that's just reached its allocated space on the tarmac and is coming to a standstill.

"Well then . . ." I can't think of anything else to say right now.

Ten minutes later, an airport staff member approaches us. Accompanying him are two men who'd look like regular, athletic businessmen if it weren't for the short hair and the serious expression both are wearing on their faces.

"Gavin," Joanna says, sighing, the relief audible in her voice. "If you only knew how glad I am that you're here," she continues in English.

The man nods at her, without so much as a glance at me. "Our flight conditions were ideal. We'll take off again in two hours."

"Good. By the way, this is Erik, my fiancé. My father told you he'd be accompanying us."

The two dark eyes focus on me, seem to bore into me for a brief moment, then look away again.

"No, Joanna. Your father specifically said: not him."

39

At first I think I must have misheard. Gavin is standing there in that relaxed way of his; his eyes are friendly, but he's not fooling me with that. Sure, he'd take a bullet for me, but there was no way I could talk him into doing something that contradicts my father's orders.

OK. I'll get this cleared up right away.

"I spoke to Dad on the phone yesterday, and again a few hours ago—it's already been decided that Erik is coming with me. You've misunderstood."

Not a muscle twitches in Gavin's face, but there's something not unlike sympathy in his expression. "I'm certain that I haven't. We have instructions to bring you home, just you. No matter what the circumstances."

Gavin has been working for my family since I was fourteen. He was there on all of our vacations—and on most of my dates. One of two silent shadows sitting at the table next to me, keeping an eye on the entrance of the restaurant while I would hold hands with my respective companion. I never managed, not one time, to convince Gavin to give me some privacy for even half an hour.

Although that was a long time ago.

I take Erik's hand. "He's coming with me. I'll be responsible for him."

A soft, barely visible shake of the head. "Sorry as I am to say it, Joanna, you won't be responsible. And it's not your decision."

Despite Gavin's Australian twang, Erik can understand every word, there's no question of that. It only takes one glance at him to see that he understands exactly what's going on here. I squeeze his hand tighter.

"I'm calling Dad," I say to Gavin, and hope he can hear from the tone of my voice that his job will be on the line. "Hopefully that will clear things up. If I can't reach him, it's my orders that count, not his. And certainly not what you understand them to be."

I let go of Erik's hand and take a few steps to the side. It takes a few seconds before the call goes through. As I press the phone to my ear and listen to the dial tone, I try to get my unbridled rage under control, otherwise I won't hit the right note with Dad. I'm half expecting him not to answer—he's organized everything; now it's up to his subordinates, and it'll all run like clockwork. Like always.

But he picks up after the third ring.

"Hello, Jo." His voice doesn't sound drowsy in the least. He was awake. Maybe he was even waiting for me to call. I grip my phone tighter.

"Hi, Dad. I'm at the airport already."

"Yes, I know. And the plane is there already as well, I just got word from the pilot."

Right, deep breath. "OK. Listen, Dad, there's clearly been a misunderstanding. Gavin is refusing to take Erik on board, even though I told him several times that you and I agreed on it. Could you please tell him that he has to follow my instructions?"

From the corner of my eye I can see Erik turning away. If it's true what he says, and he has known me for almost a year—he properly hasn't seen this side of me. He'll probably like it just as little as I do, but that doesn't matter right now.

My father hasn't responded yet, only cleared his throat. That's not a good sign.

"No, no, that's all correct," he says now.

"Excuse me?"

"Come on, Jo. We can always bring this Erik over later if we really have to. But for now, just you come home. Alone. I want to speak to you in private."

I try to stop myself from the yelling on the phone. "We have a deal. I'm expecting you to keep it."

No, that wasn't a good move. It would have been smarter to play the daughter he'd like to have: obedient, full of admiration for her daddy, and possibly not bright enough to have a will of her own.

"We did indeed have a deal." All trace of fatherly understanding has disappeared from his voice. "That you're allowed to have your fun in Europe and none of us would ask you any questions. That you would marry Matthew as soon as you got back. And yesterday you suddenly tell me about some fiancé? Who you want to bring with you?" He bursts out laughing, only to shout even more angrily into the phone afterward, "Forget it, Jo. You reneged on your side of the deal, and I'm not going to keep my side of it. You're flying home now, and if Gavin even thinks about letting your lover on board, then God help him."

I close my eyes for a moment. I can no longer feel the burning rage inside me, just cold. And an intense clarity.

"You lied to me. On purpose. Yesterday and now again today."

He laughs again. "Don't try to make me feel guilty. It won't work. Unfortunately you still don't know what's good for you, and so you just have to rely on the people who are better able to judge."

I still don't feel any rage, despite what he just said. But the fear is coming back with a vengeance. The realization that it's not yet over.

"Have a nice life, Dad."

I hear him gasp for air. He understands, of course, he knows me. "You're flying home, just so that's clear. Don't even think about putting up a fight, I'll block all your accounts, and if it's necessary Gavin will just have to force you onto that damn plane—"

I hang up. See Gavin shrugging in commiseration. *I told you, didn't I?*

It will be just a matter of seconds until his phone rings and Dad gives him new instructions. We need all the head start we can get. Once Gavin's on the phone, he'll be distracted. That's our only chance, and even that's just a tiny one.

I nod to him. "You were right. He tricked me."

Gavin tilts his head. "I'm very sorry."

"It's not your fault." I look over to Erik, who's looking out over the airfield, his expression stony. He caught onto exactly what happened, of course he has, and his disappointment must be even greater than mine. In two hours I'll be safe, while he won't have anywhere he can go.

"Gavin?"

"Yes?"

"Give us five minutes, OK?" I gesture toward the panoramic window at the other end of the room. "This isn't going to be easy for me."

He quickly checks the surroundings, assesses the situation, then nods. "OK. Take your time."

I pick up my purse, then walk over to Erik, reach out and touch his shoulder. He turns his head around to me slowly.

"Come, please." I pull him along with me and, as expected, he resists. "Where to?"

"Please. Don't look at me like that. Come on, we don't have much time."

Finally he gives in. Reluctantly. "I knew it," he says softly. "Somehow I knew it even yesterday. But at least you'll get out of here, and you are the one they're looking for, after all."

I pull him toward the glass wall; the terminal hall is right below us. A cell phone rings; I hear Gavin saying "Sir?" I fling my arms around Erik's neck.

For a moment we stand there, holding each other close, then Erik pushes me away. "Are you trying to make it even harder for me?"

"No." I don't let him go. "The door is over there. I'm not flying back without you. They're going to try and force me, so we have to run as fast as we can. Out of the building. Gavin and his people haven't properly entered the country yet, so they won't let them through the checkpoint just like that, and that's our chance."

Erik remains silent. He puts his arms around me. "That's crazy, you can't stay here, that would be—"

We don't have time for this discussion now. I tear myself away from him and go over to the door, with a pointedly casual gait. As soon as I've opened it, I start to run. Out of the lounge, down the steps, taking two at once. Erik is right behind me, I can hear his breathing, as well as Gavin cursing, but that doesn't matter now, because passport control, which we passed a few hours ago in the other direction, is just ahead.

Still, the two officers try to stop us. One of them manages to grab hold of Erik's jacket, but he quickly pulls himself free again.

Gavin's calls become louder. "Stop, Joanna, there's no point to this!"

Another fifty feet to the exit, then twenty. How lucky that we're in General Aviation and not the public terminal. Erik is beside me now; he grabs my arm and pulls me along with him. The doors open; darkness and a rush of cool air greet us; out of the corner of my eye I see the alarmed customs officers intercept Gavin and his colleagues; then we're outside.

There are no taxis here, it's no-man's-land, but we just keep running, keeping to the left. Anywhere, just not toward the airport, because anyone acting the way we are would seem suspicious in the airport. Especially two days after a terror attack.

So we simply stay by the edge of the main road, slowing down bit by bit, then finally come to a halt. Car headlights wash over us from behind, and with every car that passes, I fear it might brake next to us and that someone will drag us inside.

Erik gestures to the right. "There's a gas station over there."

I nod, gasping. We walk the rest of the way at half speed, on the sparse patch of green by the side of the street. Again and again I feel Erik looking at me, but now is not the time for explanations. I ask myself if it would have been any different if I had come clean with Dad and told him about Gabor. About the boiler and about me attacking Erik with a knife. About the fact that he was inside the station at the time of the attack. About the fact the both of our lives are in immediate danger.

I try to imagine it.

That might just have yielded a flight ticket for Erik—to a completely different country. To Paraguay or Chile, maybe.

But if I'm completely honest with myself, I have to admit that it probably wouldn't have changed anything. Deep down, George Arthur Berrigan would have been delighted that someone else was going to get rid of the problem of Erik for him.

40

What the hell was Joanna thinking? For a long time I had thought I knew this woman, who right now is trudging alongside me toward the gas station. The sudden change in her a few days ago had been hard to deal with, but I had still wanted to stay with her at all costs. Help her. Even though she could no longer remember me, she was still my Joanna.

But then the knife, the one that was meant to kill me, had cut such a deep rift between us that I almost gave up on her. After that, I'd thought her capable of anything, even being in cahoots with the people who are clearly trying to get me out of the way.

And now, even though she's in mortal danger, she has rejected the chance to get herself to safety. She's even running from her own people, just because the man she can't remember isn't allowed to come along. Suddenly, she's once again the woman I thought she was all along. The woman who's prepared to overcome any obstacle that might be in our way.

The woman who might even have remembered who I am?

"Where should we go now?" she asks, interrupting my train of thought. We've almost reached the gas station. I stop, glance back in the direction we came from. The illuminated GAT building is several hundred yards away. Hardly anything is visible in the darkness between us and the terminal. But it doesn't look like anyone is chasing us.

I turn to face Joanna, who's also turned around to look behind us.

"Why did you do that?"

She looks at me like I've asked a completely absurd question. "Because I didn't want to leave without you." Her breathing is still uneven from running.

I wouldn't know where to begin describing the turmoil inside of me. "But why?" I want to get at least a tiny glimmer of clarity. "I don't understand. You couldn't remember me anymore, you even tried to . . . Has something changed? Have you remembered something from the time we spent together?"

"No. Unfortunately not." She shakes her head and raises her hand in a dismissive gesture. "We don't have time for discussions right now. Neither of us is going to leave Germany, by the looks of it, so we should really see to it that we get out of the immediate area right away. It won't be long before Gavin shows up and finds the gas station. There's not much else here, after all. I'm going to call us a cab, and you have to think about where it should take us."

I'm surprised by the matter-of-fact way in which Joanna is dealing with the situation. And she's right, too. Right now it's important that we make ourselves scarce from the area surrounding the terminal. Gavin didn't really give me the impression of being a man who gives up all that easily.

"All right, but let's at least walk over to the gas station. We're sitting ducks out here."

We walk the remaining three hundred feet and stop at the rear of the building. While Joanna's taking care of getting a cab, I think about what we should do next. There's no way we can go back home. To get to Munich by cab will take us about half an hour. The city's probably still in chaos, but still . . .

"The taxi will be here in five minutes," Joanna says, sliding her phone back into her pocket. "It's probably best if we get a hotel room in Munich, what do you think?"

"Yes. There's this hotel at the Isartor I stayed at once. It's OK and it's fairly big."

"OK. The Isartor it is, then."

"Oh, and—Jo?"

Her arms are crossed in front of her chest; it's obvious she's feeling cold. "Yes?"

"Take the battery out of your phone. I don't think your father's going to find anyone who'll be able to pinpoint your phone that quickly, but let's not take any risks."

She hesitates for a moment, then takes the smartphone out of her pocket again and pulls the battery out of its casing.

"Good idea."

We walk around the gas station, and wait beside it in the shadows of a recess. After about ten minutes, the taxi pulls up.

We get in; I tell the driver our destination. Then we sit in the back in silence. Shaken up, yet at the same time totally dejected by the events of the past hour. The past few days were bad, but as far as hopelessness goes, they don't even come close to how I'm feeling right now. Just in the moment we thought we were finally safe, we were thrown right back into peril.

Toneless darkness rolls past my window, punctuated only by the light of a streetlamp or a lone house here and there.

As we drive onto the expressway toward Munich, I put my hand onto Joanna's forearm. "Now will you tell me why you decided to stay?" I'm speaking so softly she can only just understand what I'm saying. She nods toward the driver and shakes her head. "Not now."

Half an hour later, Joanna pays the driver sixty-three euros for the journey. "I'm running low on cash," she says, once we've gotten out and I've slammed the taxi door shut. "I didn't bring that much with me. My father told me over the phone that he's going to have all my cards canceled as well. Normally he makes good on his threats fairly quickly, but I should still be able to pay for the hotel with my MasterCard if we're lucky."

"I don't think that's a good idea. I don't know what means are at your father's disposal, but it might be possible for him to find out where we are if you use your card."

"You're right; I hadn't even thought of that. And just to give you an idea, my dad has all the means a person could possibly have at their disposal, and then some."

The image I have of Joanna's father is becoming clearer and clearer. And with every additional detail I find out, the more I get the feeling I wouldn't like to meet him.

"I can take care of it," I say. "I don't think Gabor can trace my card."

I feel around for my wallet. It's not where it should be. "Damn it." I pat down the few remaining places in my clothes where it could be. Nothing. Just what we needed. It's hopeless.

"My wallet's gone. Either it's still in the taxi, or I lost it before that."

"Are you sure?"

"Yes I'm sure. I mean, it's not here. Or I could have dropped it while we were running away."

"OK, hang on." Joanna approaches the first friendly-looking person walking by and speaks to him. The man smiles and hands his phone to her, and she types in a number. Two minutes later we've ruled out the possibility of my wallet being in the taxi.

I feel a crippling sense of resignation. It drains my energy, tries to lure me into sinking to the ground right where I'm standing, into no longer doing a single thing.

"And there was me thinking things couldn't possibly get any worse." Joanna is wearing a thoughtful expression on her face. "All right then, so let's go in and pay for a room before Dad cancels my cards. We'll just have to hope he doesn't pick up on the transaction."

She seems to be adjusting to the shitty situation we're in much better than I am. And she's still here, even though she could be sipping champagne in her father's fancy Learjet by now.

She stayed. Because of me. So I pull myself together and enter the spacious, modernly furnished hotel lobby at her side.

The young man standing behind a reception desk made of light brown wood smiles and gives us a friendly greeting. Various types of rooms are still available, he tells us, and we opt for a standard one. He shoots a quick glance beside and behind us, probably to check for luggage, of which we have none.

He asks us to leave credit card details, so Joanna takes out her MasterCard and puts it on the counter. My pulse quickens. This must be how a crook trying to pay for something with a stolen credit card feels.

The hotel employee swipes the plastic through the slot on the card machine and presses a button. The seconds ebb away at an agonizingly slow speed while the man, his expression unchanging, stares at the small screen. This is taking way too long. He's going to shake his head in a second, tell us there's a problem with the card. With the streak of bad luck we've been having, I'd even be surprised if he didn't. I wonder if it will show him that the card's been canceled. And if . . . "Thank you," says the man, handing the MasterCard back to Joanna. "Your card hasn't been charged yet; that will be done when you check out. And here's your room card."

We smile at each other. It worked. Relief is written all over Joanna's face. And on mine as well, probably.

"Breakfast will be in the restaurant, from six thirty until ten," the man explains. "Your room is on the third floor. The elevators are just here on the left. I hope you have a pleasant stay."

The room is fairly spacious. Joanna takes a quick look around and lets herself fall down onto the king-size bed.

"At least we're out of the line of fire for now."

I pull up a leather armchair that's diagonally opposite to her. There's so much I'd like to tell her, but I don't know where to begin.

"Jo. You can still go back. If you—"

"No chance."

That's what I thought she would say. And yet . . . now that I finally know she's standing by me again, all I want is to see her safe. But at the same time I'm very happy she's with me.

"I can't begin to tell you how happy it makes me, what you did. But I still don't understand why."

"Erik—"

"No, please let me finish. If you still can't remember us, that means you've only known me for a few days. A lot has happened in that short time; we've been through an awful lot together. But that doesn't change the fact that I still must be a stranger to you. And the fact that there's nothing in our house to remind you of me either, however that happened. So why on earth are you not just snubbing your father, but also risking your life, all for a stranger?"

Joanna looks me straight in the eyes the entire time I'm speaking.

"I hate having my father try and dictate how I should live my life. He's a patriarch, and he's used to everyone dancing to his tune. I put up with it to a certain extent; I mean, he is my dad after all. But I'm not having him determine the lives of people who mean a lot to me."

Is this the part where I get hit with the sobering reality? "Does that mean you only stayed because you wanted to defy your father?"

Joanna shows no reaction whatsoever, and I'm just wondering if she even understood the question when she grabs hold of my hands.

"You must have blocked out part of what I just said." Her voice doesn't sound reproachful, but gentle. "The most important part, at that. Is that one of your character quirks? I'll gladly repeat myself in case you didn't understand. I said that I'm not having my father determine the lives of people who mean a lot to me."

Sometimes, words can really do a world of good. I think of everything Joanna said, all the things she did over the past few days. Of all the times she pushed me away when I tried to get closer. And now . . .

"I mean a lot to you? After such a short time? After everything that's happened?" My hands are still in hers. They feel very warm, all of a sudden.

"Yes, you do. But that's not really a surprise, is it? I don't know what happened to me, but whatever it was, it seems like I'm still essentially the same person. And if what you say is true, I've fallen in love with you once before. So why shouldn't I do the same thing again if, from my perspective at least, we get to know each other all over again?"

41

I wait for Erik to say something, but he doesn't. He leaves my confession hanging there in the air, and just looks at me silently, with a mix of hope and distrust.

I can hardly blame him. I can still see the bandage under his right sleeve; I imagine the pain is still troubling him, even though he never complains about it.

And yet we make physical contact, without him flinching or freezing up, for the first time since the knife incident. He gently squeezes my hand back, but lets go immediately when I stand up to draw the curtains. We're on the third floor, but I still feel more comfortable if the windows are covered. And the door locked, but Erik has already seen to that.

For a moment I just stay there by the window, looking at him.

I wasn't lying. He means a lot to me; more than I can explain even to myself. My decision back then at the airport was neither made on a whim nor based on an act of spite. I wouldn't have been able to bring myself to get on the plane without him. Not just because I would have been abandoning him. But because the thought of being separated from him was, all of a sudden, unbearably painful.

I go back over to him, sit on the broad arm of the chair he's in. Right now, nobody should have any idea of where we are, even if my father can check up on the booking via the credit card—that would only be possible once we check out. Until then, we're safe. I had completely forgotten how that felt.

Was Erik feeling the same thing? Probably not, after all, he was in a room with the woman who had almost stabbed him to death. Who could become violent again at any time. Hurt him. Hurt herself. A woman who wasn't right in the head. It was no wonder he was being cautious about the confession I'd made.

"What I said just then, I meant it." I brush a strand of his hair off his forehead, letting my hand linger for a moment longer than necessary. "I can't tell you exactly when it started, but it's getting stronger all the time. You're becoming more and more important to me . . ."

Erik closes his eyes for a few seconds at my touch. "Jo, I . . ." He interrupts himself. "Does this room remind you of anything?"

I look around. It's a five-star hotel, the furnishings are tasteful and expensive—but not particularly memorable. "No. I'm sorry."

He nods, as though that was the response he had expected. "Of course not. I shouldn't have asked you. It's just—it looks very similar to our hotel on Antigua; even the lighting is the same." He gestures toward the funnel-shaped lamps on the walls, which cast their warm light over the cream-colored carpet. "Back then you said those things looked like torch holders."

Something inside my rib cage tightens. *Torch holders*, that was the first thought I'd had when I saw the designer lights upon walking in. Except that, in *my* mind, I'd only just thought of it now.

"I proposed to you on that vacation. Beneath one of the most beautiful and tacky palm trees I could find. We had just done a cocktail class at the beach bar together, and you'd single-handedly broken five bottles of rum because you were absolutely hell-bent on throwing them around like the barkeeper. We had our first fight too because at some point you decided to go off and explore by yourself, without telling me. I was out of my mind with worry, and you simply couldn't understand why."

I can see how vivid the memories are for Erik, while none of the things he describes ring a bell with me, not even a little.

"It was ours, all of it. Our life, our story. Sometimes we'd only have to look at each other to know what the other was thinking. When you tell me now that you're starting to fall in love with me, I know that's wonderful, but . . ."

This time, I'm the one who doesn't let him finish. It hurts me to see him grieving for our shared past, but I can't change that—I can only share the here and now with him, that's all we have. Who knows for how much longer.

I rest my forehead against his. "Our life," I say, "is this, right here." My lips brush against his, as if by instinct, very softly. A touch like a whisper, but it suddenly makes me aware how much I've been longing for him. Longing to be as close to him again as on that one precious afternoon.

For what feels like an eternity, the kiss is mine alone. My tongue tentatively moving forward; my hands stroking over Erik's shoulders, his neck, his hair. He doesn't move, as though he's waiting to see whether there's anything else hidden behind my attempt to get closer to him. As though he has to stay alert and be prepared for anything.

Gradually, though, the tension starts to leave his body. His hands glide down my back, around my waist; then he pulls me so close to him that I almost gasp for air.

I bury my face in his neck, begin to open the buttons of his shirt, breathing in his scent, which for me is the most familiar thing about him.

"Joanna." He holds me, like he has to make sure I don't slip away. "I've missed you so much."

As I strip the shirt off of his shoulders, he stands up, pulls me up with him and over to the bed. This time, our kiss is no longer a playful way of getting closer, but a prelude, making it clear that we both know and both want what's about to come.

Erik's hands beneath my shirt, on my skin. I barely notice him undressing me, little by little, I only feel his lips, his hands, his tongue. With every touch it becomes harder and harder to think, but one thing becomes utterly clear: this man must know me. He knows exactly where and how to touch me to make me lose control. I'm the only person in the room for whom this is new.

For a while, I still try to resist letting go, try to be stronger than the sensations Erik is awakening within me. With his lips and then, oh so softly, biting gently against my neck. With his hands on my breasts. I feel him pressing against me, feel how aroused he is. And all of a sudden I want nothing more than to feel him on me. Inside me.

He notices my agitation. He straightens up a little and looks at me.

"Come here," I whisper, pulling him toward me, but he shakes his head with a smile. His hand glides down from my breast over my stomach, where it lingers briefly, and then between my legs.

I feel his touch throughout my entire body, like an electric shock; my breathing sounds like sobbing; Erik kisses me as though he wants to comfort me, while his hand does the exact opposite, more and more, stopping only at the point when my entire being is pure desire, a scream for more; at the point where I've long since lost control.

"I love you so much," he whispers. Strokes my face. Looks me directly in the eyes as he lies on top of me and slowly pushes inside me.

It's like flying, going up and up, a little bit more with each of his movements. I feel my body trembling in his arms, everything in me just anticipation now, a silent plea for him not to stop now, to please never stop again.

And then it's like the world is shattering into pieces and me with it; I hear myself screaming as Erik grabs me tighter, holds me; the first and the second time.

Only then does he seek his own rhythm. Harder, quicker. Giving up all consideration and control, his body tenses, his fingers dig into my shoulders, and he groans my name. Screams it out, as though he is afraid of losing me again.

But he won't. Never again.

Afterward, we lie there intertwined, my head on his chest. I gently stroke the spot where I can feel his heart beating. And I suddenly know that I've done it before, on more than one occasion. I don't know when or where. But I'm sure that I'm not wrong.

"Erik?" He's running his hand lazily through my hair, and now he turns to look at me. Smiles. "Yes, my darling?"

"I think I just remembered something. Nothing specific, although it is in a way. A situation like this."

His smile widens. "You don't remember anything that is connected to me, but you do remember us having sex?" He laughs. "My God, I must be good."

I give him a playful shove. "Not the sex, silly. This, here. Lying together with you, and—" I stop, and wonder whether I should say what's on the tip of my tongue, whether it sounds stupid. I decide it doesn't matter. "Stroking your heart."

He moves away from me a little. Looks at me in disbelief, and I immediately regret not having held my tongue.

"Did I say something wrong?"

Erik shakes his head. "No, Jo. No, completely the opposite in fact. That's what you always called it, it's very typical of what you would say. . . . Do you really remember?"

Not really, no. It's more like having déjà vu. But it's the closest thing I've had to a memory in the days since I've known Erik.

"Yes, I think I do."

42

I'm lying on my back, holding Joanna close to me. Her face is resting on my chest, her breathing is calm and even. I don't want to risk moving, as she may have fallen asleep, and because I don't want to ruin this indescribably wonderful moment. I feel as though, if I lie there quietly, I can hold on to the bliss that's currently surging through my entire being.

I eye the whitewashed ceiling. The stucco rosette in its center and the matching molding make for a stylish contrast with the room's modern furnishings. Past and present can be compatible, even if they're so different that at first glance they seem irreconcilable.

Does that apply to people, to relationships, as well?

I find it hard to resist the urge to pull Joanna even closer to me. To feel even more of her naked skin against mine. But even that probably wouldn't be close enough. Not now, now that she has chosen to stay with me despite the danger, now that suddenly at least a tiny flash of *my* Joanna has come back. And with it, the hope that everything between us might turn out to be all right again after all.

It's crazy just how little you need to be happy, at least for a moment.

But then, all of a sudden, there's something else. No more than a notion, but it still threatens to destroy this wonderful moment. I fight the impulse to let the notion turn into a more concrete thought, but I can't stop it from happening.

What if this brief spark in Joanna's memory wasn't the starting point for her to regain all of her memories of me, but instead the last little twitch before the history we shared disappears once and for all into a black hole in her mind?

What if, say, in an hour's time, she goes crazy again and plunges some sharp object into my heart, the very heart she was stroking just minutes ago?

No. Whatever happened to Joanna, it's wearing off. She's in great danger now, and that's because of me. If she wasn't with me, Gabor and his people wouldn't be interested in her, she knows that. And despite that she's passed up her one chance of leaving the country.

What more proof do I really need to be sure that *my Joanna* is on the way back to me?

The sex, just now . . . it was exciting, just as it always is with her, and yet very different. I felt like she was exploring me in a very inquisitive way, and yet at the same time she seemed to know exactly what I like. She'd let herself go the way you only can with someone you trust, but had still watched how I was reacting to her body and what she was doing.

I picture her beneath me again, eyes shut, her hips thrusting against me, her hands on my waist, directing me.

I can feel my body reacting to these images in my head; crazily enough I'd almost find it a little embarrassing if Joanna noticed. I don't want her to think I'm insatiable; she hardly knows me, after all. Not yet. But hopefully that's going to change again soon.

Joanna's eyes are shut; she doesn't react to the movement.

She really is sleeping again, despite all the hours we already spent asleep during the day. Or perhaps she's just pretending because she wants to think in peace. To try to remember.

I set my eyes on the ceiling again, and suddenly I can't help but think of Nadine. I don't want to; it's as though she's pushing herself in between Joanna and me in this intimate moment.

It's unfathomable to me, the fact that she's dead. I'm still finding it hard to believe. It reminds me once again that this isn't some Hollywood movie, but real life.

"Are you feeling as good as I am?" Joanna asks softly, and starts to stroke my chest again.

"Yes, I . . ." I start to say. "I'm really happy you remember me at least a tiny bit. And I'm really enjoying this moment."

Our eyes meet. The love I feel for this woman is like a warm current flowing through my body. I can't help but pull her closer. And closer. She's on top of me now, her hair brushing over my face, her mouth so close to mine I only have to shift upward a little for our slightly parted lips to meet. When they do, it's so tender, so soft, that it barely feels like we're touching. I drink in her breath, move closer to her; we seem to melt into each other. My hands wander down her spine, grab hold of her buttocks, gently press her hips against my own. Joanna reacts, matching the thrust of my abdomen. The arousal I feel is nearly making me lose my mind. I start moving to a slow, steady rhythm, enter her almost instinctively, hold her as she arches her back, moaning. Then, there is only feeling and movement, losing ourselves in each other.

Joanna eventually falls onto her back next to me, spent. We're both breathing in quick bursts, our bodies gleaming, dripping with sweat.

I want to do nothing, to not have to brood over anything, to just lie there in the certainty that she's with me again. Finally.

After we've been lying there for a while, I have no idea for how long exactly, she asks me, "What are you thinking about?"

"I'm trying to put the feelings I have for you into words," I reply, keeping my eyes fixed on the stucco rosette above me.

"And?"

"I can't do it. Everything I can think of is either trite or too tame." Now I turn to face her. She does the same.

"I love you, Jo. But it's more than that. People use these words so carelessly for every little surge of emotion they might feel."

"I know what you mean." She raises her hand, strokes my forehead with the tips of her fingers. "And it's such a wonderful feeling. I'm so sorry."

"About what?" I ask, both surprised and confused at once.

"That I can't make you feel loved. But you have to believe me, there's more than . . ." She breaks off as I put my finger to her lips.

"What are you talking about? You can't make me feel loved? Jo, you just ran away from your own people with me, to stay here with me, in a place where you're risking your life. You think that doesn't make me feel anything?"

"They're not my people, they're my father's people. And yes, I couldn't just leave you here. But—"

"It's all right," I interrupt her gently. "You're here, in spite of everything. Because of me."

As I say the words, I realize, maybe for the first time since we fled from the terminal, what it would do to me if something happened to Joanna all because she stayed with me. The realization both terrifies and shames me in equal measure. I just accepted the fact that she's putting herself in mortal danger. For my sake.

I sit up and lean against the padded headboard.

"Jo, I really think what you did is amazing, but . . ."

"But?"

"But I'd feel better if you were safe."

"You want me to fly to Australia with Gavin? Without you?"

"No, I want the two of us to fly to Australia together, but it seems that's not going to work. So at the very least I want you to be safe."

I lean forward slightly, stroke her cheek. "I can't bear the thought that something might happen to you."

Joanna takes my hand, pulls it away from her face, and sits up. All trace of softness has disappeared from her eyes. "If I go back now, we'll never see each other again. You understand that, don't you? Is that what you want?"

"No, of course not. I'd be coming after you. On a normal flight. Tomorrow even." I hope my words sound more convincing than they feel to me. Joanna shakes her head, giving a bitter laugh.

"You don't know my dad. Once I'm back in Australia, he's going to move heaven and earth to make me marry Matthew. Just like he planned. Everything either happens the way Dad planned it or not at all."

"But you're a grown woman, surely he can't just—"

"I'll say it again—you don't know him. My father can do everything he wants to do. And he gets his way just about every time."

Joanna's words rouse a kind of defiance within me. I refuse to accept that this man on the other side of the world could determine our fate, determine our lives so easily.

"We'll find a way, Joanna. If he disowns you, let him, we can take care of ourselves. I'll find work in Australia, somewhere far, far away from your father. It's a huge country, after all. We'll look for a small house somewhere and—"

She interrupts, shaking her head. "No, Erik, there's no way. I'm staying here."

43

We sleep very little that night. Erik tries another three or four times to convince me to go back to Australia, but eventually gives up when I threaten to get my own hotel room if he doesn't let it go.

I realize, of course, that my decision isn't a very clever one. But I found it hard to ask Dad for help even when I still thought I'd be able to rescue Erik in the process. And now that the battle lines are clearly drawn, I wouldn't want to take even a crumb of bread from my father from now on.

The chances that we would be able to make it alone aren't that bad. Of course we have to get out of the city, if not the country too, and then . . . Maybe contact Bernhard. *All the information you want is available, and if you stay alive long enough you'll get it too, but for now you just have to believe me. Get yourself to safety, otherwise you'll soon be dead, just like Erik.*

We were still alive. How long is long enough?

I'll call him first thing tomorrow, I resolve at around four in the morning, as tiredness begins to catch up with me after all. And after that we'll get out of here.

When I open my eyes again, it's light outside and Erik is already awake. He is lying next me, watching me, stroking my arm softly. Smiling. I snuggle up close to him. "What time is it?"

"Half past eight, almost." His hand wanders down over my shoulders to my waist, and then down to my hips.

"No," I say, in as firm a voice as I can manage in my drowsy state. "Not now. There's so much we have to take care of."

"Yeah." Erik closes his eyes. "But who knows when we'll next be able to be together like this. I don't want to let you go, Jo."

We give ourselves another ten minutes. Ten minutes in which I feel the fear and anxiety slowly growing stronger inside me again, despite Erik's proximity. The fact is, we have no time to lose.

I have to really push myself to go down to the breakfast room and leave our room, where we were invisible to the world.

"There's a computer with an Internet connection in the lobby," Erik says as he stirs his coffee. "We can book flights from there. Maybe to Italy or Spain, to begin with."

"Do you still have your passport?"

"Yes. It was in the inside pocket of my jacket." Erik smiles. "Safe and sound."

It could work. We would need to buy a few essentials—some clothes, toiletries, a suitcase—but then we could take a taxi to the airport. After all my calls to the police and the next-of-kin hotlines, his name was sure to be on the list of missing persons. Would they let him through regardless? I mean, he wasn't a suspect, after all.

Unless, of course, my father had contacted the German police and reported my running away as a kidnapping. I wouldn't put it past him, not in the slightest.

But fine. We'll deal with each problem as it comes.

The computer in the lobby is in use, by a visibly irritated businessman who is trying in vain to call up his emails. I can see Erik's impatience building, can see how hard it is for him not to interrupt the man. Maybe he's feeling the same as I am—the people coming in and out of the hotel are making me nervous. As are the headlines on the newspapers laid out on a table next to the reception desk. They're all about the attack. I pull Erik toward the elevators; one of them is already on this floor. "Let's make a phone call first."

"Why, who do you want to call?"

"Bernhard. Do you remember what he said? He knows something, and I want to know what it is."

After we get to the room, I sit down on our rumpled bed and reach for the telephone on the nightstand. "Do you know his number by heart?"

Erik nods, closes his eyes briefly, then writes the number down on a notepad with the hotel logo, rips off the page, and gives it to me.

I dial zero for an outside line and then the number. But the phone is unreachable. I try it four times, and get the same result each time.

"Did you and your coworkers usually keep your cell phones turned off at work?"

Erik shakes his head. "No, just on silent mode during meetings."

That's not a good sign. I replace the phone handset. Silently we make our way back downstairs, where by now the computer has become available. Erik browses to the booking page for Lufthansa. "Where to?"

Rome is my first thought. But Dad knows that I've always wanted to go there. The same applied to Barcelona. "Florence," I say.

Erik enters the requested details, chooses a preferred return date, albeit only for show. We both know that we won't be coming back to Munich.

"There's a flight at ten past three this afternoon," he says. "Four and a half hours from now."

"Great." I take my purse out of my bag. Four credit cards, three of them belonging to accounts which, although they may have my name on them, are funded by my dad's money. For me to use whenever I wanted. The fourth is different, that's where I put my savings. Gifts, earnings. The balance on this account is by far the least impressive, but it could still allow a family of four to survive a year without any problems.

I press the card into Erik's hand and he enters the number. Clicks on *Secure Payment*.

We wait for the confirmation. I'm just looking around for a printer where we can print out our online tickets and boarding passes, when the error message appears. In red.

Your credit card has been declined.

I feel my pulse quickening. Erik looks at me; his hand moves up in front of his mouth.

Maybe he typed in the number wrong? I check the card number, but no, it's all correct; I start from scratch, and enter the details myself this time. With the same result. That means there's no point in even trying the other three cards.

We've gone through far worse in the past few days, but for some reason this, right now, is the moment I feel like giving up. I don't know what to do, I don't even have the strength to hold back the tears that are welling up in my eyes.

Erik closes the browser window and takes me in his arms, guiding me out of the lobby. He's right. A crying woman would only attract attention.

"We're trapped," I whisper once we're back in the elevator. "We can't even pay for the hotel, let alone leave the country; we're done for."

Erik looks down at the floor, his expression solemn. He is frowning, as though he's in pain. "Listen to me, Jo. You're calling your father now and telling him that you're coming home. You have a little cash still, right? If it's not enough for the taxi, then Gavin will have to wait in front of the General Aviation building for you and pay." He looks at me. "It's the only sensible thing to do. I'm not going to let you risk your life here in Germany."

I don't think Erik realizes it, but his words are a huge help to me. Differently to how he intended, but that doesn't matter.

By the time the elevator doors open, there's barely any trace of my despair left; instead I'm filled with such an intense rage it almost takes my breath away. I hang the *Do Not Disturb* sign on our room door, take out my phone, and ram the battery back in, despite Erik's protests. As soon as I get a signal, I dial the number. He picks up after the second ring.

"Damn it, Joanna. It's about time you called. Where the hell are you?"

I take a deep breath. "That no longer concerns you. So you blocked my accounts? Even the one with the money I earned myself?"

"Yes. I warned you I would. Do you really think I'd waste my time with empty threats?"

"But you don't have access to my account!"

He laughs. "Jo, darling. The account is with our family bank. Do you really think they would say no if I asked them for a favor? Do you think they would take the risk that I'd transfer our money to their competitors?"

I feel an intense desire to destroy something, yet at the same time, I have never felt so helpless.

"Right, listen to me now." My father no longer sounds amused, but businesslike. "You make your way to the airport, Gavin will meet you there, you're flying home. End of discussion."

He doesn't know what he's doing. Otherwise he wouldn't destroy the very last chance he had to win me back.

"No, Dad." My voice is calmer than I even dared to hope. "I'm staying here, and I might soon be dead because of that. The people who are after Erik and me are the same ones who blew up Munich station, and they've already nearly succeeded in killing us a few times. And by cutting me off, you've considerably raised their chances. Congratulations. But you know what? I'd rather get shot than spend my whole life being blackmailed by you. Good-bye."

I hang up before he has the chance to say anything. Imagining the look on his face right now, I begin to laugh. A laugh which just about holds back the tears beneath the surface; nonetheless, it feels liberating.

Erik doesn't laugh with me. He looks at me skeptically, shaking his head gently. "That was a bit dramatic, what you just did."

My phone rings: Dad, of course. I reject the call. "Yes, you're right. I acted like a fourteen-year-old. Possibly because that's what I should have done when I was fourteen."

Erik points at the phone. "It's possible he might give in, now that he knows how serious the situation really is. Joanna, don't throw away your chance of safety because of spite. Or our chance, even."

I understand Erik's thought process, but he doesn't understand my father's. Giving in just wasn't in his programming. Not at any price. "Well, we'll find out soon enough," I say. "If he's worried about me, he'll unblock the accounts, right? That's what any other loving father would do in his position. But I'll bet anything that he won't."

I let the phone fall onto the bed. The feeling I had a few moments ago, of having won the battle, even if it had been an empty victory, has now disappeared. "We'll somehow have to manage without money. I've no idea how, but—"

"No, we don't have to do," Erik interrupts me. "You have money, don't you remember? You threw it at my head the day before yesterday. Almost."

My God, of course. The tapas cookbook. The twenty thousand euros. We had that much, except . . .

I look at Erik. "How are we going to get it?"

44

Yes, how are we going to get to the money?

The irony of the whole situation is hard to beat. Twenty thousand euros that could make the difference between life and death, just lying around in our house, in our very own kitchen. But the money might as well be lying around somewhere on the moon, for we have no chance whatsoever of getting our hands on it.

By now, Gabor's people know that Joanna was in the house and that she isn't there anymore. And they must assume she's not going to be coming back, because she's scared. Because she knows someone broke in. Are they still going to be lying in wait there? Or have they taken off?

In any case, there's no way she can risk going there. The danger is far too great. And I'm dead, in their eyes, and need to stay that way if possible.

"I don't know," I say with frustration. "There's absolutely no way we can go back to the house."

Joanna starts chewing her lower lip. She always does that when there's an important problem needing to be solved. There's so much familiarity within that little quirk that, for a brief moment, it makes everything around us seem completely unreal.

But then her eyes widen, and I know she's had an idea. "You're right. There's no way *we* can go back to the house. But what about if somebody else went to pick up the money for us?"

"Somebody else?" I echo, to give myself a bit of time to think. "That could work, maybe, but who did you have in mind? Besides, there's still a risk Gabor's people might be hanging around."

"Ela."

Ela. Of course. But a thought makes my euphoria evaporate the very next moment.

"It's just that Ela thinks I'm dead."

Joanna shrugs. "So we'll have to fill her in. Or you can hide when she gets here."

I don't even need to consider that option. "No. If she's going to be putting herself in danger for us, we're not going to lie to her on top of it all. I already felt bad about doing that anyway."

"Yes, you're right. Once we explain the situation to her, she'll understand that we had no other option. I'll call her and tell her you're still alive. And then—"

"No. Call her and tell her you're in trouble and need the money. When she brings it here, I'll be here as well and we can explain it to her together. OK?"

"OK. That's probably best." With one swift motion, Joanna leans forward and kisses me on the mouth. "Everything's going to be all right. You'll see, everything will be all right in the end."

She already has her phone in her hand when something else comes to my mind. "Wait." Joanna stops midmotion and looks at me with confusion.

"We have to think of something to make sure Gabor's guys don't intercept Ela when she arrives. I don't really figure they'll still be there, but you never know."

Joanna quickly thinks. "The police?"

"What?"

"Just before Ela gets there, I'll call the police for help saying I think someone's breaking into my house. Ela will wait until after the officers have been in the house. Gabor's people should have cleared off by then at the latest."

That does sound like a good plan, but Joanna has overlooked something. "That's not going to work. If you make a distress call saying someone's breaking into your house, you'll have to be there yourself. But if they ring the bell and nobody opens the door, they're going to assume something happened to you. What are they going to do then?"

"Damn." The disappointment is written all over her face. "They'll break open the door and turn the whole house upside down. And then it'll take them forever to leave again."

"Exactly. Unless . . ." I've had another thought while she was echoing my misgivings. Something that could be the solution. "Unless you're in another city, at a friend's place. Say you got a call from an acquaintance of yours who drove past our house and saw some men hanging around. You're worried; after all, I've been missing ever since the bomb attack, and you already spoke to the police a few days ago and told them you were scared."

She thinks for a few seconds. "Right, that sounds plausible. And the story checks out, too."

"And if Gabor's people really are still hanging around the house, the police will pay them a nice, friendly visit."

"OK. But I'm calling Ela first."

"Please tell her to be careful. If she sees anyone she thinks is strange or suspect, she should leave at once."

Joanna doesn't turn the phone on speaker, but from her reactions and replies I can more or less figure out what Ela's saying. The conversation only lasts a few minutes. At the end of the call, Joanna explains where we hid the spare key, then hangs up. "She's seriously worried about me, and about you as well. And yes, she said of course she'll get the money. It's going to be a real shock for her when she sees you here."

"Yes, but she'll understand we didn't lie to her without good reason." I try to pass off my hope as conviction.

Joanna calls the police ten minutes later. She sounds confused and anxious, afraid and distraught. The act she puts on is so convincing that my thoughts briefly stray in an unwelcome direction. Only for a few seconds, then it stops. I know I can trust her, and that's that.

When Joanna puts away the phone, a smile flashes over her face. "They're going to check it out right away. My goodness, the poor guy on the phone was so worried about me, he wanted to deploy a hundred uniformed officers around my hou—around *our* house."

"I'm still a bit worried about Ela. Hopefully everything will go well."

Everything does go well. After about an hour, Ela calls back and lets Joanna know that she has the money and is on her way to Munich. Apparently the policemen only walked around the house for ten minutes and then left again. She didn't notice anyone else. Another ninety minutes later, there's a knock on the door of our room.

I nod at Joanna, who's looking at me with a questioning expression on her face, and disappear into the bathroom. We'd agreed on me doing that.

The sounds that follow suggest that the two of them are hugging tightly. The door is pushed shut. Then, Joanna's voice: "I have to tell you something. Please don't get upset, OK?"

"What's the matter?"

"It's about Erik. He's alive." She tacked on the second part so quickly that Ela didn't even have time to misinterpret the initial part.

"What? That's amazing! He's alive? You're sure? I'm so happy. Is he OK? Where is he?"

I open the bathroom door "I'm here, Ela."

She freezes, looks at me like I'm a ghost. Then she rushes into my arms, flinging hers around my neck. We stand there for a while, silent, in a tight embrace. When we break away again, she takes a step backward and looks me over from head to toe, as if she has to convince herself everything is still the way it should be. Her eyes only briefly rest on the spot where the bandage can be seen under my shirt.

"Where were you, and what happened?" Her voice is calm and she's composed herself again.

I point at the armchair. "Have a seat, I'll explain everything."

I wait until she's sitting down, then tell the story. Starting with the strange email I found on Gabor's laptop. I leave out nothing. Ela interrupts me twice to ask questions; otherwise she just listens, completely alert. When I wrap up the story with our escape from the terminal, she takes a few moments to let it all sink in, then finally nods. "I see. It's unbelievable, really. And you really think Gabor's involved in the attack at the train station?"

"I don't know if he's responsible, but he definitely has a hand in it somewhere. Now do you understand why we told everyone I'd been missing since the attack?"

"Yes, of course. Although I do think you could have told *me* the truth, at least. I was really, really worried."

"We didn't want to drag you into it as well," Joanna explains.

Ela gives me a grim look. "But now you had to anyway. Three days earlier and you could have saved me a few sleepless nights."

I go over and put a hand on her shoulder. "I'm sorry. We were only thinking of your safety, really. Be on your guard, OK? Maybe you should sleep at Richard's place for the next few days."

She dismisses my concern with a flick of her hand. "What about Joanna's amnesia? And the other . . . strange occurrences?"

"No idea. We're still completely in the dark there. I have no idea what the connection could be. The most important thing right now is that we get away from here, as far away and as quickly as we can."

Seeming to take my last words as a request, Ela pulls the envelope containing the money from her bag, gets up, and gives it to Joanna. "Here. What are you going to do now?"

Joanna gives me a prompting look, one that's saying *you answer.*

"We're going to leave the country as quickly as possible."

"How?"

"By plane."

Ela emphatically shakes her head. "From Munich? That's not a good idea. Not after what happened."

I sense what she's getting at, because the same thing quickly went through my mind before, when I was trying to book the tickets for us. "You mean because airport security is going to be on high alert? I don't reckon that's a problem. I mean, we're not wanted or anything."

"But what if somebody's called the police claiming you two were involved in the attack?"

I hadn't even thought that far ahead. "You mean Gabor?"

Ela shrugs. "It's a possibility, at least. I wouldn't put it past him if he really is part of the whole thing. He might even have posted some of his people to wait for you at the airport. Is that a risk you're willing to take?"

No, we definitely don't want that. Joanna's face is telling me the same.

"Ela's right," she says. "It's probably easier to leave the country by car. We could rent one."

"Hmm . . . you don't think there are going to be stricter border controls as well?" I object.

Ela nods. "Maybe, but not as strict as at the airport. I think a rental car is a good idea." She pauses briefly, then adds, "Oh, I just thought of another thing. You said you lost your phone at the train station. Do you want to take mine, just in case? If you get separated or . . ."

"No, thanks. That's really nice of you, but we do have a phone. That should be enough."

"Hang on," Joanna interjects. "Ela's right, we shouldn't take any risks. What if something happens to my phone? If I lose it, or if it breaks? Or if Dad manages to get my contract canceled as well? We'd be stranded without a phone then, so I think you should take Ela up on her offer. Just in case."

"My thoughts exactly." Ela reaches into her pocket and holds the device out toward me. Eventually I take it and slip it into my pocket. "You'll get it back."

Ela's voice is playfully insistent. "I'd better."

A quick hug for me, one for Joanna, then Ela's at the door already. She turns around once more. "Good luck. And please, check in with me." Before either of us can reply, the door falls shut behind her.

I stand by the window and wait until I see her walk out of the hotel entrance, along the street, then get into her car a short distance away and drive off. There's nobody following her.

"OK," I say. "Now, how are we going to get a rental car? Perhaps the best idea would be if I check online where the nearest car rental place is and—"

"I'll get us one," Joanna interrupts, putting on her jacket as though underlining her resolve. She fishes a few notes out from the envelope containing the money and hands the rest to me. "Here, hang on to this, please. I'm going to get a cab from downstairs and get it to take me to the closest car rental place. We're in Munich, it can't be that far. I'm sure the taxi drivers know their way around."

"OK. I'll come with you."

"No, I can do it by myself." Her voice sounds unusually energetic, like she's used to giving orders, almost. "You're dead, remember? We can't take any risks here. I'll get us a car and come pick you up from here. OK?"

I'm averse to the thought of letting her go out on her own, but I guess in the end she's right. However unlikely it might be that one of Gabor's people will run into us, it's still probably better if I wait at the hotel.

"All right, then."

"Great. Back soon." Joanna plants a kiss on my mouth. Before I can react, she's already heading to the door.

With robot-like motions, I fold up the envelope and slide it into my front pocket, walk over to the bed, then sit down on the edge of it.

Ela, Gabor, Bernhard, Gavin. Joanna's father. My goodness, what have we gotten ourselves into here? How wonderful and tranquil our life had been until last week, and how I'd taken being with Joanna, being engaged to her, for granted. The things I'd give now to have that life back. I'd fulfill all of her wishes, every last one of them. I'd . . .

An impulse makes me get to my feet again, go back over to the window. I want to see her get into the taxi. Not a minute passes before she appears below. The taxis are all farther down the street, on the other side. Joanna purposefully makes for the cars; she doesn't turn around, doesn't look up.

She's only about fifty yards away when suddenly the door of a parked car right in front of her is thrown open. I see legs clad in a dark pair of pants, a torso. A hand grabs hold of Joanna and drags her into the car, so quickly she has no chance to fight back. The door isn't even slammed shut again before the car pulls out of the space and races away.

It all happened much too fast, and there were virtually no people in the street either. No one saw it. No one but me. Gavin and his people really know what they're doing.

The whole thing took maybe ten seconds. More seconds pass until I get over the shock.

I storm out of the room, down the little corridor to the elevators. I press down hard on the call button, decide it's taking too long, yank open the door to the stairwell. Third floor. I run down two stairs at once, support myself against the rail. Between the second and first floor, my senses kick back in, telling me I'm acting like a complete idiot. What the hell am I running for? Do I think I'll still see the car with Joanna inside drive away when I finally reach the space it pulled out of two minutes ago? And isn't it clear who dragged her into the car and where they're taking her, anyway?

I knew turning the phone back on was a mistake. Unbridled fury takes hold of me, burning so fiercely it nearly consumes me.

I reach the ground floor. Pay the bill first, that should only take a minute. Don't risk any trouble with the police, not under any circumstances. Good, my common sense is working again.

I walk over to reception, tell the chubby lady at the counter my room number, and impatiently watch her type away on the keyboard. A hundred and twenty euros. I pull the envelope out of my pocket, put a hundred and a fifty down on the counter. "Keep the change," I say, and leave, but not before noticing the confused look she gives me.

"To the airport. General Aviation Terminal," I bark at the taxi driver. He turns around and raises an eyebrow. Then he nods.

No talking, no conversation. He understood.

As we drive I stare out of the window, not registering the things I'm seeing. My anger at Joanna's father grows with every mile. As does my sense of powerlessness. But I'm not going to let them get rid of me, I'm going to scream at that Gavin person and, if need be, go at him with my fists. Although, even now I know I'm not going to be able to do a thing. If they're still there. Yes. If they're still there in the first place.

I pay the driver generously and dash out of the cab. My injured arm collides with the edge of the door; the pain and the anger make me curse in equal measures.

The terminal hall, the passage through to customs. The officer gives me a skeptical look. But there's no way he could recognize me, it's not the same man as yesterday. "I have to get in there, to Mr. Berrigan's plane, please."

"What's your name?" His tone sounds much more friendly than I would have expected, judging from his facial expression at least.

"Thieben. Erik Thieben."

The man looks down at a list in front of him.

"I'm sorry, I don't see you on here anywhere."

"No, I was on the list yesterday. I was here then, but I forgot something."

He shakes his head. "Sorry, I can't let you through."

"But I have to go see these people. It's important."

"There's nothing I can do."

"Damn it, this is a life or death situation," I burst out. "Don't you get it?"

I see the man's eyes looking past me, searching. And I know what that means. Security. I'm an idiot. It's all over.

"Excuse me." I suddenly hear a familiar voice, speaking English, with an Australian accent. "Could you please let the man through? He's with us. Mr. Berrigan sorted everything out yesterday."

The officer briefly scrutinizes Gavin, then turns back to me. "Your ID, please."

The name Berrigan obviously works on German customs officers as well. I get my ID back, walk past the counter and toward the stairs, alongside Gavin. Once we're at the staircase I position myself in front of him, practically snorting with anger. "Where's Joanna?" I say in English.

Not a muscle twitches in Gavin's face. His gaze literally drills into me. "Why are you asking me? You're the one who ran away with her."

"And you just kidnapped her from outside the hotel, so now you're going to tell me—"

I don't even see the hand coming. I only become aware of it when it grasps my throat and mercilessly squeezes the air out of me.

"What's that you're saying? Kidnapped? Where? By who?"

I wheeze, make a grab for Gavin's hand, try to pull it away. No luck. At the point where I fear I'm about to lose consciousness, his grip finally loosens. I cough. I'm starting to suspect things aren't the way I thought. They're much worse.

"I . . . I don't know. There was a dark-colored car outside the hotel. Someone dragged her into it. Then the car disappeared."

Gavin stares past me. For four, five seconds. Then he nods. "Wait here. We'll set off in two minutes."

45

The dark fabric of the back seat, my face pressed against it. Pulse racing in my temples, my neck, everywhere. Strange hands like iron clamps. One of them is closed around my wrists, the other holds the back of my neck tightly. I'm paralyzed with horror on the inside, but my body resists, making me kick against the back of the driver's seat, brace myself against the grip of the man who's holding me, fighting with more strength than I thought myself capable of.

"That's enough, little girl, or I'll have to hurt you." The voice is unfamiliar. Despite the almost friendly tone, I have no doubt that the man won't hesitate in following through with what he said.

So I keep still. My head is still pressed against the back seat, my face turned to the dark-tinted side window of the car. I only briefly saw the face of the man who pulled me into the car and didn't recognize him. I can barely think at all, I just know that it's over for me.

They didn't cover my eyes.

They're not going to let me live.

And then there's that smell, a smell that makes me feel sick, that spells evil.

Once again, my body reacts without me telling it to. It begins to tremble uncontrollably, intensely, as though someone were shaking me.

The man loosens his grip a little. "She's about to collapse on me here," he says to one of his accomplices in the front seats.

"Make sure you don't squeeze her neck too hard, we need her without brain damage," one of them answers. I know the voice, I've heard it once before, and combined with the smell, the picture falls into place with a fear-inspiring jolt—

Joanna. The most important thing here is you and your safety. Do you want my help?

The psychologist. The one Erik argued with and threw out of the house. Bartsch.

The man next to me lets go, slowly, as though he's waiting to see if I'll start to resist again. But I remain motionless. My breathing is so quick, it's as though I've just been running, as though I'm still running, and inside I am.

Gabor's people have found us. Found me. And it was our own mistake—they must have followed Ela, from our house right to the hotel. The hotel I strolled out of just half an hour later without taking any precautions. After all, it was only a hundred feet to the taxi rank.

I feel like hitting myself in the head for my own stupidity. We were so careful the whole time, only to make this terrible mistake.

"Joanna, is everything all right?" Now Bartsch once again sounds as polite and concerned as he did a week ago, in our living room.

I don't answer him, but instead just concentrate on the world outside the car. We're slowing down. The car stops at a red light.

Don't think. Just do it. I thrust myself away from the seat, grab the door handle—not locked, you stupid assholes, it opens easily, wide enough to slip out.

One of my legs and half of my upper body are already out when the man grabs me by the arm and pulls me back inside. I hear myself scream; it feels as though he's ripped my shoulder out of its socket. The next moment, he throws himself on top of me and slams the door shut with a bang.

"You do that one more time, you stupid bitch, and you'll see what I'm made of." He hits me in the face, hard, first with his palm, then again with the back of his hand. I can taste blood.

"Lambert! Stop that at once!" Bartsch has turned around in his seat. "It was your mistake, why did you even let go of her in the first place?"

"Because I didn't expect Wickers, that idiot, to forget to lock the doors!" bellows Lambert. He's still lying on top of me with all his weight, pressing the air out of me. "But don't worry," he says, quieter now, "it won't happen again."

He pulls my hands behind my back and slings something narrow and hard around my wrists, then pulls it tight, so hard that it hurts. "It's your own fault," he says.

I touch my tongue against the spot where my lip has burst open. Yes, it's my own fault, but it was worth it. Perhaps someone noticed my attempt to flee and made a note of the license plate. And maybe they'll inform the police.

A phone rings up front. After two rings, Bartsch picks it up. "Yes? Yes, we have her. It all went smoothly, better than we'd hoped." He stops, shakes his head. "What? No. That wasn't what we agreed, that . . ."

The person he's talking to must have interrupted him. Bartsch tries several more times to say something, but without success. "You really should have made that clearer," he says eventually, sounding defensive. "No, I . . . That wasn't . . . I wouldn't presume to do something so arbitrary."

He's getting more and more nervous with every word, and it's contagious. The tension in the car is palpable anyway, and if one of these three men loses their head . . .

My hands are starting to feel numb; I flex them into fists and then stretch out my fingers to keep the blood flowing.

"I understand," says Bartsch into the phone. "Yes, I think that's doable. Of course. We'll be there shortly."

He puts down the cell phone and turns around to me. "What's the name of the woman who was in your house? The one who went to your hotel just now?"

I was right. We had been naïve enough to believe that Gabor had withdrawn his people. And that the police had thoroughly checked the area. "Why?" I ask.

"That's irrelevant. Just tell me her name."

My thoughts are tumbling through my mind. Should I not say anything? Should I lie? I couldn't betray Ela, no question of that; there was no way I could warn her about Gabor, and nor could Erik.

The thought of him burns like fire. He has no idea what's happening; he is sitting there in the hotel waiting. Looking forward to my return.

A hand clasps my hair, tearing my head backward. Lambert. "He asked you something!"

"Stop it." Bartsch's warning sounds dangerously soft. "That's not necessary yet."

Lambert lets me go, grinning; he heard the *yet* just as clearly as I did.

Bartsch doesn't ask a second time. He turns back to face forward again, crossing his arms in front of his chest.

I haven't paid any attention to our surroundings for a while, and only now do I see that the landscape has changed. We are no longer in the city, but probably quite a way outside it by now. Industrial buildings line up against warehouses, and most of the vehicles approaching us are trucks.

"Patience," says Bartsch, and I don't know whether he's addressing Lambert or me.

They park the car by one of the warehouses. It's huge, and a little way back from the road, on a plot of land which is surrounded by high walls. Far away from anything. There could be no hope of running away from here.

At the other end of the compound, I see a truck driving out of one of the warehouses. But it's so far away that I can't hear the engine, not even when the driver opens the car door.

Is there any point in yelling? As loudly as I can?

Lambert seems to guess what's going on in my mind. "You try anything, make one attempt to escape, and I'll break your bones."

So I don't try. The chance that someone could hear me is tiny, and it's obvious that Lambert would make good on his threat without giving it a second thought. He enjoys his sense of power. And I'm sure he'd like to feel a little more of it.

We walk up over a ramp and into the building. Lambert is shoving me roughly ahead of him. No one stops him, not even Bartsch, who goes past us and enters the building first.

Shelves that stretch up high, almost to the ceiling. Huge boxes, some of them wrapped in plastic. It would be very easy indeed to make someone like me disappear in one of these.

In an open space in the middle of the building there are three forklifts, and Bartsch goes to lean against one of them, striking a pointedly relaxed pose. "So. We still have a little time. And I'd like to use it to repeat my question from before: who was the woman who went to see you in the hotel?"

I barely have a chance to take a breath before Lambert pushes me so hard in the back that I fall to the floor. My hands are still tied, so I can't break my fall, only turn to the side to protect my face. My right shoulder crashes against the floor with such force that tears shoot into my eyes. Lambert laughs and kicks me, not too hard, more symbolically. "Aww. Now the little girl's crying."

"That's enough." Bartsch strides over, pushes Lambert to the side, and squats down next to me. He looks down at me.

There's some image in my head, something that I would be able to see if it would only just come a little closer to the surface. I shut my eyes, and at that moment Bartsch puts his hand under my chin and turns my face toward him.

"Tell me, Joanna. Her name."

His smell. This aftershave, which had already bothered me in our living room, now almost makes me retch.

Another kick, this time against my thigh, stronger now.

"I said stop," Bartsch snaps at Lambert. At the same moment, I hear steps approaching.

"What's going on here?"

A familiar voice, albeit only from the telephone. Gabor is here, and he's not alone. Two men flank him, and there are more in the back; one of them is sitting on one of the crates. "Just how incompetent are you people?" he says quietly.

Gabor casts a look full of irritation back over his shoulder, then turns to Bartsch. "Why is Frau Berrigan lying on the floor, and who did this to her?" He looks around. "Gentlemen, you can't be serious."

With exaggerated care, he helps me up, even brushes the dirt off my right sleeve. "I'd like to apologize for my colleagues. If there's something I can't stand, it's bad behavior." He looks around to Bartsch. "And? I'm assuming you now know who the woman was that you let get away?"

"We were just in the process of finding out."

Ela, my God. We put her life at risk, even though we should've known better. What would I do if she didn't get away? How would I feel?

If they ask me, I decide, I'll say that the woman was called Susanne Jäger. A neighbor. I'll act like it's hard for me to betray her. . . .

But Gabor doesn't even bring it up. He gives his people a contemptuous look before stepping in front of me, as close as though he wanted to hug me. Or kiss me.

Instinctively I take a step back, and stumble into Lambert, who holds me by the arms, not as roughly as before, but enough so that I can't get away when Gabor begins to pat me down. He's quick and to the point. First my jacket, then the pockets of my pants. From my right pocket, he pulls my phone. Which is locked.

I get ready for Lambert trying to beat the code out of me. I decide to stay silent for as long as I can.

But Gabor doesn't even ask. "Turn her around," he says.

As he reaches for my numb hands, I realize I've lost. My phone can be unlocked by fingerprint too. I try to break free, all along knowing how foolish the attempt is. I can barely feel what Gabor is doing with my fingers, let alone pull them away. It doesn't even take thirty seconds.

"Thank you, Joanna. So, let's see."

I turn around, wanting to slap the phone out of Gabor's hands and stamp on it with all my strength.

"Last calls. Oh—someone called Manuela. Was that your visitor? Was it?"

I don't answer. Only shake my head, thankful for the fact that I didn't save Ela's surname in my contacts.

"Well, let's check. Let's see what Manuela has to tell us."

This time Lambert has to hold me back with all his force as I try to throw myself on Gabor. I can't let him dial the number. I can't let him hear who will pick up, impatient and full of anticipation.

I fight against Lambert's grip. "No, please."

Gabor looks up, smiling. "Yes."

46

A million things are running through my head all at once as I wait for Gavin. If it wasn't him who kidnapped Joanna, there was only one possibility remaining.

But why would Gabor's people do that? Just to take her someplace they can get rid of her without any problems? Or does Gabor still need her? Could she be of use to him in some way? If so, there's a chance she'll stay alive for a while.

When Gavin returns, there are two men accompanying him. I recognize one of them; he was in the airport lounge as well yesterday. The other one's older by a good few years. Just like the other two, he's athletically built and wearing a dark suit. They stop; Gavin gives me a nod. "Let's go."

"Where?"

"There's a car outside. First we're driving to the spot where they kidnapped Joanna." After the first few steps, he adds, "It was very stupid of you two to run away."

"Have you already talked to her father?" I ask as we approach customs.

"Yes."

"And? How did he react?"

The look Gavin gives me is answer enough. *Don't ask.*

The customs officer waves us through. We exit the building and head toward a black SUV parked only a few feet away from the entrance. Gavin uses a remote to unlock the car and pauses in front of the passenger door. "You're driving."

He's right, that's easier than me explaining the route all the way to the hotel. I get in the car, and I've only just fastened my seat belt when my phone, no, Ela's phone, rings. Either somebody is trying to get hold of her, or . . . I hastily feel around for the phone in my pocket, pull it out, stare at the screen. "It's Jo." I exhale nervously. I press the green button and hold the device to my ear. "Jo, thank goodness. Where are you? Are you OK?"

Silence on the other end. "Jo? It's me, Erik. Say something."

Why isn't she answering? Did they tape her mouth shut? Maybe she's tied up and somehow managed to hit redial . . .

"What a surprise. Erik."

My stomach cramps up, as though caught in an iron vise. That voice. It's . . . "Herr Gabor?"

"Yes indeed. And I have to say, I'm greatly surprised to have you on the phone. On dear Manuela's phone, at that. You know, I should really be angry at you. Not informing me, your employer, of the fact that you're still alive . . . it doesn't exactly stand testament to a sense of duty on your part."

Gavin gives me a nudge, makes a questioning gesture. I emphatically shake my head and place my forefinger in front of my lips.

"Why do you have Joanna's phone? Where is she? How is she? If you hurt her in any way I'll—"

"Please, Erik, do stay calm. Joanna is merely enjoying my hospitality. And I'd be very happy if you came to join us as well. Then we could all have a nice little chat."

I look over at Gavin, who glowers back at me.

"I want to talk to Joanna," I say as assertively as I can. "I'm not doing anything before that happens."

Instead of a reply, I hear a scraping sound, then Joanna's voice, distant at first but moving closer. "You son of a bitch, let go of me." The last few words are perfectly clear. Gabor must be holding the phone to her ear now.

"Jo. My God. Are you all right? Did they hurt you? Where are you?"

"Erik. Don't come here, you hear me? You can't come here at any—"

She breaks off abruptly, somebody must have put a hand over her mouth. I hear Gabor's voice again shortly after.

"It seems your fiancée doesn't want you at our nice little get-together. But I do." He makes it sound like an invitation to go for lunch. "Where are you right now?"

I feel unbridled rage boil up within me. That bastard tried to kill me, several times. And now he's got Joanna. For the first time in my life I feel like I want to cause someone pain. Terrible pain. "Sure, like I'm really going to tell you."

"That's fine. Then let's do this another way, your location doesn't matter. I'll give you . . . let's say fifteen minutes to show up here. If you're not here with us by then, you needn't bother coming at all, at least not where Joanna is concerned. Now listen up, I'll tell you how to get to where we are."

"No, wait. I'm near the airport, fifteen minutes won't be enough."

"Well, well. Near the airport. What are you doing there?"

"When Jo didn't show up again, I thought she might already be here," I lie. "We were going to fly out today."

Gabor is silent for a while, during which I feel sick with fear, then he speaks again. "I'll be expecting you in half an hour. We're in a warehouse at the edge of town. You can definitely make it in time."

He describes the route, speaking slowly and with pointed clarity. He gives me the address right at the end. I mentally repeat it three times. "Oh, and Erik . . . I find the phrase rather childish because those dim-witted crooks on TV always use it, but I don't know how else to put it. If you call the police, your fiancée's dead." Then, the signal tone. He hung up.

"That was Gabor," I say, and lower the phone. "He kidnapped Jo, and he's demanded that I go to him. Within half an hour. He'll kill her if I don't."

"Would he do that?"

I nod. "Yes, I think he would. He said that he'll also kill her if I call the police."

The corners of Gavin's mouth turn downward. "No, no police. Not yet. We'll deal with this. Can you make it there in half an hour?"

"Yes, I think I can."

"Good." He takes a pen from the inside pocket of his jacket, opens the glove compartment, and pulls the car instruction manual out of a leather file. He swiftly tears off the cover sheet and holds it out toward me. "The address. Write it down. And your telephone number. When you're done, get going, I'll call you."

"And what are you—"

"Write. Now."

While I'm doing what Gavin demanded, he turns around to face the two men in the back seat of the car.

"Call Riley. Everyone except the pilot out at once. Full equipment. And we need three vehicles. I expect us to set off in five minutes. Let's go."

As the men slam the doors shut behind them, I hand the sheet back to Gavin. He takes a quick look at it and nods. "Now, you're going to drive to the place and do everything just as this Gabor guy asked you to. We'll be following you in a few minutes' time. I'm going to call you while you're on the way, and then you're going to explain to me in detail why this Gabor guy kidnapped Jo. And what type of a person he is. Clear?"

My mind is in such turmoil that nothing's really clear anymore, but I hope I've understood him. My instinct tells me the best plan is to follow Gavin's instructions. He, as opposed to me, obviously knows his way around situations like these.

He gets out of the car; I start the engine and drive. On the highway toward Munich, I key the address into the navigation system. The device is set to English. Of course.

Twenty-four minutes to my destination, the display informs me. Thank goodness.

When Gavin calls me, he's en route as well. I hurriedly tell him what I know about Gabor, which is obviously not as much as I thought I knew about him, not by a long shot. I tell him about the attempts to kill us, about the email I saw on Gabor's computer. And about the explosion at the train station.

Gavin asks me how many people Gabor has at his disposal. But how am I supposed to know that?

By now I've reached the periphery of Munich. The GPS is showing just under a mile to go before reaching the destination. I enter some kind of industrial area. Rows of auto repair shops and car dealerships of every brand, a large metalworking shop, a bathroom fittings company. Larger and smaller warehouses in between, unmarked, windowless.

Eight hundred and fifty more yards. No more car dealerships here. Just warehouses.

I try to picture what will await me when I get there. Are they going to beat me down once I'm trapped? I break out in a sweat. The closer I get to my destination, the more difficult I'm finding it to think straight. It's the fear. It's taking control of me more and more, threatening to paralyze my mind entirely. All of me, my entire being is screaming at me, telling me to turn around, to put as much distance between myself and Gabor as I can, and to do it as quickly as possible.

But, Joanna. She's completely at the bastard's mercy. No. I'm not going to run, no way. I manage to stifle my fear, to make room for anger at Gabor and his henchmen. Those fuckers.

Another three hundred feet. I glance at my watch. I got through the traffic OK, and have six minutes left until the half hour runs out. I stop the car, pull out my phone, dial the last number.

"I'm here," I say when Gavin takes the call after a single ring. "What should I do now?"

"How much time do you have left?"

"Five more minutes."

"OK. Wait for another two minutes, then go in. We're almost there now. Do everything the man says. Pretend like you'll be perfectly compliant. Try to get close to Joanna as well. Once we're in, it's going to get unpleasant. You'll have to protect her, do you understand?"

"Yes, I'll try."

"Very good. Once we've hung up, hide the phone somewhere in your car and go."

"The phone? Why would—"

"Have you forgotten that Gabor called you from Joanna's phone? He's going to search you too. He'll find the phone and hit redial. An Australian number. He'll suspect what's going on if he's not a complete idiot."

"But the call log can be—"

"For fuck's sake!" Gavin suddenly bellows. "You're the one who put Joanna in this situation. Now stop babbling and do what I've told you, or I'll fucking tear you a new one."

I want to scream back at him and tell him to go screw himself. Tell him that the reason why Joanna ran away from him at the airport in the first place was because he was so stubborn. Tell him I'd asked Joanna more than once to go back to him. But I need him. Joanna needs him.

"OK," I say, emotionless, and hang up. I hide the phone underneath the floor mat behind the driver's seat, take one final deep breath, then get out and walk the last three hundred feet. Maybe it's a good thing if they don't hear me coming.

My knees feel shaky. But I wouldn't dream of running away anymore.

Because Joanna's there somewhere, just up ahead of me.

47

Lambert's hand, which is pressed over my mouth, smells of cold cigarette smoke. I try to bite it, try to kick behind me, but he's unimpressed by both attempts. Instead, he just laughs. "Just you wait until Gabor gives me free rein," he whispers into my ear.

Gabor has just finished his conversation with Erik and is carefully putting my phone into the inside pocket of his jacket. "That was more productive than I expected," he says, turning toward me.

The man who was sitting on the crate earlier has now stood up and is ambling toward us. He's tall, dressed like a businessman, and his dark hair is very short, buzz-cut.

"Did I get that right, Gabor? This Thieben guy you assured me was dead is actually still alive?"

Gabor shrugs, clearly trying to keep his cool. "Yes, but he won't be for much longer than the next half hour. He's on his way here."

So my warning hadn't helped. Erik was going to fall into these people's hands—probably believing that he was saving me. As if Gabor would risk letting either of the two of us leave alive.

"It was a mistake to entrust you with this much responsibility," says the man with the buzz cut. "It's not going to be easy to straighten all of this out again. I hope you realize that—"

"Enough." The voice is coming from the entrance. I hadn't noticed that the gate to the building had been opened again, and it seemed that the others hadn't either.

The man walking in toward us acts like he has all the time in the world. He had only said one word, but it was enough to make everybody there freeze, including Gabor. Lambert's grip on me becomes increasingly merciless.

The man is old, in his mideighties for sure. His posture is very rigid, almost military-like, even though he has a walking stick, though he's not leaning on it; he strikes it onto the floor with every second step, as though he's wanting to create a rhythm as he walks.

The three-piece suit he's wearing reminds me of my father's tailored suits from London. This man has money. And power which far exceeds Gabor's. I can see that in people. I've met some of these sorts before, though admittedly no one whose appearance alone causes this much fear. As he walks past, the men flinch, not visibly, but internally. Like school kids trying not to get noticed by their teacher.

"I find it very regrettable that I've been forced to clean up your mess, Gabor." The man's voice is soft but powerful, as though it would be beneath him to raise it in order for the people around him to understand. "You said you were up to the task. Clearly it was a mistake to believe you." He comes to a stop, both hands on the pommel of his stick. "You are endangering the success of the project. The elections will be in two weeks, and in light of recent events we'll be celebrating our biggest victory in seventy years—unless, that is, your mistakes prove to be our downfall."

Elections? What do the elections have to do with all this? I have no idea what the man's talking about, but I can see that Gabor is struggling to regain his composure. He clears his throat several times, but still sounds hesitant when he finally speaks.

"I can assure you, Herr von Ritteck, that I have everything under control. There were just a few unpredictable incidents—"

"Unpredictable?" The man takes three leisurely steps toward Gabor. "You gave an employee access to our confidential correspondence. If you mean unpredictable in the sense of being stupid, then I agree with you. And then, instead of immediately dealing with your mistake, you let the man go."

Gabor keeps shaking his head. "But I took measures. There was a downright genius idea of how to get rid of Thieben if it had turned out to be necessary."

Von Ritteck takes another step toward Gabor, who clearly needs all his willpower not to flinch. "*If?* Your role was to keep all risks far from the squadron. Or to at least immediately inform me of your failure and obey my orders. And believe you me, they would have been clear."

Gabor tries to interject, but von Ritteck silences him with a quick hand movement. "As far as I know, Thieben isn't the only problem. What's the situation with the other two workers?"

"Both dead," explains Gabor hastily. "They think Nadine Balke committed suicide, and Morbach's body will never be found. Not in the next ten years, at least."

For a moment I'm glad that Lambert is holding me in such an iron grip. Bernhard Morbach. The man with the laptop bag, the one who warned me. *You have to disappear, as quickly as you can. Please believe me. This isn't a joke, you have to get yourself to safety.*

It seems that he hadn't managed to do the same himself.

"Morbach." A trace of regret appears on von Ritteck's face. "He was promising. Very dedicated to the German cause; I liked him. Another few years and he would have had the necessary hardness to not lose his mind over a few deaths when the well-being of the homeland is at stake. He would have understood that they died for their country like soldiers. Victims of a necessary war against these subhumans with their prayer mats and veils, who presume to enjoy the same rights on German soil as we do." He stomps his walking stick on the floor once more. "Who dare threaten us, strike fear into the hearts of our wives and our children with their terrorism. But this time they will suffer the consequences."

Slowly, very slowly, it was dawning on me. The project. Project Phoenix, that must be it. That's what this man is talking about. Over a hundred dead, in order to fuel the hate of the population—toward Muslims primarily, but also toward anything foreign.

Absolute madness. And yes, the elections were in two weeks. . . .

I haven't read any papers in the past few days, and I've barely been online—the desire to survive had left no room for anything else. But I can imagine what a surge of emotion there must have been on social media. How fertile the ground must have been for right-wing populist politicians and their simple solutions, even hours after the attack. *Die for their country like soldiers.* I think of the pictures on television and of what Erik told me. I hope against hope that this von Ritteck and all his helpers will get caught, exposed, that they will pay for what they've done.

The only thing I want more than that is to survive. But considering what I now know, this is even more unlikely than before.

Gabor seems to have regained his composure a little. "That's all as close to my heart as it is to yours," he explains. "That's why I volunteered for this mission. Why would I have done that if our goals weren't more important to me than my own well-being?"

Von Ritteck looks him up and down. "Desire for recognition, perhaps?" he says dryly. "And, of course, you also know how influential the people are who you're trying to get in with."

Gabor looks genuinely hurt. "Is that what you think of me? I assure you, I would sacrifice myself for the cause without a moment's hesitation. And I will; I'll take the blame and protect everyone else if Phoenix should fail because of my mistakes."

It's hard to say whether von Ritteck believes him. He just stands there in silence. Then he slowly turns his head.

Until now, the man hasn't so much as glanced in my direction, but now he looks at me for the first time. For a long while. Without expression.

I don't avert my gaze; after all, I have nothing left to lose now. "Phoenix cannot be allowed to fail," he says, before turning to look at Gabor again. "Just out of interest: do you realize who you have in your custody here?" He points the head of his stick toward me.

"Yes, of course. That's Erik Thieben's fiancée. Her name is Joanna."

"Aha." Von Ritteck slowly shifts his weight from his right leg to his left. "Joanna what?"

It's clear from Gabor's face that he considers this question to be no more than an annoyance. That a response like "but that's irrelevant" lies on the tip of his tongue, and that he only stops himself from saying it out of respect and, most likely, fear too. "Joanna Berrigan. She's Australian, a photographer, and she's been living in Germany for about a year."

"Correct, except unfortunately you seem to have missed the most important detail," von Ritteck says, interrupting him. "So maybe I should fill you in, then. Berrigan, huh? Think for a moment, Gabor." He waits for a few seconds. "Doesn't the name mean anything to you? No? Just as I suspected. I have no intention of making a speech about the influence and fortune of her father, so I'll just say this: she is not the kind of person you can simply make disappear without having to face consequences to surpass your wildest imaginations."

He's caught Gabor out, that's obvious. His gaze flits over to me, then back over to von Ritteck, who is pulling his pocket watch out of his waistcoat pocket. "How come I know that and you don't, Gabor? Can you explain that to me?"

"No." Gabor draws himself up. "Clearly this oversight is my responsibility. But if the plan that I initiated months ago had worked, this problem would have been solved all at once."

Von Ritteck sighs. "And so I'll solve it for you. Because I have to. You're incompetent, Gabor. You're not worthy of being part of Squadron 444."

For the first time, the rage which Gabor must have been stifling with all his might starts to surface. "Yes, I failed. But it wasn't just me. You sent me Bartsch with the assurance that he was first-class. An expert on the human psyche, those were your words. But if he had fulfilled his task correctly . . ."

Bartsch had remained in the background until that moment. Now he steps out of the shadows and goes to stand next to von Ritteck. "I fulfilled my task exactly as was required of me. The idea was yours, Gabor. It was good, I don't question that. But it wasn't airtight."

Gabor, who suddenly sees himself confronted by two opponents, laughs mockingly. "Oh, so all of a sudden it wasn't airtight? That's not how it sounded two months ago. Back then you couldn't wait to get on the plane."

Bartsch shakes his head. "Stop it, you're not putting the blame on me. I didn't make any mistakes here."

"Oh no?" Gabor stretches out his arm and points at me. "If that were true, then we'd have a killer here with us."

48

Gabor had said that the warehouse was located behind a high wall, and the wall I'm standing in front of right now has to be the one. Once I walk around it and have a clear view of the site behind, I spot a black limousine parked right in front of the warehouse. I instinctively take a few steps to the side and conceal myself behind a pile of stacked pallets.

Are the occupants of the limo some of Gabor's people?

I look at my watch. In two minutes' time the half hour will be up; I'm going to have to chance it. There's no more time to lose.

Soon I'm standing in the driveway, which is roughly ten feet wide.

The warehouse is set a little off to the back. Entrances painted in different colors and loading ramps indicate that several companies share ownership of the building. The open space outside, however, is mostly empty. There are only a few cars at the far right end of the warehouse, near where I'm meant to go to, according to Gabor's instructions.

He said I had to go to a blue gate. There it is, up ahead, right where the limousine is parked.

I get to the spot one minute after the time limit expires. The gate is locked. I look around, have no clue what I'm supposed to do now. Gabor didn't tell me anything, and I hadn't thought of asking him either.

Time is running out. I ball my fist and hammer on the gate several times. To minimal effect. The steel of the gate almost completely swallows the sound of my knocking, and my hand starts to hurt. I turn around and kick it with my heel. The result barely differs from my first attempt.

"Hey, stop that."

I don't know where the man came from all of a sudden. He's standing off to my side, and the weapon in his hand doesn't leave me with any doubt about who he's with.

"My name is Erik Thieben," I carefully tell him. "I'd like to see Herr Gabor."

"Shut up and come with me."

He directs me away from the gate and around the corner of the warehouse. The distance between the outer wall and the actual warehouse wall is only about six and a half feet here. There's another man standing in front of a door. He's tall, heavyset, stone-faced. He takes a step aside, freeing up the entryway.

A narrow passage lies ahead of me, ending in a set of swinging double doors. About halfway through, a smaller corridor branches off to the right.

"Go straight," the guy at my back orders.

The doors swing open without any effort, revealing an area of the warehouse which is divided off from the rest. I quickly look all around me, trying to get an overview of the situation.

This section of the warehouse is about four hundred feet in length and breadth. Narrow skylights on the right-hand side as well as a few glass panels in the roof diffuse the steel and concrete construction with a dull, colorless light. It smells of oil; the stone floor is almost completely saturated with dark stains. High shelves are on either side of the room, wooden boxes and loaded pallets in front of them, which seem to be full of machines or components for building some type of large equipment. The middle of the room is empty, right over to the opposite wall, which has a built-in roll-up door, high and wide enough to let a large truck through.

Two forklifts are parked nearby. A group of people are standing in front of them, and the entire group turns around to look at us. I think I recognize Gabor and Bartsch. But where's Joanna?

Not even waiting for an order from the man behind me, I start moving. I only suppress the urge to run with difficulty. What have they done to Joanna? My steps get faster and faster. "Hey, slow down!" the guy behind me shouts. Screw him.

Then, finally, I see her. One of Gabor's men had obstructed my view of her. One of them is holding her from behind, with his hand over her mouth.

The relief I feel lasts for just a second; then I see the weapons pointed at me.

If only Gavin and his people were already here! But how should I react once they were? And, more important—how will these men react? Won't they simply start shooting when the Australians suddenly storm the warehouse?

"Ah, Erik. You're here." Gabor raises his arm, looks demonstratively at his watch. "And almost on time, as well. I hope you were sensible enough not to inform the police. My colleagues have the warehouse surrounded; they'll notice any approaching special response units right away. And if that happens, we'll execute both of you on the spot."

There are still about thirty feet between us. I'd focused all my attention on Gabor and Joanna, so it's only in this moment that I notice the old man. He's behind Gabor, seemingly supporting himself on a walking stick. But he's not hunched over, and doesn't show even the slightest sign of frailty. Given his firm posture, the walking stick seems like an ineffective prop, one used only to feign weakness.

And it's from the walking stick that I recognize him. The man I saw in Gabor's lobby. Back then I'd barely paid any attention to him, and he'd paid even less to me. Now, though, he's looking at me, maybe he even recognizes me, but there's no trace of human interest in his gaze. His eyes are cold and emotionless, in a way that makes my hair stand on end. An aura of power surrounds the man, and it would probably be the same even if he were wearing rags.

I stop and turn to face Joanna. I see the fear in her eyes. Tear my gaze away from her and face Gabor.

"Are you going to tell me the meaning of all of this? I have no idea what you're playing at here, but I'd very much like to understand why you tried to kill me. And why you kidnapped Joanna. What have we got to do with your scheming, what did we ever do to you? Or what did *I* do to you?"

"Well," Gabor begins, but the old man interrupts him right away: "Hold your tongue."

His tone is just as emotionless as his eyes were when he looked at me just now. It doesn't sound agitated in the least, it's almost casual, and yet something resonates within it, something that scares me even more than the guns pointing at me.

"I will shed some light on the darkness of your ignorance, young man. Let me put it like this—you were in the wrong place at the wrong time. A twist of fate, one for which you are not even to blame. What's all the more tragic now is that you and Frau Berrigan will have to lay your heads on the block because of another person's bungling carelessness."

The man only looks at Gabor for a mere two seconds, but there's more contempt in his gaze than can be put into words.

He takes a few steps toward me, stops when he's about two yards away. I'm aware of the odor emanating from him despite the distance between us. He smells old.

"Herr Thieben, what I'd like you to tell me now is the name of the woman who paid your fiancée a visit at the hotel. Although, you were probably there yourself the entire time, while we all thought you were dead." There's that look at Gabor again.

I glance over at Joanna, who, despite the hand over her mouth, manages to shake her head, her eyes wide. *Do everything the man says*, Gavin told me. But he also told me to stall them. I shrug. "I don't know who you're talking about. And I'm not saying anything while that man has his hand over Joanna's mouth."

A gesture from the old man, barely noticeable, makes the man holding Joanna lower his hand. And yet the old man didn't even look at him as he made the gesture.

"Erik, why did you come here?" The words burst out of Joanna. "They're going to kill us both. You realize that, don't you?"

"I'm afraid your fiancée is right, Herr Thieben, we're going to have to kill the two of you, one way or another. What she doesn't know, however, is the following. I'm going to ask you again in a second who that woman was. If you don't answer, or if you give me the wrong answer, I'll have one of my men cut off one of your fiancée's fingers. Then I'll ask you the same question again. Being a computer specialist, I'm sure you'll have calculated by now it will take us about fifteen minutes to get to the last finger. Let's say twenty, as I'm certain we'll have to take action from time to time to make sure Frau Berrigan regains consciousness."

I feel sick to my stomach.

"Then we'll take off her shoes and ask the same question another ten times; that should take another twenty minutes. So I think it should suffice if I tell you how we'll proceed from there in about forty minutes' time."

Without waiting for me to react, the old man turns and nods at a group of three men who are leaning against some large crates off to the side. The three spring up and walk toward a pilot's bag a few feet away from them on the floor.

"Now, Herr Thieben, I'm going to ask you for the first time. What's the name of the woman who came to see you in the hotel?"

"Manuela," I say without a moment's hesitation. "The woman's name is Manuela Reinhard. She's an old friend of mine."

Gabor had seen the name Manuela on the screen of Joanna's phone, but he doesn't know her last name. Which means that nobody could know that the surname Reinhard isn't the right one. I had to say something, one way or another.

"Erik!" Joanna screams. "What are you doing?" I admire her for having the nerve, even in this situation, to play along. The old man gives me a nod. "And what is Frau Reinhard's address?"

I give him the name of a street where a casual acquaintance of mine lives, all the while hoping Gavin and his people will show up here as quickly as possible. These men here are going to check if Ela is in fact registered at the address I gave them. If they check online phone books, I can always claim she doesn't have a landline in the house.

So they'll have to drive over there. It will take maybe twenty minutes until they figure out I lied to them. If Gavin hasn't shown up by then, it'll get tight. But all will be lost by then anyway.

Gabor is still standing next to the old man, silent, staring daggers at me.

"Where do we go from here?" I ask, deliberately in his direction.

"I'll tell you in two minutes," the old man responds in his place.

I don't understand. "Why two minutes?"

He doesn't respond, but it isn't necessary.

I realize that I've miscalculated when another young guy with close-cropped hair walks over to us. He's holding a phone to his ear and speaking into it as he approaches. "Yes, understood," he says quietly. "And that's for certain? OK."

He lowers the hand holding the phone and shakes his head, and the old man raises an eyebrow. "You've just forfeited one of your fiancée's fingers, Herr Thieben. There's no Manuela Reinhard living at that address, as a good friend at the police department just confirmed for us. Consequently, I would assume that the surname is not correct either."

"No, that's . . . that's . . ." I start to say, not even knowing how to end the sentence. But it doesn't matter, as one of the men steps up to Joanna. He has a pair of shears in his hand.

"No, wait, please," I say, frantic now. "I'll tell you the—" But I don't get any further, because at that very second, the roll-up door explodes.

49

The bang is so painfully loud that at first I think someone has thrown an explosive charge into the building. But then I see the truck.

It has crashed through the closed entrance like an enormous, aggressive animal, tearing the gate to bits, and now it's racing toward us, the motor revving.

I struggle against Lambert's grip, which he has involuntary loosened. I just need to get away from here. Away. I no longer understand what's happening; my instincts have taken over; the panic gives me enough strength to pull myself free.

But the momentum of breaking free makes me stumble. And then there's another deafening bang that fills the building, and seconds later someone crashes to the floor, half next to me, half on top of me.

Lambert. His eyes half-open, unseeing. Blood is spurting out of a hole in his skull, just above his right eye.

I should be happy that he's dead and I am, but the sight of him, his lifeless face so close to mine, is unbearable. I try to wriggle out from under him, but in vain. My hands are still tied behind my back, it's useless, I can't get away. I feel the scream rising in my throat.

The building is filled with other screams, part fearful, part . . . commanding. And in my native language.

It slowly dawns on me what the appearance of the truck could mean: That it's my people, Gavin and his team, that Erik must have somehow managed to inform them.

Yes. Gavin's first shot would certainly have been at the person who posed the most direct threat to my life. He must've immediately seized the opportunity as long as there was no more danger he might hit me.

Gabor has raised his arms into the air, and is trying to explain in clumsy English that he has nothing to do with any of this, but Gavin pays no attention to him, he's running toward me—and the very next moment I realize why.

Someone yanks my head back. Something hard and cold is pressed against my throat. "Stay where you are," the man kneeling over me bellows. I can't see him, but I think it's the same man who was holding the shears. "One step closer and I'll slit her throat."

His English is almost perfect, and Gavin reacts immediately. He freezes midmovement, raises both hands. He's still holding his weapon in one of them.

"Well done, Becker." Von Ritteck goes slowly over to Gavin, and I hate the fact that I'm the reason he has to stand there, motionless, and watch the old man pull out his pistol. He aims at it Gavin, who still doesn't move a muscle.

Von Ritteck cocks his head in approval. "Take a look at that, men," he says, turning to his people. "That's loyalty. This man doesn't even hesitate to die in order to fulfill his mission. Head held high. My respect. I wish I had one of his kind among my ranks."

I've no idea if Gavin understands anything of what von Ritteck is saying. But I'm totally sure that he hasn't given up yet. Neither on my life nor his.

With every breath, I feel the blade against my neck more. I try to fight back the idea of how it would feel for it to cut, first through the skin, then through blood vessels and tendons . . .

One way or the other, it was going to happen. Von Ritteck had made it clear that he would let neither Erik nor me live. And now the same fate is in store for Gavin and his people.

I can see two of them. One of them is just behind Gavin, the other is by the truck.

Get in and run over everybody, I think. *Don't worry about me or Erik or anyone.*

If Erik was even still alive, that is. I can't see him anywhere. Maybe he's lying unconscious behind one of the forklifts. Or between the piled-up pallets.

I haven't yet finished the thought when a whistle blows through the building. At that moment, one of the shelving units in the building tips over, teetering toward us, but especially toward von Ritteck, who notices it a little later than I do.

He jumps to the side, quicker than I would have thought him capable of, and Gavin dives in the opposite direction, bringing himself closer to me—and at the same moment, the blade is gone from my throat. The hand of the man who was holding onto me goes slack, he slumps to the floor, his head dented in on the left. . . . The shears slip out of his fingers.

Although I know that I should jump up now and find cover, I can't manage it. It's as though my body were made of concrete and time was molten lead—I'm aware of the fact that everything around me is happening at breakneck speed, but every detail still embeds itself in my mind.

The shelving unit buries Christoph Bartsch beneath it, right in front of my eyes. The man who, according to Gabor, had failed in relation to me. *Then we'd have a killer here with us.*

Two of Gavin's people shoot at the men who are covering von Ritteck, while the old man himself calmly sets his walking stick aside and checks the contents of his revolver.

Then there's a hand on my shoulder. Someone grabs me under the arms, tries to pull me up. "Come on, Jo. Quickly." Erik, it's Erik. I turn around, see his pale face. In his right hand he's holding something that looks like an automobile jack. There are hairs stuck to one end of it.

"Please." He puts down the jack and pulls me up a little. "We have to find cover, quickly."

The shears, I want to take the shears, it could be useful to have some sort of weapon, but my hands are still tied.

As if Erik understood me without any words, he reaches for them, lifts me onto my feet, and pulls me behind one of the large piles of crates.

More gunshots, this time followed by screams. *Can no one outside hear this? Someone has to be hearing it!*

"Hold still." Erik grabs my hands, and suddenly they're free. I can't feel them still, but I can see them. Blue and red and swollen. My wrists are chafed raw and bloody.

Erik lets the cable tie he's cut fall to the floor. "Those assholes," he whispers.

More gunshots. This time there are no screams.

But there is . . . a metallic grinding sound. Not in front of us, but behind us. One of the gates to the ramps is slowly going up, although only halfway.

An escape route. If we can make it out there, we can call for help.

Have von Ritteck's people noticed? Can they see it too, from their position?

A black shadow dashes past the half-open gate. Reinforcements from this ominous-sounding squadron maybe, paramilitary fighters, against whom Gavin's team wouldn't stand a chance.

If they come through the gate, they'll see Erik and me right away.

"We need a new hiding place." Without waiting for Erik's response, I squeeze through the crates, which have been stacked to form something resembling lanes . . . and from here I can see Gavin again. He's entrenched himself behind the crates with two of his people; they're conferring quietly—do they even have any ammunition left? And if they don't, how long will it take for their opponents to realize?

No one has pulled Bartsch out from beneath the shelves. One of the heavy crates is covering his body from the waist down, blood is oozing out of his mouth, but he's still alive. Trying weakly to push away the ton of weight that's slowly crushing him.

And then suddenly they're there. Without any sign, without warning.

"Attack," somebody roars, and the special police commando swarms the building like a horde of black ants.

They barely meet with any resistance. Gavin and his people immediately lay down on the floor with their hands behind their head, and after a brief moment of hesitation, Gabor does the same. Only one of von Ritteck's men tries to flee, through the hole made by the truck. Three policemen set off in pursuit.

The only glimmer of calm in the middle of all the chaos is the old man. He looks at the policemen with a smile, still holding his pistol in his hand. The machine guns which are pointed at him clearly don't impress him.

"Drop your weapon!" bellows one of the special unit people.

"Of course," says von Ritteck. "Just a moment, please."

He glances over at the dead Lambert, then at the man who Erik attacked. A jolt goes through his body, as if he were standing at attention, as if he's about to salute. "The seed I've planted will grow regardless," he says. "For Germany."

In one quick motion he lifts the pistol, puts it in his mouth, and pulls the trigger—simultaneously, the police open fire on him.

I turn away. *The seed I've planted will grow regardless.* We're going to have so much to explain, Erik and me.

The battle ends almost as quickly as it began. The policemen drag all of von Ritteck's collaborators out of the building. An officer from the police unit comes toward us. "You're Joanna Berrigan? Erik Thieben?"

"Yes." Erik stretches out his hands, palms up. "We're unarmed. Both of us."

The man makes sure of it himself, before nodding toward the open gate. "Go outside, you'll be looked after there."

Yes, and I have to take care of Gavin and his people. Are they all alive? Will they get into trouble for saving me? I have no idea how legal it was, what they did.

But first . . .

"I have to speak to the man who's lying under the shelving unit," I say. In a friendly tone, without any hint of bossiness or arrogance. "Please. It's very important."

The special unit guy shakes his head. "Under no circumstances. We have orders to empty the building immediately."

"Please." I put all the despair that has filled me for days into this one word. "I have to understand why all this happened to me, and I think he knows. Please give me the chance to talk to him."

The man glances over his shoulder, toward one of his colleagues, who nods briefly.

"OK. It will be a little while anyway until we can get hold of a crane that will be able to lift the crate off of him. It doesn't look good for him." He hesitates. "You can speak to him briefly, but only in my presence."

Gabor is led past; his gaze flits over us. He must know what's awaiting him. Erik and I are alive. We know what really happened at Munich station, but will we be able to prove it all? So much of what has happened could be explained differently. What we have to tell sounds so improbable that I'm sure Gabor's lawyers would take great pleasure in tearing every sentence apart.

And then what?

Simply going back into the building is harder for me than I thought. But none of the four dead bodies I can see are my father's people.

From outside, I can hear the sirens of a whole fleet of emergency vehicles as I kneel down next to Bartsch. His face is waxy and white, his cheeks drawn; his breathing is shallow and fitful, but I think he recognizes me.

The thought of demanding something from a dying man seems repugnant, but this is my only opportunity. "Dr. Bartsch?" I wait until his eyes meet mine. "Please. Please, if you can, tell me what happened. What's wrong with me. You know, don't you?"

No reaction, at first. Then a tiny, barely visible nod. I lean over closer to him.

"The ambulance is here now," says the policeman behind me. "You have to go."

"Yes. Of course. Right away."

Bartsch's lips move. His voice is barely a whisper. "Forget it," he says. He almost smiles, as if he had made a joke. "You forgot so much already. Forget this too."

"Please," I say, a little too loud. "Please don't do this to me."

There's something wet in his breath. As though he's sucking in air and water at the same time. "It's a shame," he whispers, "that I won't live to see you kill him after all. Because you will."

50

I'm standing in front of a police van and Joanna's a few feet away, just inside the sliding door of an emergency vehicle, sitting on the floor. A woman wearing an orange paramedic's jacket has draped a blanket over her shoulders and is talking to her in a calm voice.

There are dark streaks and marks all over Joanna's face. Dirt and blood, mixed with tears, smudged all over her cheeks and forehead. Her hair is pasted to her head in strands. Something inside me is screaming to go over and take her into my arms. To press her against me, so tightly that I can feel her with every fiber of my being. To close my eyes and let the liberating certainty wash over us that we came through it, that we survived.

"Over here please, Herr Thieben." One of the two detectives who led me over to the police vehicle points inside it. He'd introduced himself as Chief König. "Let's take a drive."

"What about my fiancée?" I ask, gesturing over toward Joanna. The policeman follows my gaze.

"She's still being treated, but you'll see her later at the station."

I take a demonstrative step back and shake my head. "No, I'll wait for her."

The second man, a somewhat portly, half-bald detective whose name I've forgotten, puts his hand on my shoulder. It's too firm to be a friendly gesture.

"That wasn't a request, even if my colleague put it politely. Get in the car now. Frau Berrigan will be brought to the station shortly."

I want to tell the man that I'm sick and tired of being ordered around. That he should take a moment to imagine what we've just been through, and that he can take his orders and shove them where the sun don't shine. Just a second later, though, I remind myself that we were just involved in a shooting that resulted in numerous casualties, and that these men probably saved our lives.

My eyes remain fixed on Joanna. "All right, but I'd at least like to go and see her quickly."

"Hurry up then," König says before the portly man can answer.

Joanna gets up as I approach. The blanket slides off her shoulders, but she doesn't seem to notice. She just stands there, looking at me. We embrace, caress each other. Hold each other in silence. Sometimes you don't need words.

Joanna breaks away from me and touches her hand to my cheek. A semblance of a smile flits over her face. *You can go*, it probably means. *Everything's OK now.*

When we get to the station, the two officers take me to a somberly furnished room and offer me a cup of coffee. Once a young man has set down the steaming cup in front of me and left again, they ask me to tell them, in sequence, what happened, and especially what I know about the bombing at Munich station.

I start with the evening when Joanna suddenly didn't recognize me anymore. I do, however, understate the seriousness of the situation by quite a bit. My fear that Joanna could be shipped off to a mental institution is still there.

The two men constantly interrupt me with questions. Can I say any more about this or that; why don't I take a moment and think again carefully. What part do I think Gabor played in the whole affair, and do I know who von Ritteck is. Whether I witnessed any part of the shootout in the warehouse. Did Gavin and his people open fire, or simply react to the shots the other men fired. From time to time, they exchange unreadable glances.

Once I've finished giving my account, they take turns asking even more questions. Why didn't I contact the police earlier, and why did I fake my own death.

As I'm explaining our motivations, the door opens and Joanna comes in accompanied by a woman with black hair. The woman puts a folder on the table and leaves the room again.

Joanna, too, is given a mug of coffee, and right away she cups it with both hands. Just as she always does.

She must have had an opportunity to wash; her face doesn't look as dirty as it did outside the warehouse.

The half-bald officer leafs through the folder with obvious interest. Pullmann. Now I remember. His name is Pullmann. After a while, he tosses the folder back onto the table in front of him and scrutinizes Joanna. "So, why don't you tell me about when you saw Herr Thieben standing there in your house and you no longer recognized him."

My folded hands clench up under the table. Hopefully Joanna will say the same thing I did.

"I don't really remember in detail anymore," she starts, giving me a quick glance. "It was very strange. But it subsided again fairly quickly." Thank goodness.

They repeat a few of the questions which they've asked me, then they want to know about the Australians.

"Frau Berrigan, how are you and Herr Porter acquainted?" König asks. I only realize who he's talking about when Joanna answers.

"Gavin heads up my father's security team."

"In Australia?"

"Yes."

"So why is he here?"

"Because I called my father and told him I was worried my life might be in danger."

Pullmann leans forward and slams the palms of his hands down on the table. "And why the hell didn't you inform the police if you were afraid for your life?"

"I did contact the police," Joanna calmly responds. "But it didn't get me anywhere."

Pullmann snorts and waves his hand dismissively, but he leaves it at that.

"What about Gavin, then?" I press. "What's going to happen to him and his people? They were the ones who contacted the police. They saved our lives."

"We don't know yet. They're still being questioned at the moment.

As are those other men." König abruptly pushes back his chair and turns to his colleague. "I think we're done for the time being." He gets up, reaches for the folder, and rolls it up.

"Someone's going to take you home now. I would, however, ask that you remain available for questioning. We're going to need to talk to you again once we've finished questioning the others."

We both nod appreciatively. As we stand up next to each other, I feel Joanna's hand groping for mine. I take her hand and hold it tightly.

During the drive home, we sit next to each other silently in the back seat of the police car. Maybe it's because of the young policewoman and her colleague that we're not talking about the things that I imagine are shaking up Joanna just as much as me. But maybe it's also the thought of our house, the fear that maybe it can no longer be *our* house after everything that's happened in the past few days, and especially in the past few hours. Maybe the place that's always been our most private sanctuary has been ruined for us by Gabor's men breaking in.

As we turn onto the driveway, it's something else entirely that I notice first, something that makes my stomach clench. The missing cockatoo.

It's a symbol of the last remaining secrets which stand between Joanna and me—the fact that she doesn't remember me, her attempt to kill me, the disappearance from the house of all proof of my existence.

We thank the officers and get out. Wait until the vehicle's disappeared. But even then, neither of us is able to move a muscle.

"It's a strange feeling, isn't it?" I ask, unable to tear my eyes away from the empty spot next to the rhododendrons.

"Yeah. For you probably even more than for me." She moves closer to me, puts an arm around my waist. I do the same. "All right then, let's see what happens."

I couldn't say what I expected, but as we look around the hall and then the kitchen and realize that barely anything has changed, I'm surprised. No closets have been torn open, no drawers are yanked out, and there are no items strewn over the floor. The living room, too—same as always. Then again, why would Gabor's people have vandalized the house in the first place; they didn't want valuables, they wanted us.

I sag down onto the couch, phone in hand. There's only one thing left to do today, call Ela and tell her we're OK. We keep the conversation brief; I don't have the strength right now to explain how the dots fit together, but I promise her I'll get in touch again tomorrow. The whole time I've been on the phone, I didn't hear a peep from Joanna. I look around but she's nowhere to be seen. My pulse quickens immediately. I exit the living room, walk through the kitchen, and abruptly stop in the entrance to the hall. The front door is open, and Joanna is standing on the doorstep. She's holding the key to the mailbox in one hand and an envelope in the other, and it looks as though she's afraid to open it.

51

My name is on the envelope, barely legible, in hastily scribbled letters. It's very light, almost like it's empty. I'd prefer to feel around before I open it, to try to figure out the contents, but I don't dare. Who knows, maybe it contains another, final attempt from Gabor to get me out of the way. Using anthrax, for example.

Erik sees my hesitation and takes the envelope from my hand. He feels it carefully. "There's something in it. But it's definitely nothing explosive."

Before I can protest, he goes into the kitchen and gets a knife from the block. No, not just a knife—*the* knife.

When he sees that I've followed him, he shakes his head. "Stay in the living room and shut the door behind you."

I'm so tired that I do it without protesting. Only once I sink down onto the couch do I realize that Erik probably sent me away to make sure I was safe.

But our concern is unfounded. Just half a minute later, Erik comes back and lays the contents of the envelope before me on the table. It's just a USB stick, black and slim. "We've often used that brand at work," he says.

We look at each other, nod silently. We should probably hand this stick over to the police, but not before we know what's on it.

Erik puts his laptop on the coffee table, opens it, and puts the stick into the USB slot.

Five files. Three pictures in JPEG format, and an audio file. And a

Word document named *For Joanna.doc.* I point my index finger at it. "Open that first, please."

Erik hesitates for a second, then opens it.

The text is no longer than half a page. It's full of typos, and some run-on words.

> I'm so sorry. Erik is dead and it's partly my fault. I acepted it as collateral damage for a cause I believe in and whos aims for our country are minetoo—the means of achieving them, however, are not. I didn't think my organization was capable of something like the attack on munich station, I didnt know about it beforehand, you have to believe me, please. But I can stil warn you, Joanna. We spoke on the phone a few hour ago, perhaps youre already in the process of hidng, I really hope you are. Probably you willnever read what I'm writing here, but I need to tell you what I knw. I didnt come by that evening because I had problems with mycomputer, but because I wanted to seewhat had gone wrong. Listen to the recording I sent then you will unnerstand. Good luck. I'm on my way out of the country. I'm really sorry.
>
> Bernhard Morbach

Erik has put his arm around my shoulders. We exchange a quick glance. "The photos first," I say. I don't know why, but I dread listening to the audio file. *Then you'll understand*—on the one hand I want to understand, I *have* to, but on the other hand I'm so terribly afraid of what I might hear. What if it turns out I really was in on it with von Ritteck, Gabor, and the others, and that I just forgot about it? Just like I forgot Erik?

The first picture. Lots of green. Lush vegetation on the beach. Palm trees. And some distance away two figures, one of which is me, or someone who looks very similar to me. The other is a man, or rather a boy, with coffee-colored skin.

I have no idea when or where the photo was taken.

"The beaches at home don't look like that," I murmur.

Erik looks at me. "That's Antigua." He opens the next photo. The boy and I are in sharper focus now: he's laughing and pointing out to sea. I'm standing there, my hands in the pockets of my shorts, and looking at what he's showing me.

"Did you take these?" I ask Erik. "That would explain why you're not in them."

"No." He zooms in on the picture. "I've never seen that bay before, I don't think."

I can feel something like a hum, a silent vibration inside me. A name. But no memory.

On the third photo, I'm standing in the water up to my knees, and something is coming into the frame from the right, probably the bow of a boat. And a hand is reaching out toward me.

"You did wander off by yourself that one time." He puts a hand on my knee, and I have to pull myself together in order not to flinch away. It's not Erik's fault I'm feeling so worked up, it's because this picture doesn't ring a bell at all. Antigua is a complete unknown to me; until recently I would have sworn I've never set foot on the island. Let alone on this beach, but there I stand, unmistakably, laughing.

"OK. Then let's listen to the file now."

Erik clicks on the file, and the audio player on his notebook opens. I lower my gaze; my heart is hammering so strongly I can actually see it rather than just feel it. I close my eyes.

At first there's just the sound of water rushing, nothing but that. Rising and falling. The sound of the sea. Then a crackle and a voice, coming closer midsentence. "That was fifty milligrams of scopolamine; it shouldn't put her to sleep." Bartsch's voice, mixed with a dragging sound, as if someone was pulling up a chair. "Are we recording?"

"Yes."

Erik takes a sharp intake of breath next to me and stops the player. "That's Bernhard's voice. I don't believe it; he and Bartsch were on Antigua? At the same time as us?"

"So it seems." I remember what Gabor had said earlier in the warehouse. *You couldn't wait to get on the plane.* "Keep playing it, please."

Erik clicks on the play button, and the voice returns. Bartsch. For a moment I even think I can smell his aftershave.

"Good. It's important to me that everything is documented." A short pause, then he speaks again, in a different, warmer tone. "Hello, Joanna. I'm very pleased to have you on board."

"Yes. I'm . . . pleased too."

It's me. Without a doubt. My voice, the soft accent, the one I always think I've managed to lose until I hear recordings of myself. I lean against Erik, he puts an arm around me; only now do I realize that I'm trembling.

"So, Joanna. Are you lying comfortably? Yes? Wonderful. You're relaxed. You feel good. Please look into the little light here."

"OK."

"Follow it with your eyes. Yes, just like that. You're doing a great job."

I reach for Erik's arm, cling onto it, because I suddenly feel as though I'm losing contact with my surroundings. As if gravity had ceased to exist, only for me.

"You're very calm. Everything that has been bothering you is far away. You're focusing only on this light and my voice."

Erik strokes my face, carefully touching my split lip. "Don't drift off, Jo. Look at me, are you OK?"

I nod anxiously, tighten my grip on his arm, and the swaying feeling recedes.

"And now listen to me closely, Joanna." Bartsch begins to speak in a tone which is friendly, but commanding. "It's going to be early morning, and the telephone will ring. You will hear my voice, which will say only two words. *Dead light.* You hang up the phone. You're feeling good. You feel well. You will have a fulfilling, enjoyable day.

"At five o'clock in the afternoon, you go into the kitchen. You—"

Something interrupts him. Sounds, a loud clatter. Then voices, not speaking German, but English. Two men, and they sound a little farther away than Bartsch. There's probably a wall between them and me, or simply a greater distance. Their voices are completely unfamiliar.

"Ben? Where's Ben?"

"Get out of here, right now!"

"But I can't find him, is he—"

"Forget about him. Do you understand? Forget that you ever met him, forget that he exists. And get rid of his stuff, everything. Quickly."

"But—"

"It's important! Do what I tell you! Now!"

Another clatter. A scream of protest, then a splash, as if something had fallen into the water. Or someone.

The whole thing only lasts ten seconds, and now the silence returns, only to be interrupted moments later by the sound of someone clearing their throat and Bartsch's voice, very close now. "Joanna. Are you still OK?"

"Yes. I'm fine."

"Please speak German to me."

"Ach so. Ja."

"Good. At five o'clock in the afternoon you go into the kitchen. You hurt yourself. You hit your head against the edge of the door, fall against it with your shoulder. You injure yourself in such a way that other people can see it. To the extent that you bleed. As if you had a fight with someone. When you hear Erik come home, pick up the longest and sharpest kitchen knife that you own. Can you see it in your mind?"

I've put both hands over my mouth, and yes, I can see the knife before me, clear as day, and I can also see it plunging into Erik's upper arm; Bartsch's scent is suddenly there again, and I feel the urge to throw up.

"Yes, I can," whispers the Joanna who I once was.

"He runs toward you, and you stab the knife first into his stomach and then into his chest. Deeply. You're calm and sure about what you're doing, as though you've done it many times before.

"You wait five minutes, then you get out your phone and call the police. You say: I've killed my fiancé, but it was in self-defense."

A short pause. "Self-defense," I repeat.

"Correct. When you get back to the hotel now, say you let one of the locals show you where the frigate birds nest. Then continue with your vacation like before."

A soft click. Probably the light I was told to concentrate on. Then noises, footsteps, a door opening.

"I think that went really well," says Bernhard.

"Yes," responds Bartsch. "She didn't struggle, she went off right away. It's because of the scopolamine as well; it's the perfect booster."

"OK, then I'll turn off the recording now," Bernhard announces, and seconds later the recording ends.

I want to move, to turn around to Erik, but I can't. I can only sit there and stare at the screen of the laptop.

"They hypnotized you," says Erik quietly. "And drugged you. My God."

Yes. I grasp my head, bury it in my hands. I wonder if I'll ever get the memories saved in the recesses of my mind back.

"Should I play it again for you?"

I shake my head slowly, so Erik closes the player. The third photo appears beneath it once more—me in the water, the boy next to me, the bow of the boat coming in from the right, and a pale-skinned hand stretching out toward me.

The boy. Ben. Yes, he has to be Ben.

"They killed him," I murmur.

"What? Who?" Now I don't need to turn my head around; Erik has taken my chin gently in his hand and is looking into my eyes.

"My island guide. The one in the photo. Didn't you hear that Bartsch got interrupted? That two men in the background were arguing?" I repeat the words, this time in English, in the way they've been imprinted in my subconscious. Ineradicable. "Forget about him. Do you understand? Forget that you ever met him, forget that he exists. And get rid of his stuff, everything. Quickly."

"But it was quiet. And unclear," Erik interjects.

I manage a smile. "Yes. But it was in English. My native language. They got rid of the little tour guide so as not to take any risks—and that's why Bartsch's plan didn't work. Two orders that got mixed up in my head. That's why I forgot you instead of killing you." I close my eyes. The world sways a little, like we were on water. "And yet the plan was a really good one. I would have hurt myself and then stabbed you. One of those cases of domestic violence and self-defense. It wouldn't have thrown any bad light on Gabor and his company."

Bartsch appears in my mind's eye, buried beneath the heavy metal shelving unit and its contents. Bleeding. Dying. *It's a shame that I won't live to see you kill him after all.*

"I'm going to go get treatment," I declare. "I mean, now that we know what happened, it should be easier. Don't you think?" I search for Erik's gaze; his smile is encouraging, and he nods, but of course he can't know if that's really the case. No more than I can.

"I'll copy these files before we give the USB stick to the police," he says, pulling the icons into a new folder. "In any case, we now know that you got rid of my stuff, don't we?" He gives me a lopsided grin. "I don't suppose you have any idea where? Dump site? Storage? Some charity?"

I shrug. "No idea, I'm sorry."

His grin grows wider. "Well, in any case you must have had to work really hard. More credit to you."

I give Erik a playful punch on the shoulder. "Well, you know me. When I do something, I do it properly."

He pulls the stick out of the USB slot, snaps the lid back onto it, and puts it on the coffee table. Then he turns to me and takes me into his arms. "That's true. You always have."

His kiss is familiar, as is his scent. I bury my head against his shoulder. I feel like I could cry, because I've been robbed of almost a year with this man, all the stories, the shared memories, the first times.

He seems to sense that my mood is shifting again. He pushes me a little way from him, and looks at me in mock accusation. "There's something else I have to know."

"Yes?"

"And I'm expecting you to tell me the truth."

The sight of his intensely wrinkled brow makes it hard for me to stay serious. "Let's see."

"Do you still remember that guessing game we played when you thought I was a burglar?"

"Yes, of course."

"I want to know at least one of the answers now. Tell me your middle name."

I shake my head decisively. "No chance."

"Now listen to me. We're engaged. I have a right to know such important things."

I kiss him on the tip of the nose. "You have a right to guess. So get started."

He smiles deviously. "A name that suits you?"

"In a certain way, yes."

"Hildegard," he says, not missing a beat.

"Another wise-ass guess like that and I'm getting the knife again."

"Oh. OK. No, wait. Probably some insane English fantasy name. Tiffany Amnesia or something like that. Am I right?"

Now I really can't help but laugh. "Not at all bad. Both of them. But still wrong. Just think about how my father made the majority of his money."

Erik takes my hand. "Diamonds."

"Exactly. But it's not Diamond, because I'm also—what?"

Erik frowns again. "Difficult? Exhausting? A danger to the public?"

"Unique, silly." He pulls me close to him, strokes my back. I can't see his face, but I feel him nodding. And I know that he's going to guess right.

"Solitaire."

Epilogue

The conversation in the room falls silent as he gets up. All of them have gathered here today; he wouldn't have expected any less. Only two of the eldest are absent—Zedwitz, who is pushing ninety, and Habeck, who is older still, and from whom dementia has robbed nearly everything, even his love for the fatherland.

He waits until all eyes are fixed on him, until he can be certain that all those present are paying him their utmost attention. Only then does he begin to speak.

"My brothers-in-arms. I thank you for your trust, and value greatly that you are entrusting me with the leadership of the squadron in these difficult times. My predecessor is a very tough act to follow—we all know what Heinrich von Ritteck achieved for our cause. Staffel 444 was his life, a life he decided, at the very end, to take himself. He chose an honorable death, and thus avoided the shame of being arrested by a corrupt police force. All of you know just how much filth the lying press have poured onto him these past weeks—and so we shall honor his memory all the more." He reaches for his glass and raises it up high. The others get to their feet—the younger men swiftly, the old men slowly and with difficulty. Again, he waits until everyone is ready, then he clicks his heels. "To Heinrich von Ritteck!"

"To Heinrich von Ritteck!"

They drink, and only sit back down when he sets his glass onto the table.

"I would like to welcome three newcomers to our ranks. Ulrich Herfurth, Max Jauner, Albert Puch—welcome!"

The men he named all bow their heads. Each of them is a man of influence, each in a different area.

"You are joining a fellowship of great tradition." He feels there is no harm in emphasizing this to the new inductions. "Our parent organization was Gladio, the clandestine army brought into being after the war, as a defense in the event that Communism should overrun Europe. Today, this threat is no longer to be feared. Staffel 444 has by no means taken up the cause of supporting the diseased pan-European construct in which we are regrettably trapped. We fight only for Germany, against foes who threaten our home from the inside and out." His lets his gaze sweep over the faces of the others, slowly, poignantly. "When Gladio blew up Bologna central station in 1980, the number of casualties came to eighty-five. Our operation in Munich was almost twice as effective; we exceeded by far our target of at least one hundred casualties. And unlike how it was for our predecessors, now the anger of the people will be permanently directed at those who it is our duty to fight. This is what Heinrich von Ritteck gave his life for, and it was not in vain."

He allows himself a slight smile, the first of the day. "Despite the painful loss of our leader, we have reason to be joyful," he continues. "The German people have taken action. At the elections two weeks ago, they have shown what they think of weakness, tolerance, and leniency toward the subhumans who threaten and overpopulate us. From the ashes of our magnificent explosion, the German spirit is rising to new heights, just like a phoenix."

Everyone present raps their knuckles on the tabletop in approval. He nods, waits until they have quieted down again.

"We have achieved a great deal, but much still lies ahead of us. I found out yesterday that Hans Gabor will take full responsibility for everything we could otherwise be charged with, due to the witnesses he didn't manage to get rid of. Gabor failed, but he is prepared to atone for his failure and exonerate the others who were arrested."

They listen, although some of them are frowning warily. He puts more emphasis into his voice. "There is no cause for concern. If Gabor should change his mind, we have members of Staffel 444 on location who we can trust to act swiftly."

He raises his glass again. "The next project will run without error, I personally vouch for that. Germany has a future, a grand future, and it lies in our hands."